Bound South

Bound South

A NOVEL

Susan Rebecca White

A TOUCHSTONE BOOK
Published by Simon & Schuster
New York   London   Toronto   Sydney

Touchstone
A Division of Simon & Schuster, Inc.
1230 Avenue of the Americas
New York, NY 10020

Copyright © 2009 by Susan Rebecca White

First Touchstone trade paperback edition February 2009

TOUCHSTONE and colophon are registered trademarks of Simon & Schuster, Inc.

Manufactured in the United States of America

ISBN-13: 978-1-60751-732-0

to Alan

Part
One

The Other Side of Town

(Louise, Fall 1998)

*P*robably it is for the best that Caroline has chosen to go to play practice rather than to attend Sandy's funeral with Nanny Rose and me. Still, Nanny Rose will give me hell when she realizes that neither Caroline nor John Henry is coming. (Nor Charles for that matter, who is only eleven and too young for this.) Sandy worked for Nanny Rose for the last thirty-three years. The last eleven of those years she worked for us too. That was Nanny Rose's gift to us after I had Charles; she sent Sandy over to our house once a week. Of course she waited until I had a boy to offer help, even though it turned out Charles was an easy baby while Caroline nearly drove me to the loony bin.

Sandy was there the day I brought Charles home from Piedmont Hospital. And a year later, when we moved from our Peachtree Hills starter house to our current home in Ansley Park, Sandy held the baby while I directed the movers with the furniture. Poor Sandy. When she walked out the door of our little house carrying Charles, our dog Cleo up and bit her on the leg. Cleo had never been a biter; the only explanation was that Cleo thought Sandy was taking away the baby same as the movers were taking away all the furniture. Most of the movers were African American, as is—was, I should say—Sandy.

After that I kept Cleo in the fenced side yard every Monday when Sandy would come. Sandy loved Baby Charles. Once he was old enough to chew, she'd bring him a candy bar every week. I would have to drive to the gas station on Peachtree and buy Caroline one too or else suffer through her tantrum. Of course I would have preferred it if Sandy had brought both children a treat, but I didn't feel that I could ask her to do so, knowing that she didn't have any extra money.

She spoiled Charles, as did I, and he seemed none the worse for it. Our spoiling just made him sweeter. Really. He was just as pudgy and smiley as a baby could be. How John Henry and I created such a sweet boy—such an open and loving little person— from the same genes that formed Caroline the Terror, I will never know.

I NEVER NOTICE how messy my car is until it is time for either John Henry or Nanny Rose to ride in it. John Henry is fond of saying that I use my car as a giant handbag, stashing all sorts of stuff in it. Well, I'm sorry. My house and my person are always tidy. There has to be one place where I can allow things to get a little cluttered. I pick the empty Diet Coke cans off the car floor and throw them into the Herbie Curbie. If Caroline were with me she would insist that I recycle them, but the recycle box is inside the house and I simply do not have time to go back in there. I honk good-bye to Charles and Faye (my other cleaning lady, who comes on Thursdays, although now I suppose I'll have to see if she can come on Mondays as well) and pull out of the driveway heading down Peachtree Circle toward Peachtree Street. Nanny Rose lives a few miles north, in Buckhead. The funeral is on the south side of the city, so it is out of the way to pick her up, but Nanny Rose is seventy-seven and both John Henry and I try to make sure she drives as little as possible. John Henry jokes that in her dotage she "speeds more and sees less."

EVEN THOUGH I was born in Ansley Park, and John Henry and I have lived here for over ten years, it still gives me a little thrill to drive through my neighborhood. I just love the tall old trees, the fine architecture, the sense that even though the skyscrapers of Midtown frame the neighborhood, when you are in Ansley Park you are *in* the South. So many of the old houses here remind me of the houses that line Franklin Street as you drive into Chapel Hill, where John Henry and I met, or rather, where we began our relationship, as we had met once or twice before we went to college. Our families, both from Atlanta, ran in similar, though not entirely overlapping circles. (Frankly, John Henry's family was "older" than mine.) Before college John Henry and I hardly knew each other. The fact that we went to rival high schools had a lot to do with that. He attended Coventry while I went to Birch.

If John Henry had his way we would probably live in Buckhead or even Sandy Springs. He complains that the houses in Ansley Park are too close together and that there are too many cars parked on the streets, especially during the weekends, when people from other neighborhoods drive over here, park, and walk to Piedmont Park. And good Lord don't even get him started on Freaknik, when students from all of the black colleges around the South meet up at Piedmont Park for a party, but not before blocking the traffic in our neighborhood for hours with all of their jumping in and out of each other's cars and dancing in the streets.

What really bothers John Henry about the neighborhood is that he's in the minority being a Republican over here. Not that Ansley Park is a hotbed of radicalism. (Lord no. Daddy, whose political views often put *him* in the neighborhood minority, still counted many from Ansley Park as his friends and allies.) Still, to John Henry's chagrin, most of our neighbors are progressive in their politics. They are usually tasteful about it, of course. Most people from Ansley Park would rather write a big check than make a big scene.

Another thing John Henry is not thrilled about is Ansley's close proximity to Midtown. Not the office buildings, but the little strip of shops on Piedmont and Tenth Street that cater to a gay clientele. Midtown, after all, has become the gay capital of the South, and John Henry is not, as my colorist, Chevre, says, "gay friendly."

But I love our neighborhood. I love the tall modern buildings peeping over the gracious old homes. Living in Ansley Park, you never forget that Atlanta actually is a city. Most people who say they live in Atlanta do not live in the city at all. Most of our four million residents live OTP—outside the perimeter. But Ansley Park is in the center of things, and consequently I never have to drive more than fifteen minutes to get anywhere I need to be. The farthest I drive is to Coventry, where Charles and Caroline are in school, and that's only about five miles away. It's like my best friend Tiny always says: "The only time I go OTP is when I'm on an airplane."

Caroline says that the whole city is one big strip mall. I say it's made up of neighborhoods, that the old homes are really its attraction. True, there isn't one spot in Atlanta where you stop and think, "*Now* I'm in the heart of the city." Atlanta isn't like a New York or a San Francisco. There's no equivalent to Greenwich Village or North Beach here.

Virginia Highlands, with its boutiques and restaurants, tries to be that, I suppose, but it doesn't have the diversity, the push and pull, the tumult. To be honest, Oakland Cemetery, over there off Memorial Drive, is where I feel most *in* the city. The cemetery is wide, hilly, and shaded with oaks. The two smokestacks of the old mill in Cabbagetown border it on one side; the modern Atlanta skyline on the other. Inside the actual cemetery are crumbling brick paths, stone gravestones, and mausoleums bearing the names of important Atlanta families. Also, there are thousands of unmarked Confederate soldiers' graves and a section where large tombstones bearing Stars of David and Jewish names are all smushed together (the cemetery was originally segregated and the Jews were only given a small plot). Bobby Jones is buried at Oakland. So is Margaret Mitchell.

I wonder where Sandy will be buried. I don't even know how you go about getting buried nowadays if your family hasn't already bought a plot of land for you. Maybe Sandy will be cremated, though I doubt it. I have a feeling that as a Baptist, she'd rather be laid in the ground so that her body will be around for the Resurrection.

I TURN RIGHT on Peachtree Street and head toward Nanny Rose's white brick house on Peachtree Battle Avenue, the same house John Henry grew up in. Nanny Rose has not redecorated since she moved in over fifty years ago. She once told me that "good taste never goes out of style," which, frankly, assumes a lot. John Henry's old room is painted egg yellow, same as it was when he slept there as a boy, and it still has two metal-framed twin beds in it, one for John Henry and one for Wallace, John Henry's twin brother, who shot himself in the head his senior year at the University of Georgia.

IT'S ONE THIRTY on the dot when I arrive at Nanny Rose's house, but even so, she is waiting outside in the ninety-degree heat. (I've lived in Atlanta my entire life except for when I was at college, yet *every* year I forget that early September is often just as hot as August.)

Nanny Rose has a way of making you feel that you are always

late. You wouldn't think such a little woman could be so intimidating.

Her hair is so black it looks almost blue in the midday sun. She must have colored it last night. I have asked her a million times to let Chevre do it, to give it a softer, more natural look, but she refuses, even though Chevre is the absolute best, able to transform my dull brown hair—embedded with lots of gray—into the glossy, rich color of polished mahogany. Nanny Rose says that hiring someone to fix her hair would be an unnecessary indulgence.

As much of it as she has, she's really quite frugal with her money.

I drive up next to her, stop the car, lean over the passenger seat, and push her door open from the inside. She stands stiffly beside it. I sigh, turn off the ignition, and get out. Oh Lord. Here we go.

After officially opening the car door for her, I hold Gunther, her blond Pomeranian, who is apparently going with us to the funeral, while she lowers herself sideways into the seat.

"Come on back to Mother," she says, holding out her hands for the dog.

Once Gunther is safely in her lap, she rotates her bottom until she is facing forward. I close her door and walk back around to the driver's side. Once in my seat, I notice that Nanny Rose's smell, a mix of floral perfume and Aqua Net, has already permeated the air.

"Hello, Louise," she says. She tilts her cheek, almost imperceptibly, toward me and I lean over to kiss it. Her cheek feels dry and powdery beneath my lips. She has applied her rouge in a red circle, much as a clown would, although on Nanny Rose it doesn't look clownish, just old-fashioned.

"Nanny Rose, I like your suit," I say.

I do. She wears a pink-and-white-checked suit—ancient

Chanel, I'm sure—nude pantyhose, and pink flats. As always she wears a thin gold chain around her neck with her diamond engagement ring and her wedding band hanging from it. Her fingers, which are bony and long, swell from arthritis. She runs her right hand roughly over Gunther's spine. He emits a low growl.

"Where are the children?" she asks, peering around to look in the back of the car as if Caroline and Charles might be hiding below the seats. "Where is John Henry?"

"John Henry has a deposition in Birmingham, and Caroline—well—she got cast in the school play, *Steel Magnolias*, and she really didn't feel that she could miss practice."

Nanny Rose looks at me as if she just swallowed something that tastes terrible. "She can't miss play practice for a funeral?"

"Apparently it was a huge deal that she got a lead part as a sophomore, and she's just nervous about it. She doesn't want to upset the director."

"Do you think it's appropriate for her to put so much time and energy into extracurricular activities when her grades are so dismal?"

I shrug my shoulders. Frankly, I have no idea what I should do about Caroline and her terrible attitude toward school, but I'd no sooner take acting away from her than I would throw her out on the street. That girl lives to perform.

"John Henry never had any scholastic difficulties," says Nanny Rose. "He was an excellent student."

"I know, Nanny Rose," I say, flashing her a smile before focusing again on the road. "He and I met at Chapel Hill, remember?"

"Oh yes. Of course. Which house were you in?"

"Chi Omega," I say. We have been over this a hundred times.

"Chi Omega is a good old house. Of course, Pi Beta Phi is best, isn't it, Gunther?" She scratches the dog under his chin.

"Chi O was a top house," I say, turning onto the entrance ramp of I-75 south.

"We're taking the expressway?" asks Nanny Rose, her voice alarmed. Nanny Rose never drives on the expressway.

"Yes, ma'am," I say. "Don't worry, this will pop us right over to the church."

"Thirty-three years Sandy worked for me and I never knew she was a Baptist."

"Sandy didn't talk much about her personal life," I say.

Nanny Rose nods solemnly. "I know. That was one of the things I liked best about her. She always showed up on time and never called to say she was sick and couldn't make it. I had this other girl working for me—Josephine. She'd come on the day Sandy was at your house, except she hardly ever came. There was always something the matter with either her child or her car. Not Sandy. Sandy was as reliable as the postman. More so!"

I glance at Nanny Rose and see that her eyes are pooling with tears. She reaches into her quilted clutch, pulls out a linen handkerchief, and dabs her eyes with it.

"I've slowed down," she says. "I can't do everything for myself the way I used to. Sandy, she used to help me in and out of the bath; she used to help me into my clothes. Why, it got so I'd even let her help me into my girdle! Now she's up and left me and I'm not going to have anyone to help me get around anymore. You can't help me, can you, Gunther?" she asks, lifting Gunther's chin with her hand.

"I'm not going to be able to go to circle or to play bridge or to go have lunch at the Club now that my Sandy is gone. No one will be there to help me get myself together."

Nanny Rose is crying in earnest now. She looks so small in the passenger seat. She looks like a child.

"You got yourself together today, didn't you?" I ask. "Look at how nice you're dressed."

Nanny Rose blows her nose into the corner of her handkerchief and then folds it over.

"We'll find you someone else," I say. "Sandy might have a granddaughter or a niece who would like to come and work for you."

I consider suggesting that Faye might be available, but I refrain. Though I'm sorry that Sandy died, I am not sorry to be done with sharing "help" with Nanny Rose. The less tangled my day-to-day life is with my mother-in-law, the better.

"No one will be able to replace her, Louise. You ought to know that."

I have never heard Nanny Rose talk about Sandy this way. They were always so formal with each other. Nanny Rose still had Sandy wear a maid's uniform, for goodness' sake, a little starched black dress with a white apron. Nanny Rose was always "Mrs. Parker" to Sandy. Nanny Rose even had a little silver bell she would ring when she needed her.

Our exit should be coming up, but I'm not exactly sure which one it is. I ask Nanny Rose if she will look in the glove compartment for the directions. She starts pulling out all the folded maps that John Henry makes me keep in there.

"No, it's just the directions John Henry wrote out for me. Look for a yellow sheet of legal paper."

Nanny Rose fumbles around in there some more, pulling out several of Caroline's CDs. One shows a close-up of a girl's tiny pink shorts, the V of her crotch evident. Nanny Rose snorts.

"They let any hussy put her picture up nowadays, don't they?" she says.

All I can think to say is "Yes, ma'am."

I spot the directions in the corner of the glove compartment, and I reach across Nanny Rose to yank them out.

"You drive," she says. "I'll look at these."

She straightens the directions with her hand. "Turn left on Peachtree Circle," she says.

"Yes, ma'am," I say, as patiently as I can. "I already did that.

We're all the way to where we exit off I-Twenty. Does it say which exit we want to take?"

Nanny Rose runs her eyes down the page. She rests the directions on top of Gunther's head, making it look as if he is wearing a paper hat. "All right now. Get on I-Seventy-five south."

"Yes, ma'am. We've done that."

"Get onto I-Twenty west," she says.

I have to hold myself back from snatching the directions out of her hands.

Gunther barks, knocking the directions off his head and onto the floor. Nanny Rose bops him on his wet nose. "Bad boy!" she says.

As she bends down to fish the directions off the floor, I pass the exit. That was it. That was where I was supposed to get off. Damn. John Henry warned me to follow his directions carefully. Otherwise, he said, it might be *Bonfire of the Vanities* all over again. I pull off at the next exit, hoping I will see an entrance ramp as soon as I do, so I can get back on I-20 heading east and backtrack to where I am supposed to be.

Once off the expressway, I notice right away that the billboards are smaller on this side of town and that they feature black people instead of white. On the side of the road, just in front of a strip mall with a Dollar General and a check-cashing business, is a man selling socks. His sign reads "100 pair for $5." He sits behind a cardboard table, bags and bags of socks stacked on top of it.

If I bought everyone in my family a hundred pairs of socks, I wouldn't have to do laundry for weeks.

"I believe John Henry Senior once owned some property over here," says Nanny Rose. "A sign. He rented it for twenty dollars a month."

It seems John Henry's daddy owned some piece of every neighborhood in Atlanta.

"John Henry Senior and I used to drive by his properties after church," says Nanny Rose. "Sometimes he would need to collect rent. Afterwards we'd stop for a Frosty Orange at the Varsity on our way back home. He called this area Colored Town, though I guess people don't say that anymore."

Where is that entrance ramp? Did I get so distracted by those damn socks that I drove right past it?

"I don't think I'd use that expression at the funeral if I was you," I say, looking for a good place to turn around.

Nanny Rose and I may well be the only white people there. I glance down at my brown Armani pants that I wear with a black silk shirt that ties in little bows around the cuffs. My outfit would pass muster at an Episcopalian funeral, but I start to worry I'm not dressed up enough for the Baptists.

I turn down a side street that appears residential. Nanny Rose holds Gunther up to the window, looking to see if they can spot any dogs on the sidewalk.

"Good heavens, Louise," says Nanny Rose. "Why are you driving us through the slums?"

We pass a house stripped entirely of its siding. We pass a boarded-up apartment marked with "No Trespassing" signs. We pass unadorned lawns, an old Cadillac, and a sleepy-eyed man in overalls whose gaze follows our car until we have passed him.

"Are the doors locked?" Nanny Rose asks.

I wish I hadn't already thought the same thing. I wish I didn't get nervous driving through poor black neighborhoods. I wish I wasn't relieved that the Lexus locks automatically, which is such an improvement over when you had to lock the door yourself, drawing attention to the act both by moving your hand to the lock and by the loud clicking noise that accompanied the action.

Up ahead by a stop sign is a group of black boys who must be around Caroline's age. All of them wear long white T-shirts, which look as if they have been bleached and ironed, on top of jeans pulled down so low the seats cover their knees instead of their rears. All but one wears bright white sneakers. The other has on black sneakers with Velcro straps instead of laces, the straps flailing to the sides, intentionally left undone. A couple of the boys wear their hair braided into thick cornrows; one has an Afro with a comb stuck in it. It is he who looks down the street and notices our car coming their way.

I grip the steering wheel even tighter while telling myself to calm down. These are only boys, only children Caroline's age, and there is no reason, just because they are black, that I should be afraid of them. We studied the perception versus the reality of actual danger once in Sunday school and how it is our internalized racism that makes us scared of those who are—in fact—quite often the most vulnerable and disadvantaged. Still, it's not as if Nanny Rose and I blend into the neighborhood. It's not as if we are driving a rusty old car. No, we are driving the new silver Lexus that John Henry gave me for my birthday.

"I would just drive on through that stop sign if I were you," says Nanny Rose. "A group of boys is never up to any good."

The boys spread out, watching us come toward them. I tap the brakes. As we roll toward the group I lock eyes with the one who has the comb stuck in his hair. He raises his hand as if he's waving me on by, then just before I drive past him, he steps in front of the car. I swerve, barely avoiding contact, and drive through the intersection without stopping. From my rearview mirror I watch him laugh and slap the hands of his friends.

The service was scheduled to begin at two. It's almost two thirty by the time we finally find the church. The small parking lot is full, but we find a space across the street. Nanny Rose takes her compact out of her purse and reapplies lipstick while I wait for her outside the car. It is so hot I am beginning to sweat. I hope there are no rings of perspiration seeping through my silk top.

When Nanny Rose has finished reapplying her lipstick she looks up at me through the window, indicating that I may open her door. When I do, she rotates her bottom once again so that her legs are sticking out. She holds Gunther in one arm and grabs my hand with the other. I pull her to her feet. It always surprises me when I stand next to Nanny Rose that she is a half foot shorter than I am.

Nanny Rose fishes Gunther's leash out of her purse, attaches it to his collar, and puts him down on the hot sidewalk. His toenails make a fast little clicking noise as we cross the street.

The church is a plain white brick building, a perfect rectangle with a pitched roof supporting a metal cross. The cross looks like a lightning rod. Nanny Rose, Gunther, and I walk to the front door. Above it "Jesus Is the Answer" is painted in red, blocky letters. A short black woman, wearing a wide-brimmed straw hat and white gloves, holds the door open for us.

"Welcome," she says. "I'm Miss Ella Watson, Mr. Brown's next-door neighbor. I'm also on the Mother Board here at Mount Zion."

"How wonderful," says Nanny Rose. "I'm Mrs. John Henry Parker Senior, and this is my daughter-in-law, Mrs. John Henry Parker Junior. Sandy worked for our family for over thirty years."

"Call me Louise," I say.

"Well, it sure is good of y'all to come," says Miss Watson. "And Sandy looks just as peaceful as can be, praise God. The undertaker did a fine job, a fine job indeed. Pastor's not here yet, so there's still time to look at the body."

Nanny Rose bends down to pick up Gunther. I doubt he's allowed in the sanctuary, but it's too hot to leave him outside. His little brain would cook in no time.

The church is packed. As I expected, Nanny Rose and I are the only white people in here. As we walk toward the viewing line, I notice that there are no hymnals tucked into the backs of

the pews. No Bibles either. At All Saints there are kneelers be-
neath each pew, but of course Baptists don't use those. There is a
portrait of a black man in a white suit hanging behind the altar.
At first I think the portrait is a rendering of a black Jesus, which
I think is just wonderful, but as we move up in the viewing line
I'm able to make out the lettering below the portrait, which reads
"Pastor Williams."

There must be over a hundred people packed into this church.
I have no idea who any of them might be. Sandy never spoke
about her home life. I probably should have asked her about it,
but I was always more comfortable having a business relationship
with her. To tell the truth, I felt guilty having a black housekeeper. I felt as if I were holding a string that connected me to
my mother and grandmother (both of whom had black maids),
all the way back to the wives of slave owners. Maybe it is silly, but
I've always felt more comfortable having Faye, who is white, clean
for me, even though Faye comes with her own set of problems
and Sandy was the much better worker of the two.

The woman directly in front of us in the viewing line wears
a blue hat with a white polka-dot band. She turns to look at us,
and I detect a flicker of surprise on her face. I don't know if she's
surprised because we are white or because of Gunther.

"Can you believe that no-good preacher hasn't showed up
yet?" she asks.

Nanny Rose sticks out her free hand. "I'm Mrs. John Henry
Parker Senior," she says. "And this is Gunther."

The woman looks at me, confused. "Gunther?" she asks.

"No, ma'am," I say, smiling. "I'm Louise Parker, Mrs. Parker's
daughter-in-law." I point at the dog. "That's Gunther."

"Lord have mercy," she says. "I'm Mrs. Evelyn Brown, and
that sure is the tiniest dog I've ever seen."

Gunther bares his teeth and starts barking at Mrs. Brown.
Nanny Rose quickly slaps his nose.

"Bad boy!" she says. "You'll have to excuse him. He is just distraught over Sandy's passing."

"Have mercy," says Mrs. Brown. "That dog must have liked Sandy a lot more than Sandy liked it."

We edge closer and closer to her coffin. I remind myself not to touch Sandy's face. Ever since I was a little girl and I went to my great-grandmother's funeral, I have had a compulsive urge to touch the dead. I don't know why. It's almost as if I can't believe the flesh will be cold instead of warm and I just want to feel it for myself. Some people, I'm sure, find it morbid to view the body after death, but I find it greatly comforting. It's just so obvious that the person—his or her spirit—is no longer present. It makes me wonder if there is indeed a place the spirit might go.

There is a stir in the church. I turn around and look at the entrance and see that the man whom I recognize from the portrait behind the altar is making his way down the center aisle of the church. Pastor Williams has finally arrived. The viewing line starts to move faster and faster until Mrs. Brown is saying a prayer over Sandy's body, and then it is our turn.

I take Nanny Rose by the hand and we walk to Sandy's coffin, stand next to it, and peer over its edge. Obviously I expect to see Sandy in it—or rather, the shell of her—wearing her best dress and curly wig.

Only, our Sandy isn't in the coffin. In her place is a petite black man wearing a dark brown suit, a mustard yellow shirt, and a slightly darker yellow tie. Attached to the tie is a small metal pin shaped like a peacock.

"Why, we must be at the wrong viewing," says Nanny Rose, but it is too late. I have looked closer and realized that no, we are at the right funeral. Placed in Sandy's hand is a pink leather Bible, just the Gospels, with her—his—name stamped on it in gold. The Bible was a present from Nanny Rose for Sandy's sixty-fifth birthday. Nanny Rose gave Caroline one just like it.

I make a quick decision. "You're right," I say. "This isn't Sandy. Let's go."

But no, Nanny Rose is peering into the coffin and reading the engraving on the front of Sandy's Bible.

She begins to shake her head. Gunther struggles in her arms, trying to get to Sandy, barking like crazy. I feel every eye in the church on our backs.

"I don't understand," says Nanny Rose. She is too confused to shush Gunther. "I gave Sandy that Bible."

"Yes, ma'am," I say, "I recognize it."

Gunther is barking again and again at Sandy, and I surprise myself by reaching over and slapping his nose myself.

Nanny Rose clutches my forearm. "Louise," she says, her voice cracking, "that *is* Sandy." She lets go of my arm and points an accusing finger at the dead man's head. "That *man* is Sandy. My Sandy was a black man!"

"Yes, ma'am," I say. "Hush now, people are watching us."

Nanny Rose's eyes fill with panic. "Louise, that man helped me into my girdle! That black man helped me into my girdle!"

She hands me Gunther, who is still barking his head off, rolls her eyes toward heaven, and faints to the floor.

CHAPTER TWO

Wherever You Go, There You Are

(Caroline, Fall 1999)

When we took the SATs, Jim got a 1560. A lot of kids in my class at Coventry scored high—our average, brought down by me, was a 1320—but Jim, it's like he goes deeper than the rest of us. He reads the Bhagavad Gita and the Bible, and the Koran, and he can put himself into a trance through self-hypnosis. He says he's working on levitation.

Jim is going to be an analyst one day, combining Western and Eastern schools of thought. For inspiration Jim built a Christian labyrinth (Jim says the center stone symbolizes heaven) and a Zen rock garden in his backyard. He spends his afternoons in solitude out there, walking the labyrinth and meditating in the rock garden. He says all of the great spiritual teachers were devotees of meditation, Jesus included. Jim is teaching me how to meditate too. He says to close my eyes and clear my mind. If I can't clear it of everything, he says to imagine a big, floating 10. Then I'm supposed to count down from there, picturing the numbers each step of the way. He says if I can just free my mind I'll be a better student. I hope he's right. I can't fail math.

• • •

JIM AND MY best friend, Amanda, started dating after they hooked up in the hot tub at Susan Ridley's house. Amanda lost her virginity to Jim, although he lost his two years ago to a girl he met at this Emerging Philosophers gathering in D.C. He promised Amanda that he was safe; he told her that he wore two condoms the first time he had sex.

About half of the girls in my class are infatuated with Jim. It's something about his eyes. They fix right on you and seem to shine when you say something he approves of. Jim's dad is Japanese, so he's half Asian. It's funny: if you were to describe Jim to me and then ask if I thought he would be popular at Coventry, I would say no chance in hell. First of all, the fact that he's Asian is one strike against him. I mean, it shouldn't be, but my school is so fucking WASPy that it is. Also, if you're actually in class with him—and I'm only in one, religion, which isn't tracked into regular and honors like all of the real classes are—you realize how scarily competitive he is, how brutally he will cut down your argument if it isn't completely solid, how he's willing to be a real asshole if it means winning the intellectual point.

Plus, he dresses like a freak.

He buys three-piece suits from this vintage store in Little Five Points, and he'll wear the suits to class too, along with wing tips. Or else he will wear something completely crazy, like the time he came to school in a Cowboy costume, complete with Stetson hat, fringed vest, and chaps over his jeans. All the guys on the football team were high-fiving him at lunch. I mean, you'd think he'd be the biggest geek at the school, you'd think he'd have to eat with Scott Seeger and Aaron Wolanksi, but he doesn't. People worship Jim.

Except me. Even though he's supposedly one of my best friends, I don't trust him. He can be mean, like the time we got drunk a few weeks ago and started talking about politics. He and

I were sitting in the kitchen, drinking my father's Scotch, waiting for Amanda to show up, and I was saying how happy I was that I have an early birthday, because that means I will turn eighteen at the beginning of next year (senior year, thank God!), and I can vote against the Republicans in the November election.

Jim said I had no right to be a Democrat.

"You can't live in a two-million-dollar house and vote for the party of the Teamsters," he said. "That's idiotic."

"My parents' house isn't worth two million dollars," I said, though I really have no idea what it's worth. "And it's not like I can help how they choose to live. Besides, my mother has never once voted for a Republican."

He snorted.

"God, Caroline, you are so naïve. You were born rich, you are rich, and you always will be rich, so you might as well just face it and vote for the party that will let you hold on to more of your daddy's money. I'm sure if your mother earned a salary, she would start voting Republican too."

I should have yelled at him, told him to shut up, told him to get the fuck out of my (parents') house. But I couldn't say anything. I felt so utterly exposed. I started to cry, and once I started, I could not stop.

Jim's words had the finality of a sentence being handed down.

GOD KNOWS WHAT my father will do when he discovers I'm failing Algebra II. Midterm grades will be sent in a few weeks, and I know I'll get a yellow slip, the color they use to indicate immediately that your average is below a 70. Dad says if I ever fail a class I can forget about going out of state for college. That means I'll go to UGA. About twenty kids go there each year from my class. They all get apartments with other Coventry kids and join the same couple of fraternities and sororities and their southern accents get thicker and thicker and by their senior year they are engaged. That's what happened to Amanda's older sister, Sarah. She was sort of a hippie in high school, but then she went to Georgia, pledged Phi Mu, and started saying "Heck ya!" all the time, her head bobbing above her pearls.

Georgia doesn't have an acting conservatory, so it's out of the question for me to go there. Acting is what I live to do—seriously. Instead of all the dead time we spend in normal life, life on stage is all about conflict and movement; every moment is bigger and more meaningful. Frederick, my director, wants me to apply to Juilliard. I tell him I don't have the grades, but he says that doesn't matter, all that counts for admission there is how well you do in the audition. Which he says I'll nail.

I AM so far behind in algebra I don't think it's possible to catch up. Plus my teacher, Dr. Mack, is always letting us get him off topic. He's a born-again, but he loves to talk about his wild pre-conversion days. He's so dorky it's practically impossible to think of him at a party. He's got greasy blond hair, which he wears parted to the extreme left and pushed across his forehead, and he's skinnier than most of the girls in my class. Seriously. He can't weigh more than a hundred pounds. Plus he's got this supersensitive skin that is always breaking out in a red rash and flaking. It's pretty disgusting.

I don't know how many times he's told us about the keg he and his roommates kept in their dorm room at college. They attached a hose to where the pump should have been, and every morning when they woke up they'd take a suck.

I know I shouldn't try to get him off topic; I should be visiting him during Coventry's so-called power hour, the time after school when all the teachers are required to stay in their classrooms in case a student wants to come by and ask questions about the homework.

Yeah right. As soon as the final bell rings I am gone. I am anywhere but Coventry, at least until play practice begins.

Today in class I ask Dr. Mack what happened to make him convert.

"I woke up one day tired of being hungover," he says.

I don't really know what that has to do with Jesus.

I STAY LATE after rehearsal talking with Frederick. He's only twenty-three, just out of Yale, but he looks older, probably because he's such a dead ringer for Daniel Day-Lewis, gravitas and all. I find it hard to imagine him ever having been in high school, but he was, only five years ago. He went to Grady, which is where I would have gone had I gone to public school. It's awesome that he got into Yale from Grady. Everyone at Coventry is so hysterical about where they will get into college, but Frederick just toughed it out at an urban public school, wrote his college essay about the experience, and was Ivy-bound.

AT SCHOOL TODAY Amanda tells me that there is no way in hell she's letting me flunk out of Coventry. She's going to tutor me. She had Dr. Mack for algebra last year (she's on the honors track, which puts her a year ahead of me in math and science) and she got an A in the course. Amanda gets A's in all her classes. She's on academic scholarship at Coventry; otherwise there's no way her mom would be able to afford the tuition. Our freshman year Amanda got a C on her first math test and I swear she was practically suicidal over it. I kept saying, "But a seventy-six means you knew seventy-six percent of the material. That's good!"

After school we go to the condo she lives in with her mom, who hasn't come home yet to pour herself a gin and tonic and curse the men in her life. We take Cokes from the kitchen along with a glass plate of salmon mousse left over from one of her mom's catering jobs. I consider taking a beer but decide that's stupid. It's only four o'clock and besides, it's a Tuesday.

I sit on Amanda's bed, rubbing my fingers against her yellow and blue flowered comforter. She stoops in front of her books, pulling a thick notebook from the lowest shelf.

"Here," she says. "Look over these, and tell me which problems you could do if Mack gave them to you." She hands me a stack of old tests.

"Oh my God," I say.

Amanda is sitting cross-legged on the floor, staring at her foot. "I know," she says. "Do you think it's a wart?"

"Not your foot, the tests. These are the exact same ones he's using this year. These first three, I've taken them all. You'd think he would have at least changed the numbers in the problems."

Amanda looks up at me. "Maybe we should just pretend you didn't see them."

I slip the tests into my bag. "Maybe you should just pretend you didn't see that."

DR. MACK SAYS the class average on yesterday's test improved by four points.

"You guys must have been paying attention," he says.

He passes them back, each folded in half so we can't see each other's grades. Mine is a 91. I could have gotten a 100, but I purposely made some mistakes. I mean, you can't go from a 68—my brilliant score on the last one I took—to a 100 without raising some suspicion. On top of my test Dr. Mack wrote "WAY TO GO!" in red ink.

DURING REHEARSAL FREDERICK takes us to the stage of the Van Dunn Theatre. The theater is new, built only two years ago. It's beautiful. The lobby has a glass wall overlooking the cross-country trails, the seating is raised so everyone can see, and the stage floor is laid with glossy wood. Muffin Van Dunn is in my grade, but she likes to pretend she's not connected to her donor grandparents. She slums it by wearing peasant tops and used Levi's.

We line up on the stage, all facing the empty seats where the audience will be. Frederick, whose black hair is slicked back from his face, stands behind the last row, holding a clipboard with the names of everyone in the cast. Frederick always forgets the names of the kids with bit parts.

"You people are not projecting," he says, his own voice booming. "We've got to make sure Grandma with the hearing aid can understand what's happening up there."

One by one he asks us what our plans are for the weekend. We are to answer loud enough so that he can hear us from back where he is. When he gets to me, I project my voice from deep in my chest.

"After sleeping with the director of *Antigone*, I'll drive home the next morning and stop at Waffle House for breakfast."

The line of cast members jerks as people laugh and look over each other's shoulders to gawk at me.

"Well," says Frederick. "Well."

I thought it would be a funny thing to say, but I was wrong. I'm burning. I want to rewind, to go back, to tell him I'm going to Bridgetown Grill with Amanda. I'm such a fucking idiot.

I DON'T TELL my parents about my 91. Mom wouldn't react anyway. She's not really that emotive, at least not when it comes to my accomplishments. With Charles it's a different story. Dad would just shake out his newspaper and smile smugly, assuming that his threats worked. Which, in a way, they did.

DURING ASSEMBLY THIS morning they announce which juniors from our class will be on the Honor Council next year. Jim is chosen. I know it's supposed to be this great privilege and everything, but it seems to me that all the kids on it are just selling out their classmates so they can get into better colleges. I had this idea that we should boycott the system. If nobody ran for the councils (Honor and Discipline—Honor to kick out the cheaters, Discipline to kick out the drinkers), the teachers would be the only ones able to bust us. And it's not like they are going to show up at our parties to see who's drinking. Well, Frederick might. But not to get us in trouble. To join in.

TODAY WHEN DR. MACK hands me back my test (I got a 92), he says, "I don't know what you're doing, but whatever it is, keep it up!" I worry he is being facetious. All day long I wait to be called in front of the Honor Council. Ever since assembly, I can't stop thinking about it, thinking about the times I've seen people summoned. Skip Peterson, a senior, will arrive at the classroom door, whisper something to the teacher, and call you out. I've seen it happen three times since I started Coventry. Skip always looks so friendly waiting at the door. He is a wrestler, short and squat with curly brown hair. He's also active in Fellowship of Christian Athletes and Monday Morning Fellowship, and he's head Honor prefect. Once I was walking down Allen Hall just as MMF was being let out, and half the girls were either holding their stomachs or crying. It turned out Skip had brought in a slide show of aborted fetuses.

FREDERICK KEEPS DAVE and me in rehearsal until seven o'clock, practicing the slap. I am so happy that Dave is King Creon. Dave is the other really good actor at Coventry. When I'm on stage with him, I feel totally safe, like anything could happen—I could even forget a line—and he'd be there backing me up.

Frederick says that essentially *Antigone* is a story about the dignity of breaking unjust laws. Sure, Antigone's brothers were violent assholes who would rather kill each other than rule together, but there was no reason why one of them—Eteocles—should be given a noble burial while the other—Polynices—was declared a traitor to the state, his corpse unburied and left to rot. Polynices didn't do anything worse than Eteocles did. And regardless of his actions, Antigone should have been allowed to bury her brother. That was the women's spiritual duty in Greek times, to bury the dead. But her uncle Creon won't let her do it, because doing so would honor "the traitor." So she sneaks out and buries him anyway. She does a crappy job with it, I mean, all she does is sprinkle a little dirt on him, but the important thing is that she refuses to compromise her principles, even though she sacrifices her own life by doing so.

That's why the slap is so important, so crucial to understanding the play. Creon slaps me when I force him to realize that he's going to have to sentence me to death, that I won't deny the crime I've committed. He tells me that we can just cover it up and pretend it never happened, but I promise him that even if he tries to do that, I'll just go and bury my brother again. When he finally realizes that I won't back down, he slaps me, and in that moment, I win. In that moment, he is the bad guy; I am the virtuous heroine, and the gods will reward me justly.

We practice the slap again and again. To make it real, Dave actually has to hit me. Hard. This isn't some cheesy high school production. I mean, it's high school, but this is Coventry, and nothing is amateur at Coventry. The only thing that softens the blow is that I know it's coming so I can turn my head when I feel his hand on my cheek. He must have slapped me twenty-five times before Frederick let us go. My face is still red when I arrive home to an empty kitchen. I find Mom, Dad, and Charles in the den, watching *Jeopardy!* Charles and Mom are practically snuggling together on the sofa. Dad is in his chair, his eyes closed, the newspaper in his lap.

Looking at Dad, who is a Coventry alum, I wonder: does Coventry make you sign a pledge upon graduation, promising you'll dress like a Republican for the rest of your life? Dad looks just like the preppy guys at my high school, only older and more dressed up. You've got to hand it to him, he keeps in good shape with his morning run; there's no gut sticking out of his blue Brooks Brothers shirt, which is still tucked into his black suit pants. His light brown hair is cut just like a football player's, short on the back and sides. The only difference is that Dad grows a comb-over to cover his bald spot.

"There's vegetable soup in the fridge," Mom says, not even looking up at me.

Mom's vegetable soup is a total misnomer. It's got two pounds of ground beef in it.

I just stand there, waiting for her to look up at me and say something about my appearance.

"Who is Stephen King," says Charles.

Mom clucks her tongue and tickles Charles's forearm. "Right again!" she says.

I want to scream. At Charles for being Mom's favorite. At her for not noticing that my cheek is red and might even bruise, and at Dad just to make him wake the fuck up.

WHEN I ARRIVE at the Waffle House, Jim is already there, sitting in a booth and sipping coffee. He's wearing normal clothes— jeans and an untucked flannel shirt—but he has on a green plaid hunting hat with earflaps.

"Are we rereading *Catcher in the Rye?*" I ask.

He points his finger at me as if it were a gun. "You got it."

I order coffee and a pecan waffle and wait for him to tell me why he wanted to meet for breakfast. I wonder if he's going to confess that he slept with Shyamala Patel and consult with me over whether or not he should tell Amanda. Shyamala and Jim were in the Inquirers' Society together, and Jim was always saying that she was the only girl he knew who was his intellectual equal. She graduated last year and went to Harvard. Jim said he saw her this summer while he was attending an enrichment program up there.

A hundred bucks says they fucked.

Jim asks if I'm still meditating and I tell him that I try.

"That makes me very happy," he says. "I think meditation will be extremely helpful for you."

The waitress brings our food, the waffle for me and cheese and eggs with cinnamon raisin toast for Jim. He eats deliberately, taking his time with each bite. I slow down my eating so I won't look like a total pig in front of him.

"There's some talk going around about your high scores in Dr. Mack's class," he says, after taking a sip of coffee.

I am chewing a bite of waffle, and it feels as if it's expanding, stuffing the inside of my mouth like a piece of foam. I wash it down with water.

"Who's talking?" I ask.

Jim shakes his head. "It's confidential," he says. "The incoming prefects, we sit in on the meetings."

Oh my God. "It came up at a meeting?"

Jim's mouth is a straight line; it almost seems as if he's mad at me. "Look, I've told you too much already. Just be careful. Don't tell anyone about Amanda's tests. Pretend it never happened. If you do get called in front of the Honor Council, remember: Deny, deny, deny until you die, you die, you die."

He takes another sip of coffee. "Besides, they've hardly got any evidence."

I CONSIDER ASKING Frederick if he's heard any rumors that I'm cheating; maybe he knows the inside faculty scoop. I am pretty sure he wouldn't turn me in, even if I told him everything. He doesn't care about Coventry. He already told me he lied during his interview with the headmaster. In order to be hired here you have to say that you are a Christian.

"You lied about that?" I asked.

He shrugged. "I'm an actor."

And he is. In a few years he's going to apply to MFA programs in acting. He would have gone right to grad school, but he needed money. That's why he took the job at Coventry, so he could live at home with his mom and save.

IN CLASS, I don't try to distract Dr. Mack with questions about his personal life. I just keep my head down and take notes, trying not to draw attention from anyone. That's hard because I arrived just before the second bell, and the only seat left was the one by Magda Miller. Magda is one of two lesbians in our class (they're not officially "out" or anything, but everyone who does theater knows) and she is always trying to be wacky. She carries plastic pieces of fruit in a straw bag—don't ask me why. Everyday before class begins she lays the fruit out in front of her on the table.

I keep glancing around the room, trying to see if anyone is looking at me strangely. Maybe I'm imagining it, but I think Becca Sanders, who is only a sophomore, is glaring in my direction. Becca is really good at math, but I outscored her on the last two tests.

INSTEAD OF GOING to the cafeteria, Amanda and I eat lunch at the Shack, which we are supposed to call the Student Center, but no one does. I buy a pepperoni pita pocket and a Coke, and she buys a Diet Coke and a bagel. I refuse to buy diet soda, even though I have gained ten pounds in the last year, even though Mom says that at some point in every woman's life you have to start counting calories. Frederick says I have beautiful curves. He says as long as my waist stays small I should not fight my hips and my boobs, that they will help me get acting jobs one day. He says I should always wear V-necks to auditions.

"Did Jim talk to you about the tests?" I ask, keeping my voice low in case someone is listening.

Amanda nods, sticking her finger into the little cup of cream cheese that comes with the bagel.

"I didn't know you were going to tell anybody that I borrowed them," I say.

She shrugs. "He's my boyfriend." She licks the cream cheese off her finger. "Don't worry. He says he doubts it will be brought to court."

"What are we going to do if it is?" I ask.

"I don't think we should talk about this in here," she says. "Anyway, I don't mean to be a bitch, but all I did was show you my notes from last year. I had no idea you would use them to cheat."

I don't know what to say. Apparently she doesn't either. She looks over my shoulder and starts waving to a group of guys walking into the Shack.

"Eric!" she says. "Over here."

At home after dinner I lie on my bed in the dark imagining what it will be like to go in front of the Honor Council. My freshman year two girls got kicked out for stealing old tests from their chemistry teacher's drawer. I remember seeing one of them, Emily, after she was expelled. Her eyes were swollen from crying and her cheeks were red and splotchy. She told me the council kept them waiting in an emptied-out office for two hours while they deliberated.

I remind myself that I, like Frederick, am an actor. Everything that happens to me I will use to hone my craft. And being an actor, I can fake my way through the hearing. I will deny ever having seen the tests. Or I will plead ignorance, say I didn't know I was cheating, that all I was doing was studying from a friend's old notes. Anywhere else, this would be no big deal. I heard that at Georgia,

SAE keeps a file of old tests for all the brothers to use. But Coventry is different. Coventry is concerned with our character.

It's OPENING NIGHT and I nailed it. I was good. I was great. I got a standing ovation. Frederick gives me a card and six pink roses after the performance. The card says that he couldn't imagine a more talented and lovely actress to play Antigone. It says that if we both end up in New York I should give him a call and we will get a drink. I bury the card in my bag after opening it. He could get fired for writing something like that.

He has the most beautiful handwriting. Each letter looks worked over.

I TELL MYSELF I'm not going to cheat again, but I end up once again memorizing the answers from Amanda's old test. I try to figure the problems out on my own, but I have no idea what any of it means. And I can't call Amanda for help. We haven't talked since that day in the Shack.

BESIDE MY 92 Dr. Mack writes, "Way to Go!" I feel frantic looking at his red words. I am sure he is being sarcastic.

I CAN'T STAND it any longer, this waiting to be kicked out. I drive to Jim's house after school, my window rolled down because it's such a nice day. The leaves on the trees are red and orange and yellow and if things were normal Amanda and I would be at the park eating ice cream or drinking beers.

Jim's dad is an economics professor at Emory, so they live near there, even though it's sort of far away from Coventry. Jim's house is smaller than ours, but it's really nice. It looks like an old English cottage—it has these little diamond-shaped windows— and it's set on this huge lot that backs up to the woods. Jim's old Jeep Wagoneer is parked in the driveway. I park behind it, noticing for the millionth time his bumper sticker that reads "Wherever You Go, There You Are."

His mother answers the door wearing a blue denim jumper on top of a white T-shirt. She looks matronly, a look my mother avoids at all costs. (My mother wouldn't be caught dead in denim anything. Not even jeans.)

Mrs. Watanabe calls for Jim, and when he doesn't answer, she says he's probably out back. She leads me through the front hall, lined with black-and-white photos of Jim and his two sisters, through the kitchen, and out the back door. The kitchen smells of melting chocolate. She says she's baking cookies.

In the very back of the yard, just where the woods come in, Jim is walking the labyrinth, his chin tucked to his chest, his eyes to the ground. I stand on the edge and watch as he makes his way to the center, coming right up to it and then hitting a wall, which is really just a line he is not supposed to step over. He doesn't. Instead he dutifully follows the course set out for him, walking toward one of its outer rings. Despite its tricks, if you continue to follow the labyrinth you will eventually get to heaven, even when it seems you are being led the wrong way. When Jim finally reaches the center he looks up, sees me, and smiles.

"Caroline. I'm so pleased that you are here. I was just thinking about you."

He sits down, Indian-style, in the center circle, in heaven.

"Come sit with me," he says. "The stones are nice and warm from the sun."

I walk to the center of the maze, stepping over the lines. I sit beside him, stretching my legs out and trying to hold my back very straight. The sun shines on my shoulders, and the warm rocks feel wonderful against the backs of my legs.

I wish I could just relax, just sit and be still, but that's not what I'm here for. I'm here for information, for reassurance.

"Jim, I'm freaking out. Every day I think Skip Peterson is going to come pull me out of class and drag me in front of the Honor Council."

"Would you like some jerky?" he asks, pulling a Slim Jim out of his pocket.

"Um, no thanks," I say, indicating with my (sarcastic) tone how odd the timing of his offer is. Then, remembering how much I need him to help me, I try to be funny. "Do you always eat snacks named after you?"

He smiles beatifically as if he is a wise old monk and I am a harmless but annoying fly. He tears the plastic wrapper off the top of his Slim Jim and takes one small bite.

"Please tell me," I say. "Is the case going to come up?"

He doesn't answer while his mouth is full, just stares straight ahead and chews and chews.

Finally he swallows. He looks right at me, his eyes darker and even more intense than usual. "You're going to be all right. I promise. Nothing is going to happen to you."

For a moment I believe him and the relief I feel is palpable. It's like being granted a pardon and knowing I get to return to the living. And then I see the partially eaten Slim Jim on the stone in front of me and I feel a pressure on my leg, which I realize is his hand, rubbing, working its way up my thigh.

"You are going to be just fine," he says and he is moving his hand up my skirt while we sit in the middle of the labyrinth, his mother only a grassy backyard away.

But what does that matter? She is busy baking chocolate cookies or washing her denim jumpers or hanging another photo of her son on the wall. And their house is private, on a corner lot, bordered by spruce trees on the neighbor's side, woods in the back. Jim and Amanda have had sex on a blanket in those woods. Amanda told me.

No one but me can see what his hand is doing, see where it is creeping, feel his fingers gently stroke my thigh.

I want to tell him to stop. I need to tell him to stop. But I realize with sudden clarity that I have a choice: it's this or the Honor Council. And I know, in my gut, that my cheating was never discussed at a council meeting. They would have called me in by now; they would have questioned me when they first got wind of it. Jim and Amanda are the only two people—besides me—who know what I did.

But that could change. Jim could turn me in. He's looking at me, watching to see how I react to his hand.

I open my legs just the slightest bit.

CHAPTER THREE

Joie de Vivre Means Pain in My Ass, Right?

(Louise, Spring 2000)

Remember Susan Smith, the woman from South Carolina who drowned her two children? Everyone was talking about carjackings back then. You were supposed to lock your door the second you got in. Susan Smith said she'd been carjacked, that a black man held a gun to her head and forced her out of the car before he drove off with her kids.

That story scared us. As I was waiting for my low-impact aerobics class to begin, the ladies stretching in front of me whispered that this sort of tragedy would never, ever have happened back when they were girls. "Maybe things weren't always fair," said the one in the purple leotard, "but the world was safer. A black man would not dare go after a white baby."

As I was waiting for Caroline to finish her acting class at the Alliance, Bootsey Brook told me about all the ways a man could get into your house when you weren't looking.

"Lock your door even if you're just going back and forth carrying groceries in from the car," she said. "You never know who might be waiting to get at you."

And then the truth came out, that there had been no kidnapping, that Susan Smith had rolled the car off the boat ramp herself, her three-year-old and eighteen-month-old strapped inside, crying for their mommy before their cries were swallowed by the cold dark water. After that only one word was heard at the grocery, at church, waiting in the carpool line at Coventry: *monster*. What kind of a monster would do such a thing?

LORD HELP ME, but I could relate to Susan Smith. Not to her actions, but to her thoughts. Once when Caroline was two and a half, she and I were in the kitchen, in our nightgowns, fixing breakfast while her daddy slept in. Caroline was standing not a foot away from me when I reached under the cabinet to pull out the iron skillet I use to fry bacon. Feeling the weight of the skillet in my hand, a thought flashed in my mind: *What if I were to bring this down on her head?*

Quick as I had it the thought was gone and I was asking Caroline how many pieces of oink-oink she wanted and I tried to write it off as that time of the month.

But it lodged in my brain. Not the urge to kill my daughter—Lord no, that was fast and fleeting—but the fact that I had the thought at all. Maybe having it meant I had inherited Mother's craziness and it was just now coming out. Maybe I wasn't fit to raise a child. Most disturbing was the fact that such a violent image could enter my mind during a time when I was not even upset with my daughter. What might happen the next time Caroline acted difficult?

Believe me, she was not an ideal child. Not like Charles, who came around five years later and was fifty times easier. There were times when I thought Caroline had it in for me, when I thought she was sent to this earth simply to make me snap.

Like the time she was four and kept trying to get my attention while I was on the phone with Tiny. Tiny was making me laugh so hard, telling me about how she clipped off her husband Anders's comb-over while he was asleep, that I ignored my daughter, told her I'd take her for ice cream if she would leave me alone for ten minutes. I should have noticed how quiet things got after she left the room. But it had been so long since I had had an uninterrupted conversation with Tiny that I decided to take the silence as a blessing.

When I walked into the living room half an hour later, the built-in bookshelves were empty. Every single one of my hardback books—their bindings, that is—was flung on the floor, the pages torn out. Paper floated in the air. I could smell it, the smell of my destroyed books from college, back when I could not wait for my future to begin, when I could not wait for John Henry to propose to me so I could become a wife and a mother. And there was my beautiful four-year-old, her eyes shining, looking up at me with an expression that showed she knew exactly what she had just done, tearing one last page from one last book while I watched, my jaw hanging.

I wanted to cause damage. I really did. And I suppose that is the difference between a child abuser and me: I didn't let myself touch her. Oh, I knew a spanking was justified, but I also knew that if my hands got hold of her I might do some real harm.

I turned and left the room and then kept on walking out the front door. I walked all the way to Peachtree Street. *That's it*, I told myself. *I'm just going to leave this time.* I wouldn't even go back to get the car. I would walk to the Amtrak station, which was just a mile down the road. I would take the first train that was leaving Atlanta.

I only made it a few blocks down Peachtree before I began

worrying about Caroline, in the house, alone. I wasn't worried that she might get hurt; I was worried that she might destroy something else. I turned around and started walking back. A car honked and I looked up to see Bootsey in her wood-paneled station wagon, waving like crazy as she sped past me. I smiled and waved, just as cheerful as I could be. I never let Bootsey see me upset. You had to be careful with that woman. She was a vicious gossip. She would believe the most ludicrous stories and then spread them all over Atlanta. Once she had Tiny practically ready to file for divorce from Anders even though we all know that Anders adores Tiny and never, ever would have slept with that niece of theirs who was staying with them over the summer.

Probably it was a good thing Bootsey drove by because afterwards I was able to transfer some of my anger at Caroline onto her. By the time I got home I had calmed down. That is, until I looked into the living room and again saw all of my destroyed books, my child trying to stick the pages back into them.

The day Caroline started kindergarten was the happiest day of my life, second only, I am sure, to the day she will leave for college.

Oh, I'll miss her. I will. And there are things I miss already about Caroline and Charles's baby years: Caroline's dark curls, which grew tight as corkscrews until she was five and they loosened, the downy feel of Charles's hair against my hand while I nursed him. (Though I would have preferred he stopped nursing sooner. At two he was still trying to unbutton my shirt at the grocery store, wanting a little midday snack.)

I miss their sticky cheeks and their warm breath and the little cards they would color for me on days I felt so down I could not get out of bed, days I would tell them they could watch as much TV as they wanted, eat cookies until their stomachs hurt, just be quiet—please, keep it down.

Probably I should have been on antidepressants. My mother was a new woman once the doctors discovered Prozac.

I USED TO worry that I might have scarred Caroline. But she's turned out better than I expected, so far. It all makes sense now; it fits together perfectly. Caroline was difficult because Caroline is an artist. Does she not have the lead role in every play at Coventry? Is it not impossible to turn away from her when she is on stage, her presence so burning, so alive? People could not stop talking about the intensity of her stage presence during *Antigone*.

I should have been credited. Surely our difficult relationship helped her develop her onstage fire.

She's still incorrigible, only now she's seventeen and gorgeous, which makes her powerful as well. Tiny says that Caroline looks like "sex on legs." I would be more offended by her description if it weren't so dead on. Sometimes I watch Caroline enter a room and I think, *Where on earth did you come from? And are those the same clothes I bought for you at Lenox Square mall?* She wears her jeans, which seemed strictly utilitarian in Macy's fluorescent-lit dressing room, so low that her hip bone is exposed. And they are so much tighter than when we first bought them, as if she put them in the dryer for hours and hours. Her shirts, nice button-down ones that follow Coventry's dress code, are always unbuttoned one too many at the neck, and she must have stuck them in the same dryer with her jeans, because they too are tight and form-fitting.

And her hair. Lord, her hair. What started out as precious little corkscrew curls when she was a child has turned into a mass of long brown tangles and knots. I am forever buying her conditioners that would allow her to run a comb through her curls every now and then, but Caroline, surprise, surprise, does not allow a thing about her to be tamed. Her hair is so messy that she can stick a pencil into it and the pencil won't fall out.

Sometimes I think she must keep her eyeliner pencil stuck

in there at all times so that she can constantly reapply it. The first time I saw Caroline with her eyes rimmed the way she likes I thought, *Thank God she goes to Coventry. Surely such distracting makeup breaks the dress code.* But she came home with it still on. And with a child like Caroline, you have to choose your battles, so even though I thought the thick smoky lines around her eyes made her look like a drug addict contemplating robbery to feed her habit, I kept my mouth shut. I figured, if Coventry is okay with it, I guess I have to be too.

Her father notices none of this, of course. He lets her get away with murder. All the men in her life do. Coventry requires that teachers send a note if a student's grade drops below a 75. Once her math teacher—a young man in his twenties—sent home a deficiency notice that ended with "Brava!"

"Your daughter is a delight," he wrote. "She has a real joie de vivre."

She has to be in homeroom every morning by 8:00 a.m. She has her license, and the brand-new Honda Accord we bought for her, but don't think that means she gets to school on time. Every morning when her alarm clock sounds, she punches it off. I go to her room, knock, and cheerfully inform her it's time to rise and shine. She doesn't move a muscle. I send her father, who taps her on the shoulder before he begins to shake her awake. She doesn't budge. Finally he will carry her, slung over his shoulder, to the bathroom and dump her in the shower. And half the time that doesn't even work! We will find her, minutes later, slumped against the shower wall, having turned the water off and fallen back to sleep. It is almost as if she has a neurological disorder.

Last semester she received so many detentions for being late that she was suspended and had to go in front of the Discipline Council. Now her drama teacher, another young man in his twenties, gives her a wake-up call every morning.

Really, it's ridiculous. I told John Henry that we needed either to send her to boarding school or to wash our hands of her. I mean John Henry and I worry so much about her bad grades and her pile-up of detentions that she doesn't have to do an ounce of worrying herself. And she doesn't. At least not in any way I can tell.

Yesterday she and I were driving to this little shop off Peachtree Road. She had seen a dress there she liked, and I was going to buy it for her. She had spent the night at a friend's house, and when she arrived home that morning she smelled like stale beer. I didn't say anything. I just did not want to get into it with her. See, I have been reading about Buddhism and have been trying to learn detachment.

But it was hard not to say anything with her sitting in the front seat of my Lexus. The smell of alcohol was overpowering. I glanced over, noticing her matted curls and the smudge of last night's liner under her eye. She was wearing an old pinstriped shirt of her daddy's, unbuttoned one too many, as always. She didn't just smell like beer. She smelled like sex. She smelled like some boy's dried semen, probably caked on that flat stomach of hers.

Lord knows what my daddy would have done if I came home smelling like a sperm depository. And then that girl had the gall to tell me that she was getting deficiency notices again in chemistry and French (but not algebra! she added, as if I should be proud of her for failing only two subjects).

"Don't worry," she said. "I've got it under control." She said all this without looking at me. Not unfriendly, just bored.

I didn't know what to say. I did not want to play the same role as always, to yell and plead and look up every tutor in town to try to get her in shape. I felt a flash of anger, but then I detached. I looked at my daughter, at the seventeen-year-old who would fit in better on a street corner than in my car, and I just did not care at all.

"I feel sorry for you," I said.

She glanced at me, mean. "Why?"

"Life is going to disappoint you, darling, and you will be the main person to blame for the hurt."

"Mom, I'm fine."

I smiled. "For now. While we pay the bills. I'm just going to feel real sorry for you next year when you don't get into any colleges you apply to. Tiny's daughter didn't get into Georgia. You remember that, don't you?"

"Helen Persons is an idiot," Caroline said. "I mean, she really is. I can't believe you'd say I won't get into Georgia just because some idiot didn't get in."

This was supposed to be the start of one of our blowout fights, where half of the time I would pull the car over to the side of the road and tell Caroline to walk home. She'd show up an hour later, smelling a little sweaty but looking satisfied, like somehow she had won the battle because she could make it home on her own.

I just kept driving, loosening my grip on the wheel. "You know what?" I said. "It's your life, not mine. And frankly, I don't give a flying fuck anymore about what you do or don't do. I'm tired of worrying. I just do not care at all."

"God, Mom," she said, and then she started crying, the panicky kind of little sobs that sound the way Charles does just before he has an asthma attack. I watched my girl cry, watched the tears run down her face, watched her glance at me through her squinted eyes, and I felt as composed as a queen. I wanted to call all my friends who had teenage daughters and tell them, *Just stop caring!*

It's a miracle, I swear to God.

CHAPTER FOUR

Clay Bird

(Missy, Summer 2000)

*M*ama is usually too tired after work to do anything but lie around and watch TV. Tonight she doesn't even make dinner, just puts two bowls, the box of Frosted Flakes, and a carton of milk on the table. After we eat she splays on the sofa, trying to cool herself with a paper fan from church. I sit on Daddy's old La-Z-Boy, the stuffing poking out of the holes in the fabric. Ever since Daddy's mama, Meemaw, died, Mama's been saying she's going to haul that thing to the junkyard. I squirt myself with water from the plastic bottle Mama uses to spritz her tomato plants. Meemaw died six years ago. That La-Z-Boy isn't going anywhere.

I go to the kitchen and get my Coke out of the freezer. Mama looks up as I walk back to my seat, holding the cold can against my neck.

"You going to be up all night if you drink that," she says.

"I'm going to be up all night anyway," I say, "unless you got AC without telling me."

Mama purses her lips. It's the lady minister on TV tonight,

Mrs. Lacy Lovehart. Her hair is so blond it looks white. She doesn't give much of a sermon. Instead she gives the *Rapture Update*. My favorite is when she reads headlines from newspapers and explains how they prove the Rapture is soon to come. Like the fact that we invented the Internet proves we've become a lot smarter. And since man's intelligence is supposed to increase tenfold in the last one hundred years, that means the end is near.

"Do you think this heat is a sign?" I ask Mama.

"In Hell," she says, "this would feel like an ice storm."

She reaches for the spray bottle she uses for ironing and mists herself.

"Sweet Jesus," she says. "If that don't look like your daddy."

I look. It is a commercial for a used car lot. All I see are a bunch of pickup trucks. Then the camera swings to the announcer. Even in a white suit and a cowboy hat, I recognize Daddy. He looks so tall and lean. His hair isn't quite as curly as I remember, but those are his eyes all right: bright blue and framed with lashes so long Mama used to say it was a shame they were wasted on a man. My lashes are just as thick, but I'm not near as pretty as Daddy is handsome. I still have chubby cheeks—baby fat, says Mama—but I figure I ought to be past that by now, considering I am twelve and am going to be in the eighth grade next fall on account of having started first grade when I was five since I could already read full passages from the Bible and spell words like *Beelzebub*.

"We've rounded up the best deals in town, so bring your posse on down to Duke's New and Used Cars. Located just off I-Two Eighty-five behind the Big Wiener."

Daddy's name is Luke, which is the same as Duke but with a D. Maybe he put together *Daddy* and *Luke* to equal *Duke*. I didn't even know he was back in Georgia, let alone that he owns a car lot. The last we heard he was living in Florida. I stand up.

"Let's drive over there," I say.

Mama looks at me. It's too dark in here to see the lines that pull down her lips, or the bump on her nose from where Meemaw broke it right before she died when she was too sick to know any better. The TV casts a soft glow on Mama's face, her yellow hair a halo behind her. She was a princess on the homecoming court the semester before she dropped out of school to have me.

"Sugar," she says, "we can't afford a new car."

"Not to buy a car," I say. "To see Daddy."

Mama's chipped tooth shows when she laughs. "That wasn't your daddy," she says. "Your daddy is long gone. That man just looked like him."

She lifts herself off the couch with a grunt and walks to her bedroom. She turns at the door.

"Your daddy don't have enough money to buy a Happy Meal. How's he going to buy himself a car dealership?"

I can't win an argument with Mama, so I do not even try. But I know that was my daddy I saw. And I know he aired his commercial on the God Is Good network because Jesus told him I would be watching.

MONDAYS AND THURSDAYS Mama cleans for Mrs. Parker in Atlanta. During the summer I go with her because Mrs. Parker lets me swim in her pool. It takes us more than an hour and a half to get there, because of the traffic. Mrs. Parker is always sighing over the fact that we have to drive so far, as if sitting in the car is the worst part of our day. I tell her that the commute isn't really that long. I don't want her feeling sorry for me.

Mrs. Parker says she likes living in town because it cuts down on the amount of time she has to spend in the car. It's true. She lives so close to downtown you can practically touch the skyscrapers from her backyard. It's a real nice neighborhood though, even if it is right smack in the city. None of the houses in it look exactly alike, but they're all big and tended to: no peeling paint or overgrown yards or nothing.

On our street in Loganville, some folks keep their front yards nice and neat like me and Mama, while other people, like our neighbor, RD, pile so much junk on their lawns you'd think they were having a garage sale. The only thing in common between the front of our house and the front of RD's is that the American flag flies from each.

In Mrs. Parker's neighborhood a few people hang flags, but not American flags usually. Theirs just show the seasons with fall leaves or spring flowers or rainbow stripes or something nice like that. At the beginning of the summer there was a flag that looked like a slice of watermelon hanging from the front porch of the house next to Mrs. Parker's. The flag itself was cut into the shape of a watermelon. It was so cute and cheerful! At dinner I asked Mama if we could buy a watermelon flag like the one we saw in Mrs. Parker's neighborhood. RD, who was eating with us, piped up and said he'd rather spend the money on a real watermelon, one that we could have for dessert. I had to bite my tongue to keep from telling him I was talking to Mama, not him. Mama would kill me if I was rude to his face. She says I need to treat him with respect.

She didn't used to feel that way. Back when RD was just our next-door neighbor, she didn't mind my teasing him. She used to tease him too. She used to look at his tiny jeans hanging on the clothesline and say she wouldn't be able to fit her wrist through the waist, let alone her hips. But then he and Mama started seeing each other. It happened fast. The week after she put in a prayer request at church for a good man—Mama started going to a real big church after Daddy left so everyone wouldn't know her business there like they did at our old church, which my granddaddy started—RD showed up for the casual worship service, the one

Mama and me go to so we don't have to wear pantyhose. When she saw RD there, she figured her prayers had been answered. I wasn't so sure, wasn't sure at all that RD was the person God meant to send. I just think RD got wind of her request and took advantage.

I'm betting God hasn't given up yet on Daddy.

Just because RD is a scrawny thing don't think he don't eat. Mama must spend half her pay on food for him, and he doesn't even come over every night. Last Sunday after church Mama fried a chicken and practically before I had a chance to say "Amen" at the end of grace, RD shot his hand out and grabbed a drumstick, not even caring that it might be Mama's and my favorite piece too. Not even caring that one of us was going to be left out.

Mama doesn't seem to mind that on top of being a puny little thing he has no table manners. Mama says what matters is that RD is a good man, a Christian.

Sometimes I wonder if he really is one, if he really accepted Jesus into his heart or just wants to work his way into Mama's. It's gotten so I'm not even sure about her anymore. I've started to think I'm the only one between the three of us who still takes church seriously. Even in God's house the two of them can't keep their hands off each other. During the sermon he tickles his finger up and down her arm. There I am, not two feet away from them, *trying* to pay attention to Pastor Finch, and they are playing X marks the spot like kids at Bible camp. Sometimes it feels like I'm the grown-up.

Right after they started dating—or courting, as Mama says—RD came over to watch the Super Bowl. When Mama walked in front of the TV during the game, he swatted her bottom. She yelped, then started giggling like a fool. He pulled her into his lap and they watched the rest of the game that way.

I was going to fix nacho dip for a snack; we had Velveeta and

Pace picante sauce just waiting to be zapped in the microwave. But watching the two of them curled up together, I didn't even bother. There's no point bringing out food for people who don't care a lick whether or not you are there. I went to my room before the game was even over.

MAMA AND I go around to the back of Mrs. Parker's house. I carry the mop and bucket. She carries the vacuum cleaner. Lord, does Mama love that thing. Last year she won $1,000 being the hundredth caller on Keepin' It Real Country. She bought herself a vacuum cleaner that cost $200. I am not joking. She said it would make her life two hundred times easier. It is so light it doesn't even strain her back to lift it, and it sucks up anything that comes near it. I bet it would suck up a dog if it got in the way, especially one of those tiny ones.

Mama fumbles through her key chain, looking for the right one. Mrs. Parker comes to the door before Mama has a chance to find it. I can't help but smile when I see her. She just looks so nice and put together, her clothes crisp and clean, her chin-length hair all dark and shiny like she polished it with Pledge.

"Hello, Faye!" she says. Mrs. Parker always greets us like we just stopped by for an unexpected visit. "And Missy! Your summer break must have finally started. Can you believe Coventry let out Charles and Caroline over three weeks ago?"

"Friday was our last day," I say.

Mrs. Parker grabs my hands and lifts my arms, as if she wants us to play ring around the rosy. She looks me up and down. "Missy, I swear you get prettier every time you come here! My daughter used to have curls like yours when she was little, but they fell right out when she turned five and now they are a tangled mess. But look at yours. Perfect ringlets, like a little doll. And your eyes! So dark and knowing and intelligent! What a wise soul they reveal. And my goodness, you're so tall for your age.

You're almost as tall as me! Of course I'm only five four, so that doesn't say that much."

I duck my head and smile. I love it when Mrs. Parker fusses over me.

"You are a flower in bloom, my dear," she says, letting go of my hands. "Just growing and growing."

"Her breasts are sure growing," Mama says. "They went from bee stings to beehives overnight."

I know it's a sin to have such thoughts, but sometimes I wish Mama would just die. Just keel over real quick and be gone. That way she'd never be able to embarrass me again and Mrs. Parker might let me come live with her.

I look around, pretending this is my kitchen, pretending that Mama is just a lady who works for me. The room smells like lemon cleaner. The red tile floor shines. Copper pots hang from hooks in the ceiling, glowing in the sunlight. Mama says there are two kinds of people she cleans for: those who need it and those who don't. As far as I can tell, Mrs. Parker's house don't even get dust.

"I've got some appointments I've got to run off to, but there's turkey in the fridge, and please, eat some of these goodies I made." Mrs. Parker points to a plate on the counter, piled high with brownies. "Lord knows I don't need them."

She laughs in that soft little way she has and runs her fingers along the sides of her pale blue shirt. The shirt is unbuttoned low enough so I can see the tops of her breasts, round and freckled.

"Missy, are you planning on swimming?"

"Yes, ma'am," I say. "I brought my bathing suit."

"Wonderful. I'm glad someone is going to be using the pool. Just make sure you are completely dry before you come in the house. These tile floors are such a hassle. They stain if they get even one drop of water on them."

Before I have the chance to say anything, Mama says, "She'll dry herself off."

Mama pulls a paper towel from the roll and squirts 409 on the sparkling black countertop.

"Faye, that reminds me." Mrs. Parker walks to the pantry in the back of the kitchen and takes out a pump bottle. "I bought this at the most wonderful new grocery store that's opened up near Emory. The store is called Whole Foods, and in addition to the most gorgeous produce you have ever seen, they sell all kinds of natural cleaning products. This one uses citric acid from lemons instead of chemicals, and it is supposed to be just as effective as what you've been using."

She hands the bottle to her with a smile. The price tag is still on it. It cost $7.95.

Mama says thanks, but if I know her, she's thinking Mrs. Parker just wasted eight bucks.

"One more thing," says Mrs. Parker. "I have shut the door to Charles's room and you should just pretend it's not there, same as you do with Caroline's. I've told him for the last time to straighten up before you come. He's almost thirteen years old, for goodness' sake, and if he leaves his room a mess he doesn't deserve to have it cleaned."

"I don't mind doing it," says Mama.

"Faye, you are so sweet, but I don't want Charles to think a woman is always going to clean up after him."

Mama laughs. I hate for Mrs. Parker to see her chipped tooth.

"You mean you don't want him to be like every other man on earth?" Mama asks.

"Oh, Faye," says Mrs. Parker, peering at her own reflection in the oven to fluff her hair. "RD isn't that way, is he?"

I glare at Mama. What is she doing telling Mrs. Parker about him?

• • •

LAST SUMMER WHEN Mama was out of the room and I was alone with Mrs. Parker, I asked her if she was a Christian. We'd been given a mission at church to bring five people to Jesus before school started up again. Mrs. Parker said that she was "Episcopalian by birth" but that she was extremely interested in Buddhism. Buddhism!

I asked her if she had a church home and she said that she was a member of All Saints but that "brunch often called louder than church."

I invited Mrs. Parker to come to our church. She said she'd think about it. Our pastor says a lot of people have stopped going to church because churches have stopped preaching the Truth. Pastor Finch says God gave the church the Gospels for a reason—to use them. He does too. Sometimes he gets so worked up about the Lord that he yells and cries and speaks in foreign tongues. It scares me near to death when he does, but I figure if I die from Pastor Finch's preaching I'll shoot straight up to Heaven.

Pastor Finch says this life is about as important as a sneeze. Face it, he says, this life is tedious. This life is boring. This life can be painful, even. And work ain't called work because it's fun. But in Heaven, anything can happen. Pastor Finch says if I want birthday cake every day in Heaven, I get it. If I want movie star silky straight hair, fine. The chip in Mama's front tooth? Fixed. And all that will pale beside the real joy of Heaven, because in Heaven I will meet Jesus, and Jesus will love me like no one has before. It will be like when I was little and Daddy would scratch my back until I fell asleep. Only Jesus won't leave. Ever.

Hell is a different story. Mama and me have this idea about how Satan is as tricky in Hell as he is on earth. We think he makes it so that when you first go to Hell it's really hot, like a heat wave in August, but it's a heat you can stand. What he's doing is making you think you can outsmart him by getting used to the heat. But what you won't know is that he has different rooms. One for people who just died, then a hotter one for people who are getting used to the temperature, then a hotter one and a hotter one still and so on for eternity.

When I first walk out of church Sunday afternoons, I feel as if I've just stepped out of a bubble bath. I feel scrubbed clean on the inside. The feeling fades when I get back in Mama's Buick. It smells like stale smoke. The front seat is sticky from spilled Cokes and ketchup, and the cleaning bottles rattle around in the back as if they're just dying to tell us that we ain't in Heaven yet.

FOR NOT BEING a real Christian, Mrs. Parker sure likes Jesus. She has an enormous painting of Him, hung smack in the middle of her living room wall. You wouldn't even know it *is* Him if His wrists weren't pierced and He didn't have long, flowing hair. Instead of wearing a white robe, Jesus is wearing a blue ball gown with rhinestones dotted along the straps. And instead of a crown of thorns or a halo, he wears a diamond tiara on his head. The blue of his ball gown is so rich you just want to stare, but I try not to. I know it is some kind of sinning to picture Jesus looking like a girl.

Below the painting is a bunch of white clay birds perched on a long wooden table. Mrs. Parker bought them at one of those art shows she's always going to. Mama was at her house cleaning when she came home with them. Mama said that each bird was wrapped first in bubble wrap and then in newspaper. The bubble wrap was taped on so tight it took Mama and Mrs. Parker forever to get it all off.

Mama told me there must have been a hundred birds, but I counted and there are only forty-two. It took me forever to count them because I kept forgetting which bird I started with, but then

I noticed that one of the birds was smaller than all the others, so I started with her.

I love the birds. They are probably my favorite things in the world. They just look so clean and pure; they look like the birds we'll see in Heaven. The runt is the sweetest of them all. I pick her up and whisper the name I gave her, Kimberly.

Kimberly doesn't have many features, just a round bird body with wings etched into her side, a beaked bird head, and little stones for eyes that are a silvery blue. None of the other birds on the table have eyes. Just this little one, and they seem to be sparkling. When I hold Kimberly I get the feeling that she belongs to me, the way a baby belongs to its mama. I stroke her polished back with my finger. I kiss her little beak.

I wonder what my daddy would think of this little bird. Mama always said he had a soft spot for creatures. She said it used to drive her crazy how he'd snatch a mouse up by its tail and drop it outside in the grass instead of killing it. She said he turned our house into Mouse Central.

Daddy would probably love my little Kimberly. Maybe I can show her to him if I find a way to visit him at the car lot. Maybe I'll give her to him. Then he'll have something to remember me by in case he goes back to Florida. He'll have to be careful with Kimberly when he packs her in his suitcase. He'll have to put her in lots of bubble wrap, build a little nest around her. He'll have to drive real smooth down the highway, to keep from jostling and breaking her little bird bones.

I slip Kimberly into the pocket of my shorts and walk to the kitchen where I left my bag with my bathing suit in it. I tuck her inside the bag, but then I get worried that she might break. I take her out and begin wrapping her in a bunch of paper towels I find under Mrs. Parker's sink. I hear a loud tapping on one of the glass windows by the back door. I look up.

Mama's boyfriend RD is looking right at me.

I jump.

He taps again.

I shove Kimberly, half-wrapped, into my bag, then open the door, my heart slamming in my chest.

"What are you doing here?" I ask, trying to sound like I'm the one who's caught him up to something.

He just stands in the doorway, looking at me with a half smile on his face, holding up a white bag with red lettering from Chick-fil-A. The front of his shirt is covered with hairs from his mutt, Li'l Dog.

"Seems I could ask you the same thing," he says.

I straighten my back. We stand there looking at each other, neither of us saying a thing, until he reaches out his free hand and tousles my hair, messing up the top part, which I had smoothed back with a barrette.

"I brought a sandwich for your mama," he says, walking into the kitchen. "I brought you one too. And a lemonade." He winks. "Don't ever underestimate the beauty of the words *employee discount.*"

He sets the bag down on the countertop and looks around. He whistles. "Nice place you got here. How much did it set you back?"

RD smiles at me. There's always something off about the way he looks because of his nose. His left nostril is half the size of his right.

"I don't think Mama's supposed to have visitors at work," I say.

"Who are you, her shift manager?" RD asks. Opening the refrigerator, he pulls out a Coke, pops the cap, and takes a long sip.

"Besides," he says, nodding toward my bag, "looks like you made yourself right at home."

"It's not—"

RD holds his hands, palms out, in front of his chest, looking for all the world as if he's about to catch a basketball. "Hey, I'm not interested in poking around, pretending I'm on *Cops* or something. Just don't do anything that might get your mama in trouble, and you and me can still be friends. Okay?"

I don't say anything, but I'm thinking that if RD thinks he and I are friends he must be even dumber than he looks.

RD begins to take the sandwiches out of their bags. I swear I can smell the butter on the buns. There is nothing I love to eat more than Chick-fil-A, even though now that Mama and RD are together I eat Chick-fil-A all the time, thanks to RD's employee discount, something he never shuts up about.

"I come have lunch with Faye every Monday," he says. "Got to take advantage of my days off."

He smiles at me like he thinks I like him.

"I'll get Mama," I say.

I climb the stairs and walk down the long hall to Mrs. Parker's bedroom. Mama is sitting on Mrs. Parker's white bedspread, reading *US Weekly*, the vacuum cleaner roaring beside her. I cut it off.

"Does RD really come eat lunch with you every Monday?" I ask.

"Lord, is he here already?" She jumps up and goes to the mirror that hangs on the bedroom wall. The mirror is framed with heavy wood and is as big as the wall of my bedroom at home. Mama lets her hair out of its rubber band and combs it with her hand.

"Do I look all right?" she asks, but she is out the door before I can answer.

I stand in front of Mrs. Parker's mirror and stick out my chest. My boobs are almost as big as Mama's.

AT HOME I try to hide Kimberly. I don't have a bed to stash her under like people do on TV, because my mattress lies right on the floor. I don't have a closet in my room, and my chest of drawers is packed so full I can't squeeze in an extra pair of underwear, let alone a clay bird that might break. I think about putting her in the closet down the hall, but it makes me nervous to have her out of my sight.

I decide to put her right on my dresser. I tuck her between the legs of the teddy bear I won at Six Flags when I went there with the Young Warriors group from my church. I put my framed photo of Daddy in front. It's impossible to see Kimberly behind Daddy, and I am sure Mama won't be picking up his photo anytime soon considering she always says that looking at Daddy is what got her into trouble in the first place.

When she was seventeen and pregnant with me, she and Daddy eloped. She didn't wear a white gown or anything. Mama says the only time she and Daddy had romance in their marriage was before the wedding. Once she found out she was pregnant and they got hitched, they moved in with Daddy's parents. Granddaddy was a minister and Mama says he was real strict.

Looking at the photo I have of my daddy back then, I don't know how she let him get away. When they first met he told her his name was Bone. Least that's what his friends called him. I figure it was because the bones in his cheeks stuck out so much. I remember once lying in bed between him and Mama on a Saturday morning when Granddaddy and Meemaw were off somewhere. I turned on my side and looked at Daddy, rubbing my finger up and down the side of his cheek.

"Be careful that don't poke you," he said.

"Your daddy thinks he's a movie star," said Mama.

MAMA MAKES MEATLOAF for dinner and sets the table with the pretty plates Meemaw left her. She has painted two pink stripes across her cheeks. Mama has never been good with blush. It looks like war paint the way she puts it on. Even I know more about blending than Mama does, and I'm not allowed to wear makeup yet.

But to tell the truth, I don't care how bad her blush looks, I'm just glad she's wearing it because I know she must be getting dressed up for Daddy. He must have called to tell her he's in town and he'd like to come over for dinner. I almost feel sorry for RD. He might have been good at keeping Mama company these last few months, but there's no way a crooked-nosed runt can compete with my handsome daddy.

"You want to say the blessing?" asks Mama as she sits down at the table.

"It's just us tonight?" I ask.

Mama smiles. "We might have some company later on," she says.

Mama and me hold hands. I try to say the blessing the way Pastor Finch would.

"Thank you, Father," I say, "for this food, Father, and for Mama, and for Daddy, and for all our relatives, Father. And forgive us for any sins we may have committed today, Father. And thank you for sending Jesus to this earth to die for them in our place. And please help Mama, Father, with the blisters on her feet. Amen."

"Amen," says Mama. "You're getting real good at that."

She scoops mashed potatoes on her plate while I squirt ketchup over my meatloaf.

"Pastor Finch is going to let me do a reading next Sunday," I say.

"I know," she says. "My girl is making me proud."

I take a bite of meatloaf. I love soft meat. Daddy does too. Mama says he used to drive all the way to Atlanta just to get a Varsity hamburger.

"Mama?" I say.

She looks tired underneath her makeup.

"What'd it feel like to have sex with Daddy?"

Mama frowns at her plate, thinking.

Maybe I shouldn't have asked, but Mama has always told me that since God knows all our thoughts and actions anyway, there's no use the two of us trying to hide anything from each other.

I was thinking about that this afternoon, about how God must have witnessed me taking the bird. I decided that God probably sees it as a toss-up between two of the Ten Commandments. On the one hand, I stole. On the other hand, I did it to honor my father.

After a minute Mama sighs and says, "It felt good. Of course it was a sin before we got married."

"Were you scared?" I ask.

"I was nervous the first time," she says, cutting a bite of meatloaf with her fork. "Mainly because it hurt. But then after a while it started to feel nice."

"Did you bleed the first time?" I ask.

"Pretty soon I stopped bleeding. It's easy to get pregnant, Missy."

She pops the piece of meatloaf into her mouth.

"I know. I know. I'm going to take the virginity pledge next year in Sunday school, so don't worry."

She waits to swallow before saying, "When you're with your husband, it will feel good. It might take a few times, but it will."

"Do you miss Daddy?" I ask.

Mama frowns. "I miss him being around for you," she says.

I AM ALMOST through washing the dishes when the doorbell rings. Daddy. Oh my Lord. I knew when I saw him on that used car commercial I'd be seeing him soon. I bet he even knows I have a present for him waiting in my room. I bet he read my mind all the way over there off I-285.

It's weird though. I've spent so much time just itching to see him, and now that he's actually here, I'm nervous. I keep the water running and scrub another plate. What am I going to say to him? What's he going to think about how I look? Last time he saw me

I was just a little girl crying at Meemaw's funeral, and now I'm twelve years old, I have pierced ears, and I wear a bra.

I hear Mama laughing in the living room, and then it gets real quiet. Then I hear her laughing so hard it sounds as if she's crying. I walk to the living room and see that she *is* crying, and it's not Daddy who is in the living room but RD. RD again. RD twice on the same day.

"Sugar," says Mama, wiping her eyes and turning toward me, her face flushed. "Guess who just asked me to marry him!"

They are both grinning like fools. My hands are still wet from the dishes and Mama doesn't even tell me not to drip on the floor.

"Daddy?" I ask, even though I know that's not the answer.

"No, sugar," she says. "RD."

RD and Mama look at each other. He steps toward me, pulling a rectangular green box out of his pocket.

The phone rings. I run to Mama's bedroom to answer it, thinking it might be Daddy calling to say that he is on his way over, that he is ready to start fresh.

"Hello?" I say.

"Is this Missy?" I recognize Mrs. Parker's voice, and I almost hang up on her.

"Yes, ma'am," I say.

"Missy, hi. This is Louise Parker. Is your mother around?"

"Um, no. No, ma'am. She's at Bible study."

"Well, you might be able to help. When I came home from my manicure appointment this afternoon, I noticed that one of the little white birds from my collection is missing. Do you know anything about it?"

My mouth gets so dry it feels like the spit has been sucked right out.

"Those birds are very important to me. I bought them to

mark the one-year anniversary of my mother's death. The littlest one—the one that's missing—has tiny moonstones for eyes. Every day when I walk by that bird I think about my mother."

I don't say anything. Even if I wanted to I couldn't, my mouth is so dry.

"Believe me," says Mrs. Parker, "I understand what a special little bird she is. I understand how by mistake someone might want to borrow her."

She stops talking but her breathing gets louder. In and out. In and out. Yoga breathing, she calls it.

"Missy, do you think you might have borrowed the bird by mistake?"

"No, ma'am," I stammer, and then I force myself to keep talking. "I didn't take anything of yours besides some of those brownies you made."

Mrs. Parker sucks in her breath. "Oh," she says. "I see."

RD is laughing so loud in the other room I am sure Mrs. Parker will be able to hear him.

"I bet RD took it," I say, surprising myself at how easy the lie comes out.

"Your mother's boyfriend?"

"Yes, ma'am. He came over for lunch today and he was asking all about those birds."

"Did you actually *see* him take one?" asks Mrs. Parker.

"He didn't do it right in front of me, no. But he was all by himself when I went upstairs to tell Mama he'd brought Chick-fil-A."

"RD? That's hard for me to believe," Mrs. Parker says. "He's always seemed so steady, so salt-of-the-earth, certainly not a thief. Nor a connoisseur of the arts, for that matter. You see I have a good instinct about people—"

I want to tell her what Meemaw used to say: that just because your end stinks doesn't mean you should follow it. But I know better than to make a joke. What I don't know is why everyone thinks RD is such a great guy.

" . . . he seems to be such a devout man."

"He hasn't been to church much lately," I say, which is the truth. Last week he insisted Mama and me stay home so he could make us pancakes. Thinking about RD wearing only his undershirt and shorts while standing at Mama's stove pouring batter into the skillet, I start to believe that he really did steal the bird. I can just see it, RD looking all over Mrs. Parker's house, finding the prettiest thing she owns and putting it in his pocket, figuring he'll surprise Mama with it, or give it to me to try and make me like him.

"Missy, are you *sure* you didn't borrow it?"

My heart races like it does when Mrs. Crawford calls on me in class and I haven't done the homework.

"I didn't take anything of yours but two brownies. And we drank three of your Cokes at lunch."

"Well, that doesn't matter."

Mama calls me from the other room.

Mrs. Parker breathes in and out real loud again. She once told Mama yoga breathing was a good thing to do anytime you feel frustrated.

"Have your mom give me a ring when she gets in, okay?" she says.

"I will," I say.

She takes one more deep breath and then says, "Maybe you should stay home next time your mother comes, just until we get this cleared up. You're old enough for that, aren't you?"

Tears push against my eyes.

Mama sticks her head in the room.

"Who is it?" she asks.

I cover the mouthpiece with my hand. "Pastor Finch," I say. "About next Sunday."

Mama strides over to the phone. "Give it here," she says. "I want to tell him the good news."

I hold the receiver toward me so Mama can't see me punch the button to hang up on Mrs. Parker before I hand the phone to her.

"It's dead," she says.

"He must have already hung up," I say.

RD stands in the doorway. He's still holding the green box, which I figure must have a ring for Mama inside it. I'm trapped in the room with the two of them.

"I bought you a little present," he says to me.

He hands me the green box. I open it. Resting on yellow tissue paper are two silver barrettes with tiny crosses etched into them. They are beautiful.

"I've noticed you've started wearing your hair pinned back in a way that looks real pretty," he says.

The phone rings.

"Don't get it," I say.

Mama shakes her head.

"What has gotten into you?" she asks before picking up the phone.

I tear out of the room before she can say hello, sliding the box with the barrettes into my pocket. I grab Kimberly off my dresser and run out to the front lawn, banging the screen door behind me.

The sun has set but the moon is bright and big. I stand still, just taking in the night. It feels so different out here than it did inside. It's as if RD asking Mama to marry him didn't really happen.

It's cooled down since the afternoon and the air against my bare arms feels as comfortable as the water in Mrs. Parker's heated pool. Someone must have barbecued for dinner; the smell of smoke and meat is strong, but not so strong that I don't smell the sweetness of the honeysuckle growing on the chain-link fence that divides our house from RD's. The fireflies are out, the glow of their rears flicking on and off. Looking down the street I spot Bo and Hunter Starr riding in circles on their bikes. They don't see me, or at least they don't act like they do. I hear the screen door open behind me, its hinges begging for oil.

I don't turn around even though I know it must be RD standing on the front steps watching me. I look at Kimberly, her tiny white body cupped in my hand. Her moonstone eyes shine in the moonlight. Her round base feels so smooth it's hard to believe she's only made of clay. I do it fast, pulling my hand behind my head to get more thrust, throwing her as far as I can into the night sky. The streetlamp captures her flight, and for a moment it looks like she might keep going, like she might just fly on out of here.

CHAPTER FIVE

Memory, a Treacherous Thing

(Louise, Late Summer 2000)

*T*iny left a message while I was at exercise to say that she just fired her housekeeper, Brenda, for not showing up to work for the third time this month, and would I please call her back and give her Faye's number?

How to respond? I know that Faye needs all the work she can get, but I also know that she will never live up to Tiny's impossible standards, that Tiny might very well fire her within a month of hiring her. Also, Tiny would not be nearly as forgiving as I was if Faye's daughter were to take something from her. (Not that I think Missy would steal from Tiny. I am almost positive that her stealing from me was a onetime deal.) But if she *were* to take something from Tiny, Tiny would probably have the poor girl arrested. She would say she was using "tough love," just as she did when she sent her daughter, Helen, to rehab at Charter Peachford after Helen got caught drinking for the third time. (In addition to the expression "tough love," Tiny is also fond of both the law and the saying "Three strikes and you're out.")

Missy needs love, that's for sure, but I'm not sure how

"tough" it needs to be. From what Faye tells me, it sounds as if Missy is extremely threatened by Faye's fiancé, RD. She even tried to accuse RD of taking the bird when I discovered it was missing. Faye says that she is fed up with Missy acting up, getting in bad moods, and talking back.

"And now stealing!" she exclaimed when I finally reached her on the phone. "That girl is going to get the belt."

I wanted to suggest some other form of punishment but I had to remind myself that that was not my place, that people from other cultures and classes handle things differently. I did tell Faye that Missy sounded like a typical preteen to me and to watch out, the ride only gets bumpier.

Faye said that Missy had actually been acting more childish than usual, that after years of seeming indifference she had become fixated on her absent father (of course Faye didn't say "fixated," she said "all broody over"). She said that Missy had this idea that she was going to see her father again and that when she did she would give him my bird. Which shows that Missy really hasn't been thinking clearly at all. I mean, what would a deadbeat daddy do with a delicate little piece of painted clay?

Anyway. That's all in the past. And that's exactly what I told Missy when Faye brought her back to our house the next week. I told her I was sorry that I had implied on the phone that she was no longer welcome at my home, that everyone needs a second chance, and that I hoped she didn't get into too, too much trouble after I phoned her mother back once Missy hung up on me. I told her that while of course I was sad that the stolen bird had shattered, ultimately it was just an object and we should all try hard not to cling too tightly to things. We should practice detachment.

"Believe me," I said. "I know how hard it can be to be surrounded by beautiful things you can't have."

I could tell by the set of her jaw and the hunch of her

shoulders that I had said the wrong thing, that I had offended her. I didn't mean to do so. I was only thinking of how I feel every time I go to the Signature Shop over on Roswell Road and am tempted to drop thousands of dollars on some fabulous piece of folk art, though it's rare for me actually to buy anything from there. It's just too expensive. The only time I actually get art from the Signature Shop is when John Henry buys me something as a gift. Granted, I have always told the salesperson exactly what it is I want so that she can guide John Henry right to it.

Though my statement to Missy about beautiful things might have been clumsy, I said it with good intention, and deep down I think Missy knows that.

Tiny would not be so well intended. Tiny thinks I let my help get away with murder. Once I told Tiny that I always have to remember to take out the recycling before Faye comes or else Faye will just put it into the Herbie Curbie with all of the other trash.

Tiny screamed, "Good Lord, Louise, you are her boss! If she is doing something wrong you need to tell her instead of driving yourself crazy proofing the house for her potential mistakes!"

When I call Tiny back she answers on the second ring.

"Louise, thank God. Did you get my message?"

The way Tiny acts you'd think she'd had no water for a week and I just showed up at her door with ten gallons of Evian.

"I did," I say. "But unfortunately you're going to have to find someone besides Faye to clean for you. Faye is completely booked."

"Lou-Lou, you are holding out on me and you know it. You said yourself that she's willing to come any Saturday you need her because she wants the extra work."

Damn my big mouth.

"Listen, Tiny, honey, I just don't think Faye would live up to your expectations. I wouldn't have hired her myself if it hadn't been for my mother pressuring me to do so."

Tiny knows a little, but not all, about that situation. I am hoping she will press me for more details so that I can tell her the full story and distract her from trying to get Faye's number out of me.

"She's been working for you for forever. She can't be that bad. And I am desperate! The silver is tarnished, my floorboards are dusty, and I really need someone to iron my sheets."

"You do not cook. You do not clean. You are an artist!" I exclaim, borrowing from something I once heard Nina Simone say in a television interview.

Tiny knows the reference (we quote it to each other often, for amusement, since both of us cook and clean and neither of us is an artist) but she chooses not to laugh. "It's just like that damn jar of marbles all over again," she says.

"Excuse me?" I ask.

"That jar of marbles your father gave you one year for your birthday. Your eighth, I think."

"I swear I am getting old-timer's. I have no idea what you are talking about."

"Are you serious? You don't remember those big old blue marbles of yours? The ones you kept in a quart-size jelly jar? Lord, you treated those things like Christ had shit them out Himself."

"Gracious, Tiny," I say, still surprised (and delighted) by her brashness even though I've encountered it my entire life. "I honestly have no idea what you are talking about."

She expels one of those sighs of hers, like I am two years old and have just knocked over a basket of folded laundry.

"You must have had two hundred marbles in that jar and not once did you give one to me, not once did you share. You said you were afraid I might lose one. And that's exactly what you're doing today, Lou-Lou. You are afraid that I'll offend your maid by actually asking her to do some work and so you are clutching her to your chest like you used to do with that jar of marbles. Well listen, honey, you're all grown up and it's time to learn how to share. So hand them over."

"I can't," I say. "I lost my marbles."

We both laugh at the inadvertent joke, though I'm a little concerned by my apparent amnesia. Big blue marbles? I have no memory of such things.

Of course it could be that Tiny's making the whole story up or that she had another friend with a collection of marbles and she's mistaking her for me. Either way, the story reminds me that we are getting old, fast. Not that I need to be reminded. New lines seem to appear on my face daily, and Tiny's already had a little work done on hers.

Of course, by the conversation's end, I have given her Faye's number. The truth of the matter is, Tiny's will has always been stronger than mine.

I HANG UP the phone, get a Diet Coke out of the refrigerator, and sit down again at the kitchen table, trying to remember those marbles. Nothing comes up. Nothing at all, though Tiny's story about them certainly makes sense psychologically. Whatever my daddy gave me when I was little immediately took on the greatest value, so of course I would have hoarded them, especially around Tiny, who was always losing things.

Unfortunately, my little flare-up of old-timer's while talking to Tiny was not atypical. Often when Tiny reminisces about experiences we shared during our youth I have no memory of what she is talking about. Which teacher or boy or put-down or triumph.

The funny thing is, there are certain moments from childhood I remember so clearly it is as if I have a video recording of them filed away in my head. The really bad moments. Those are the ones that stick with me. Like that spring day when Tiny and I were riding our bicycles in front of my house and Daddy drove by with another woman in the front seat of his convertible. Though I was only six, I knew that woman was not supposed to be with him, knew that Daddy was lying when he said that her car was in the shop so he was giving her a ride home from the office building where they both worked, he as a doctor, she as a clerk in the pharmacy on the bottom floor of his building.

I remember too the smile she gave me, open and eager, though her teeth were bad, little and sharp, as if she had filed them into points. I remember thinking, *That lady must not brush two times a day like I do. She must have bad dental hygiene.* (*Dental hygiene* was a term I had picked up from a film we watched at school titled *Healthy Mouths, Healthy Citizens!*)

It was one of those spring afternoons that make Atlanta exceptional, when every tree is budding, when the azaleas are flagrantly pink, when the sky is blue, blue, blue, and the temperature is seventy-two degrees and nothing but being outside will do, riding your bike up and down the street with your best friend, seeing who can go the longest with no hands, pretending you are acrobats by lifting one leg behind you (toes pointed!) while you speed through the air.

And then Daddy and that woman ruined everything. Driving by as if they didn't have a care in the world, as if Daddy's own wife weren't upstairs "resting" in her room at that very moment. I was so embarrassed after they left, so embarrassed that Tiny had witnessed it all. We didn't suspect Daddy of having an affair, nothing like that. We were too young, too unsophisticated to jump to such an (accurate) conclusion. What we did know was that Daddy was spending time with a woman who spoke with a gravelly, unrefined (*hick* would have been the word we used) accent, whose canary yellow blouse was so tight it strained at the buttons, who smiled at me as if it mattered whether or not I liked her. After all, I was only a child, and back then, children did not count.

Tiny and I only had a brief encounter with her and yet afterwards we knew, knew that she was someone our mothers would consider below them, someone they might whisper was "trash."

Daddy handed me a dollar bill before they rode away, an enormous sum of money back then, at least for a child. It was bribe money, though he said it was to get ice cream at the soda fountain down on Peachtree. Tiny and I rode over there, me pedaling furiously in the hopes of exorcising all the feelings I was left with after seeing Daddy. I felt mean after seeing him, mean and loaded, a pistol with its safety off. Later, after we returned from ice cream, I made Tiny cry by blocking her from leaving my bedroom, stretching my arms in front of the door and refusing to let her pass even though she said she really, really, really needed to go to the bathroom down the hall.

Bullying Tiny (something she never let me forget, especially once we were teenagers and she was tall and gorgeous and had boys rushing to light her cigarettes while I was relatively short, only "nice-looking," and much too much of a goody-goody to smoke) gave me the same sort of mean satisfaction I experienced when Mother's housekeeper, Mamie, came to our home early one morning to tell us that she needed a few days off work. Her son had died in a construction accident in Detroit, and she needed to go to the funeral. I was seven years old and hearing of her tragedy pleased a small, mean part of me. It satisfied me to see her so distraught. It was a terrible thing to derive satisfaction from. If I were religious I would say it was a sin. The only justification I can allow myself is that I always felt so exposed by what Mamie knew about my family. She was one of the few adults in my life to give me constant and steady affection, and yet I resented her for seeing what a mess my mother was, for seeing how obvious it was that my father felt so burdened by

Mother, burdened because of what he called her "weak spirit."

Mamie came to clean on Mondays, Wednesdays, and Fridays and would often stay past dinner to care for me because Mother was in one way or another incapacitated (too depressed to get out of bed was usually the case) and Daddy was still at work. From our kitchen phone Mamie would telephone her daughter to tell her she was coming home late. Again.

"It's the child I've gots to stay for," she would say, her words followed by a series of low sighs and mumbles. "Lord knows what happens to her the days I'm not here."

Sometimes she would add, "Poor baby," before she hung up the phone. I always assumed the "poor baby" referred to me. But maybe not. Maybe Mamie was consoling her daughter. Maybe she was the "poor baby," the poor little black girl whose mama had to spend so much of her time taking care of an otherwise unloved white child.

How I hated being that child, the unloved little girl. Perhaps that is why I have such a hard time remembering much of anything that was good about my childhood.

Yes, only the very worst memories are sharp and clear: the day I found Mother in Daddy's closet, lying beneath the tightly packed row of his dress shirts, all ironed and starched by Mamie, arranged by color: whites, blues, then stripes. I tried to get Mother to sit up but she would not. I tried to make her talk but she would not answer me. Daddy was at work, it was one of Mamie's days off, and I was alone with this woman who acted exactly like a corpse except for the fact that she could breathe. It was soon after that she went away for the first time, just to "rest up," just to "revitalize" her spirit. Did she go to the hospital or to some private beach? No one ever said. Soon after Mother went away Daddy brought home a kitten for me, whom I named Gray-Gray because of her color.

Gray-Gray. Thank God for that kitten. She would arch her

back and rub against my legs and sleep with me at night, her warm body relaxed next to mine, her heart beating fiercely in her chest, as if to proclaim, *I am alive. I am with you.*

While Mother was away—or maybe it was after, after she came back—the woman who was riding in the front seat of Daddy's car came over to the house before Daddy got home from work. I answered the door and she was there, looking very glamorous with a red painted mouth and an orange pencil skirt that hugged her hips. She was friendly and flirtatious, she cooed over Gray-Gray, and she gave me a pack of Wrigley's gum. I warmed up to her. I let her in, ushered her to the living room, and offered her a drink while she waited for Daddy.

How funny. I was all of seven years old and I already knew the difference between a bourbon neat, and one on the rocks. Daddy used to have me make his friends' drinks whenever he and Mother entertained, which was not that often (though when they did, they certainly *looked* the happy, handsome couple). It was a party trick of his, getting his baby daughter to serve the gentlemen bourbon, the ladies gin and tonics.

It sounds terribly exploitive, I know, but I actually loved doing it, loved getting the heavy cut crystal glasses out of the antique armoire where Daddy kept them, loved using the silver tongs to plunk one, two, three cubes of ice per drink. It was just one of those things parents could get away with back then. If I had, say, trained Caroline to mix a martini when she was little she would have mentioned something about it at school and a group of counselors from Social Services would have shown up at our front door. And Caroline would have let them in and probably would have asked if they wanted their martinis made with vodka or gin. And the next thing you know, I would have been hauled off to jail.

Miss Winnie, that was what the woman told me to call her, did not want a drink. She said that all she wanted was for me to sit right next to her and let her pet the kitten. Gray-Gray was not supposed to be in the living room. It was the nicest room in the house. The curtains were made of silk and if Gray-Gray were to run up them, they would be ruined.

But I must not have cared, must not have worried about getting in trouble. I hardly did, anyway. Mother would threaten sometimes but rarely followed through. Daddy once tried to spank me but stopped short, though I was already hoisted over his knee.

"Promise to try and always be a good girl," he said, after lifting me back up and sitting me on his lap. "Your old daddy just can't bear to hurt his little lamb."

Funny, considering some of the things he *could* bear to do. Including cheating rampantly on Mother and, after Gray-Gray had babies, whisking away her kittens to an undisclosed place, most likely the bottom of some murky body of water.

Miss Winnie and I tried to talk, but she was distracted and kept looking up at the entrance to the living room, anxious for Daddy to come. And then he did and I could tell right away that he was mad at her for being inside our house.

"Louise, you know you're not supposed to answer the door to strangers," he scolded. I had to remind him that Miss Winnie was not a stranger. Hadn't he introduced her to me just last spring, when they drove by in his convertible? Hadn't we all smiled at each other and then hadn't he given me a dollar so Tiny and I could go and get as much ice cream as we could possibly want?

He sat on the farthest sofa away from us, eyeing the decanter of brandy, which rested on a small table just by Miss Winnie's elbow. He looked at that decanter like he looked at pretty women, but he didn't rise to pour himself a drink. I thought about asking if he wanted me to get a drink for him, but I didn't. Instead I held Gray-Gray close to my heart, trying to send a message to her that everything was okay.

Daddy and Miss Winnie talked in forced, cheerful tones.

And then something shifted. Daddy's voice rose and he was using bad language. "What the hell do you think you're trying to prove?" he asked and she just smiled at him like his words did not bother her one bit.

"That's not very nice, Daddy," I said. "Miss Winnie is our friend."

He turned on me with such rage I thought I might use the bathroom in my pants. He was screaming. *"In your room!"*

Gray-Gray bolted off my lap and raced straight up the silk curtain.

"Letting that goddamn cat into the goddamn living room! Answering the door by yourself! You are in big trouble, young lady. Big trouble! You go right to your room and stay there until I come up to deal with you."

He was so large, so furious, that though he was on the other side of the room it seemed as if there was no distance between us at all, that he was going to smash all his weight against me, that he was going to crush me beneath him.

It was all I could do to get my legs to work. I only wanted to sink to the floor.

"Now," he roared, and I ran, not turning around to check on Gray-Gray. I ran out of the living room, into the front hall, and up the curved staircase with the iron railing. I ran up, up, up, and then down the upstairs hall, passing Mother, who must have been roused by Daddy's screaming, who was walking unsteadily toward the stairs, her blond curls unkempt, her long white nightgown still on. She looked like a little girl.

I shut myself into my room, wailing, and waited for either my mother to come and comfort me or my father to come and beat me (which surely he would have had the heart to do on that night). But no one came. No one came to my room at all. Only Gray-Gray showed up, mewing at the door. I let her in and put her on the bed with me and cried some more, only softly this time.

Gray-Gray watched me anxiously and then licked my cheeks where the tears had been.

At breakfast the next morning no one said a word about what had happened the day before. And after a few weeks went by with no one mentioning that day, I began to wonder if I had made it all up.

A year or so later when Winnie arrived at our door again, this time to see Mother, I knew I had not.

CHAPTER SIX

No Lolita

(Caroline, Fall 2000)

*M*om thinks Frederick is hot for me.

"No twenty-four-year-old man shows such interest in an eighteen-year-old girl without romantic intentions," she says. "You should know that before you go on your date."

"It's not a date, Louise."

I am sitting at the kitchen table. She is standing at the counter, making brownies.

"I'm not Louise to you," she says, measuring out a teaspoon of salt and using the back of a knife to scrape off the excess. "If going to dinner and then a play at the Alliance Theatre is not a date, then the definition of dating has changed since I was single."

She smiles at her own joke and then walks to the pantry to retrieve the cocoa powder. She turns toward me after closing the pantry door.

"Frankly, darling, I think it's fabulous. Six years really isn't that much of an age difference. Of course, it might become a problem if he's looking to get married."

"Mom," I say in my slowest, most drawn-out, pretend-I-am-talking-to-a-six-year-old voice. "You are insane. He is a director and I am an actor. Tonight we are going to see a performance of *The Glass Menagerie*, which the Coventry players are staging in three weeks. It makes total sense for us to go together, as professionals."

Mom raises her right eyebrow. "Professional whats?" she asks.

"Oh my God, I can't believe you just said that."

"Just see if he pays for your meal," she says.

I HEAR THE doorbell ring at 6:15, the exact time Frederick said he would arrive. I have to say that I find his promptness a little unappealing; it makes him seem really desperate. I have just stepped out of the shower and haven't even towel-dried my hair. I hear Mom start exclaiming over him as soon as she opens the door. She actually says, "It's lovely to see a young man in a shirt and tie."

Jesus. It's like *she* wants to do him.

I was planning on wearing jeans and a tank top but after hearing how dressed up he is I put on a blue cotton sundress that I bought in Little Five Points. It hangs loose on me and looks sort of hippy-dippy, but it shows off my tan, which is fast fading since summer vacation. Adding to the hippy affect, I go braless, more to see Mom's reaction than anything else.

Downstairs, Frederick, wearing jeans with his slightly frayed shirt and tie, sits at the kitchen table with Louise, eating from a big plate of brownies. My mother's brownies are so good they almost make you forgive her for everything she's ever done to you. She puts three different kinds of chocolate in them, chocolates that she special-orders from Williams-Sonoma.

Frederick looks up at me, a brownie halfway to his mouth.

"Your mother is a culinary genius," he says.

"Oh hush," she says. I swear to God she bats her eyelashes.

I grab a brownie and put it whole into my mouth.

"Caroline," says my mother. "These aren't single-bite bits."

Frederick laughs while he stands up, pushing his chair back underneath the table. Brownnoser.

"Thank you so much for these," he says, touching my mother on the shoulder with his long delicate fingers. "I guess we better go if we want to eat before the play. Although seriously, I would be pretty happy if I could just eat brownies for dinner."

"You are too sweet," says Mom. "To be completely honest, I don't think this batch is up to par. Do they taste as good to you as they usually do, sweetheart?"

"They're perfect," I say, annoyed. I have never once heard my mother claim that anything she has cooked meets her standards.

She walks with us out the front door and stays there, beside the house, waving until we have backed out of the driveway. I wouldn't be surprised if she slipped Frederick a condom while I wasn't looking. Dad stayed in the den the whole time, watching sports on TV. In the movies fathers are forever doing idiotic things to try and stop their teenage daughters from having sex. My father isn't like that. Much as he hates Clinton, he seems to have adopted the Don't Ask, Don't Tell policy when it comes to my life.

Which suits me just fine.

FREDERICK TAKES ME to the Bridgetown Grill near the theater. I order jerk chicken with raspberry sauce. Over dinner Frederick makes me laugh so hard with his imitation of Coventry teachers that I snort a bite of jerk chicken up my nose. I start sneezing chunks of chicken into my napkin! It is totally disgusting, but Frederick laughs and calls me a "delight." And then he puts his Visa on the table and tells me the meal is his treat.

EVERY TIME I go to see a performance I tear up when the actors first come on stage. It has nothing to do with the material, it's just—I know how they are feeling. Lit. Alive. Doing what they are supposed to be doing. Afterwards I usually feel a little depressed. I don't like being a member of the audience. I want to be one of the players.

I tell this to Frederick as we walk from the theater back to his beat-up Jeep. He says that during his first year at Yale he didn't get a part in any of the plays he tried out for. But he went to see all of the performances, regardless. He had to. He was trying to be part of the theater scene. Still, he says, his stomach would knot up while watching the other actors. All he could think was *That should be me.*

"Hold on to your jealousy," he says. "Sometimes casting comes down to who seems to want it the most."

We stand by the side of his car. Even though it's late September the night air is still warm. Cars buzz by us on Peachtree. Frederick unwraps a piece of Trident and pops it in his mouth. He holds the pack out to me. "Want some?"

"I'm good," I say.

It's late, almost midnight, my curfew. (Which is retarded. I mean, that I'm a senior and I still have a curfew.)

"I think you are beautiful and smart and talented," Frederick says, all in one rushed breath. "And I know I should wait until you graduate—"

He swallows his gum, leans in, and presses his chapped lips against mine. I don't pull away but I don't lose myself in the moment either. Maybe it's that I can't get over the fact that I'm kissing my *teacher.*

I WAKE TO the smell of something baking, something sweet. Waffles. Dad used to make them every Sunday morning but he stopped completely when in junior high I refused to eat any because Mom had forgotten to buy syrup and was trying to convince me that strawberry jam would work just as well. I asked for a PowerBar instead and that was it. Dad had one of his "Jesus, I didn't see that coming" anger attacks. Waffles ended up in the garbage; Dad stormed out of the kitchen. Tradition ended.

Downstairs Charles, Mom, and Dad are all sitting at the kitchen table. Charles wears boxers and a T-shirt; Mom and Dad wear the matching fuzzy robes they bought at some ritzy hotel.

"Good morning, darling," says my mother.

"Ready for a waffle?" asks Dad. He is unusually upbeat, making me wonder if before breakfast he and Mom did the nasty. Which in itself is nasty.

"Sure," I say. "Smells good."

Dad jumps up to pour batter in the iron.

Mom, winking, asks, "And how was your night?"

"God," I say, "it's like you're just itching for me and Frederick to fuck or something."

For a second everyone stares at me, like they aren't sure if I really said what I just said. (*I* wasn't sure I said what I just said. It just came out.) Then my mother starts crying—crying, like she is some delicate flower who can't be exposed to such language even though last spring she told me that she didn't give a *flying fuck* what I did with my life.

Dad turns from the waffle maker, his face red, shaking a plastic spatula at me like he is going to come after me with it. He wears a comb-over to try and make it look as if he's not so bald, and every time—every time—he starts screaming at me he shakes his head around so much that the comb-over flops to the wrong side and he looks like he's just got this random piece of long hair growing out of his corporate crew cut.

"Jesus," I say. "Sorry."

Mom looks right at me and says, "I would appreciate it if you just left the table."

"Fine," I say, and I do.

• • •

WHICH IS NOT to say that I don't cry in my room or feel as if I can't breathe or even hold a pair of orange-handled scissors up against the inside of my arm and make a small scratch. (I could never be a serious cutter. It hurts too much.) This is not to say that I don't stand in front of my bathroom mirror with a fistful of hair in my hands, ready to cut it all off until I remember how horrible I looked in the third grade when I let my mom's stylist give me a haircut "just like Mary Lou Retton's."

Sure, I feel like shit after the Parker family attempt at breakfast but eventually the feeling becomes less intense and I hear dishes being rinsed and I know that each of the other three members of my family will soon be off doing whatever it is they do on a Sunday. So once I am pretty sure I'm not going to burst into tears or anything, I call Frederick's house to see if he wants to hang out.

His mom answers, which is kind of creepy when you think about it—that Frederick still lives at home—but she doesn't try to talk to me or anything, thank God.

As soon as I hear his voice I start crying again.

"Caroline?" he asks.

Why does he assume the crying girl on the other end of the phone is me? I've never cried in front of him before, except last year when I finally told him about Jim and the whole Honor Council thing.

"What is it? What's the matter?" he asks.

I tell him that I have just had a massive and ugly fight with my parents.

"Come over," I say. "Come get me."

"Was your fight about me?" he asks. "Did you tell your mom about—about what happened last night? Between us?"

Yeah, Frederick. Louise and I curled up in our jammies and discussed the fact that my teacher stuck his tongue in my mouth.

"Look, it had nothing to do with you. It was about my—as my mother would call it—my potty mouth. Don't worry. Louise still loves you."

He says to look for him in twenty minutes.

FIVE MINUTES LATER, someone knocks on my bedroom door.

Before I say anything, Dad walks in holding a bottle of water.

"I brought this for you," he says.

I reach out to take the bottle, feeling my throat tighten the way it does before I cry. I do *not* want to cry in front of my father. I do *not* want to have a heart-to-heart with him.

He sits on the edge of my bed. "Honey," he says, "you've got to think before you say things."

Oh great. He's here to lecture me about holding my tongue even after Mom makes all sorts of sexual innuendos about me and my teacher.

"The thing is," he says, trying to make deep and meaningful eye contact with me, "there is nothing less attractive than a woman with a foul mouth."

"What about a woman who smokes?" I ask, remembering that he once said that the least attractive thing a woman could do was smoke cigarettes.

"Well, that too," he says, not understanding that I am ridiculing him to his face. "Listen, babe. You are going to be out of here in less than a year. Can't we make these last months peaceful? Don't you think you can try and get along with your mother?"

No. I really don't. The thing is, Louise is totally unpredictable. It's like she switches roles from day to day. Sometimes she wants to be all close and girlfriendish with me, and then other times she suits up as Tough Mom. And I'm sick of it. Sick of dealing with her. Sick of being the guinea pig while she figures out which parenting philosophy she's going to embrace on any one particular day.

"You know, I could be doing a lot worse than occasionally saying a bad word," I say.

I *am* doing worse things, but as I said, my father is clueless when it comes to my life.

"Hey, I know you are a good kid," he says.

He smiles and I remember him saying those exact words when I was little, after Mom went apeshit because I got a grass stain on my white Easter sundress. All of a sudden I want to cry. Everything just seems impossible, including the fact that I love my father. I love him so much, yet I don't think I can stand living with him and my mother for even the next night.

Dad stands and stretches his arms behind his back. "There are some leftover waffles downstairs," he says. "Why don't you go eat?"

I WAIT FOR Frederick on the front porch. Sandy used to smoke out here while Mom was running errands (translation: getting a manicure, getting her hair colored, or shopping at Neiman's). Sometimes I'd smoke with her. Once Charles caught me and threatened to tell Mom unless I let him try a drag. I handed my lit cigarette over to him, and the minute he inhaled, Sandy said in that growl of hers, "Now if you tell your mama about Miss Caroline she'll whip your butt for smoking."

She wouldn't have, but Charles still kept his word.

THE MINUTE I see Frederick's Jeep making its way down Peachtree Circle, I run down the driveway to meet him at the curb, climbing into the front seat as soon as he stops the car.

"Hi," he says.

The inside of his car smells like he just sprayed orange air freshener. I wonder if he farted on the way over and is now trying to cover it up.

"Let's go get drunk," I say.

He rolls his eyes. "Caroline, please," he says.

"Oh, would that be inappropriate?" I ask, widening my eyes in mock innocence.

"Wow, I'm so glad you called me to come get you. You are in such a terrific mood. So upbeat and sunny."

"Sorry," I say. "I just had a shitty morning. Let's get Chick-fil-A."

"It's Sunday," he says.

Damn it. I always forget that Chick-fil-A is closed on Sundays. Fucking Christians.

"What else can we eat? Fried chicken? Want to get a bucket at Fry Daddy's?"

"I don't know how you stay so skinny," he says.

"Let's go to your house to eat it," I say. "We can have cocktails with our chicken. Unless your mom will be there."

He shakes his head. "I think she's got some church thing, but it doesn't matter either way. I've got private access to my room."

"Well, well, well," I say. "Why didn't you tell me you had access to a mom-free bachelor pad?"

"Being a smartass will serve you well in New York," he says.

"Do you really think I'm going to get to go to New York?" I ask. "That I'll do well at my audition?" I hate how high-pitched my voice becomes anytime I talk about my chances of getting into acting school.

"You are going to kick ass," he says. "And you're going to have a great recommendation from your acting teacher."

He turns his attention from the road to smile at me.

"I can't believe I am actually going to get away from this fucking city."

"Atlanta's not so bad," he says. We are driving on Ponce toward Fry Daddy's. As always there are a lot of homeless people—men mostly—on this street.

"Why are they all here?" I ask. "It's like a homeless convention."

"Atlanta likes to keep their homeless zoned."

"They're zoned? That's the most retarded thing I've ever heard in my life."

"Yeah, talk to me next year after one of them is living on your doorstep in New York."

Frederick pulls into the parking lot at Fry Daddy's, where there are even more homeless people milling about. They are almost all black, and none of them are eating chicken.

I get out of the car thinking about how half the kids at my school don't even know there *is* a Fry Daddy's, and if they did they probably wouldn't ever go to it because they'd be scared of getting shot or something.

"They're so fucking annoying," I say just as Frederick is locking the car doors.

Frederick looks frantically around the parking lot as if he thinks I'm talking about the homeless men.

"I mean the kids at Coventry," I say. "The Crispy Christians especially. They're such hypocrites. I mean, they all drive Ford Explorers or BMWs and the girls wear those James Avery crosses around their necks. I mean, instead of spending money on a gold cross, why don't they give the money to the poor? Haven't they read that part of the Bible where it says that it's easier for a camel to go through the eye of a needle than for a rich man to enter the gates of heaven?"

"Ansley Park isn't really the slums, is it?" he asks.

"I never said I was a Christian."

"There's that group that volunteers at Habitat once a month," he says.

"Yeah, but that's just so they can put it down on their college applications."

"Don't get too cynical, Caroline," he says as he holds the door to Fry Daddy's open for me.

"Okay, Dad," I say.

Frederick looks so annoyed by my comment that he actually resembles my father.

Fry Daddy's smells like old grease. The girl behind the counter is black, like everyone else who works there, and like everyone else, she looks bored.

"Hello and welcome to Fry Daddy's," she says, not bothering to differentiate her words with inflection. "Would y'all like our Daddy-O of a deal?"

"What's that?" I ask.

"Buy two Whoa Daddy buckets of chicken for only the price of one plus five dollar," she says.

"Gee, that's a lot of chicken," says Frederick, sounding like he's in a commercial.

Suddenly, I feel inspired. "Let's get the extra bucket and give it to the men in the parking lot. We can just pass it around and people can take a piece."

"How many pieces are in a bucket?" asks Frederick, leaning into the counter. I hope he doesn't get a grease stain on his R.E.M. T-shirt. The shirt is a classic. It's designed to look as if it were inside out, like the song.

"The Whoa Daddy has sixteen pieces: four thigh, four leg, four wing, four breast," the girl says.

"Okay," he says. "Give us the Daddy-O of a deal."

FREDERICK WAITS IN the car with our bucket of chicken in his lap while I stand in front of the restaurant, trying to figure out how to offer the second bucket to the homeless men. I sort of assumed people would just line up for it, but nobody is paying any attention to me.

I walk over to the guy standing closest to me and ask if he wants a piece of chicken. I must have asked in too low a voice because he doesn't say anything. But then this other guy, who's wearing overalls with no shirt, asks if he can have some.

"Sure," I say. "Let me get you a piece."

I pluck out a breast and hand it to him. And then I am surrounded by men, all saying things to me at once.

"Hey, can I have some of that?"

"Look at this little angel with her chicken."

"Hey, over here, you wanna share more of that bird?"

"Give me one of them legs."

"What's somebody so sweet and pretty doing over here at FD's?"

"You got yourself a husband, honey? I be your husband."

I keep handing out chicken, like it's Halloween and I am distributing Snickers to the ankle biters. It occurs to me when I am almost at the end of the bucket that we definitely didn't order enough to feed everyone. More and more men seem to be gathering in the parking lot, surrounding me. For a split second I wonder if maybe the bucket will become bottomless, like Jesus with his five loaves of bread that fed five thousand.

Right. The gospel according to Caroline: teenage fuck-up aided by lecherous teacher feeds thousands with only one Whoa Daddy bucket of chicken.

A man approaches me, taller than the others and wearing a little black knit hat over his short hair.

"Y'all don't crowd this nice lady in," he says. "Back up, make a line."

He looks at me. "You want me to finish handing out this bird? It might be easier for me to be holding the empty bucket than you."

"Okay," I say. "Thanks." The bucket only has two pieces left in it, anyway. Most likely this guy will just eat them both himself.

"We thank you kindly, ma'am," he says. "And you be careful out there."

He glances at my skirt, which makes me suddenly aware of how very short it is. I walk back to the car, where Frederick waits. One guy calls after me, asks if I will please, please, please marry him and be his wife.

"THAT WAS AWESOME," I say. I'm practically jumping up and down in my seat I'm so pumped up. Frederick is heading east on Ponce toward Little Five Points. I know a guy who lives near there who sells pot. I wonder if Frederick would be into buying some.

I glance at his profile, noticing the faint acne scars on his gaunt cheek.

"What were you like in high school?" I ask. "When you were at Grady?"

"Total loser," he says, giving me a quick smile before focusing again on the road.

And just like that, bang.

I want him.

Not because he'd been a loser, obviously, but because he didn't try to pretend that he wasn't one. I thought he would.

I thought he would try and impress me, because he's always sort of seeming to do that, but right now he's just driving the car without even looking at me.

Oh God.

I really want him. I want him to pull into a parking lot so I can climb on top of his lap and feel his cock against me.

Fuck.

I am pulsing.

I put my hand on his thigh. He glances down at it but doesn't say anything. I move my hand up toward his crotch. He still doesn't say anything. I rub it over the bulge where his penis is.

"Caroline," he says.

"Frederick," I say, imitating his pained tone.

He pulls into the Kroger parking lot, parks the car, and turns in his seat toward me.

"I told you last night how I feel about you. But right now, this afternoon, it's not a good time for us to start anything too intense. You were really upset when you called me. You seemed distraught."

"So what? We fed the masses. Now I feel better."

"I think you're too much of a mess right now for us to do anything. I would feel as if I were taking advantage of the situation."

It takes me a minute to get angry. But when my brain finally catches up to his words, I feel so angry that I want to punch him in the nose. And then I start crying, crying as hard as I cried after this morning's waffle incident.

"Caroline, I really like you," he says.

"Oh, fuck you," I say.

"Watch yourself," he says.

"Or, what—you'll give me a detention?" I ask, aware even in my anger of the drama of our situation. Of how this would be the *big climactic moment* if we were in a play. Of how I tend to be my most clever when I'm feeling rejected.

His face is scrunched up as if he's in physical pain. If I were directing I would tell him he was overacting.

"I masturbate every day thinking about you," he says.

Oh my God.

"That's not how you're supposed to talk to your student," I say, trying to joke, but I'm floored.

He grabs my wrists with his hands, holds them tightly in front of me. "Caroline," he says. "You've got to stop that. I want you. I really do. But I'm not going to play along as Humbert Humbert to your Lolita."

My instinct is to make another joke, to say something about how I'm too old to be Lolita, how he'll have to teach much younger kids if that's the kind of relationship he's looking for. But for once I shut up.

I lean in and start kissing him. It's different from last night. This time I want it. I want him, Frederick, not my teacher, not my director, but Frederick the man who bought the two buckets of chicken so I could give one away to the homeless, Frederick the man who is in this car with me.

And the strangest thing is how surprising it all is, that this— this affair, as my mother would call it—is really happening. Even though we kissed last night, even though we flirted all last year, back then it felt like a game, like something that would never really happen.

It's the difference between standing near a fire and being the wood that burns.

CHAPTER SEVEN

Far from the Tree

(Louise, Spring 2001)

I keep the necklace in the blue velvet bag it came in, buried in a dresser drawer among my seldom-worn winter sweaters. Tonight at the party I will give it to Caroline, though I will not tell her the story of how it came to hang from Mother's neck. Caroline will have no idea of its significance, and I plan to keep it that way. I could tell her Daddy gave it to Mother for some anniversary or another, though the truth is Daddy hated that piece of jewelry.

I suppose I will have to come up with some sort of a dramatic story to tell my daughter. Because knowing Caroline, unless the necklace is infused with drama and intrigue, she won't deign to wear it at all. It's not exactly her taste in jewelry. It's not ethnic enough.

Caroline would love the drama of the real story, but telling her that would be too disruptive in too many ways. Plus, I don't want to ruin her memories of her grandfather. She still thinks of him—who died when she was only six—as a sweet, genteel old man who loved to buy her candy bars and challenge her to games of checkers.

So why give her the necklace at all, if I am going to lie about its origins, if I have doubts about whether or not she'll wear it?

I need to give her a gift, that's why. After all, the party tonight is held in honor of her, to celebrate her admission to the acting program at Juilliard.

She found out yesterday. This August she will leave for New York.

When she first told me her good news I was awash in jealousy. I thought, *Is this what it means to be a mess your whole life, that someday you will be rewarded with a big white envelope saying that truly you are one of the special few?* My whole life I turned in papers on time and followed the rules. Caroline was nearly kicked out of Coventry every year for poor attendance, and yet she is admitted to arguably the best drama program in the country.

I kept thinking, *I am forty-seven years old and what do I have to show for myself besides a daughter whose life I envy?* I will always be a spender. Never a creator. The closest I ever came to being an artist was getting an art history minor at Chapel Hill.

But then it hit me: Caroline is leaving home. This girl whom I love but who drives me crazy is moving out of my house, most likely for good, for surely she will not return to Atlanta after living in New York, at least not for years and years to come, at which point we will have both mellowed out. *Louise*, I told myself, *you have reason to celebrate.*

Inspired, I went to the kitchen and poured myself a glass of champagne from one of the bottles I was keeping in the refrigerator to open at the party. Pop! went the cork and I started to laugh. Putting the bottle down on the kitchen counter, I started dancing, just shaking like a two-year-old, feeling so good in my body, which is strong, if not terribly thin, from years and years of Bodypump and low-impact aerobics. *Mission accomplished!* I thought. *I am almost done with this phase of my life!*

And for some reason I thought of Mother's necklace, buried

in the back of my dresser drawer. I thought, *That little artifact does not belong in this new, lighter chapter of my life.* I am turning a page, I have raised one daughter and will soon enough have raised my son, and I just do not need to be reminded of that piece of my (well, Mother's) history anymore.

It's not a necklace I can just give to anyone, of course; it should stay in the family, but with someone who *doesn't* appreciate its significance, who can actually wear it, who will have no idea of the real weight it carries.

BEFORE I WRAP it up for Caroline, velvet bag and all, in white tissue paper with gold dots, I try on the necklace one more time, struggling with the clasp as Mother did the first time she wore it. It is hard to believe that I am older now than Mother was on the day she received it. Harder still to imagine how young I was on that day, just eight and a half years old. (Young enough to still mark half birthdays!)

Young and foolish enough to hope that because Mother was up that morning she would remain up for every morning to come. And not only was Mother up, she was up and bathed and dressed, lipstick applied, long curls tied back with a scarf the color of heavy cream. She was in the kitchen making breakfast, making breakfast and *humming,* and in addition to bacon and eggs, she was also making me my very own pancake shaped like the letter *L.*

I remember how, setting the table that morning, I took great care to fold the napkins just so, not wanting either side to stick out more than the other. It was important that everything go well. It was important that nothing upset Mother, that no mishap occur that might send her back to the solitude of her dark room.

Despite my fear that Mother might once again retreat upstairs, I was happy. Happy to the point of giddiness. Happy that I was still on spring break and did not have to go to Miss Ann's

School that day. Happy that I had awoken to the feel of Mother's soft lips on my cheek. ("Good morning, sleepyhead," she had whispered.) Happy that I was about to eat a pancake that Mother had made for me. Happy that Gray-Gray was expecting kittens and was so close to delivering that Mamie had placed a large cardboard box in the far corner of the kitchen near the laundry room for her to use when it was time to give birth.

I had already decided that I was going to name the kittens after Donald Duck's nephews: Huey, Dewey, and Louie. When I told Mamie this, she asked what would I name the kittens if they were girls? I said that one of them would have to be named Daisy. This made Mamie smile and click her tongue against the roof of her mouth.

"You a smart thing, ain't you?" she said.

After breakfast I planned to ask Mother if we could walk down the street to Winn Park. There I could show her how good I was at pumping, how high I could go on the swings. All the other children who lived in the neighborhood would watch the two of us and be jealous that I had such a fun mother to play with while they only had their weary housekeepers to keep track of them.

I heard Daddy stomping down the stairs, as loud as usual, although this morning it did not matter how thunderous his footsteps might be, he was not going to disturb Mother's rest. Daddy could march down the stairs playing a trombone for all it mattered; Mother was not lying alone in bed, the pillow over her head to block out the noise and light. Mother was up.

I cannot tell you what a miracle it felt like for her to be up.

Daddy, who slept in a separate room from Mother and did not yet know that she had risen, stopped short at the kitchen doorway, the familiar smell of his Royall Lyme cologne already making its way to my nose.

"Well, well, well," he said. "Look who's awake and about."

I remember holding myself very still, making a quick deal with God that if I did not move one inch Daddy's tone—he often spoke to Mother as if she were a child—would not upset her.

"That would be me," said Mother, her voice (thankfully! wonderfully!) light. "Would you like just bacon and eggs for breakfast or would you also like a pancake?"

Let him sit down and eat with us, I prayed. *Let him sit down and eat every bite on his plate.*

"I suppose I have time for a pancake," he said. "That sounds good."

I exhaled, aware that in addition to holding my body still, I had also been holding my breath.

Daddy walked over to the table and was about to sit down when his gaze landed on the empty cardboard box in the corner of the room.

"What's that box doing there?" he asked.

I didn't tell him that it had been sitting in the kitchen for the last four days, that he simply hadn't noticed it before.

He walked over to the box, poking it with the toe of his leather shoe.

"It's for Gray-Gray to have her kittens in," I said. "Mamie says cats like a warm, cozy place to deliver their babies."

"I could find that cat a warm, cozy ditch by the side of the road to have her babies in," said Daddy.

Immediately I was blinking back tears and experiencing a familiar tightening in my throat. And then Daddy was by my side, kneeling, stroking my cheek with his finger. "I'm sorry, sweetheart. That was a silly joke. It's just when I brought Gray-Gray home I never intended for her to have a litter of kittens."

"But I'll take care of them!" I said.

"I know, I know, sweetheart. It's fine. Pretend Daddy didn't say anything. It's a nice box. It's a perfect box for Gray-Gray's kittens."

• • •

AT BREAKFAST I ate three pancakes and would have eaten a fourth had Mother not said that little girls shouldn't eat more food than their tummies could hold. Daddy ate his pancake in three big bites and then rushed off to Piedmont Hospital, where a year ago he had relocated his practice.

Mother and I sat at the table, Mother drinking coffee and staring off into space.

"What do you want to do today, Mama?" I asked, though I rarely called her that.

She smiled at me and I tried not to notice that her pink lipstick was not applied precisely, that it bled into the faint wrinkles around the sides of her mouth.

"Why don't we get dressed up in our very best clothes and white gloves and go to Rich's? We can buy you a new dress for Easter Sunday and afterwards we'll have lunch."

I knew that shopping for an Easter dress would also mean shopping for white shoes, for while girls at All Saints never wore white shoes during winter, it was almost a mandate that they don a pair to celebrate the Resurrection. The idea of trying on pair after pair of white patent leather Mary Janes sounded beyond tedious to me, but I quickly brushed away all thoughts of impending boredom. It didn't matter how, Mother and I were going to spend the day together and that would be great no matter what.

It was so nice when Mother paid attention to me. It was so nice when she looked at, rather than through, me. In the early days of her bad moods, I used to do all sorts of naughty things just to get her attention: draw on the walls, cut my own hair, mash Mother's lipsticks against the bathroom mirror. Most of the time she didn't even notice, and Mamie ended up cleaning up my mess. Mamie was always cleaning up the mess.

• • •

THE KNOCK CAME just as Mother was finishing cleaning up from breakfast, her face flushed from the steamy water she used to rinse off the dishes. I was helping, placing each rinsed dish into the dishwasher. We both turned our heads at the same time when we heard the knock, but only I seemed to recognize who was knocking. It was Miss Winnie.

The reappearance of Miss Winnie, more than a year since she first visited the house, frightened me. What if Daddy discovered her there? What if it turned out he had forgotten something he needed for work and when he returned home to retrieve it he saw Miss Winnie in his house? Or what if Miss Winnie did something to Mother, something to get even with Daddy for being so rude to her the last time she was here? Seeing Miss Winnie through the glass panels of the kitchen door, I wanted more than anything to secure the chain lock and walk out of the room.

"Don't worry about her," I would say, my voice full of false assurance as I led Mother out of the kitchen. "She's probably selling encyclopedias or something like that. Let's just pretend that she is not here."

But I said nothing and while I said nothing Mother walked to the door and opened it. I followed behind, wanting to stick as close to her as possible.

"I hope I'm not disturbing you," said Winnie, her southern accent even stronger than I had remembered.

Winnie not only sounded different, she looked different: thinner and more severe, brittle almost. And the clothes she wore, a navy turtleneck tucked into a long pleated skirt the color of sand, were much less stylish than the pencil skirt and black patent leather heels she had worn the last time she had come to our house.

"No, of course not," said Mother, who was always unfailingly polite to everyone, even those she considered below her. "How may I help you?"

"Lord, I don't know how to begin," said Winnie. She glanced down at me and smiled. "Hey, you."

Mother looked at me and frowned, the expression on her face a cross between curiosity and suspicion.

"Sweetheart, do you know this lady?" she asked.

I did not know what to say in response.

"I'm sorry," Winnie said. "I was thinking you might remember me, but anyway, I should have introduced myself. I'm Winnie Meadows. Course, up until last year I was Winnie Hicks. Still getting used to the new name."

She made a motion with her left hand so that we could see the thin gold band she wore around her ring finger. It had no diamond.

"I used to work at the pharmacy downstairs from your husband's office," she added.

"Ernie has changed offices," said Mother.

"I don't work there anymore neither," said Winnie.

We all hovered by the door. For a moment, no one said a word.

"Won't you come in?" Mother finally said. "I was just going to have a cup of tea. Would you care to join me?"

Why was she inviting Miss Winnie inside? Mother didn't even know this woman. She wasn't a neighbor or a member of our church or the Club or anything.

Winnie said yes, she would like to come in, and then she was inside, walking across the red tile floor, looking around at the many-paned glass windows, the sleek linoleum countertops, the brand-new dishwasher and the electric range-top stove, and she was saying how nice everything was, how fancy and new.

"All my husband's doing," said Mother, standing by the sink

and filling the kettle with water from the faucet. "He insists on the latest gadgets and appliances."

"That sounds just like Ernie," said Winnie.

Mother turned off the water and stared for a moment at Winnie before putting the kettle on the stove.

Gray-Gray, who had been asleep underneath the dining room table, appeared at the kitchen door. She was so heavy with kittens that she hardly had any energy to do anything besides sleep and eat. How different she was now, fat and lined with swollen nipples, than she was two years ago when Daddy brought her home to me as a tiny two-pound thing. I walked over to where Gray-Gray's food and water were kept to make sure that there was food in the bowl. There was. Gray-Gray walked slowly toward it.

"I can't believe this," said Winnie, giving me her eager smile, her voice light and animated. "The last time I saw that cat she was thin as a rail, and now she's about to be a mama!"

Mother gave Winnie a quizzical look as she walked from the stove to the table and sat down, indicating that Winnie should sit as well. "You said I might remember you. When did we meet?"

I wanted Miss Winnie to lie, to say that no, she had never been to the house before, that she knew about Ernie and Gray-Gray because she was the one who gave the kitten to Daddy to give to me. Yes! That would work. Miss Winnie could say that her cat had had kittens and she had asked around the doctors' offices in her building and Daddy, who loved new things, had agreed to take one. It would make sense. After all, Daddy did bring Gray-Gray home from the office. For all I knew Gray-Gray might have once belonged to Miss Winnie. Maybe, I thought (hoped), that *was* the reason Miss Winnie was here, maybe she was here simply to check up on Gray-Gray.

"Listen," said Winnie, who had sat in the seat next to Mother. "I need to talk with you about something, woman to woman."

She reached out her hand and touched Mother on the fore-arm.

I watched for Mother's reaction. Mother did not really like to be touched. She casually retracted her arm so that it was no longer resting on the table.

"The water will be ready in a minute," she said. "Then we can have our tea."

"The main reason I come here," said Winnie, "is to ask for your forgiveness."

She began crying, a wet, noiseless cry.

Mother glanced at me.

I had sat down at the table when Mother did. Now I turned in my chair and stared at the cat eating her food. Maybe if I looked as if I wasn't paying any attention to the adults, Mother would let me stay in the room with them.

"Louise," she said.

I pretended not to hear her. Pretended that I was so absorbed watching Gray-Gray that I had just blocked out every sound.

"Louise, go upstairs and play."

I still did not respond. I didn't care whether or not Mother got mad. I did not want to leave her alone with this woman who seemed only to bring trouble to our family.

"On the count of three I want you out of this room, do you hear me?" warned Mother.

I turned in my chair so that I was looking at Mother face to face. I tried to give her my saddest eyes. Her own eyes were hard, Miss Winnie's soft and forgiving. I felt a deep urge to kick Miss Winnie's chair. Better yet, I wanted to kick Miss Winnie.

"One. Two. Three." Mother counted slowly, giving me plenty of time to run.

I did not move from my seat. Mother looked for a moment as if she might rise from her chair to make me move, but the moment passed and Mother was still sitting, glaring at me like I was the one who had ruined the day.

It was all too much and I began to cry. The day had started so well. We had eaten pancakes and we were going to go to Rich's and wear white gloves and now this, this interruption, was going to ruin everything. Soon I was crying harder and certainly louder than Miss Winnie was, and that felt good, because if anyone deserved to cry it was me, not Miss Winnie. Mother stayed seated but opened her arms and I jumped from my chair and ran into them, burying my head in her neck, feeling her soft skin, which smelled of cherries and almonds, the fragrance of Jergens lotion.

"I don't mind if she stays," said Winnie.

I turned around so that I was facing Winnie, positioning myself between Mother's legs, pressing my back against her breasts. It had been a long time since I had been so near my mother's body.

"Well, all right," said Mother, sounding the same as she did when Daddy phoned to say he was going to miss dinner, again. "Just, whatever you need to say, be aware of little ears."

Winnie nodded.

Mother whispered to me, "You can stay with me, but if I end up telling you to leave, you better do as I say, understand?"

I nodded, secretly knowing that I wasn't going anywhere. Mother wrapped her arms around me and I could tell she was glad I was there. "Tell me again why you came?"

"I came because, because I want to tell you about this girl I knew. She—her life—well, she was sort of connected to you and I thought you ought to know about her." Winnie ran her finger along her simple wedding band. "This girl was young and easily tempted. She was the type of gal who didn't even know how to recognize trouble, forget about trying to avoid it. She was the type of gal who took to drinking when times got hard. She didn't have no family, none she could rely on, and she lived by herself in a boardinghouse on Juniper Street filled with other women like herself. Half of them were looking for a man to take care of them, no matter if he was married or not so long as his wallet was full."

A low whistle that fast grew shrill interrupted Winnie. It was the kettle, steam rushing through its spout.

"Excuse me a moment," said Mother, pushing me out of her lap when she stood. She walked toward the stove and I sat back down in her chair.

After she took the pot off the burner, Mother walked out of the kitchen and into the dining room, returning a moment later with two porcelain cups and the hand-painted teapot. I could not believe it. Mother hardly ever used her best china, only at Thanksgiving and Christmas. She set the empty cups on the table near Winnie and then walked back to the stove, where she placed the teapot on the counter beside it.

She pulled down the box of Lipton tea from the cabinet and put three bags into the pot. She poured water over the bags and secured the lid. She brought the pot to the table, placing it on top of a place mat left over from breakfast.

"Do you take lemon and sugar?" she asked.

"Just sugar," said Winnie.

Mother disappeared once again to the dining room and returned with the porcelain jar that contained sugar cubes. She placed it on the kitchen table and then sat in the chair across from Winnie, the chair where Daddy usually sat.

"We'll give it a minute to steep," she said.

For a moment nobody said anything.

"We need spoons," said Mother. Once more she rose, but instead of walking to the drawer where she kept the stainless steel flatware, she again went to the dining room and returned carrying two sterling silver spoons with flowers engraved on their handles. Buttercup, the pattern is called. Same one I have. And like Mother, I only use it for special occasions and very special guests, which I did not consider Miss Winnie to be.

"There," she said.

She poured tea first for Winnie and then for herself. I wanted tea too, but I knew better than to fuss about it. If I did, Mother might easily decide that it was time for me to go upstairs and play.

"All right," said Mother, once the tea was poured. "Now tell me more about this woman you once knew."

Winnie looked nervously at her. She seemed to have shrunk further into herself ever since Mother had brought out the good china and sat in Daddy's chair. (Now that I am an adult I know what Mother was doing pulling out all her treasures. She was making a power play, same as men do.) Winnie rubbed her finger against the handle of her teacup, which was painted with real gold. Mother took a sip of her tea and sat up very straight.

"Well, you see, this girl, see, she got wrapped up with an older man, a family man who took an interest in her. He was a doctor, and he acted like a doctor around her; he kind of acted like he was *her* doctor. He kept saying she didn't eat enough; she was 'malnourished,' he said. Some days he would buy her lunch. And then it got to be that they were having lunch together almost every day. Then he started taking her out to dinner. He took her to places she never thought she'd see the inside of, least not as a guest. He did other things too; he sent her flowers and bought her candy from the pharmacy where she worked."

Mother and Winnie exchanged glances.

For a moment the only sound in the room was the soft lapping of Gray-Gray's tongue as she licked water from her bowl.

"One day he bought her a house," Winnie said.

"A house?" asked Mother, obviously startled. "A real house?"

"Yes," said Winnie. "A real house. She allowed him to buy her a house and she was fool enough to believe that soon he would come join her in that house, that he would leave his wife and his child and he would come and live with her instead."

"Come sit in my lap again, sweetheart," said Mother. I climbed down from my chair and once again enveloped myself between Mother's legs. I was eight and a half, too old to sit like this, but I didn't care. Mother wrapped her arms around me, holding me tight.

Winnie's voice picked up speed. "Any fool could have told her that this man was not going to leave his family, but this friend of mine was the queen of excuses. She always had an answer for everything, an answer that fit the way she wished the world would work."

"Where was this house?" asked Mother. Her voice, which had been warm and confident just moments ago, now sounded flat and far away.

"In Virginia Highlands. Not two miles away from his. It wasn't a big house but it was her own."

"With strings, I'm sure," mumbled Mother.

Winnie's cheeks flushed. At that moment it occurred to me that despite her old-lady clothes, Miss Winnie was still pretty.

"Would you like a piece of shortbread to go with your tea?" asked Mother.

"I do, Mommy," I said. I couldn't help myself. I loved shortbread, which also happened to be Daddy's favorite cookie. Mamie made some once a week and left it in a tin box in the pantry.

"You already had pancakes," said Mother. "More hot water?" she asked Winnie.

Winnie shook her head.

"Well I'm going to get some," Mother said, once again pushing me off her lap when she stood.

"Has Miss Gray-Gray ever had kittens before?" asked Winnie, focusing her attention on me.

"No, ma'am," I said, staring at the table. I knew that Mother might fuss at me if I was openly rude to Miss Winnie, but that didn't mean I had to act like I liked her.

Mother came back to the table, steam rising from her freshened cup of tea. She put her cup down and walked to the pantry, where she took out the red tin can of shortbread.

"Just one, Louise," she said, bringing the tin can to the table. I pried its lid off and looked for the biggest piece. I pulled it out, a golden stick with tine marks along the top, and bit off a piece of it, savoring its salty sweetness.

"So what else do you want to tell me about this girl?" asked Mother, sitting back down at the table next to me. I could tell from the weariness in her voice that she really didn't want to hear anything more.

"What I want to tell you—the main reason I come here—is that when this girl was seeing this man, after he'd bought her the house, after they had, after their relationship changed—"

Winnie glanced at me and then looked at Mother.

"After their relationship changed how?" asked Mother, and though I couldn't have told you why, it seemed to me that there was something mean about the question.

"After it lost all innocence. Not that it ever was innocent, but something happened—an act, an act reserved for marriage. . . ."

Winnie paused, trying to lock eyes with Mother, who gave no indication that she was catching Winnie's look.

"After that, this girl would call his house on the nights when she didn't get to see him. When his wife would answer she wouldn't say anything, she'd just stay on the line so his wife would know there was someone there. Every night after calling she felt as if she was trapped in a deep hole, like she had fallen into the worst kind of sin, but she couldn't stop herself from doing it. It was like she was stuck down there in that hole and all she could do was try to pull someone else down into it with her. One night she called his house must have been twenty times. She'd hang up when no one picked up and then try again. She knew they were around, maybe not him but his wife and his little girl."

There was a foreign noise, a sudden cry from the corner of the room. I looked at Gray-Gray. Her stomach was heaving and her eyes were wild but she was purring like she did when I stroked her under her chin.

"Mama," I said.

"Shh," said Mother.

"She'd driven by the house earlier that day, saw his little girl out playing in the front yard."

Gray-Gray walked over to the table and lay on the rug beneath it. Her stomach was pumping up and down and then, still purring, she began to use the bathroom on the floor.

"Mommy, she's not using the litter box!" I cried, knowing Daddy would be furious if she made a mess on one of the rugs. "Bad Gray-Gray!"

"What in the world . . . ," said Mother, turning her attention to the cat.

"She's not doing anything wrong, sugar. She's just having her babies," said Winnie.

I jumped from my chair and crouched underneath the table beside Gray-Gray, gently touching the top of her head with my finger.

What I had thought was Gray-Gray's, well, excrement, was actually her first kitten, a wet bubble of a thing that once birthed resembled a rodent more than it did a cat. The kitten was covered in a clear sort of film that dissolved as soon as Gray-Gray started licking her.

"She knows just what to do, don't she?" asked Winnie, her

voice soft. I turned my head and to my surprise there was Winnie sitting on one side of me, Mother crouched on the other.

Gray-Gray's eyes widened and she let out meows that were low and long. Her stomach was pumping up and down again and then another kitten bubble dropped out of her, this one black instead of gray. Again Gray-Gray licked it all over, just as she had the first one, her rough red tongue rubbing the embryonic sack right off her baby. The other kitty, the first one, had already climbed onto Gray-Gray's stomach and was sucking away at one of her teats.

"She found that fast," observed Mother.

"How many do you think she'll have?" I asked.

"Five or six is about usual," said Winnie.

"Your father is going to have a heart attack if we have six kittens around the house. We'll have to find someone to take them."

"Mama, no! I want them."

"Sweetheart, we aren't keeping all of those kittens. You may pick out one, but once they're weaned, we've got to find the others a home."

"Look, there's another one!" I said as another sack twisted its way out. So involved was I with watching the births that I didn't really let Mother's words about giving away the kittens sink in.

(I should have.)

"Wonder if it's as painful for her to deliver kittens as it is for us to deliver babies," mused Winnie.

"Do you know about childbirth?" asked Mother, her voice spiked with alarm. "I mean, firsthand?"

"Yes, yes I do. Last year I had me a little boy. Named him Luke after the Gospels. My husband is pastor at Sweetwater Church of the Fallen and Redeemed, out in Loganville, so we knew we'd go with a biblical name."

"You had a baby—with your husband?" asked Mother.

"We baptized him in the church. Swore we'd do our best to raise him in the name of Jesus."

Gray-Gray pushed out another baby, while the other three stayed attached to her nipples.

"Isn't that the truth about being a mother," said Winnie, looking at the cat covered in nursing kittens. "Afterwards your body is never again your own."

Carefully, Mother made her way out from underneath the table, stood, and walked to the little desk by the back door where the telephone and her pocketbook were kept. She fished around inside her pocketbook, looking for her wallet. When she found it she pulled three twenty-dollar bills out of it.

"Here," she said, walking back across the room, the hand that held the bills shaking slightly. "Take this. There's more upstairs, hidden away. There's more than a thousand dollars up there. You can have it all, just take it and use it to raise your boy. Just take it and leave us alone, all right?"

Mother had money hidden somewhere upstairs? I wondered where she kept it.

Winnie worked her way out from under the table in a crouch. She rose, standing beside Mother, leaving me alone under the table with Gray-Gray, her four offspring sucking away, another baby dropping from her.

Winnie held her palm out in front of her. She looked like a crossing guard stopping traffic so that the kindergartners can waddle by.

"I don't want your money," she said. "Lord no. I'm not here to take anything from you. I've already done too much of that. I'm here to tell you how sorry I am."

I was busy trying to watch both Mother and the cat, when without warning, Gray-Gray jumped up and walked to the cardboard box that Mamie had left in the corner of the kitchen, knocking her kittens off her chest, leaving them in a blind, hungry jumble.

Gray-Gray circled the outside of the box and then jumped inside it. Once inside she turned around two times and then jumped back out. She returned to where her kittens lay and grabbed one by its neck with her teeth.

"Mommy!" I cried, terrified that Gray-Gray was trying to kill her baby.

Mother turned to look at Gray-Gray, who was now carrying the kitten to the box, looking much the same as when she killed a mouse and carried it in her mouth to eat it on our front porch.

"Don't worry," said Winnie. "That's just how mama cats carry their young."

It bothered me that Winnie answered for Mother, almost as much as it bothered me to see how rough Gray-Gray was with her newborn baby. That didn't seem like the sweet Gray-Gray I knew. After dropping the first kitty into the box, she returned to the pile of kittens and grabbed another by its neck.

Winnie reached into the pocket of her tan skirt and pulled out a small velvet bag. "My husband and I, we sold that house in Virginia Highlands. He's a preacher, after all, and it was a house born of sin. We donated most of the money from the sale to our church, though I held on to a little of it. I was so scared of being back where I was when I was young, of not having a dime to my name. What I didn't realize was, I had something—I *have* something. I have Jesus Christ and by holding on to that money I was holding on to my past life, before I was born again through his blood. And if I was holding on to my past life, then I was holding on to my past sin."

Winnie handed Mother the small velvet bag. "I bought this for you," she said.

I watched as Mother pulled out a small velvet board with a chain of gold looped around it.

"You bought it with money you held on to from the house?" asked Mother.

Winnie nodded.

Mother unwrapped the chain from the cardboard. Dangling from its end was a pendant shaped like the letter *A*. It looked like the pancake letter that Mother had made for me that morning, except of course that it was Mother's initial and not my own dangling from the end of the chain, and it was delicate and gold.

"It's the scarlet letter, but reversed," said Mother, her voice so soft that I could barely hear her.

"I know I can't make up for what I did," said Winnie.

"Ernie is going to have to look at this every day, isn't he?" mused Mother.

Clasping each end of the necklace, Mother brought the chain around her neck. She tried to fasten the ends together, but her fingers fumbled with the tiny lock.

"Would you help me?" she asked Winnie.

She turned so that her back was facing Winnie. Winnie took the ends out of Mother's hands and depressed the tiny latch that opened the lock. After slipping the ring into the lock she released the latch. The necklace hung taut from Mother's neck, the tiny *A* resting in the indentation between her collarbones.

That evening when Daddy came home from work, Mother showed him the necklace and told him who gave it to her. Daddy stiffened and then told her to take it off, that it looked cheap. But then Mother flipped the pendant around and showed him what was stamped on the back: *18 karat gold.*

CHAPTER EIGHT

Trouble

(Louise, Spring 2001)

*S*ometimes I wish Caroline attended public school. Surely if she were at Grady I would not have to interrupt my afternoon to come in and talk about her lack of scholastic effort or her chronic tardiness or her blatant disregard of the school dress code or whatever it is they are calling me in about this time. Lord knows Caroline is a handful, but sometimes I think Coventry makes too big a deal over relatively minor infractions. Like the time last week when they made Caroline call me from Dean Brown's office to tell me that if she was late one more time she would have to go in front of the disciplinary committee.

Frankly, now that she has her acceptance to Juilliard, I don't really care how many tardies she has. And it being the spring of her senior year, I'm not really sure why Coventry cares anymore either.

But still, off I go to meet with the dean of the school, Miss Brown. This really is inconvenient. There are no groceries in the house, I have a bag full of John Henry's dirty shirts to take to the cleaners, and now I won't be there when Charles gets home from school to make him a snack. Of course I know he's thirteen years old and is perfectly capable of getting the bag of Chips Ahoy out of the pantry himself, but I take pleasure in feeding my son, in being with my son. There has always been such a marked ease in my relationship with Charles. I suppose it's that he accepts me so completely as his mother, his nurturer and caregiver and natural authority figure. Caroline resists my authority at all costs. She put a bumper sticker on the back of her car that said so much. "Question Authority," it reads, and when I saw it I had to laugh. Question authority she certainly does.

THE TRAFFIC IS not too bad getting to Coventry, and so twenty minutes after leaving my house I pull into the back gates of the school. The campus is enormous, as big as a college. I pass six tennis courts on my way to what used to be the Girls' School, where Caroline and Dean Brown are waiting. On my way up the front steps of Robinson Hall, I pass Amanda, who used to be one of Caroline's good friends.

"Hey there, Amanda," I say.

"Oh, hi, Mrs. Parker," she says. She looks away from me when I try to make eye contact. She must be embarrassed that I know that she and Caroline had a falling out.

I walk through the hall filled with beige lockers. It is narrow and smells faintly of sweat. The lockers seem too small to belong to gangly teenagers. There is a cluster of girls sitting in a circle on the floor, holding a copy of the school newspaper and laughing like crazy. I don't know any of the girls. From what I can tell, Caroline has always sort of held herself above her classmates. Which is the opposite of how I was. I remember how carefully I would get ready in the morning before high school, how I would curl my hair under with a hot iron and practice my smiles in the bathroom mirror. I had three different kinds: one for girls (confident and sure), one for boys (mysterious), and one for teachers (quick and no-nonsense).

I'm not supposed to meet with Miss Brown until four o'clock, and it's only three fifty. I pop into the girls' bathroom to freshen up a little. Standing in front of the mirror I reapply my lipstick, blotting it with one of the brown paper towels from the dispenser.

Okay. Time to face the music. It's funny, isn't it, how having a delinquent daughter makes me feel like *I'm* the one in trouble.

I walk into the reception area of Miss Brown's office and am greeted by a young girl seated behind a large desk with a phone, a computer, and various boxes for dropping off forms. Surely this girl is a student. A prefect.

"I'm Louise Parker. I'm here to see Dean Brown."

A look flashes across the girl's face, a look that makes me wonder if I have lipstick on my teeth. When she turns to knock on Miss Brown's office door, I slide my finger quickly across my teeth, hoping to wipe off any errant color.

Miss Brown opens the door just enough to stick her head through.

"Yes, Samantha?" she says. You can tell that she is a formidable woman just by the way she styles her hair. It is dark and cut short, winged on the side and held perfectly in place with hairspray. Aqua Net, I'd be willing to bet.

"Hello," I say, holding my hand up to give a little wave. "Samantha was just letting you know I'm here."

"That's right, Miss Brown," says the girl.

"Thank you, Samantha. And hello, Mrs. Parker. I appreciate your coming on such short notice."

She has the clipped accent of a New Englander. She opens the door just wide enough to let me squeeze in.

Her office is a big room, large enough to hold a desk with a computer and two sofas that make an L, separated by what looks to be a good-quality antique end table with a porcelain lamp on it. Caroline is sitting on the sofa nearest to me. Her shoulders are hunched and when she looks up I can see that she has been crying.

"Hello," I say.

"Hi," she says. Her voice is meek.

"Mrs. Parker, sit down, please," says Miss Brown. I sit next to Caroline on the sofa. She scoots over a little to her left to give me more room.

"Let me start by telling you how upset we feel about this situation," Miss Brown begins. "Of course Caroline is responsible for her own actions, but that doesn't mean that we aren't all grieved by what happened."

Caroline's posture is terrible: shoulders slumped, eyes trained on the floor.

"Again, our grief does little in the way of rectifying this matter."

I am trying to nod and look concerned, but I am utterly confused as to what is going on. And Miss Brown is certainly acting elusive; she sits on the far end of the other sofa and she, same as Caroline, refuses to make eye contact.

I put my hand on Caroline's leg, hoping to convey by my touch that I am on her side. At least, I think I am. I certainly don't care much for Miss Brown's manner.

"Sweetheart, what happened?"

Caroline looks at me, finally, her eyelashes wet from crying. "Frederick and I . . . someone saw us," she says. And then she starts crying again, crying and sniffing. I pull a travel pack of Kleenex out of my purse and hand it to her.

Oh dear. I wonder if I should pretend not to know what she is talking about. It would look better, I'm sure, if I were in the dark about their relationship. I try to give Miss Brown my most quizzical expression.

"Mrs. Parker, this is a difficult thing to tell you, but we found your daughter in a quite compromised position with Mr. Staunton. Frederick Staunton."

Lord knows what a compromised position means to this woman. Did she catch them kissing or did she catch them having sex? I can't really tell.

"Well," I say, "I'm sorry to hear that." After a minute I add, "Sorry and, well, shocked. I hadn't realized that their academic relationship had taken on a . . . romantic element."

"*Romantic* is a generous word. I think *inappropriate* is more fitting. Mr. Staunton will be asked to resign immediately, of course."

"Oh," I say, wishing John Henry was here. He always knows exactly what to say and exactly what not to say in these situations. He knows how not to become legally embroiled.

"We've never had any . . . any problem of this nature arise before," she says, and the naughty little girl in me snickers at her word choice: *arise.* "We are unsure yet what the disciplinary action against Caroline will be. We consider this, of course, a grave offense."

I nod, wondering if it's possible for them to kick her out over this. And then I think, *If they try to, we'll sue.*

"And of course I'm sure that Coventry will decide it has an ethical responsibility to inform all the colleges that Caroline has received acceptances from about this situation."

"But she's going to acting school," I say. "I mean, we're all very upset about this, of course, but I hardly see the point of informing a drama school about a dramatic situation. Surely they're used to such things."

Caroline gives me a shy half smile. She looks so wounded and small sitting here. Of course, perhaps she's just acting contrite in the hopes that Dean Brown will go easy on her, but if she is acting she's doing such a good job of it that I feel large next to her, large and in charge and wanting to protect my girl from this uptight woman who probably never got caught doing anything bad in her life because she didn't have anybody to do bad things with.

"Miss Brown, I don't mean to tell you how to run your school, but I hope you give it some serious thought before informing Juilliard," I say. "My husband is a lawyer. Perhaps we should check with him first to see if there is any legal precedent for such an action."

My heart is beating fast. I hope that we are able to end this meeting quickly so I don't cry in front of this woman. I always cry after confrontations. Especially when I speak my mind.

Miss Brown's voice becomes—incredibly—even more clipped. "We are each responsible for our own actions," she says. "Caroline must face the consequences of her decision to engage in such inappropriate behavior."

I grab my bag and stand. "Well, Caroline and I have a lot to talk about, obviously," I say. "Thank you for calling this distressing matter to my attention. Come on, Caroline."

Caroline stands. I walk toward the door but turn to face Miss Brown before I exit her office. "Perhaps you should talk things over with the headmaster, with Dr. Johnson, before making any concrete decisions about informing Juilliard," I say. "My mother-in-law is an extremely generous donor at Coventry, and I would *hate* for the school to lose her contribution over something Caroline did."

"Our donors are well aware of the moral fiber of this school," says Miss Brown. "They have given in the past and continue to give now because of Coventry's explicit mission to raise boys and girls of integrity and faith. It is a sad time when a student veers so far from our mission, Mrs. Parker. I'm sure it is upsetting to you."

Bitch.

I'm sorry. I don't like to use that word but there is no denying it. This woman is a Grade A bitch and if I weren't better raised I would tell her that to her face.

"Is Caroline to be in class tomorrow morning?" I ask.

Caroline shoots me a pleading look but I ignore it. Of course she won't want to go to school tomorrow but she must. Absolutely. There is truth to the adage about getting back on the horse once you have been bucked.

"Caroline should continue on as a student until we have decided officially what the school's action will be."

"Thank you," I say. "She'll be there."

We walk through the nearly empty hall; Caroline keeps her gaze trained to the floor as if she were a murderer being led through a crowd of her victim's family.

"You are going to wind up an old lady with a humpback if you keep walking that way," I say.

"That's what you're worried about? My posture?"

I can't help it, I laugh. I know I should be distraught over the upcoming scandal. I know I should be furious with my daughter for being so reckless with her relationship with Frederick (were they caught on campus?), but none of it seems that serious. Caroline is only months away from starting Juilliard, Frederick is a sweetheart, and I—I just don't have it in me to get too worked up over this.

Once we are in the car with the doors closed and the windows rolled up, I ask her what "compromised" position she and Frederick were found in.

She shakes her head. "I can't tell you," she says.

Good Lord. As if we're not going to learn about it. "Should I just call Frederick and ask him?"

I put the key into the ignition and turn the Lexus on, not to start driving but to get the air conditioning going. It's only May and already it is hot.

Caroline starts crying. "Oh my God. I feel so bad for Frederick. He's going to be fired. Because of me. They are going to fire him and they are going to make sure he never teaches anywhere else. I know it."

It probably wouldn't be a bad thing if Frederick found another career besides teaching. Teaching has never seemed to me to be a viable career option for a man. I mean, I hate to sound sexist, but I don't see how a teacher's income could ever be considered anything but supplemental.

"Did they actually catch you in the act of making love?" I ask.

She gives me a look of utter scorn, the mascara smudged beneath her eyes. "No, Mom, we weren't 'making love.'"

I ignore her sarcasm, for now.

"Were genitals involved?"

"Oh my God, I can't talk about this with you. I'm sorry, but I can't."

Whoosh. There goes my patience.

"Darling, if you didn't want to talk with me about such intimate things, you shouldn't have been doing whatever it was you were doing with Frederick in a public place. I'm not asking about your private life out of personal curiosity, I assure you. What you do in your bedroom is your own business, but when you take it out of the bedroom, well, it becomes a lot of other people's business, whether we want it to be ours or not. I wish things were different, but you are in a lot of trouble with the school and if you want me to help you best navigate your way through it, you need to tell me exactly what happened."

I soften a little. "There is nothing new under the sun, sweetheart. You aren't going to shock me by telling me about whatever you were doing with Frederick."

She says something so softly I can't make out the words.

"What?" I ask.

"I was going down on him. They walked in on me while I was going down on him."

"Does that mean you were giving him a blowjob?" I ask, wanting to make sure I completely understand what happened.

Poor Caroline. Her face is bright red she is so embarrassed.

"God, Mom. You're not supposed to know that word."

I laugh. As if the whole world wasn't talking about blowjobs after that trashy woman was caught giving one to President Clinton. As if Tiny doesn't tell me how she uses them to help persuade Anders every time she wants a new piece of jewelry.

"This is such a nightmare," she says. "It was my English teacher, Mr. Lyons; he was the one who walked in on us."

"He's young, right? African American? The one who was a Jefferson scholar at UVA?"

Caroline nods. I am wondering if there is any way to get Mr. Lyons to keep quiet about the whole thing. After all, he and Frederick can't be that far apart agewise. Maybe they are friends. Then again, they can't be too close if Dean Brown was already informed.

"Did Mr. Lyons go straight to Miss Brown?" I ask.

Caroline lets out a huge sigh. "It's worse than that, Mom. It's much worse. He was giving an admissions tour. There were at least six potential Coventry students with him. I mean, I've never heard of them including the green room as part of the tour. No one has ever walked in on us there before."

Oh dear Lord.

This is much worse than I realized.

All those eyes—those young eyes, those young potential tuition-paying eyes—on my daughter. Oh dear. I feel a heavy weight settling on my chest. They are going to let Frederick and Caroline hang for this. What choice does the school have with so many witnesses?

"How many people saw you?" I ask. "You said six students were on the tour? Were they all in the green room when you were caught?"

"I don't know, Mom. It's all kind of a blur."

She's crying, lost in her grief, and I don't think she's acting. And suddenly, it all seems like too much, too much for her to have to go through at so young an age. I reach out my arms and she grabs onto me.

"WELL I JUST think we should have Frederick over so that we can all talk about it as a family," I say. "I mean we knew the situation all along. It's not like just because they were caught he's now a pariah."

"I didn't know the situation, Louise. For God's sake, do you think I would have given approval to my little girl having sex with a grown teacher?"

"Oh, don't act so innocent. You knew they were seeing each other."

We are in the sunporch with the door closed. Caroline is up in her room, where she has stayed ever since I drove her home from school. John Henry stands from his lounge chair to walk to the liquor cabinet.

"I thought he was helping her with her acting!" he says, reaching for an old-fashioned glass and the bottle of Knob Creek bourbon. He pours himself at least four fingers of the stuff and takes a long swallow.

"Don't you try to get out of this by getting drunk," I say.

"Louise, today my daughter was caught at my alma mater performing fellatio on one of her teachers. I think I deserve a drink. Frankly, I think I deserve to drink as much as I goddamn please."

The man has a point.

"Well, pour me one, then," I say.

He gets out another of the old-fashioned glasses (a wedding gift to us from my parents, so many years ago) and pours me two fingers of bourbon, neat. He walks to where I sit on the sofa and hands it to me.

"Cheers," he says, clinking his glass against mine. "To a second generation of Parker family scandal."

I smile. John Henry always makes jokes in grim situations. He was his funniest self the first few months after his twin brother, Wallace, shot himself in the head.

"Look," I say. "We need to focus on making sure that Caroline graduates and goes to Juilliard and that Coventry doesn't lynch Frederick just for tarnishing its reputation."

John Henry throws his one free hand up in the air in exasperation. "Louise, you act as if he did nothing wrong. He was taking advantage of our daughter, a student of his, for Christ's sake, on school property. I mean what if he blackmailed her into giving him sexual favors? What if he told her he would write her a good recommendation if she—you know, if she did what he wanted her to do?"

I take a sip of the bourbon, enjoying its sliding warmth. John Henry's thought has some appeal, but it's not the truth. I mean I'm sure girls are taken advantage of all the time, but not Caroline. She's got too much backbone to let herself get exploited.

"I tell you, John Henry, the two of them really like each other. They're a good match. He's only six years older than she. I blame the school. They were fools to hire a red-blooded young man to teach eighteen-year-olds, half of whom are blossoming, beautiful girls. What did they think would happen?"

John Henry stares at me for a moment.

"I'm really surprised that you're defending her so with such zeal," he says.

"Well, I am her mother."

"I know, I know. I'm not criticizing you. To tell the truth, it's nice to see you being so much on your daughter's side."

I suppose I could take his comment as an insult, the flip side of it being that I'm not usually "for" Caroline, but I know what he means. It feels good and right to be fighting for her instead of against her.

AFTER I FINISH my drink I go upstairs to her room. The door is closed and, I'm sure, locked.

I knock.

No answer.

I knock again. "Caroline," I say. "Open the door. We need to talk about what's going to happen tomorrow."

I wait. Finally I hear the lock turning and I push the door open.

We are standing face to face. I reach out to push her hair out of her eyes. She lets me before backing away and sitting down on the bed. She is submissive in a way that I've never seen before. And because of her weakness, her helplessness, I feel the same as I did in Miss Brown's office, that I *must* take charge. As if she's going to be eaten by the wolves unless I step in the way.

"Have you talked to Frederick?" I ask.

She nods.

"What did he say?"

"He just kept saying how sorry he was. How he fucked up— sorry." She looks up at me quickly, assuming, I suppose, that I'll fuss at her for cursing.

"I'm sure he feels terrible," I say. "Poor thing."

"Um, I don't mean to sound rude, but I'm really surprised that you're not worried about the scandal that's going to come from all of this."

"Oh honey," I say. "Coventry is not going to let this out any more than they have to. Their reputation is on the line more than yours, believe me."

"But a group of visiting students *saw* me."

"Well, that was unfortunate, but there's nothing you can do

to change the circumstances of how you got caught. You know, darling, this is exactly the reason my mother always told me it was important to keep up with the little things, to say your *ma'am*s and *sir*s, to write your thank-you cards on time, so that people would feel generous toward you when the big things happen that you can't control. I mean, think about her. She spent time at a mental institute. And do you think she got kicked out of the Junior League? Do you think she was ostracized at the Driving Club?"

"Mom, Coventry isn't a social club. I mean, sometimes it seems like it is, but it's not. It's high school. People aren't just going to pretend nothing happened if I'm polite on the outside and keep up with my thank-you notes."

We are both silent for a moment.

"Besides," she says, "I was never good at keeping up with the little things. I kind of suck at the little things."

"Oh, but you are strong," I say. "Listen, you have less than a month left of school. Just pretend that you are in a play, that you're Hester Prine in *The Scarlet Letter* and your part lasts for three weeks, okay? And then when you get to New York next fall, all of this will be behind you."

I will tell Caroline the story behind the necklace I gave her—surely she's earned the right to know—and knowing that story will give Caroline strength, will make her realize that everyone has their own shame to bear. Caroline will probably wear the necklace to school tomorrow, claim her *A* like the bold girl she is.

"They're going to kick me out."

"Believe me, sweetheart, your father and I are not going to let them kick you out."

"Even if they do somehow let me graduate and Juilliard still lets me enroll for next year, what I don't get is why you're not worried for you. You don't get to leave Atlanta. I promise, Mom, everyone is going to know about it. I mean, ten minutes after Frederick and I were caught, everyone at school knew about it.

They were all trying not to stare at me when I walked down the hall to Miss Brown's office."

"Honey," I say, "if scandal was going to bring our family down, don't you think it would have happened when your uncle Wallace killed himself?"

Caroline shrugs.

"I'll let you in on something," I say. "During these next few weeks you should make a real effort to look as good as you possibly can. I'm serious now, darling. Sometimes a put-together exterior makes you feel better about whatever mess you're dealing with on the inside."

She starts to laugh and I laugh a little too, aware of how—well, how shallow I must sound. Afterwards she straightens her shoulders. Some of her natural dominance is back. I hope it doesn't curb my warm feelings toward her.

"You're going to go back to school tomorrow and hold your head up straight, aren't you?"

"Yes," she says. "Yes, ma'am."

I smile at my sassy girl.

WHEN I GO to her room the next morning to make sure she has gotten up and not just punched snooze on her alarm and fallen back to sleep, her bed is empty and made and on one of the pillows is an envelope addressed to "Mom and Dad."

I open it quickly and scan the letter she has left us. She is with Frederick, it reads. They are on a plane to San Francisco, where, she assures me, she will do whatever she needs to finish up high school, to get her GED. John Henry and I are not to worry about her. She is eighteen, she is with the man she loves, and she is strong. "I'll be fine," she writes. "I promise."

Part Two

CHAPTER NINE

Every Woman Has Some
Jesus in Her

(Louise, Fall 2002)

*T*iny has been my best friend since we were practically babies, so under normal circumstances I would be insulted that I wasn't invited to the party she had last Saturday. But that party was a Republican fund-raiser, and years ago I told Tiny that while there is no arguing that the Republicans throw a better party than the Democrats, she should just stop sending me invitations to them. John Henry may vote the Republican ticket every time, but that doesn't mean I have to support the GOP. No one knows this but Tiny, but back in college I dated, briefly, a Jewish boy named Ben Ascher who tried—in his words—"to make a bra-burning liberal out of a sweet Georgia peach." Well, I have never burned a bra, but if my loyalty to the Democratic Party is any sort of sign, he at least partway succeeded.

In lieu of my attending her party, I tell her that I will come over for an early lunch today—Monday—and help eat the leftovers from it. I drive to Brookwood Hills, Tiny's neighbor-hood, just a mile or so down Peachtree from Ansley, and park the Lexus in front of Tiny's mock Tudor house on Palisades. Walking along the stone path that winds from her front yard all the way to the back garden, I feel nothing but envy for Tiny's landscaping. Everything that grows on the property is planned and deliberate, but it is planned in such a way that it looks completely natural, as if this little piece of paradise just sprung up of its own accord. I would love to hire Tiny's gardener, Nancy, who does such a fabu-lous job, but she is booked solid for the next five years.

Tiny's back door is open but the screen door is closed. I push on it—it's rarely locked—and let myself into the kitchen.

Facing the opposite direction from me, Tiny pushes a tray of something yummy—I'm sure—into the oven. She has an apron tied around her waist and from this view she looks a bit like Julia Child in her prime. She's certainly tall enough to pass for Julia.

"Hello!" I say.

Tiny turns from the oven, her bright pink lips formed into a surprised O as if I've been missing for years, as if we didn't just this morning talk on the phone and confirm our plans for lunch.

"Lou-Lou!" she cries. "Wait one second, let me just set the timer on these little quiches."

She closes the oven door, twirls the timer, and rushes over to me, throwing her arms around me in a full-out embrace. It oc-curs to me as I take in the familiar smell of Joy perfume, Tiny's preferred fragrance for the past twenty years, that she is the only woman I know who *really* hugs.

"I love this," she says, towering over me while she touches the sleeve of my pale blue blouse. I look down quickly at where her fingers were, hoping she didn't leave any quiche grease on the silk. She didn't.

"Neiman's," I say. "On sale."

"It's perfect," she says. "Now what are we drinking?"

She walks to her refrigerator and opens the door. "I've got a wonderful pinot gris, a very delicious champagne, or if we want to be poops, Perrier."

Even though I know I shouldn't drink in the middle of the day, there's no real point in my saying no to the wine. Tiny will eventually wear me down.

I gaze at the items in Tiny's refrigerator while considering whether or not to go ahead and give in to an afternoon of alcohol. As always, I envy the contents of Tiny's Sub-Zero. The top shelf holds drinks: eight-ounce glass bottles of Coke, Perrier, two bottles of wine, and three bottles of champagne. The second highest shelf holds prepared foods. I know that inside the large Tupperware container is homemade gazpacho, which Tiny will have on hand until the weather finally cools down, which can be as late as mid-October. Today there is also a glass bowl filled with chicken salad, along with a plate of the sliced leftovers of a molasses-marinated pork roast, Tiny's favorite dish to serve at parties.

Below the prepared foods are fruits and vegetables. Unlike me, Tiny does not just buy her produce and then stick it into the refrigerator. She washes the grapes and separates them into snack-sized bunches. She cuts the carrots, celery, and peppers into sticks; she rinses the lettuce and stores it stacked between paper towels in the salad spinner.

Truly, hardly anything escapes Tiny's will.

"Let's go ahead and have the pinot gris," I say, resigned.

"Oh goody!" says Tiny. She pulls the bottle out of the fridge, opens it with her one-hundred-dollar high-tech opener, and pours it into wine glasses that she must have set out earlier.

"I get the Baccarat?" I say, noticing that she is using her very best crystal. Tiny has hundreds of wine glasses but only twenty-four pieces of Baccarat.

"Only the best for Lou-Lou," she says, taking my free hand.

"Come. I want to show you the fairy bowl Anders just bought on eBay."

"Good Lord, another one?" I ask.

"First it was jewelry," she says. "Anything I wanted he'd get for me as long as he could bid for it. You know how competitive that man is. Finally it got to be I had so many new bracelets and earrings I didn't have any room left in my jewelry box. So I told him he needed to find a new outlet for his bidding, and Wedgwood Fairyland Lustre pieces have been it."

"But surely a bowl is bigger than a piece of jewelry," I say.

"Ah, yes, but I still have a spare shelf in the living room display case. It's all about where there's room to put things, darling."

We have to walk through the dining room to get to the living room. The dining room is wallpapered with a scene from the Revolutionary War. Tiny doesn't much care for the paper. She thinks that the fierce Indians depicted in full war paint, complete with feathers sticking off their rear ends, look as if they are pooping, but before ripping it out she had it appraised and realized the antique paper was worth over ten thousand dollars.

She and Anders decided to live with it.

We walk into her wood-beamed living room. Sitting on the glass coffee table is the new bowl. It practically glows it is so brightly painted with blues, purples, and golds. Painted around the edge of the bowl are wispy angels and nymphs.

"It's gorgeous," I say, picking it up to admire it more closely.

I wish John Henry would think to buy me something this beautiful.

"I caught Anders screwing the tenant," says Tiny.

I set the bowl back down on the coffee table and turn to Tiny.

"What?"

Tiny takes a sip of her wine, leaving a pink stain on the lip of the glass. She nods.

"He was always going back there to check on things; I knew something was up."

Tiny and Anders's house includes a one-bedroom garage apartment that they rent out for eight hundred dollars a month.

"You mean that little girl? Ashley? How old is she?"

Tiny smirks. "Twenty-two years old. Just graduated last year from Georgia. Still has a Kappa Kappa Gamma sticker on the back of her car."

"Are you sure they were having an affair?"

Anders is devoted to Tiny. He has been ever since they met their sophomore year at Chapel Hill, right around the same time John Henry and I started dating.

"You should have seen Anders's face when he looked over his shoulder and saw me standing in the doorway." Tiny touches her upper lip with her pointer finger and pulls away a drop of white wine. She touches her finger to her mouth, and the drop is gone.

"Come," she says, "let's get our lunch ready, and I'll tell you all about it."

I look for signs of distress on Tiny but see none. Her face holds the same bemused expression it always does. In fact, her eyes seem to be sparkling. It occurs to me that Tiny is glad to have caught Anders, is glad to have this thing to hold against him. It's as if she has checked him in a long-standing game of chess they've been playing.

"I've got things set up in the sunporch," she says. "Bring your wine."

THE SUNPORCH HAS two walls of windows. Tiny fusses with the silhouette shades until the blinding sun is blocked. "There," she says. "Sit."

Surrounding a vase of delicate dendrobium orchids are plates of food Tiny has set out on the small round table, much more food than we could ever eat. There is a plate of asparagus glistening with hollandaise sauce, a plate of sliced pork roast, a bowl of apricot compote, and a beautiful green salad with grapefruit, candied walnuts, and avocados. Tiny has also put a cheese board and a bowl of glazed strawberries on a foldout tray by the table.

"This looks wonderful," I say.

"I forgot to bring the bottle of wine," she says. She rushes back to the kitchen while I put food on my plate, eyeing my portions carefully. Ever since I reached my forties I have realized that being thin is a product of youth, not virtue. But that doesn't mean I don't resist my thickening middle.

Tiny returns from the kitchen with the bottle of pinot gris and a small platter loaded with mini quiches. "I almost forgot these," she says, sliding three onto my plate and refilling my glass.

Lord. I should probably just forget about my diet for this lunch. She's probably got more food waiting to bring to the table; the cheese and strawberries she set out will probably be only a part of our dessert.

I eat a bite of the meat with a little apricot compote. Tiny works wonders with pork roast. She marinates it for a full day before cooking so that it comes out of the oven tender and flavored throughout.

"Oh, this is so good," I say.

"Junior League recipe," she says. "Same thing I've been making for fifteen years."

Even sitting down Tiny is a good head taller than me. When I was a little girl the term for ladies her height was "statuesque." Tiny has always claimed that she is actually short-waisted, that it is only her long legs that make her loom above everyone. Once, when we were sixteen, we were eating hamburgers at the Varsity and she got a booster seat *for herself* and then sat in it for the duration of the meal.

Tiny has always been crazy like that.

I want Tiny to start up again with the story about Anders and the tenant, but I don't want to ask for details she doesn't want to give. So I just eat and tell her how delicious everything is, and she replies again and again that everything she fixed was simple, simple. If I so much as take two sips from my wine glass, she refills it.

Finally I put down my Francis I fork, so full I absolutely cannot take another bite.

"Tiny, I'm dying. You have got to tell me about Anders and that girl. Unless it's too painful. I don't want to open back up any ugly wounds."

"You think they've had time to heal?" Tiny laughs. "Lou-Lou, I caught the two of them two days ago, on Saturday, the day of the party. I had to play host all night with the image of my husband pressed up against that girl's hiney."

"No," I say.

"I think the term is 'doggie style,'" she says. "I warn you: refuse a position and your husband will find someone else to do it with."

"Oh Tiny," I say, squeezing her wrist. "What did Anders say when you caught him? What did that girl say?"

Tiny barks out a laugh, grabs the cheese plate off the tray, and sets it on the table between us. Using a delicate ivory-handled knife, she lobs off the nose of the Pierre Robert and spreads it onto a thin slice of French bread.

She must be really upset. She never cuts the nose off a piece of cheese but always slices it down the side of the triangle, the way our eleventh-grade French culture teacher taught us to do.

"That girl hid her head under the pillow. Which was the most sensible thing she could have done. Anders started sputtering that things looked worse than they really were."

Tiny pops the piece of bread and cheese into her mouth. She points to the wine bottle, but when I pick it up to pour, I realize that we have already emptied it.

Even though she's in the middle of a bite, she talks anyway, holding her hand in front of her mouth so I won't be exposed to her half-chewed food.

"Do me a favor, Lou-Lou. Go to the fridge and get out a bottle of Veuve Clicquot."

I am already feeling light-headed, but I love champagne. And obviously, Tiny *needs* me to drink with her.

I return with the bottle. Tiny motions toward the liquor cabinet. I open it and take out two crystal champagne flutes from the bottom shelf. Once Tiny's cat, Barbara Bush, jumped in there and knocked over a whole shelf of crystal. Amazingly, only one glass broke.

Tiny removes the hood from the champagne bottle, takes her white hemstitched linen napkin out of her lap, and uses it to twist the cork off with a pop.

"Cheers," she says after pouring two full glasses. We clink rims and each take a sip. The champagne is delicious, cool and bubbly with just a hint of yeasty sweetness.

"Did Anders buy the fairy bowl as a way of saying he's sorry?" I ask.

I plop a glazed strawberry into my champagne flute and let it float.

Tiny shakes her head. "It came days ago. Anders hasn't known what the hell to say to me since I caught him."

I stick my fork into my glass trying to fish out my strawberry, but it bobs out of the way every time I try to spear it.

"Sometimes I wish John Henry would cheat on me and then we could just get a divorce," I say, surprising myself. The champagne must be going straight to my head. "Lord knows it's been easier with Caroline out of the house and across the country, but ever since we gave up on trying to get her back home, John Henry and I haven't had much to discuss."

Tiny raises her eyebrows. She has them shaped every other

week into two perfect crescents. "Well maybe Charles will fuck up and then the two of you can bond over worrying about him."

I let out a little laugh, though it is rueful and not really amused. Charles, if not exactly "fucking up," has become more and more distant. It started when he began high school, and now that he's a sophomore it's as if I hardly know him. He spends all his time in his room with the door closed, playing terrible music that sounds like human misery itself.

I stick my fork back into my champagne glass, trying again to jab the strawberry. Again it bobs away.

"Don't you know not to stick sterling silver into champagne?" asks Tiny, and then sticks her own fork into her glass. I laugh and pour myself some more Veuve.

"Excuse me, Miz Persons?"

Standing at the entry of the sunporch is Faye, wearing baggy shorts and one of those terrible T-shirts she has, this one proclaiming, "1 cross + 3 nails = 4 given."

"Sorry to interrupt you ladies, but I'm going to head out. I just mopped the kitchen floor so be careful you don't slip if you go back in there."

All this time I didn't realize anyone else was in the house besides Tiny and me. It must be the alcohol dulling my senses, or maybe it's the music—*Frank Sinatra's Greatest Hits*—that Tiny has been playing so loudly.

"Thank you so much, Faye. I'm sure you did a terrific job. Now did you manage to get to that little pile of delicates I left on top of the washing machine?"

"Yes, ma'am," says Faye. "I washed them out with Woolite. Hung them up in your bathroom."

"Perfect," says Tiny. Faye turns and walks away but Tiny calls after her.

"I have some leftover bacon from this morning's breakfast,

which you are welcome to take with you if you like. Just pop it in a Ziploc bag; there's a box of them in the drawer to the right of the stove."

Tiny is always trying to fob off her throwaways on the help. That might be one of the reasons her maids often stop showing up. That, or the fact that she expects them to handwash her underwear.

"Okay," says Faye. "Missy just loves bacon."

WHILE SIPPING CHAMPAGNE and eating strawberries and chocolate brownies (I was right, Tiny did bring out another dessert), Tiny tells me that Earl LeTrouve is soon going to make it big. I love Tiny, but she has really gone over the top with this folk art thing. Probably she's just trying to irritate Anders, whose taste is more refined. That or she truly thinks she's going to one day make a mint on the pieces she's collected. I don't know why she's so sure that certain artists—Earl for instance—will eventually gain mass appeal. Maybe it's just that Tiny has a bedrock trust in her own taste.

I already own one LeTrouve piece, which Tiny convinced me to buy a few years ago at the Big Angel Blowout over in Inman Park. As is often the case when I am with Tiny, my judgment *was* impaired by the three glasses of white wine I'd had, and truly I probably would not have bought the piece had I been sober, but regardless, I do like it.

It's a big, bold portrait of Jesus, wearing a bright blue ball gown, a diamond tiara on his head. The title of the piece is *Every Woman Has Some Jesus in Her*, which I thought was clever. John Henry, of course, *abhors* the painting and would like nothing more than to rip it off the living room wall, where I had it hung. He claims it's sacrilegious, but I told him so is having sex on Sunday mornings, when we should be at church. He backed down after that, not wanting to give up a good thing.

"So are you game?" asks Tiny, her eyes shining. "Because I can speed-dial Jose and he'll be here in twenty minutes."

Jose is the driver that Tiny and Anders use for special occasions and trips to the airport (technically, Jose is a driver at Anders's firm, but he and Anders have worked out some sort of an arrangement). Beyond that I'm not sure what she's talking about. I've had too much to drink.

"I'm sorry," I say. "This champagne went straight to my head. Game for what?"

"For going to see his home studio. It can't be more than an hour and a half away from here; Stephen said he lives just past Eatonton, toward Milledgeville."

"You want to go to Milledgeville?" I ask. "To see Flannery O'Connor's house?"

"Good Lord, Louise. How much champagne have you had? Not to see Flannery O'Connor's house, to see Earl LeTrouve's studio. He'll sell his stuff right out of it and we won't have to pay a gallery's markup. Seriously, Stephen says that Earl is going to be huge one of these days and that we should buy up his stuff now while it's still cheap enough to do so."

"Stephen?"

"Is your old-timer's acting up? I've introduced you to him I don't know how many times."

Right. Stephen. Stephen. Stephen is Tiny's gay friend, the one who runs the framing shop.

I look at my watch. It is already one thirty. Charles will be arriving home from school soon, and I haven't done anything productive with my day, let alone made any plans for dinner tonight. I should go home and get things done, except when I think about it, about the reality of what I will do (go to the dry cleaner, watch *Oprah*, attempt to get Charles to answer me with more than a single word), I feel sad, lonely.

"Okay," I say. "I'm up for an adventure."

The truth of the matter is it's good Jose can drive us around for a few hours. I am way too inebriated even to drive the mile and a half back to my home.

BEN ASCHER, THE Jewish boy I dated, was incredulous that I had never visited Milledgeville before. He thought I should pay tribute to the hometown of Flannery O'Connor.

"I can't believe that you haven't yet made a pilgrimage!" he said. "My God, you grew up in Georgia, *and* you're an English major at a southern university. What more do you want?"

What Ben didn't understand was that girls in Chi Omega—at least not my circle of friends—did not make literary pilgrimages. Maybe girls in the less popular sororities did such things, but the only pilgrimages we ever made were to Myrtle Beach to attend fraternity formals.

Tiny holds forth during the entire drive. Her daughter, Helen, is getting married next spring, and Tiny is in charge of the wedding because Helen is living in New York. Helen is marrying a boy who also grew up in Atlanta, so his guest list is as long as hers. Tiny thinks they'll end up inviting over five hundred people.

"We have to have the reception at the Driving Club," she says. "Which kills me, because the food there is so mediocre. But what else can we do? It's the only place that will hold all of us."

"I went to a wedding reception there last month and the food was actually quite good," I say. "Plus as long as you give people those buttered saltines they'll be happy."

Tiny moves on to the subject of flowers, while I think about Caroline and how she will never have a big Atlanta wedding, how she probably will never get married. I used to think that she and Frederick would marry each other—not that their wedding would be a Driving Club event—but they broke up not one year after they ran off to San Francisco. When she called to tell me about the breakup I thought that meant she might move home, but instead *he* moved and she stayed put.

To be perfectly honest, San Francisco is a better place for her than Atlanta ever was. It suits her. It seemed that the moment she stepped off the plane and onto California soil she got her act together. She earned her GED, not that we're exactly beaming with pride over that, but then she enrolled at San Francisco State University. She's majoring in something called American Studies, although judging by what she's learning it should be called American Sins.

I don't mean to sound negative—I think it's important to learn about indigenous cultures and to take a skeptical stance toward government, and so on and so on—but I do sometimes get a little tired of being lectured so often by her on the Complicity of America in all things Evil.

If Ben Ascher and I had ever consummated our relationship, I would swear she was his.

She has a steady job waiting tables at an adorable little Middle Eastern restaurant, and she is forever acting in different "important projects" (her term) around the city. I thought that without Frederick's support she wouldn't be able to afford San Francisco, but she seems to be okay. Of course we pay for her college classes, and John Henry sends her a small check each month to cover part of her rent, but other than that, she's on her own.

It's funny looking back on the first few months after she ran off. We did everything short of kidnapping her to get her to come home, but she wouldn't and we couldn't make her since she was eighteen and legally an adult. So then we waited for her to fail so that we could go clean up the pieces and straighten her life out for her. But so far she hasn't failed. It's as if away from all our worry she's finally started looking after herself. I find myself wondering if I ever could have done what she did—defied my parents and run off with, say, Ben Ascher. Well obviously I couldn't.

I didn't.

Ever since she left—after I stopped wanting to kill her with my bare hands for running off in the middle of the night—I've been so proud of Caroline, so proud of her independent spirit. Truly, it is a thousand times easier having a rebel daughter who lives across the country than it is having one living down the hall.

EARL LETROUVE'S HOUSE is a plain brick ranch just off an empty stretch of 441. I would not have guessed that a folk artist lives here. There are no steel structures in the yard, no prophetic messages spelled out across the roof in white Christmas lights, no painted cars with Barbie doll heads glued to the front hood. There is an American flag flying from a tall flagpole stationed in the front yard, and a white pickup truck parked in the driveway.

Tiny double-checks the address and tells Jose to let us off, that this is it. "I'm sure we'll be at least an hour," she tells him. "Feel free to go get yourself a bite to eat."

We get out of the car and walk up the concrete path that cuts through the grass and leads to the door. As I watch Jose pull away, I have a terrible thought.

"Tiny, we do have an appointment, don't we?" I ask.

Tiny looks at me, all wide-eyed innocence. "His home is his gallery, Louise. He welcomes drop-in visitors."

I am suddenly aware of the stretch of highway before us and the fact that there are no other houses on either side of Mr. LeTrouve's. Oh Lord, please don't let him be like that man who made the skin suit in *Silence of the Lambs*.

Tiny rings the bell while I stand back a bit. I really, really wish she had not sent Jose off to get a burger. I want us to be able to drive away in an instant if need be.

"No one's answering," I say, praying that no one will. "He's probably not home."

Just then the top half of the door swings open and a tremendously fat man with dyed black hair stands before us.

I wait for him to say something, but he does not.

"Mr. LeTrouve?" asks Tiny.

"Yes," says the man. He is wearing red suspenders over a plaid flannel shirt. His hairy stomach is so big that it pokes out between his shirt buttons.

"I'm Tiny Persons and this is Louise Parker and we are both just the biggest fans of your work. Stephen Pollard, the owner of Frame!—you know, that adorable frame and print shop in Atlanta—well, he said that you sometimes open your studio to the public, and we were just wondering if we might peek in and take a look at some of your marvelous creations."

Tiny's southern accent doubles in intensity when she is putting on the charm.

"Y'all want to come in and check out the studio?" asks Mr. LeTrouve.

"We would love to!" says Tiny. I try not to roll my eyes at her breathlessness. She is turning into a folk art whore, I swear to God.

"Well, come on," he says. "You don't mind dogs, do you?"

"I adore them," says Tiny.

I like a dog as long as it's not trained to attack and as long as it's not a pit bull.

Mr. LeTrouve unlatches the bottom half of the door and steps back to let us into his house. It smells of dust and clutter, like someone needs to go through and open all the windows. The second we step inside, three Doberman pinschers come running out to the hall, their toenails clicking against the wood floor.

"Halt!" says Mr. LeTrouve, and they all skid to a standstill and look up at Mr. LeTrouve for his next instructions.

I have to admit, I'm impressed.

"Go to bed," he says, and the dogs turn and run back down the hall and into a room at the very end of it.

"Pardon the mess," he says, motioning to a room to his right that must be the living room but that is filled with so much junk it would be impossible to get through it, let alone to sit on one of its sofas. "I can't seem to keep the front of this place clean the way Mama did."

"Is your mother, is she deceased?" asks Tiny.

Mr. LeTrouve nods.

"I'm so sorry," says Tiny. "When did she pass away?"

"Nineteen ninety-three," says Mr. LeTrouve. "When she died she had eight cats. I promised her I'd take care of them, which is one of the reasons I stayed in this house. Six of them are still alive, and one of them had a litter a few years ago, so we've got fourteen around here somewhere."

Oh Lord. Tiny has trapped us in a house with a cat-loving Norman Bates.

"Y'all come on back to the studio," he says. "Can I get you something to drink? Some water or a Co-Cola?"

A Coke sounds so good after all that champagne and driving that I agree to take one even though my better judgment tells me not to imbibe anything from this house.

"I'll have one too, please," says Tiny.

"Just keep walking straight back and you'll hit the studio," says Mr. LeTrouve. "I'll meet you there."

There are all sorts of photos on the hall wall. From the giant physiques of most of the people in them, I'm assuming they are members of Mr. LeTrouve's family, but intermingled with the family photos is a rather large portrait of Robert E. Lee.

Why some people are still so attached to that man I will never know.

There is a china cabinet at the end of the hall. I can tell, even from a distance, that it is not filled with Earl LeTrouve's mama's china, but it is not until I walk up close to it that I realize what it is filled with: death. The shelves are lined with death. On the lowest shelf are little stuffed mice, standing on their little hind legs. The second shelf up is lined with chipmunks, these turned in profile to show off the black stripe down their backs. The third row has birds, wrens mostly but two robins and one bluebird, and the fourth is filled with squirrels. The squirrels are at eye level with me, and I know, staring at their black beady eyes, that I will have nightmares about them tonight. On the final row is a framed photo of a large black cat, lying on its side—contented as can be—atop a pile of brown leaves.

I feel a wave of nausea. I motion to Tiny to take a look, glaring at her as soon as she does.

"Listen," I say. "This is beyond the pale. I think we should get out of here as soon as we can."

Tiny takes a good look at the display case. "They're stuffed," she says. "Really, it's not much different than the deer head Anders has hanging in his study."

"Well I don't like that either, but this *is* different. This is vermin in a china cabinet."

"Don't be a snob, Louise. Have a sense of humor. What kind of southern upbringing did you have if you can't find the humor in this situation?"

Tiny is forever lecturing me about how I have abandoned my southern heritage. Mainly because I don't vote Republican (which only became a southern thing to do a few years ago) and because I don't believe in heaven and hell. ("You went to church every Sunday growing up!" she says. "How did the truth not sink in?")

"As a matter of fact," I say, "my southern upbringing explicitly forbids displaying dead animals in the china cabinet."

"It's art," she says. "Look, it has a title."

Indeed, engraved into a little brass plaque just above the cabinet doors are the words "Sassy's Treasure: Everything but the Rats."

I shudder.

Thank God he did not include the rats.

Thank *God* he did not include the rats.

Why did Tiny tell Jose to take an hourlong break? If he were still parked in the driveway I could march back out there and wait in the car while Tiny subjects herself to the imagination of a lunatic.

"Come on," she says. "Let's see more of his stuff."

We find the studio at the end of the hall. It appears to be a new addition to the house. Its floors, walls, and windows are free of the years of caked-on grime that the rest of the house has. Indeed the studio is light and airy, neat and organized. The shelves that line three of the walls are stacked with, among other items, paintbrushes and tubes of paint and boxes of pastels and little plastic tubs and scrapers and turpentine and rolls of chicken wire. Pushed against the one spare wall is an old farm table with four tiny paintings resting on it.

I walk over to the table to examine the paintings more closely. Each depicts an apple tree, one for each season. They are so small and so vibrant; it looks as if layers of color and light have been applied to each one. There's nothing impressionistic about the paintings. I can tell exactly what they are trying to portray: apple blossoms in the spring, bright green leaves in the summer, fruit in the fall, and bare branches in the winter. As I look closer I notice that each painting has the same blackbird in it, though he shows up on different branches in three of them, and on the ground, in the grass, in the summer scene.

The more I look at the four paintings, the more I like them. I focus on the depth of color and the precision of each image. Even though their techniques are completely different, there's a generosity of spirit in these pieces that reminds me in some ways of Hank Huffington's work, the now-acclaimed portrait artist who started out as a mail boy at John Henry's firm and whom I hired to paint Charles's and Caroline's portraits. (It took me weeks to persuade John Henry to spend the $6,000 Hank charged for painting the portraits. John Henry could not understand Hank's exuberant, almost cartoonish style, using every color in the rainbow to paint something as seemingly simple as brown hair. You see, John Henry has philistine tendencies and could not recognize how fabulous Hank's paintings were until they started appreciating in monetary value. Which they did.)

I am drawn to Mr. LeTrouve's work just as I was drawn to Hank's. I am drawn to Mr. LeTrouve's paintings the way a child is drawn to candy, the way a woman is drawn to jewelry. Indeed, there is something jewel-like about each one, as if you might find it wrapped inside a Tiffany's box.

"I hate to admit it, but I love these."

"I told you he's fabulous," says Tiny.

"It's the colors even more than the subject matter that I'm drawn to. The four seasons are nice, of course, but it's the luminosity that's captivating. And I'll tell you, Tiny, this does not look like folk art to me. It looks to me like egg tempera, like Earl LeTrouve was inspired by Botticelli."

I stare at the paintings for a minute more before turning my attention to the other pieces in the room. Leaning against the far wall are three large oil paintings, each depicting a terrifyingly dark and shadowy forest. There is a tiny girl in the corner of one of the forests wearing a red cape, like Little Red Riding Hood.

Propped against the edge of the farm table is a small wood sculpture of a naked woman, nothing too special, although when I touch it I am pleased to feel that the wood has been polished so smooth it feels like silk.

Tiny notices me touching the sculpture and walks over and picks it up. She turns it over and stares at the crack of her rear.

"If I bought this," she says, "it would never have to be dusted because Anders would pet it day and night."

Mr. LeTrouve walks into the studio carrying a tray. "I thought y'all might like some banana pudding with your Cokes," he says.

"I adore banana pudding," says Tiny.

Good Lord, has this woman lost all sense? Much as I like his paintings of the apple tree, that doesn't make me willing to eat food prepared with the same hands that stuffed those squirrels.

Mr. LeTrouve hands me my glass of Coke, filled to the top with ice cubes. "Banana pudding?" he asks. "I got a little creative and used colored Nilla wafers."

I look at the pudding. There are bright pink and green wafers floating in it, along with browned slices of banana. The food coloring in the wafers is leaking into the gelatinous pudding. I don't think it would be possible to make something less appetizing if you tried.

"Thank you so much," I say, "but I'm afraid I have a banana allergy."

"Well, I don't," says Tiny, glaring at me. She grabs one of the bowls and eats a bite with a bright pink Nilla wafer in it. "Delicious," she says. "Just like Mama used to make."

Ha. As if Tiny's mother, former president of the Junior League and cochair of the Piedmont Ball for years, would have ever made banana pudding with colored wafers.

I clear my throat, hoping to change the subject from the pudding, which is nauseating me more than the stuffed animal display. "Mr. LeTrouve, would you mind telling me about this series of apple trees? I am just so drawn to each of those paintings."

He scratches the top of his head while he walks over to the paintings, giving them a look-over. "These here are my egg drawings," he says. "I mix powder pigment with egg yolk and water. That gets me the paint, and then I apply it thin as I can, layer by layer, to these little gesso boards. You got to use true gesso boards—the ones made with rabbit skin glue—to get that nice, reflective quality."

"So it *is* tempera," I say. "I absolutely adore them."

"You see I read this book that said the shock of the Gospels has worn off after all these years of us hearing it every Sunday. That's why we get bored in church. That's why we're unmoved. So, I got to thinking I might make me some Jesuses that would startle me into believing. I started with my party dress series, and now I've moved on to this."

"Excuse me?" I ask, having no idea how we jumped from talking about tempera to talking about Jesus.

He points to the painting of the tree in spring. "Can't you tell that's Jesus?" he asks.

"The bird?" I ask.

"No, the tree. Look at it along the trunk for His body and then follow those two branches that are reaching out like His arms stretched on the cross. Don't you see it?"

I pick up the picture and examine it closely. The trunk looks like a trunk, varied and patterned, yes, but not like a body. I can, however, make out Jesus's arms, two long branches with tiny red puncture marks about where the wrists would be. I look at the tree in winter, and yes, Jesus's arms are in it too.

The discovery makes me gasp, which is a wonderful feeling, as I am not one to be taken over by religious sentiment. Try as I might I don't feel much of anything in church and I feel even less during the Eucharist. I will look at others as the wafer is placed in their mouths and I can tell by their simple earnestness that they are believers. And believe me, I have yearned for their earnestness. But I've never been able to convince myself, to convince my gut, really, that there is any existence beyond this earth.

"Are they for sale?" I ask.

Mr. LeTrouve turns toward me and smiles. "It takes a mighty long time to put down the layers for tempera. And it takes months and months for the paint to dry completely. And seeing as how I'm a bit partial to those pieces, well, they ain't going to be cheap."

"How much for all four?" I ask, feeling my heart start to race because I want them so much.

"And this," says Tiny, holding up the naked statue and smiling wickedly. "For my darling husband."

Earl names the price and I reach into my bag for my checkbook, my hand shaking at how much I am willing to hand over.

CHAPTER TEN

Salt of the Earth

(Missy, Summer 2004)

I peer into the kitchen, checking to see if Mrs. Parker is in there, hoping she is not. Even though it's been a long time since she called to say that she overreacted about the bird, I still feel embarrassed when I see her. Especially after that talk she had with me the first time Mama dragged me back to her house. It's been years, but I still feel ashamed thinking about it. If Mama didn't make me, I wouldn't keep coming to Mrs. Parker's house with her, but Mama says sorry, I'm too good a help to leave at home, at least during the summer when there's nothing else for me to do.

I open the fridge and take out the roast beef and the mayonnaise. Then I take one of the croissants from the bag Mrs. Parker left on the counter and make a roast beef and croissant sandwich. One thing I can say about Mrs. Parker, she always has good food in her house, and she doesn't mind if me and Mama eat it. I put the sandwich on one of Mrs. Parker's pretty green plates (she says she doesn't like to use paper plates because of the landfills) and walk to the den so that I can watch TV while

I eat, but I stop short at the door. Charles Parker is already in there, sitting on the sofa and watching a show.

"Hi," he says, glancing at me. He's dyed his hair again. This time it's white blond, so bright it's hard to look at. He's cut it supershort too, almost like he's in the army (as if that boy would make it in the army). He's wearing a necklace of all things, made of little silver balls linked together. He looks faggy, and then it occurs to me that maybe he is one, a fag.

"Sorry," I say. "I didn't know you were in here."

"There's room for more than one," he says. "Come in. Sit down. Take a load off."

His words are friendly, but his tone is not. He doesn't sound mean exactly, more like he's making fun of everything he's saying while he says it, like he's making fun of himself.

Even though there's room on the couch to sit next to Charles, I sit in one of Mrs. Parker's upholstered chairs, resting my plate in my lap. The fabric on the chair is printed with little orange monkeys.

"What are you watching?" I ask, thinking I'll just eat my sandwich real fast and go. I take a bite. It tastes really good, the roast beef all soft, the croissant so tender.

"It's this hilarious new show I found," he says, stretching out to lie down on the couch. "It's called *Salt of the Earth*. It's a Christian soap."

I watch the GIG network all the time and I've never heard of *Salt of the Earth*.

"I thought the *Rapture Update* was on at eleven," I say.

In fact, I know it is. It comes on twice a day, at eleven in the morning and nine at night.

"Oh my God! You watch Lacy Lovehart? She's hilarious. She's totally my apocalyptic hero!"

Lacy Lovehart is a lot of things—upbeat, smart, prophetic— but she's not hilarious.

"*Salt* isn't aired on the GIG. It's on this cable access show filmed somewhere near Chapel Hill. Most mortals outside of North Carolina don't have the privilege of watching it, but my dad bought a satellite dish so he can pick up UNC lacrosse games. Hence, I picked up this little gem, and believe me, you are in for a treat. This is even better than Lovehart. Promise you'll watch, okay?"

"Okay," I say, shrugging.

"Okay, so we just found out that Dawn, the preacher's daughter, is pregnant. Her brother, Matthew, discovered her home pregnancy test in her trash can. That's them."

A boy and a girl, Dawn and Matthew I guess, sit on a big pink bed in the middle of a pink room. Over the bed is a white cross with pink flowers painted on it. Dawn and Matthew both have the same blond hair, a color that looks like it came out of a bottle. I figure they dyed their hair the same color so that they would look more like brother and sister, because otherwise they don't really look alike. He's big and muscular while she's just a tiny thing.

In Dawn's hand is something that looks like a thermometer, and Dawn looks like she's been crying.

"*How'd you find it?*" she asks.

"You left it on top of your wastebasket, you idiot," says Charles, making me miss Matthew's line.

"Will you turn it up a little?" I ask.

Charles grabs the remote off Mrs. Parker's glass coffee table, which has magazines fanned out on it: *Martha Stewart Living, Veranda, The New Yorker, Atlanta*. Charles punches the volume up so it's really loud. I take another bite of sandwich.

"Their mom, Mary, stays at home, big surprise. Dad is a minister at the ROCK church, where they 'rock out' for Jesus."

I keep missing what's happening on the show because Charles is blabbing. "What did she just say?" I ask.

"She said her boyfriend raped her."

"That's horrible."

"Isn't it?" asks Charles, but he doesn't sound like he thinks it is. He sounds like he thinks it's funny.

"I'm going to kick his butt!" cries Matthew, standing up from the bed, his hands in fists.

"Thataboy," says Charles. "Put a boot in his ass for the Lord!"

"Wait!" cries Dawn. The camera zooms in on her face. Her cheeks are chubby, like she still has baby fat, but she has wrinkles around her eyes like Mama.

"My God, how old is she? Twenty-eight?" asks Charles. "Hello? Has she heard of Botox?"

"How old is she supposed to be?" I ask.

"Sixteen," he says, smirking. "A sixteen-year-old with crow's feet."

I turn sixteen next month. Dawn could be me.

"Do you know what we need to do?" she asks.

"Pray?" says Matthew.

"That too. But first we need to tell Dad."

She looks down at her belly, rubs it, and then looks back at her brother.

The scene freezes.

"Intermission," says Charles. "Just like a play. I think we're supposed to read our Bibles during this time."

He's pierced his nose since the last time I saw him. He has a tiny silver ball stuck in his right nostril that matches the silver balls around his neck.

"What do you think?" he asks.

I'm careful with my words, realizing that this might be my chance to help bring Charles to Jesus. I mean, even if he is making fun of it, he *is* watching a Christian TV show. That means the seed has been planted.

"I'm wondering what you think might happen to you when you die."

Charles rolls his eyes. "Oh God," he says. "You're one of *them*."

"I'm a Christian if that's what you mean."

"Jesus. You and everyone else I go to school with. I thought I was done with this for the summer."

"I'd like to know how you can say 'Jesus' if you don't believe in Him?"

"Hon, hate to break it to you, but I've heard that argument like ten million times. I go to Coventry, remember? Anyway, it's a figure of speech. I can hardly escape a word that's become a part of the American vernacular, can I?"

Pastor Finch says the unsaved are always trying to use fancy talk to trip you up, but as long as you understand their tactics and don't get flustered, you can give it right back to them.

"What does going to Coventry have to do with whether or not you know Jesus?" I ask.

"Don't you know Coventry is a Christian preparatory school for boys and girls? Home of metal fish slapped on the backs of luxury SUVs?"

"It's not a sin to have money," I say. "It means God trusts you with earthly affairs. There's a whole show about it on GIG; it's called *Growing Your Talent*."

"Oh honey," Charles says, as if he's much, much older than me, when I know he's only seventeen. "Shh! We're back on!"

Dawn and Matthew walk down the stairs and into a nice living room. In it there are potted plants by the windows and framed photos above the mantelpiece and a braided rug on the floor. In the middle of the room two sofas are pushed together to form an L, and there's a big entertainment center against the wall. They walk through the room and knock on a closed door on the other side of it.

"Pops is very hip," says Charles. "You'll like him. He's all *Jesus is my homeboy* and shit."

"Dad?" asks Dawn, pushing open the door.

"You better knock," says Charles. "He might be in there whacking off."

I try to ignore him and concentrate on the show.

The camera shows the back of a man's head. His curly hair is the exact same color as Dawn's, like it's been dyed to match too. Nailed above his desk is a wooden cross, and there are all sorts of band posters framed and hanging on his wall. I recognize some of the names of the bands from listening to the Loaf FM: Yes, Sir! and Holy Howl and Plant a Seed.

The man turns in his swivel chair so that he's facing his children. He is wearing a black button-down shirt tucked into black jeans. He's got cowboy boots on and . . . oh my God.

"Yes?" he asks.

My stomach drops.

It can't be.

"Dawn has something to tell you," says the boy.

The father smiles at his daughter.

Oh sweet Jesus. This isn't like that time way back, back before RD and Mama got married, when I was convinced that some man in a car lot commercial was Daddy. That was just wishful thinking. This is . . .

Oh sweet Jesus.

He has the same slight gap between his two front teeth. Not a chip like Mama, just a cute little gap making his smile special. Making it so he could spit a stream of water that would arc like a fountain, driving Mama crazy at the dinner table.

"He's cute, huh?" asks Charles.

"Shh," I say, waving him away with my hand. I get up and walk to the TV. I want to see his face up close. How many times have I dreamed about seeing him since he left so many years ago?

"You two look like you have something serious to discuss," he says. *"Shall we start by taking it to the Big Guy?"*

"What is up with you?" asks Charles. "Never seen a rock 'n' roll preacher before?"

I'm having a hard time getting the words out because my mouth is so dry. "That man," I say, touching his face with my finger. "That man is my father."

CHAPTER ELEVEN

Box

(Louise, Labor Day Weekend 2004)

*P*oor John Henry. When Caroline asked if we would come to San Francisco to see her new show, *Got Freedom?*, she did not warn us that she would be naked for the majority of her time on stage, not to mention that at one point during the performance she would leap into a pile of other naked bodies and proceed to writhe on the floor.

Granted, it wasn't sexy—wasn't supposed to be—but it was shocking. Although maybe not as shocking as the director intended. Maybe only shocking because Caroline is our daughter and we are used to seeing her dressed and upright.

John Henry and I wait in the lobby after the show, not saying a word to each other for fear that someone who knows Caroline might overhear us criticizing the performance. Eventually Caroline emerges from the greenroom, her face scrubbed of her stage makeup. She wears a pair of faded jeans and a faded red T-shirt that I am sure she bought at Goodwill. Tied around her waist is a lightweight cashmere cardigan I gave her for Christmas last year. It seems crazy to need a sweater in the summer, but that's San

Francisco for you. (Not that I really know much at all about San Francisco. This is only our second trip out here since Caroline ran away.)

"Hey!" I say. "Our star!"

I can tell she's nervous because she doesn't start grilling us for feedback like she usually does after one of her plays.

"Y'all hungry?" she asks.

"Not starving," says John Henry, "but I could eat."

I try to eat only when I am very hungry, but look at which one of us is skinny and which one of us could stand to lose ten pounds.

"There are a million good restaurants around here," Caroline says. "There's crepes, there's sushi, there's a sort of American supper club dealie, there's burritos—"

"No burritos," says John Henry. "Your mother will have gas all night."

I do not even dignify his comment with a response.

"Sushi sounds nice," I say. John Henry shoots me a look. Raw fish is not his favorite, but let him order chicken teriyaki. He'll live. "Are we dressed for it?" I ask.

John Henry is wearing a blue blazer over a polo shirt and I am wearing an Armani suit I bought three years ago at Neiman's.

"You both look great," says Caroline. "Come on. It's just a few blocks up this way."

She leads the way to Sixteenth Street and Valencia. It shouldn't surprise me that Caroline navigates the city so well; surely she's been doing it since she was eighteen and left for San Francisco. Still I feel a certain pride in my girl. I put my hand on John Henry's arm. He glances at me, smiles. He's proud of her too.

The sidewalks are crowded with people, mostly young. In fact, the only old people I see are pushing shopping carts filled with empty bottles and cans. I notice how deftly my daughter avoids the beggars, and it makes me think of the first time I took her to New York when she was ten. It was a girls' weekend, and she and I stayed at the Waldorf. Her father had given her fifty dollars for spending money. She must have given half of it away to the beggars on the street. Whenever someone asked, she gave. I figured it was hers to spend however she liked, but John Henry had a fit when I told him about it.

"What if some drug addict stuck an AIDS-infected needle in her arm?" he demanded when I called home that night.

"Honestly, darling," I said. "How do you come up with these things?"

WHEN WE GET to the restaurant—Sue Su's Sushi—the hostess seats us at a low-lit table in the back. On the wall behind us is a painting of a white ship afloat on a black sea. Before sitting, I examine the painting, trying to decipher whether or not the ship is in danger. Caroline takes her cell phone out of the canvas bag she uses as a purse and dials her new boyfriend, Davis, to see if he can join us. The waitress approaches our table and before she has a chance to say anything Caroline—the phone still pressed against her ear—orders three Asahis.

"And a huge water," adds Caroline.

"I'd like water too," I say.

"Me too," says John Henry. "With lemon."

"Oh that's good," I say. "Lemon all around."

Caroline gives the waitress an apologetic look, as if John Henry and I are demanding too much by ordering a garnish. As if using a cellular telephone in the middle of the restaurant makes her a paragon of good manners. I hear her whisper "love you" before she hangs up the phone, which surprises me—I thought they'd only been dating for a few months—though it shouldn't. Caroline has always rushed into things.

"Davis is coming," she says.

"What did you just order for us?" asks John Henry.

"Japanese beer," she says. "You'll like it."

"Can't argue with that," says John Henry just as the waitress brings us the bottles.

"I'll be back with your waters," she says.

"And could you bring us ladies a couple of glasses for our beer?" I ask.

"I don't need a glass," says Caroline.

"It's unbecoming for a woman to drink beer from a bottle," I say, doing a dead-on imitation of Nanny Rose's lockjaw accent (an admittedly ungenerous thing to do considering I wholeheartedly agree with the rule).

My daughter sticks her tongue out at me, but she is only teasing. It occurs to me to consider it a minor miracle that we have finally reached a place in our relationship where neither one of us wants to strangle the other. She's grown so pretty these last few years. Even with her dark hair pulled into a messy knot on top of her head, the wisps that usually curl around her face slicked back with sweat, she looks becoming. Her cheeks are flushed and her eyes are alert. She looks alive.

"You worked hard tonight, didn't you?" I ask.

"Ugh," she says, then takes a sip of beer. I do the same thing even though it's out of the bottle. It's cold and crisp.

"This *is* delicious," I say.

She smiles. "Isn't it? I wish y'all had seen a better performance. The cast was off tonight."

"Are there any shows where you don't take your clothes off?" asks John Henry. "I'd like to see that one."

Caroline sighs, exaggerated on purpose. "Daddy," she says, "the nudity wasn't gratuitous. We were showing how unsexy the body can be without rosy light and candles."

"I could have told you that," I say, thinking of my mushy belly and the cellulite that has started creeping up the backs of my thighs.

"Hey!" says John Henry. "Who are you calling unsexy?"

"I'm talking about me, darling. You should be studied. With the exception of that teeny-tiny bald spot of yours, you don't seem to age."

"Four miles a day," says John Henry. "Rain or shine."

I'm surprised the man doesn't beat his chest.

"Mom, first of all, you are beautiful. Second, talking about bodies, there's something I've been wanting to ask you."

She twists a stray piece of her hair with her finger. "I have this friend Deidre who is making a book about women's vaginas. The working title is *Box*. What she's planning on doing is photographing the vaginas of twenty different women and then interviewing each of them about their relationship with it."

"This is a conversation you and your mother should have in private," says John Henry, staring at the illustrations of sushi on the menu.

"Are you suggesting I let a stranger photograph my 'rhymes with Carolina'?" I ask, using Nanny Rose's term just to make Caroline laugh.

"Deidre is a friend of mine, not a stranger," Caroline says. "She put out a photography book showing women in various states of orgasm. It won a major prize."

"Various states?" asks John Henry. "Like Missouri?"

"Yeah," says Caroline. "And Ohio, and Vermont and Georgia."

"Really?" I say.

"Louise," says John Henry, "you've got to work on your wit."

"So do you want to?" asks Caroline.

"What, work on my wit?"

"Ha," says Caroline, though I wasn't meaning to be funny. "Have your vagina photographed for the book."

"Darling," I say, "have you gone completely insane?"

A NICE-LOOKING young man walks into the restaurant wearing a seersucker jacket over a crisp white shirt tucked into linen pants. Seersucker. My father used to wear seersucker from May through September. The fabric would leave lines on my cheek when I hugged him.

Besides Daddy, I can't remember the last time I saw a young man wearing seersucker outside of a J. Crew catalog. I know plenty of men John Henry's age who wear it, but no one who doesn't yet have a bald spot or a paunch, and certainly no one in San Francisco, where ill-fitting thrift store finds seem to qualify as the epitome of fashion.

Even from a distance I see that this man's eyes are blue and alert.

And then the young man in seersucker walks to our table and Caroline jumps up and kisses him hello.

"Mom, Dad," she says, "this is Davis."

John Henry stands up as far as the table will allow him to and reaches out his hand. I can tell just by watching their shake that Davis has a firm grip.

"Excuse me if I don't get up," I say. "I'm not sure if there's room for me to stand without bumping the table."

"Oh, please stay where you are," he says. He reaches into an inside pocket of his jacket and pulls out a purple box the size of a small book. He hands it to me and then slides into the booth next to Caroline.

"Caroline told me that you are a connoisseur," he says.

I open the box. Chocolate.

"Ooh, *fleur de sel* caramels," says Caroline.

"Sea salt," explains Davis, as if I don't know what *fleur de sel* is. "Harvested by hand off the coast of Brittany. They put it into the caramel and it is just amazing."

"Well, I shall have to have one right now," I say. I bite into one. The chocolate surrounding the caramel is slightly bitter, the caramel buttery with salty little crunches.

"I could die happy," I say.

Caroline smiles and squeezes Davis's arm. John Henry reaches over to my box of chocolates and pops one in his mouth. I want to bat his hand away. That man doesn't know the difference between a Hershey Kiss and a hand-dipped truffle.

"Good stuff," says John Henry. Before he can grab another one I put the lid on the box.

"Are you hungry, sweetie?" asks Caroline.

"Starving," says Davis. "What have you guys ordered?"

"We haven't," I say. "But I just love California rolls."

"Great," says Davis, but Caroline flattens the corners of her mouth.

"What?" I say. "What's wrong with California rolls?"

"Not hip," answers John Henry, as if he is the king of cool in his blue blazer with gold buttons.

When the waitress returns Caroline orders all kinds of things I've never heard of, and John Henry orders another round of beers for the table. I never think I like beer until I am actually drinking it and then I love it.

I look across the table at my daughter and her boyfriend and it occurs to me that the two of them look a lot like John Henry and I did when we were young. Caroline has let her hair grow long enough to wear it up, and it is no longer cut in a deliberately unattractive style. It has been so long since I've seen her with long hair—two summers ago, the first time we visited her in San Francisco, her head was shaved, and when she came to Atlanta for

Christmas it was still quite short—that I almost didn't recognize her when she picked John Henry and me up at the San Francisco airport.

Davis is better looking than John Henry was, but there is a definite resemblance. They both have square jaws and blue eyes, and they both hold themselves in a way that exudes authority. Not rigid exactly, just assured of their place in the world, assured that they know how the universe *really* operates. He is not at all someone I would have imagined for Caroline. He is so immaculately put together, so well polished. He is probably the type of man who uses a lint roller before meeting with clients. And he is a man, not a boy. Indeed, he looks as if he might be a decade older than Caroline.

"How was the show tonight?" asks Davis.

I jump in before John Henry can say anything negative. After all, we flew all the way out here to lend our daughter support.

"Provocative," I say. "Was it supposed to make me think of those prison abuse photos?"

Caroline shrugs. "It's not an exact parallel," she says. "But yeah, those photos are now definitely in the American collective unconscious, and the director was aware of it."

"I don't know what people expect," says John Henry, leaning forward in his seat and looking right at Davis. "We're at war."

Oh Lord. I try to detach my feelings, to let them just drift away while my husband talks. I have heard this speech before.

"Exactly," says Davis. "I mean, what do you think the Iraqis are doing to our soldiers?"

I almost spit out my beer. I look at Caroline, who is rolling her eyes.

"Can you believe he actually voted for Bush in two thousand?" she asks. "He and probably three other people in this city."

"The few but the proud," says Davis, smiling.

"What?" exclaims John Henry. "My little Bolshevik is dating

a Republican?" He motions for the waitress. "This news calls for a toast. Let's get another round."

THE SUSHI IS wonderful. It comes on a white oval platter, arranged as artfully as an exhibit in a museum. Davis ordered California rolls for me, but I have to admit, they are a little boring compared to the other things on the plate. My favorite is the rainbow roll, fried shrimp inside rice with pieces of salmon, tuna, eel, and avocado on the outside. John Henry, who will never go with me to get sushi in Atlanta, who claims to hate it, eats more than his share and then orders seconds, along with a fourth round of beers. I tell the waitress I'm going to stick with water from now on, knowing that I will be sick as a dog if I drink any more. John Henry says my tolerance for alcohol has never been the same since junior year at Chapel Hill, when I drank four Tom Collinses before the formal and danced with him so provocatively I was issued a reprimand by the head of Chi Omega standards.

The more Caroline drinks, the cozier she becomes with Davis. She keeps her hand on his thigh—high up on it—and she periodically leans over to kiss him on the cheek. It occurs to me that her breath must be fishy, and I wonder if Davis minds.

"Tell Mom the story about your mother's champagne truffles," says Caroline. "She'll relate."

At one point the words *champagne truffle* would have sent Caroline into a long lecture about the gap between the rich and the poor, but I have a feeling that's not the direction this story will take.

"Did someone say 'truffle'?" I say, widening my eyes for effect. I am aware that I am coming across as slightly keyed up. Caroline says I have two states of being: hyper and flat. Of course the girl doesn't know what flat really is. My mother spent most of my childhood in bed with the curtains drawn. *She* was flat.

"My mom is as big a chocolate fan as you are," says Davis. "Her favorite is Maison du Chocolat."

"Louise once bought a box of those," says John Henry. "When I saw my Amex bill I thought she must have bought an actual house in France."

"Shush, dear," I say. "Davis is telling a story."

Davis smiles as if John Henry and I are putting on an act for him: kooky old married couple. John Henry holds up his empty bottle of beer, indicating to the waitress that he'd like another. His fifth.

"She's not a fetch dog," says Caroline.

"Actually, that's what your dad's paying her to do," says Davis. "Fetch things for him."

I tense, waiting to see how Caroline reacts. It surprises me, but I actually want to see her get mad at him. Instead she smiles.

"Can you believe him?" she asks.

Frankly, I can't believe her. She's become so—so compliant.

John Henry looks at Davis as the waitress approaches the table. "Up for another?" he asks.

"All right," says Davis. He turns back to me. "So you know Maison du Chocolat are really expensive."

I nod, acting as if I am eager to hear the rest of the story, while inside my head I'm thinking, *Wait, wait, wait. What's the catch? Why is this not-so-young Young Republican with my rebel daughter?*

" . . . went to visit my youngest brother, who lives in New York. While she was there she bought a pound of their champagne truffles and took them back with her to the Bay Area."

"Your parents live out here?" I ask.

"They do," says Caroline. Davis takes a sip of beer.

My God. Caroline is going to marry this man and never come back to Atlanta. She is going to marry this man and become a

California housewife. She probably won't even finish up her degree at San Francisco State.

"In Walnut Creek," says Davis, putting his beer bottle back on the table. "Just over the Bay Bridge."

"And through a tunnel and a lot of traffic and suburban sprawl," says Caroline.

I practically raise my fist in the air I am so relieved to hear a little attitude coming from her. There's the girl I know.

"So my mom took the truffles back with her through the sprawl"—Davis smiles at Caroline, indulging her criticism—"and only allowed herself to eat one a day. Of course she could have eaten the whole box in one sitting, but she wanted to savor them."

"What self-discipline," I say.

The waitress appears with the beers and asks if we want to order more sushi. Davis checks with John Henry before telling her no.

"Maybe they will have champagne truffles for dessert," I say, joking.

"Not at a sushi restaurant," answers Davis, as if I were being serious.

"So what happened to your mother? I'm dying of curiosity."

"Tell her, she's *dying*," says Caroline.

John Henry is staring off into space, dreaming about God knows what. In the early years of our marriage I used to squeeze his knee whenever he spaced out around company, but eventually I realized it was better just to let him be on his own little planet.

"So she has this friend, Eric Ryder, who is a man of excess. He loves steaks, he loves cigars, he loves booze—"

"He really loves booze," adds Caroline.

"Do you think he's an alcoholic?" asks Davis, turning to her.

"Uh, yeah," says Caroline, her tone taking me back to her high school years, when every question I asked her was answered with sarcasm and disdain.

"Really?" asks Davis.

"What happened?" I ask, trying to steer them back to the story.

"He came over for dinner. My parents made steak. They opened a good bottle of wine. After dinner, my dad poured the single malt Scotch and Mom put out a little bowl of her prized truffles. Well, Mr. Ryder picks up the bowl and starts popping the truffles into his mouth as if they were peanuts. He just throws them back, one after the other."

"Dear Lord," I say. "Is that justifiable cause for homicide?" I turn to John Henry, the lawyer.

"What?" he asks, jerking to attention.

"His mom was furious," says Caroline.

"She slammed the door when he left," says Davis.

I take a sip of my water. "Do you know the, um, Davis's parents well?" I ask.

"The Hamiltons," says Caroline. "We go to dinner at their house about once a week."

"My mom loves Caroline," says Davis, popping the last California roll in his mouth. He holds up one finger while he chews, indicating, I suppose, that we shouldn't start talking until he's finished with what he has to say. "I want Mom to come to one of Caroline's shows."

Caroline grimaces and shakes her head. "She'd be so uncomfortable," she says. I am about to ask her why she thought *we* *would* be comfortable watching her roll around on the floor with a bunch of other naked bodies, but then I realize: I'm glad she asked us. I'm glad she thought we could handle it.

"Have you asked her to pose for *Box*?" I ask.

"Mom!" says Caroline.

"I see where you get your sense of humor from," says Davis, squeezing Caroline's knee.

THE NEXT MORNING we take a cab to Caroline's apartment in the Mission. When John Henry gives the address, 202 Shotwell Street, the driver looks confused.

"That's a ways from here," he says, making a left out of the Ritz.

"Our daughter said it would take fifteen minutes, tops," I say. I want to make sure he doesn't try to take us on an unnecessarily long and expensive ride.

"Not distance," he says. "What I mean is, you folks are on top of the hill right now, and the Mission is a long way down."

"Well, that's where our daughter lives," I say.

"Making her pay her own rent, huh, Pops?" he asks.

"You got it," says John Henry although that's not exactly the truth. He sends her three hundred dollars each month, to help cover expenses.

"The Mission is completely gentrified," I say, which are the exact same words Caroline said to me after she called to tell me she was moving out of the apartment she shared with two other girls in the Inner Sunset, and into a studio in the Mission.

Then she told me the name of her new street. "Shotwell?" I had asked. *"Shot well?"*

We go over the hills of San Francisco at an alarming speed, and I am nauseated by the time we get to Caroline's place. The beers I had last night aren't helping. God knows how many John Henry and Davis drank by the time dinner was over. I stopped counting.

We pull up in front of her new place, which I recognize from photos she sent home. It is a yellow Victorian, newly painted, with a surrounding wrought iron fence. It is actually quite charming, although the house to the left of it looks—as John Henry would say—one step away from the wrecking ball.

Caroline buzzes us in and we climb the two flights of stairs to get to her studio. The stairs are carpeted and smell of mildew. We knock on Caroline's door, and she opens it immediately, as if she were waiting for us just on the other side.

Caroline's apartment holds none of the dinginess of the stairwell. It is small but perfect with gorgeous dark wood floors, a high ceiling, and crisp white walls decorated with art I have bought for her. Of course the bed is in the living room—it's a studio, after all—but she's arranged it in such a way that there is a clear delineation between where she sleeps and where she lives. And the place is so spotless I am convinced that Caroline must have hired someone to clean it for her.

"Darling, this is adorable!" I say.

"I recognize that," says John Henry, pointing at the sofa. It is an old one, inherited from my parents years ago and finally passed along to Caroline when we had our house redecorated. In truth, it probably cost me more to ship that sofa out to California than it would have cost to buy her a new one.

"There are a lot of Atlanta touches in here," says Caroline. "Remember this?"

She points to the Earl LeTrouve painting I bought her for Christmas last year. In it, a winged angel with hair as dark as Caroline's wears a red poofy party dress and holds a Bible in one hand and a martini glass in the other. Written in cursive across the bottom of the piece are the words "party without ceasing."

(When I saw Earl last year at the Big Angel Blowout, he said that no one was buying his tempera pieces besides me, and tempera was too taxing to do anyway, so he had decided to go back to his party dress series, which he paints with acrylics. "Got to get everyone dressed for the Marriage Supper of the Lamb," he said, and I pretended to know what he meant.)

"Mr. LeTrouve lives near Milledgeville, not in Atlanta," I say.

"Well, Georgia touches," Caroline says.

John Henry is already sitting on the sofa. "No TV?" he asks.

Caroline purses her lips. "Davis keeps threatening to buy me one," she says. "He's such a Giants fan, it kills him not to be able to watch the games."

He must spend a lot of time over here.

"I have to admit, I never thought you would date a sports man," I say.

Caroline laughs. She is wearing a crisp white button-down shirt on top of her blue jeans and she looks so pretty it makes me a little sad.

"I know. It's crazy," she says. "Y'all take cream in your coffee, right?"

"Yes, but I'll fix it," I say, walking to the teeny kitchen area. "I know just how your father likes it."

"I made Nanny Rose's chocolate chip coffee cake," she says. "Does she still pretend she doesn't start with a mix?"

I nod and then roll my eyes. Caroline smiles. Her teeth look so white I wonder if she's been bleaching them.

JOHN HENRY READS the newspaper over breakfast while Caroline and I talk about Charles.

"It's almost as if he's moved out," I say. "I hardly ever see him. The only reason I know he's still living at home is that his room is a mess and I'm always having to buy groceries."

Caroline laughs. "It's good he's going out," she says. "It means he has friends."

"Yes, but he never brings anyone over to the house. I don't know a single one of them."

"I don't think he has any," says John Henry, looking up from his paper.

"I'm sure he does," I say. "He just doesn't want us to meet them."

"God, I really don't know Charles at all. I mean, he was what—thirteen when I left? Maybe I should call him."

"Send him an e-mail," says John Henry.

The phone rings.

"Could it be the power of suggestion?" she asks, walking to the kitchen to answer it. It's immediately obvious that the person on the line is not Charles. Caroline is gushing, reminding me of a girl during sorority rush.

" . . . just wonderful. Yes. They got in just fine. Thanks for asking. At the Ritz. Oh yes, only the best. No, no. Not yet."

I'm thinking it must be Davis's mother. Ten thirty on a Saturday morning and she's calling my daughter's apartment? For no apparent reason other than to check in and see if we arrived?

I wonder if Davis has moved in here with Caroline.

Surely I would have picked up on his presence in this space, some aura of maleness that they couldn't hide. But maybe that's why she had the apartment deep-cleaned before we arrived. And maybe he hid all his things under the bed—the queen-size bed, a bed awfully big for one, especially in a studio this small.

I walk to the bathroom thinking he might have left his tooth-brush. It's ridiculous, I know, my sleuthing. I should be direct with her. I mean, if she can ask me if I'll have my vagina photo-graphed by a stranger, surely I can ask her if she's living with her boyfriend.

Does she plan to marry this boy? The thought makes my chest ache. I'm being ridiculous, I know. Davis is the type of boy— man—every mother wants her daughter to marry. Obviously, he's close with his parents, he's awfully cute, and he has nice manners. Plus, he's an investment banker. He could provide Caroline with the type of life she grew up with, the type of life she's used to.

It's just—he's so sure of himself, so arrogant, so conventional.

I walk into the bathroom and sit down on top of the closed toilet. I begin kneading my shoulders with my fingertips. This was how I felt on my own wedding day, right before Daddy walked me down the aisle. He kissed my cheek and said, "Guess this is the last time I can call you Amelia Louise Lawson."

I wanted to turn around right there, turn around and walk out of All Saints in my silk gown and kid leather gloves. I wanted to leave John Henry standing at the front of the church in his black tuxedo, his Phi Delt brothers flanked behind him. I wanted to leave Tiny in her blue silk bridesmaid dress. She would have understood. She would have dashed home to change and met me somewhere dark and unknown where she could tell me how everyone reacted, the three hundred guests I left high and dry.

I sigh and lean back, letting the back of my head touch the tiled wall. I look up and am startled. There must be sixty wire birds dangling from different-colored ribbons, hung from hooks in the ceiling. I stand to look at them more closely, surprised that I didn't notice them when I first came into the bathroom.

The birds are made from thin wire coiled together to form dense bodies and small, dense heads. Some birds are made from silver wire, some are made from gold. Attached to the tail end of each bird is a feather, some small and wispy, some large and bold, all different colors. The feathers add a marvelously ethereal contrast to the birds' metal structures. It is as if the birds' tail feathers have plotted against their bodies to achieve flight.

"Caroline?" I call.

She doesn't answer.

I open the bathroom door. She is standing by the kitchen sink, washing our breakfast dishes, the steam from the water flushing her face. John Henry is stretched out on the couch, his eyes closed, his mouth half open.

"Caroline!"

She turns to look at me, the water still running.

"Would you mind coming in here for a minute?" I ask.

She turns off the water and walks toward me. "Do you need toilet paper?"

I wait until she is at the bathroom door. "Tell me about the birds," I say.

"Oh those." She laughs, shrugs. "I was just playing around in my friend's art studio. Deidre, the woman who's making the book, she runs a jewelry-making camp for kids and she had some extra supplies."

"You made these yourself?" I ask. I look up at them again, the hanging flock.

"First I made that one right there—the one with the peacock feather for a tail—and then I just felt inspired and kept going."

They are so pretty, I don't want to stop looking at them, touching them. Just little balls of coiled wire, really, though so whimsical, so sweet.

"These are wonderful," I say.

Caroline looks pleased. I think of all the origami cranes I folded for John Henry's and my first Christmas. All that effort for our home. Did he even notice? Would it have made any difference to him if I'd just hung the gold balls Nanny Rose gave us?

"Darling," I say, "if I let your friend take a photograph of my vagina—"

Caroline's eyes widen at my use of the actual word.

"Will you promise me to wait at least two years before you marry Davis?"

"I could tell you didn't like him," she says. "I could tell last night. God, Mom."

"It's not that." I sit back on the toilet. I have the urge to pull her into my lap, to hold her as if she were a little girl. "I just think you should stay single a little bit longer."

I am hurting her, I can tell. She thinks I am judging. She must think nothing she does will ever be good enough for me. How do I tell her that what I want is to know her, to know the woman who made these birds, to see who she might become if she is allowed to spread out, to expand. How do I say, *Darling, please. Don't shrink yourself so soon.*

CHAPTER TWELVE

The Odd Couple

(Missy, Labor Day 2004)

*I*t hits us the minute we walk in the kitchen. The place smells like old beer and throw-up. There's a black Hefty bag waiting by the back door filled with Bud cans and liquor bottles. Mrs. Parker's red tile floor, which usually shines so clean, feels sticky beneath my shoes. Mama shakes her head looking around at the mess.

"I expect he thinks we'll clean this up," she says.

We will too. We did it last time Mrs. Parker went away and Charles threw a party.

Charles walks into the kitchen, looking down at the floor and scratching his head. He's wearing flannel pj pants and a white undershirt, even though it's already one o'clock in the afternoon. He looks startled to see us.

"Oh, hey," he says. His voice sounds like he's got something thick caught in his throat. "Sorry about the mess."

Mama doesn't say anything, just starts organizing the bottles in her cleaning bucket.

"Why don't you go ahead and vacuum the downstairs

rooms?" she says to me. I'm still holding her white vacuum cleaner.

I give Charles my best look when I pass him, like I'm disappointed in him but love him all the same. I figure that is what Jesus would do.

"Have you been keeping up with that show?" he asks in a low voice.

Mama doesn't even look up from the sink, where she is filling the mop bucket with water.

"I told you we don't have a satellite dish," I say.

"It's on at four o'clock today," he says. "Come watch it with me."

"If I'm through cleaning your house, I will," I say.

This time Mama looks up long enough to glare.

At 3:58 I go to the library. Charles is already lying on the couch, his right hand inside his pants. He takes it out when he sees me standing in the doorway. I hope he feels embarrassed.

"Come in," he says. "Show's going to start. Hand me the remote, will you?"

The remote is sitting on the coffee table, not two feet away from him.

"You sure are lazy," I say, handing it to him before sitting in the armchair on the other side of the room.

He punches a button to turn on the TV. His hair is greasy and flattened to his head. "I'm extremely hungover," he says. "My friends decided I was having a party last night."

I don't even want to know. Pastor Finch always says it's not drinking itself that's the sin, it's that inebriation takes our minds off God.

"They invited, like, half my class from Coventry. People who wouldn't give me the time of day at school were showing up. I'm so fucking pissed at them."

"Is the TV on the right channel?" I ask.

"Yep," he says. "I mean, Thorton Bowers was at my house. What the fuck?"

"What kind of a name is Thorton?" I ask.

"It's a name for an asshole. He was the one who started calling me Butt-Fuck Chuck."

I turn to him. He's staring straight ahead at the screen even though it's only showing a preview for a show about dollhouses.

"That's terrible," I say. "Why would he call you that?"

The theme music for *Salt of the Earth* starts. This is my first time to see the credits, and I just love them. They start with a giant drawing of a hand spread over the top third of the screen. The screen is black and the hand is white and big. At first it's turned upward, so it can cup the salt in it. Then the hand turns over and starts sprinkling the grains of salt over the black nothingness below. First a white cross shoots up from the ground. Then a church builds itself around it, so the cross ends up the steeple. And then a man shoots out of the ground, white and cartoonlike at first, but the wavy lines of the drawing change into a real image of my daddy, Pastor Praise. Now a guitar is drawn in his hands and then it becomes real and he's wailing on it. He plays a few chords and his wife springs up from the ground and then his two kids. They all start as cartoons but end up as real people. Once they are all together they join hands and go inside the church.

"This is just what I need to cheer me up," says Charles, placing a throw pillow beneath his head.

The show starts at Matthew's school, at the track. Matthew, dressed in running shorts and a tank top with the number 3 on it, is sitting on the bleachers, cheering on his team. But he seems nervous and keeps looking around as if he is expecting someone.

A wiry man with red hair and a whistle around his neck walks up to Matthew. *"The four-hundred relay is in two minutes,"* he says. *"Any sign of Andrew?"*

"No sir," says Matthew. *"But I'm sure he'll show up."*

"Otherwise, we'll have to forfeit," says the coach.

Matthew puts his head in his hands as the coach walks away.

"My God," says Charles. "Look at those muscles."

Matthew's arm muscles *are* big.

Someone makes an announcement over the loudspeaker. *"Up next, the four-hundred-yard relay!"*

Matthew takes one last look around before going to consult with the coach. They talk in whispers while the camera turns from them to a dark wiry guy wearing jeans and a leather jacket. He's spying on the meet from underneath the bleachers. I just know the guy must be Andrew.

"You want to know why they call me Butt-Fuck Chuck?" asks Charles.

I don't say anything, hoping that if I ignore him he will shut up and watch the show.

"Because once I got drunk at a party and I kissed a guy."

I knew it.

"You know, God still loves you," I say.

Charles starts laughing. "Jesus," he says, "you just keep plowing forward, don't you?"

"God has special plans for homosexuals," I say. "We studied about it in Sunday school. He's testing you extra because your task is even harder than most of ours."

"What, to get a guy to fuck you? That's not that hard," says Charles.

I cannot believe he just said that to me. "No, to *not* let a guy do that to you," I say. "To turn away from the temptation and to put all of your longing and lust toward God."

Charles turns toward me. "Are you for real?" he asks. "I mean I know you are a little fucked up about your dad. . . ."

"Do you know any other word besides *fuck*?" I ask.

He starts rubbing his forehead. "Let's just watch the show," he says.

Matthew and the coach are shaking their heads. They walk over to a bunch of boys, all in track uniforms, and say something to them. One of the boys pounds his fist into his hand.

The camera cuts again to the guy sitting beneath the bleachers. He has an odd smile on his face, as if he is enjoying watching his team lose.

Next thing we see, Matthew, Dawn, Mrs. Praise, and Daddy (Pastor P.) are sitting around the dinner table with their heads bowed, holding hands. Daddy says "amen" and everyone looks up.

"So how was your meet?" asks Daddy.

"Andrew didn't show up!" says Matthew. *"We had to forfeit."*

"That doesn't sound like Andrew," says Dawn, reaching for the bowl of mashed potatoes.

"Eat up," says Charles. "You're eating for two now."

"I know," says Matthew.

"Is this enough?" asks his mom, looking up at her son as she ladles vegetables on top of a piece of roast.

"Great," he says, smiling at her. *"Thanks, Mom."*

"Maybe we should stop by Andrew's house after dinner," says Daddy. *"See if anything is wrong."*

"Maybe he has the flu," says Dawn. Especially with the table blocking her belly, you can hardly tell she's pregnant.

"I have a feeling it's something else," says Matthew. He piles his fork with roast, carrots, and mashed potatoes, and takes a bite.

"Why do I watch this crap?" asks Charles.

"Maybe God wants you to," I say.

"What we have to figure out is how to get on it," says Charles. "As guest stars."

My heart starts beating faster. I've been having the exact same thoughts, thinking that maybe Daddy could incorporate me into the story and I could work as a Christian soap opera actress and be reunited with him and make a lot of money so Mama won't have to clean houses anymore. But I hadn't thought about Charles being in on it.

Daddy and Matthew are standing in front of Andrew's door. He lives in a house that looks a lot like theirs, brick on the first floor, siding on the second, but his front door is yellow instead of red.

Andrew doesn't look sick at all when he answers the door. He's wearing the same pair of jeans he had on at the track meet, but he's taken off the leather jacket, revealing a shirt that's so tight it hugs his muscles.

"*Oh*," he says, looking at Daddy and Matthew without even smiling. "*Hi.*"

"*May we come in?*" asks Daddy.

"Let me just clean up the crystal meth I'm making," says Charles.

"Shush," I say, smiling.

Andrew sticks his hands deep into his pockets and walks to the couch in the living room. Daddy and Matthew follow.

"*We had to forfeit the match*," says Matthew.

"You bastard," adds Charles. I giggle without meaning to. It's the way Charles says it; he sounds just like an outraged woman on a soap opera.

"*Son*," says Daddy, "*is something going on?*"

"I have a hard-on for you," says Charles.

"Shut up!" I say. I almost add, *That's my daddy*, but I hold back. Maybe Charles forgot about what I said the other week.

"Sorry, sorry," he says.

"*I have AIDS!*" screams Andrew.

"*What?*" say Charles and Matthew at the same time.

"*When I went on that trip to visit different colleges, I met this guy, and I thought he just wanted to be my friend but then he got me drunk, and . . ."* Andrew starts crying. *"We, we had sex with each other and now I've got AIDS and I'm probably going to die young and go to Hell and that's why I didn't show up to the track meet because, well, I don't want anyone else to feel good about themselves when I feel so terrible, and I didn't want the team to win! I made it so we forfeited the match because that's the kind of terrible person I must be."*

"No, he did not just say that." Charles talks as if he is trying to sound black. "What, he has a little man sex and suddenly he has full-blown AIDS? Where do these guys get their stats?"

"No offense, but I really think you should be taking this seriously," I say. "I mean, after what you just told me."

"Are you for fucking real?" asks Charles. He sits up so he can look straight at me. "Can you snap out of it for one minute?"

"What?"

Charles slumps back down into the couch. "Never mind," he says. "You and I are just very different people, okay?"

I want to watch my daddy but I am also very aware that Charles needs me right now. I wonder what my daddy might do, what Jesus might do. I kneel beside Charles on the sofa.

"We're not different," I say, trying to concentrate on Charles and not the TV. I look him straight in the eyes, just like Pastor Finch taught me during his missionary training course. "You and I are both sinners who have no chance of getting into Heaven on our own. Sometimes the sinner is even better off than someone who tries to do good, because the sinner at least doesn't fool himself into thinking he's perfect."

"Jesus Christ," says Charles.

"That's right," I say, even though I know he wasn't praying. "Jesus is God. And Jesus came to this earth to take away our sin," I say. "He died on the cross for us to pay for our sins against God. God loves us, but God cannot have us all stained with sin. But Jesus took it away. That boy you kissed? Jesus took it away. I mean, he will, if you just ask him to do it. It will be as if it never happened in God's eyes. God will look at you and he won't see the sinful person you are, he will see his perfect son in your place."

"I liked kissing that guy," says Charles. "And he"—he points his finger to Andrew on the screen—"I bet he liked fucking that guy on the college trip."

I stand back up.

I can feel the tears on my face. I don't want Charles to see me this way. This is not how Pastor Finch said it would be to bring someone to Jesus. And I want someone to believe with me. Mama says she does, but half the time she and RD sleep in on Sundays.

I know Jesus is with me always, but it's not the same as having someone on this earth to share Him with. Even if this world is just a sinful blink before Eternity, it gets lonely.

"I got to help my mama," I say, and I am amazed at how strong my voice sounds.

I WALK STRAIGHT out the library, through the hall, and down the three steps that lead to the enormous living room. It's always colder in this room than in any other, and the ceiling is higher in here too. Standing directly in front of me is the life-sized portrait of Jesus in a dress. No wonder Charles is so confused. I finger the edge of one of the orange and red silk throw pillows Mrs. Parker has on her sofa, but then I don't pick it up. I don't want to mess it up with my tears.

"Hey."

I look up. Charles is standing in the doorway. I can see the dark circles under his eyes even from here. He walks down the stairs and sits down on the couch. He pats the space next to him.

"Sit down a minute," he says.

I sit.

"Look, I'm sorry," Charles says, and when he talks I smell the peppermint from his chewing gum. "I was being a jerk. I just—almost everyone I go to school with is some kind of a Crispy Christian, and I—I'm different from them. I'm sorry. I'm sure you have good intentions, but I've heard it all before. Believe me, a lot of people have quoted John three sixteen to me."

"If you know about it why don't you believe?" I ask.

Charles shrugs. "At my high school, the biggest assholes are always the Christians. It's like this thing all the popular kids do together. They go to Young Life and they slap those stupid metal fish on their Ford Explorers. The boys play football and wear cowboy boots and have Confederate-flag license plates, and the girls are all white and rich and wear lots of silver jewelry and are cheerleaders or else they play volleyball or some such crap."

"But you're white and rich," I say.

He looks surprised, as if I wasn't supposed to say that. "We're not really rich," he says. "You should see how much money some of the kids at my school have." He blows out a big puff of air, as if he's been holding it in for a long time. He looks at his finger-nails as if they are really, really interesting. "I mean, even if my dad *did* have a lot of money, even if I was a trust fund baby or something, he wouldn't leave it to me. Not if he found out I like guys."

He makes quotation marks with his fingers around "I like guys," his voice high as if he's making fun of himself.

"How do you know you like guys?" I ask.

"How old are you?" he asks.

"Sixteen," I say.

"You act a lot younger," he says, and then shrugs. "It's the same way you feel about boys, that's how I feel about them."

"I don't really think about boys," I say. "I think about God. And my daddy, I've started thinking about him again."

"Do you still think that guy on the show is your father?" he asks. "For real?"

His eyes light up a little.

I chew on my lip, considering what all I should tell him. I hear a voice in my ear, a soft *Do it*, and I know Jesus wants me to tell my story just like Charles told me his.

"Mama says that Daddy always wanted to be an actor. When he was younger he got to perform a lot: he started a theater troupe at my granddaddy's church. But Mama says he always wanted to be on TV. He thought it was the perfect place to evangelize. Plus, Mama says my granddaddy never really supported Daddy's theater group. He wanted Daddy to focus more on the Gospel than on entertainment. Mama was in the group. That's how they met. She used to be a real good singer.

"The theater group would travel around together to different churches, performing. And I guess what happened was one night after a performance they got carried away with sin, and Mama got pregnant with me. She was only seventeen. Daddy was ten years older, twenty-seven. Anyway, once he got Mama pregnant, Granddaddy didn't let him have any responsibilities at the church anymore, and he shut down the group. Daddy took a job as a loan collector. Mama says there wasn't anything he wanted to do more than move out of his parents' house, but he didn't make enough money, not to afford rent and support me and Mama."

"Do you still live with your grandparents now?" Charles asks.

I shake my head. "They're dead. But we still live in their house, in Loganville."

"Jesus, that's a commute."

I shrug.

"Anyway, Daddy was really, really good-looking, so he started auditioning for commercials. He always wanted to be on TV. And then when he got this chance to be in an educational movie they were filming in Florida, it was too expensive for him to take us with him so he went down on his own. But then Mama says he must have stopped getting work and he was too embarrassed to come back with nothing to show. So he didn't."

"You never saw him again?"

"A couple of years ago I saw a commercial for a used car lot. The guy in that looked just like the photo I have of my daddy, but Mama said he just resembled him. And she was right about that. But I took out that photo after I watched *Salt of the Earth*, and I swear it is the spitting image of Pastor Praise."

"When was the last time you saw him?" he asks.

"I just saw him on TV," I say. "Duh."

"No, in person."

"Oh. When I was six. He came to Meemaw's funeral. She was his mama."

It shames me still that I cried each time he tried to pick me up during his visit. He had a stuffed white bear and a Snickers bar to give me but he had to leave them with Mama. Mama says I acted scared of him.

Charles scratches his hair. "What's his name? It's not really Pastor Praise, is it?"

I smile. "Nah. It's Lucas Son Meadows. He goes by Luke."

MAMA AND RD are watching some reality show in the living room when the phone rings. I figure it's a telemarketer, so I don't answer, but then RD yells to say the phone is for me. Must be Crystal calling about our next Young Warriors meeting. She always wants to go together and I always say yes even though Crystal aggravates me. All she ever talks about is how she can't wait to get married so she can experience "mind-blowing" sex. She's been saying this ever since this young pastor came to talk to our Young Warrior group about how Christians have better sex than anyone else because they achieve true intimacy by saving their virginity for their spouse. I'm sure that's true, but I don't really want to think about Crystal and her future husband blowing each other's minds. I told her that too, but she still won't shut up about it.

I walk to the kitchen, where the phone is. RD is standing

there, holding the phone, wearing just a thin robe and a pair of flip-flops.

"It's a boy," he says, smirking. "Kissy, kissy."

I snatch the phone from him. "Hello?"

"Hey, it's me."

Oh. Charles.

"Hi," I say.

RD waggles his eyebrows at me and then returns to the spot on the couch where his butt has made a permanent dent in the seat cushion.

"Guess what," says Charles.

"You decided to accept Jesus as your personal savior?" I ask, but I'm only kidding. Sort of.

"That would be a negative. Guess again."

"I already guessed," I say.

"Lucas Son Meadows is indeed Pastor Praise on *Salt of the Earth.*"

Here it is, the middle of summer, and I have goose bumps on my arm. "How do you know?"

"I Googled him."

"On your computer?"

"Yep. It took me all of ten seconds. The show's filmed near Durham, North Carolina, which is about four hundred miles from here, and Mr. Luke Meadows is also a youth minister at— let me make sure I'm getting this right—the Holy Faith Church of the Redeemer and Eternal Cup of Life."

"Oh, sweet Jesus."

I need to sit down.

RD walks back into the kitchen and opens the refrigerator door. He's just standing there, looking at the jars of pickles and the pack of bologna. I am freezing cold. Rubbing my hands up and down my arms, I try to warm up.

"Who's the fellow, peewee?" he asks, turning away from the

fridge. I don't know why he calls me that. I'm five seven—tall as he is.

"Friend from school," I say.

Charles is saying something but I can't listen to him because RD keeps bugging me.

"Is he your boyfriend?" he asks.

I glare at him and he hoots. "I knew it!"

"What'd you say, Charles?" I ask.

RD finally decides on a piece of bologna. He peels it off the loaf, rolls it into the shape of a cigar, and pops it in his mouth. He makes kissing noises as he walks by me on his way out of the kitchen. His kisses smell like bologna meat.

"What I mean is, we've got a couple of options."

"Wait. What are you talking about?"

"I think we should go to Durham this weekend," he says. "My parents are going to Hawaii after San Francisco; they won't be back until a week from today."

"Your mama left you alone for two weeks?" I ask.

"I'm very responsible," he says.

"Hardy har har," I say. Mama once grabbed my hand and slapped it at the dinner table after I said that to her.

"I can drive us to Durham. It's straight up I-Eighty-five."

"What would I tell my mama?"

"How about that we're going on a Christian retreat?"

I shake my head, although he can't see me. Mama would know if our church had planned a youth function.

"That won't work," I say.

"Well, what if you just leave? She won't have any way of figuring out where you are. Then once you get back you can tell her that you went to see your dad."

"Yeah and have her beat me black and blue," I say.

"Really?" asks Charles, his voice panicky, like he might be about to speed-dial child services.

"Wouldn't yours?" I ask, but then I think about it, think about Mrs. Parker and her soft perfumed skin, her hands that are always manicured, that look as if they've never been rubbed raw and red from cleaning chemicals and hot water. No, she would not.

And then I start thinking about what Charles is offering. Mama *will* kill me if I sneak out and don't come back for the night. But what can she do to me if I am with my daddy?

"Look. Do you have proof that Luke Meadows is your real dad?"

"I have pictures of him."

"Is he listed on your birth certificate as your father?"

I glance into the living room. Mama's asleep, her head cocked back on the edge of the couch. RD is rubbing her knee. "I don't know," I say softly. "My mama's got all that stuff."

"Well, tell her you want to see it. If you have a birth certificate proving Luke Meadows is your father, they'll know you are serious. We could do DNA testing, but that's expensive. We'd have to get some talk show to pay for it."

"Charles, what are you talking about? Why would a talk show pay for a DNA test to prove my daddy is my daddy?"

"Look, right now *Salt* is just on some crappy little cable access channel, but it could get big. I'm telling you, this Christian entertainment shit is big business."

"I don't know why you need to curse so much," I say.

"It's going to be a long car ride," says Charles, sounding exasperated. I hear him take a deep breath and let it all out. He sounds just like his mama, doing her "yoga breathing."

"Look, do you want to see your daddy?"

"Yes," I say.

"Then we need a way in. We need a way to make the producers at *Salt* let us in while they are filming."

"Why not just go to his church?" I ask.

He's silent for a minute, and then he says, "That's brilliant.

We show up at his church—the Holy Eternal Waterfall, or whatever it is. I'll Google it right now, find out where it is."

I can't help it, I laugh. I don't know what that boy would do without his Google.

"I was thinking we'd leave Friday," says Charles. "Can you skip school without someone there calling your house? If not, I guess Saturday might work. Saturday might even be better since we really don't have to be there until church on Sunday. Church is on Sunday, right?"

"Ha," I say. "I think Friday will work best. That's the day Mama cleans Mrs. Black's house in Dunwoody. It's the biggest house I've ever seen, and it takes Mama all day to clean it. I'll just pretend I've got really bad cramps and then she'll let me stay home from school and she won't know I'm gone until she gets home that night."

"Sounds like a plan," he says. "I'll drive to your neighborhood that morning. You call me on my cell as soon as your mom leaves."

"She always leaves around eight," I say. I glance into the living room one more time. Mama's still asleep, only now her head is cocked to the side. RD is holding the remote. I just know he's punching through channels, not even stopping to look at what's on.

"I'll get to Loganville around seven thirty, and I'll just camp out down the street from your house until your mom leaves."

"Just come at eight fifteen," I say. "I know she'll be gone by then."

"It's more fun this way. It will be like that time I skipped class two days in a row just to wait by my own mailbox to retrieve a deficiency notice from my math teacher. I had a disguise and everything; I wore a fake mustache and a fedora."

I really don't know what he's talking about.

Finally he gives me his telephone number, and I tell him how to get to my house. It surprises me that he knows where

Loganville is. He tells me that there is a guy from his high school that lives in one of the new developments out here who sells pot.

"Charles," I say, "don't you talk to me about drugs. And don't even think about bringing any with you on our trip. You do not want to know what I would do to you."

"You'd forgive me," he says. "I mean, you're a Christian, right?"

CHAPTER THIRTEEN

Patron of the Arts

(Louise, Labor Day Weekend 2004)

"*A*re you sure you want to do this?" asks Caroline. "Because there are plenty of other shops in the neighborhood for us to go to."

"Caroline, I promised Tiny I would get her something from here. Now come on, let's go."

I push through the swinging door that leads into Good Vibrations, San Francisco's "sex positive" outfitter, a place that Ray, the leader of Tiny's singles group in Sea Island (where she is staying until her divorce from Anders is finalized), claims is "all orgasm, no sleaze."

"Get me one of those Rabbit vibrators like Charlotte had in *Sex and the City*," said Tiny when I told her John Henry and I were going to visit Caroline. "I'd order one off the Internet, but it's illegal to have them shipped to Georgia."

I am thinking about picking up a little something for myself too. Just something small and discreet. John Henry doesn't even have to know about it.

John Henry doesn't even know about this—Caroline's and my little shopping spree. He is off having coffee (although more likely a beer) with Davis, and I fear that Davis is right this moment asking his permission to marry Caroline. Davis seems the type to do such a thing. He seems to me to be—sorry, Caroline—a real kiss-ass.

I don't know. I suppose I should see asking the father's permission as respectful but it reminds me too much of horse trading. Like Davis might agree to have Caroline immunized as part of the deal.

Tiny says somewhere along the line all of my southern blood just dripped right out of me. That's not entirely true. I still have standards. You wouldn't catch me dead wearing white shoes after Labor Day. And if you invite me to your house for dinner, you'll receive a detailed thank-you note, exclaiming over the food, the flowers, the wine, and the company—even if I only had a so-so time.

"My heavens," I say, once inside the shop. "This is quite a selection."

"There's probably a hundred different models of vibrators here," Caroline says. "You can test them all."

"That doesn't sound very sanitary," I say.

"Oh gross, Mom. No, you can test them by turning them on in your hand."

I walk over to the far right wall, which is loaded with boxes of vibrators and tester models. Right away I spot the Rabbit, although there are several models to choose from. I pick up the Rabbit Pearl, which has what looks like a string of pearls curled into the base area—the balls—of the unit. When I turn it on the pearls rotate around the base. I can see how it would feel good.

Good Lord. This thing costs almost eighty dollars. I wonder if Tiny knew what an expensive gift she was asking me to pick up. Oh well. I grab one of the boxes and continue looking for a smaller, more delicate thing for myself.

Caroline, who buried herself in the book section the second we walked in, comes bounding up to me with an extremely tall woman wearing a leopard print coat, skinny black pants, and chunky red heels.

"Mom, I want to introduce you to my friend Deidre. She's the artist I was telling you about last night."

Deidre, Deidre, Deidre. Oh, right. The vagina woman.

"Nice to meet you, Deidre," I say. I would hold out my hand to shake, but I am clutching the boxed Rabbit. I hold it up. "This is for a friend," I say.

"Yeah, sure it is," says Caroline.

I give her a stern look.

"I love your daughter," says Deidre. "You know, she's got some artistic talent of her own. I mean, in the tactile arts, not just with acting."

"Did you see those birds she made?" I ask. "I just adore them!"

Caroline is blushing, which is sweet.

"Would it be too much of an imposition to show my mom your studio?" asks Caroline. She turns toward me. "Deidre works just a few blocks from here."

"Fine, fine," says Deidre. "Let me just get the things I need from here and I'll meet you in front of my building in, say, an hour?"

She needs an hour in the sex shop?

"Okay," says Caroline. "We'll get a coffee and then we'll come over."

Once Deidre is out of earshot I ask Caroline how often she runs into people she knows while shopping at Good Vibrations. She blushes.

"It's not like I'm a frequent shopper or anything, but I swear

every time I come in here to buy a gag gift or whatever, I see someone I know. Or someone who knows me. Once I did this guest
spot on my friend's cable access show, *Vegan Nation*, and later I was
in here and this guy who must have been the show's biggest fan
comes running up to me, going on and on about whether or not
honey counts as vegan because of the bees."

"How odd," I say. I'm not entirely sure what a vegan is and I
don't think I want to ask.

"So are you ready?" she asks.

I really want something for myself, but somehow, having run
into Caroline's friend—even though she obviously *is* a frequent
shopper—has made me self-conscious. "Sure," I say. "Let me just
buy this thing for Tiny."

The woman who rings me up is enormous. She wears a T-
shirt that says "If you want the job done right, do it yourself."

I hand her the box. As she scans the price code she says,
"This doesn't come with batteries but we sell them here. A buck
apiece."

"Thank you, but this item is for a friend," I say. "So I'll let
her purchase her own batteries."

The woman looks at me as if I am a child caught telling an
amusing lie.

"No judgment, no judgment," she says, smiling.

DEIDRE'S STUDIO IS on Harrison Street, which is more like ten, not
"a few," blocks from Good Vibrations. The studio is in a large
warehouse, up a metal staircase that clangs when you step on it.
The studio is big, at least two thousand square feet, and it has
little tables and chairs set up where Deidre teaches art to school-
children. It amuses me to think of taking one's child to so raw a
space for art class. When Caroline was little she used to take art
from Miss Bitsy, a divorced woman who lived in a cute little bungalow in Peachtree Hills.

The art that Deidre has hanging on the walls is fairly unin-
spiring, in my opinion. The canvases are painted gray with wispy
black lines that vaguely resemble telephone wires. I guess I'm just
a concrete person; abstract images have never done much for me.
Still I murmur and cluck over them and Caroline points out a
few that she absolutely loves. I wonder if she is giving me a hint,
if she would like for me to buy her a piece of Deidre's art for
Christmas.

There is a corner of the studio with a little kitchenette and a
fifties-style linoleum table. After we look at Deidre's art we sit at
the table and Deidre puts on a kettle for tea. She is so tall that I
feel abnormally little around her, as if I am from the munchkin
species. It is nice to be sitting. At least now I don't feel as if I
should be standing on my tippy-toes.

"Hey Caro," says Deidre. "Guess what time it is?"

Caroline glances at her watch and then looks furtively at
me.

"What?" I ask. "What?"

"Do you really want to know?" asks Caroline. She is wearing a
blue T-shirt that reads "Shalom Y'all."

I wonder, *Does she want people out here to think she's Jewish?*

"Is your mom not four-twenty friendly?" asks Deidre, smiling
at me.

"Four-twenty what?" I ask, blinking. I feel like my first year at
summer camp, when I tried so hard to fit in with the girls who
had been going there for years.

"Okay, so some people smoke a joint at four twenty in the afternoon," says Caroline. "Not all the time, of course, but there's a
little bit of a tradition of doing it at this time."

"Okay," I say. "Let's do it."

"Okay?" asks Caroline, looking stricken.

"Okay!" says Deidre. She walks to a drawer underneath the
kitchen counter and pulls out a long white cigarette.

"Have you ever smoked pot before?" asks Caroline.

Once I did. With Ben Ascher. But I don't want to get into that with her.

I shake my head. "No, but I don't mind giving it a try. If it's what San Franciscans do."

"Has something gotten into the water in Atlanta?" asks Caroline. "You have turned into, like, groovy Mom."

"And my daughter's dating a Republican," I say.

Deidre, who was occupied lighting the marijuana cigarette, pulls it from her mouth. "Davis is a Republican? I knew it."

Caroline shakes her head, her mouth open in protest. "No, I mean, he's not like a registered Republican or anything. He just doesn't adhere to any one party's line. He's voted for Democrats plenty of times. And yes, he's voted for Republicans too. But he's not like a crazed right-winger. I mean, he won't vote for Bush this time."

"He voted for him the first time?" asks Deidre. There is venom in her voice.

"How old is he, sweetheart?" I ask, trying to defuse the tension. "To have voted in so many elections?"

Deidre passes the cigarette to Caroline, who inhales and then blows out a puff of smoke. "Thirty-one."

"And you're what, twenty-one?" asks Deidre.

Caroline passes the marijuana cigarette to me. "About to turn twenty-two," she says.

Deidre raises her eyebrows. It occurs to me that she is not a subscriber to the "no judgment" policy of Good Vibrations. Truth be told, it seems to me that many of the people who live in San Francisco are second only to the membership committee at the Driving Club in terms of being judgmental. They just have different qualifications for what they think makes a decent person.

"So what you are going to do is put the joint in your mouth and just inhale. And then once you have as much as you want, hold the smoke in your lungs for a minute before you exhale. Okay, Mom?"

I put the cigarette—or joint, I suppose it is—into my mouth, trying to ignore the soggy feel of the paper. I inhale and immediately want to cough out the sweet smoke, but I manage to hold it in my lungs for a few seconds before doing so.

"Way to go, Louise!" says Deidre, drumming the palms of her hands on the linoleum table.

I pass her the joint. "May I have a glass of water?" I ask.

Deidre jumps up. I imagine her bumping her head against the ceiling when she does, and I giggle. "Iced water coming up," she says. "And how about some chocolate-covered graham crackers."

Caroline and I split a piece of cake when we stopped for coffee before heading over to Deidre's studio, but still, a chocolate-covered graham cracker sounds wonderful. It sounds fabulous in fact, like just what the doctor ordered.

"Oh yes!" I say and Caroline bursts out laughing.

"What?" I ask.

"Nothing," she says. "Just welcome to the munchies."

ONE JOINT AND an entire tin of chocolate-covered graham crackers later, Deidre pulls out the photos for her *Box* collection. She spreads them on the table so we can compare the different subjects.

"That one looks like the Grand Canyon," I say, and start to giggle.

Caroline starts giggling too and I am reminded of being at school with Tiny when we would both get so tickled over something we couldn't help but laugh even though our teacher threatened to send us to the principal's office.

"I used a close-up lens with that one," says Deidre. "So you see all of the nooks and crannies."

"And grannies," says Caroline.

"And nannies," I say. "Nanny Roses."

Caroline and I start giggling again.

"You are two of a kind, aren't you?" says Deidre.

"Hey," I say, lifting my gaze from the photo and looking right at her. "Are you still interested in me posing for you?"

Deidre is fishing through the box of photographs, looking for more examples to pull out. She stops and returns my stare. "Did Caroline tell you I was looking for an older woman for the project?"

"Oh honey," I say. "Please don't tell me you just said 'older woman'!"

Deidre shakes her head as if she is ridding it of a bad idea. "Did I say older woman? Excuse me, that's not what I meant to say. What I meant to say is that I'm looking for a sexy, sophisticated southern dame. That's who I'm looking for."

"Well I might just know one of those," I say.

"Don't you think you should wait until the pot wears off to think about doing this?" asks Caroline.

"No," I say. "But listen, Deidre, I don't want my face in it. And I don't want you to use the Grand Canyon lens."

"Mom," says Caroline. Her voice sounds panicked. "I didn't agree to that deal you wanted to make. If Davis asks me to marry him, I'm going to say yes."

Oh good Lord. Does this child think every decision I make is about her?

And damn. She is going to marry him. She's going to marry him and lead a boring life.

"Darling," I say. "I'm not doing this to stop you. I'm doing it for the sake of art."

And then I don't know what comes over me, but I can't stop laughing, my shoulders shaking, my eyes running. Oh, oh, oh, oh, oh, oh, oh, oh, oh!

Oh, it's all so ridiculous.

Part Three

CHAPTER FOURTEEN

Pilgrims

(Missy, September 2004)

*C*harles picks me up at 8:14 a.m., ten minutes after Mama and RD drove off. He doesn't even turn off the engine, just waits in the driver's seat while I lock the front door to my house, walk to his dark green Honda, and place my bag in the trunk, which is popped but which I have to open. First thing I do after I settle into the front seat is start poking at the buttons on his radio so I can figure out how to tune it to the Loaf. The Loaf FM is a Christian station and listening to it might do Charles some good. Now I'm no fool, I know the Loaf won't bring Charles to Jesus by the time we get to Durham or anything like that, but I figure he ought to at least get some exposure to the kind of contemporary praise music I am sure we will hear at Daddy's church, the kind of music that Pastor Praise—Daddy—plays with his band on *Salt of the Earth*.

Believe me, if Charles's first experience listening to live praise music isn't until we are actually at Daddy's church, surrounded by the faithful, that boy will make a scene. I know it. He'll laugh and point out the corniest lyrics and then he'll keep making fun throughout the singing, whispering nasty things in my ear like he did when we watched Daddy's show and the whole time he was saying, "Is this for fucking real?" and "You can't make this shit up."

He will draw attention to the two of us for sure. And who knows? Maybe an usher will think we are being too disrespectful and will kick us out of church and I won't even have a chance to see my daddy after having spent six hours trapped in a car with Charles Parker just to do so.

"Missy," says Charles, just as soon as I find the station, "don't you know the golden rule of the road? The driver chooses the music."

His engine is still running while he flips through the pages of a black leather CD carrier. He ought to cut the engine off. He's wasting gas.

"I only know Jesus's golden rule," I say.

(To anyone but Charles I wouldn't say something so outright preachy. It's just that Charles gets downright itchy when I preach at him and—well—I sort of like watching him itch.)

He pulls a CD out of the carrier and slides it into the player.

"Sorry, but I'm not driving six hours listening to saccharine ballads to JC coupled with not-so-subtle right-wing propaganda."

He puts the car in reverse and backs out of the driveway, barely missing the mailbox on his way out.

"If that's the kind of leader you choose to be," I say, as he turns right on Stevens, "I guess that's your right as a man."

Lately Pastor Finch has been talking up this book called *Born to Be Wild*. It's all about man's true nature. Men are born to be leaders, of course, but Pastor Finch says that they are also born to be adventurers and warriors. That's why all little boys want to grow up to be firemen or astronauts or soldiers. God implanted the heart of a hero inside all of them, but both secular society and, sadly, the church do their best to rub righteous manliness right out. That's why it's hard to find true leaders anymore. We've nagged the leader gene right out of our men. Least that's what Pastor Finch says.

I wonder if Charles has a warrior hidden deep inside of him. I wonder what would happen if he read *Born to Be Wild*, if it might wake up some sleeping part of him, the part that likes football and girls.

Thing is, I know exactly how Charles would react if I told him about the book. He'd make fun of it like he does with everything else. Then he'd say something just to aggravate me, like he thinks a woman should be the next president of the United States and it's okay for boys to dress up like fairy princesses.

Knowing Mrs. Parker, when Charles was a little boy she probably let him dress up like a fairy princess, if that's what he wanted to do. And she probably let him play with whatever toys he wanted, whether or not they were pink or had unicorns on them or were covered in glitter or whatnot.

That might be what got him so confused about everything in the first place. Maybe Charles grew up thinking he was a little girl and his mama went right along with it, letting him dress in tutus and high heels, and pretty soon Charles started thinking he liked boys the way girls are supposed to.

Then I realize something that surprises me, something that makes me wonder if maybe I've been spending too much time with Charles, if maybe he's been a bad influence. What I realize is deep down I don't really care whether or not Charles believes that he has the secret heart of a warrior. I'm just glad to be driving in the car with him, right now.

Aggravating as he can be, I (mostly) enjoy his company.

Last night I was so nervous thinking about today, about the trip, about seeing Daddy, I could hardly eat any dinner. But this morning I feel so happy, so excited to be going to Durham, to be getting away from Mama and RD and RD's smelly dog and our little house and all the problems that go with it: the bills we never get caught up on, the old toilet that overflows at least once a week (it's always RD who stops it up), the neighbors two doors down who own that mean German shepherd who sometimes sits on our front lawn growling anytime one of us tries to step out the door.

I don't even care that Charles has chosen the most depressing music in the world to play, just one man singing whiny lyrics.

And then I realize something else: with all our fussing over what music we were going to listen to on the drive, I forgot to feel ashamed of my house while Charles was parked in front of it (taking in every last detail, I'm sure). Last night I could not stop thinking about Charles seeing it, about Charles judging it against the one he lives in. I was worried Charles would feel sorry for me, after he saw how run-down our house is, with its patchy roof and peeling paint and broken blinds that you can see from the outside. And you can bet RD hauled all of his outdoor junk over to our front yard once he moved into our house. So now *our* front yard is filled with statuettes of boys in overalls and girls in dresses, too many pink flamingos to count, and a duck made out of concrete that must weigh a thousand pounds, because believe me, I have tried to move it.

RD's nasty old truck is *still* parked out front, in the same spot it's been since its engine didn't turn over two weeks ago. RD says he'll get around to fixing it soon enough—Mama has been dropping him off at work every day—but for now his Chevy sits. I wouldn't be surprised if RD never got around to fixing it, if one day he decided to put cinder blocks under the wheels instead. RD says it's got all kinds of things wrong with it under the hood, not to mention all those dents in the side and the cracked back windshield. On its bumper is a peeling sticker that reads "Durn Tootin' I'm a Rebel." I told him he should take the sticker off considering that a black family just moved in across the street and they're likely to get offended. RD says he doesn't mean no offense, he's just got a rebel spirit, and as long as a man's a Christian, he doesn't care whether he's black, white, purple, or whatever.

I bet a hundred dollars Charles made fun of that bumper sticker the second he pulled into our driveway. I bet he wrote it down in one of those notebooks he's always recording things in.

"Neiman's," says Charles.

We've been riding in silence and it startles me to hear him talk.

"What?" I ask.

"The bag you put in the trunk," he says. "It's from Neiman Marcus, right?"

"It's not mine. It's your mama's. From when she cleaned out her closet last spring and gave us a bunch of her sweaters."

"May I just take this moment to apologize for how clueless my mother is?"

I pretend not to know what he's talking about, even though I do. He thinks it's embarrassing for his mama to use a bag from a fancy shop when she's giving us her old clothes.

"It's a good bag," I say. "It's got a handle on it."

We're driving on Grayson Highway, about to pass by my church, though I'll keep that information from Charles. Otherwise he might pull in and try to introduce himself to Pastor Finch, tell him that he "likes guys." Just before the church there's a housing development with a sign in front of it that says "Homes from the 400's." That's 400 as in four hundred *thousand* dollars. I told Mama she ought to drop off flyers advertising her cleaning services in the mailboxes of those new homes. If someone's willing to pay over four hundred thousand dollars for a house, I bet they're willing to pay for someone to clean it. There are so many nice new developments going up around here, Mama could probably get all new clients, all within ten miles of our house.

I wonder if the boy Charles knows who lives out here—the one he told me about who sold him those illegal drugs—I wonder if he lives in that new development.

"You know where you are?" I ask him.

"I just keep following GA-Twenty, right?"

"Yep," I say. "Just keep going. You'll hit signs for Eighty-five."

We drive for a few miles without either of us saying anything, the only sound in the car the music Charles has chosen, which in this case means a man singing "needle in the hay" over and over again.

We drive past Big Chuck's BBQ and all of a sudden I am hungry something fierce. I was too excited to eat any breakfast this morning, not even when Mama offered to fix us eggs. I should have eaten, packed my stomach for later. I've only got thirty-two dollars for this whole trip and that includes helping Charles out with our hotel room tonight.

At least I thought to pack those Lance snack crackers. Peanut butter with cheddar and original flavor.

"Leather pants will work for church on Sunday, right?" Charles asks.

I start to say something, like *You had better not be planning to wear leather pants to my daddy's church*, but then I decide to try something else for a change. I pretend that Charles is RD's mutt, Li'l Dog, and he's jumping all over me and I'm just standing there, my arms wrapped tight around my sides, looking up at the ceiling until he calms down.

"Yep," he continues. "They're called 'second-skin' they fit so tight. Especially over the part that really counts. If you know what I mean."

He turns his eyes off the road to look at me, moving his

eyebrows up and down like some kind of a fool. I can't help myself—I laugh. He's relaxed, smiling, one arm on the wheel. It occurs to me that he's been looking forward to this trip. That he's been looking forward to spending time with me too. That he likes baiting me almost as much as I like baiting him.

CALL IT A miracle, but by the time we cross the state line and roar into South Carolina—Charles has a lead foot—we have finally discovered a band that we both find tolerable. The band is called Belle and Sebastian and their songs are real catchy. It ain't music you'd hear on the Loaf—that's for sure—but it's a lot better than that needle-in-the-hay guy.

Charles says that he once went to a Belle and Sebastian concert and everyone there looked just like him.

"We were all wearing highly ironic T-shirts," he said. "You know, ones with big-eyed does on them or a silhouette of a wolf against a mountain backdrop. It was a little disturbing. Made me realize I'm not as original as I thought I was."

I want to tell Charles, *Don't worry, you're an original,* but I don't. Somehow saying that might sound like I am calling him a fag, and even though he's used that word in front of me before, it doesn't seem right.

I wonder: if everyone looked like Charles at the Belle and Sebastian concert, does that mean everyone there was gay? I study Charles, trying to figure out if I would have known he was gay if I was meeting him for the first time. This summer when his hair was bleached and he wore that beaded silver necklace, he sure looked queer, but his hair doesn't look *all* that strange anymore. It's dyed almost black (a little too dark for his pale skin) and it's grown long enough to cover his ears. To tell the truth, he doesn't stand out too, too much. Don't get me wrong, no one would mistake him for the captain of the football team or anything like that. But he doesn't look any stranger than that group at my school who wear black all of the time and walk around looking like they are trying to figure out a way to blow the place up. And he doesn't act prissy or squeamish or anything.

"Play that song about the minister again," I say.

"I think you're missing its point," says Charles, but he smashes the return button on the car stereo until the song starts up again. When the chorus comes around I sing along:

But if you are feeling sinister, go off and see a minister, he'll try in vain to take away the pain of being a hopeless unbeliever. La, la, la, la, la, la, la.

I know Belle and Sebastian aren't a Christian band—not if Charles Parker owns a copy of their CD—but nevertheless the song makes good sense. Think about it: If you feel that you are about to commit a sin—to do something *sinister*—you *should* go off and find a minister. But there's nothing a minister can do with someone who's chosen to turn his back on God, with someone who is a "hopeless unbeliever." (And aren't all unbelievers hopeless?) So the minister probably *would* be trying in vain. But he'd try; you'd bet he'd try. By teaching you about Jesus, he'd try to help with the pain of being a hopeless unbeliever, which, sadly, is what most people in this world are. Or if they're not hopeless unbelievers then they believe in the wrong things—like Osama bin Laden and the people in Iraq who go around bombing our soldiers.

Then I think: Charles and me are on our way to find a minister (my daddy), yet what we are doing might be considered sinister, or at least a sin. Lying to Mama. Taking advantage of Mrs. Parker being out of town. Spending tonight together in a hotel room though we are neither related nor married.

That's a big one, but there's nothing I can do about it. I don't have the money for my own room. And Lord knows nothing's going to happen between Charles and me.

Even if I wanted it to.

• • •

ALL DURING THE trip Charles points out—and laughs at—the billboards with godly messages written on them. There are lots of them in South Carolina, and we've passed a couple in North Carolina too. My favorites are the ones with the black background with a quote—in white letters—smack in the middle. In every one the speaker of the quote is God. One of them says, "Why don't you stop by my house on Sunday before the game?"

Charles thinks the God quotes are "hilarious." I think that they are funny too, but in a different way from him. Charles wants me to write them all down in a little black-and-white-speckled notebook he pulled out of his glove compartment. I'm torn. A part of me wants to write them down, mainly because I think Pastor Finch might like to copy one of them for his sign in front of our church.

Right now his sign says, "Sign up for a Free Trip to Heaven. Details Inside."

But Charles doesn't want me to write down the signs for any righteous reasons. He's just making fun of them, like he does with everything.

And all of a sudden, I start to feel tired. Tired of him. Tired of that way of his, always teasing, always saying little things that don't make any sense to anyone but him, always putting on different voices and accents.

All of a sudden, the thought of being with Charles straight through the weekend is wearing me out.

Or maybe I'm just tired from thinking about seeing my daddy. Wondering what he will do when he sees me in my white dress, the one I packed in Mrs. Parker's old Neiman Marcus bag, the one I wore two years ago on that Easter Sunday when I recommitted my life to Christ. I kept thinking, all during that Easter service, that maybe Daddy would slip in the back so that he could witness me, down at the front of the church, making all those promises to God in front of Pastor Finch and the whole congregation.

Daddy would have been proud of me standing up there. That's what Mama told me after the service.

Mama. I'm trying hard not to, but I can't stop wondering about her. Wondering what she's doing right now. Wondering what she'll think when she calls from work to check on me (I told her I was feeling sick) and I don't answer the phone. Wondering at what time of the day she'll actually get home and read my note, which I left for her on the kitchen table.

Wondering what she'll do to me if Daddy makes me go back home.

SOMEWHERE IN NORTH Carolina I must have fallen asleep. I remember us passing the exit for the Billy Graham highway near Charlotte, and I remember Charles putting in another album, this one with a man singing in a real soothing voice, *pink, pink, pink, pink, pink,* and I remember talking with Charles about food, saying something about how much I love green bean casserole with the potato sticks on top, and then I must have started dreaming because the next thing I knew I was sitting in Mrs. Parker's living room with that portrait of Jesus on the wall. But then Jesus's face became Daddy's and then Daddy was sitting on Mrs. Parker's sofa with me and he was wearing a giant marshmallow strapped on top of his head like a train conductor's hat. I asked if he was home for Thanksgiving and he said yes, he came home to see his girl.

I reached out to give him a hug and for a moment he stood still while I wrapped my arms around his middle and felt his chest against my cheek and breathed in his smell, which was sweet like Aunt Jemima syrup. At that moment, everything was okay. Daddy was home and he still loved me and I still loved him. Then he sort of evaporated into the next room and I went following after him just wanting to grab on to him again. I kept going room to room looking for Daddy but then suddenly I was in the lobby at DeKalb Medical Center where Meemaw was when she died, and I was waiting for the elevator and there was a couple next to me arguing about whether or not they were supposed to go to the third or fourth floor. And then Charles must have started poking me in the shoulder because I feel his finger jabbing into me and I hear him say, "Wake up, Missy. We're here."

When I open my eyes he says, "Welcome to the Church of the Holy Rolling Waterfall of the Graceful Durham Bulls."

And we are parked in front of a long, low, windowless building that I guess must be Daddy's church but that looks more like a giant version of one of those trailers they use at school when they run out of classrooms.

"Well, shall we venture inside?"

"It's a Friday afternoon," I say. "There's not going to be anyone in there."

Charles is combing his hands through the front of his hair, making it lie sideways across his forehead. He really ought to cut it. Not shaved like it was earlier this summer, just short and neat. He would look real cute that way.

"Your dad might be in there," he says, "writing Sunday's sermon."

I know, I know. That was our plan from the beginning, to first go to Daddy's church and see if we can find Daddy or anyone else who knows where Daddy might be. But the inside of my mouth tastes like old McDonald's from when we stopped in Greenville. And that means my breath smells like old hamburger and french fries. I can't see my daddy after all of these years with nasty breath.

"Do you have any gum?" I ask.

Charles reaches into the side pocket of his car and pulls out a pack of Extra.

"Here you go," he says, tossing the pack onto my lap. "There's a mirror in the visor if you want to freshen up before we go in. Or we could see if there's a bathroom in the church."

"Freshen up" is something Mrs. Parker says. Every time Mama and me have stayed late at Mrs. Parker's house, usually when Mrs. Parker wants Mama to do a deep clean, Mrs. Parker always goes upstairs at 5 p.m. to "freshen up" for when her husband comes home.

I pull down the passenger side visor and look at myself in the mirror. My curls are frizzed at the ends, so I comb them back into a ponytail and secure it with the rubber band I keep around my wrist to pop any time I talk back to Mama.

(See, I am working on following the Ten Commandments more faithfully—including the one about respecting your mother and father. All of us in Young Warriors are doing it. We are supposed to pick a commandment that we often break and then pop the band any time we start to do so. Since I'm away from home and obviously can't sass Mama, maybe I should pop it every time I get aggravated with Charles. Then again, if I did that, I'd be popping that thing all the time and my wrist would get all red and swollen like Darren's, who is trying to stop thinking impure thoughts. Plus, it's not breaking any commandment to get aggravated at Charles.)

I'm wearing my favorite T-shirt, one from Old Navy with a little American flag on its front, on top of a pair of jean shorts, which are actually an old pair of Caroline Parker's that Mrs. Parker gave to me. Mrs. Parker says that she was saving Caroline's clothes in case Caroline wanted to wear any of them when she came home to visit, but she hardly ever comes home. The shorts are real cute. Still, they are pretty short, and I worry I don't look dressy enough for church even though it is Friday and there's no service happening or anything like that.

I give myself one more look in the visor mirror. Before Charles came this morning I put on a little blush and some lipstick, but it looks like all my makeup wore off during the drive. I pinch my cheeks just to give them more color, swallow my piece of gum, and tell Charles I'm ready.

ONCE INSIDE I am immediately hit by that new house smell—like the smell of Mrs. Black's house in Dunwoody. We are standing in the lobby. The floors are covered in gray carpet and there are bulletin boards on all of the walls advertising the special programs run by the church. There's a whole board dedicated to *Salt of the Earth*. Someone did a nice write-up about it, saying it stars "Holy Faith's favorite youth pastor, Lucas Meadows." Beside the write-up is a photo of the entire cast of the show, Daddy standing in the middle with his arms around his "children," Matthew and Dawn. Looking at this picture of Daddy, inside his church, in Durham, North Carolina, is almost too much. I feel a little dizzy. I feel like I might need to sit down.

In the photo Daddy's eyes are piercing but kind. I imagine Jesus's eyes will look the same.

"Missy, come here," Charles calls from the other end of the lobby. It seems wrong for him to be saying my name out loud in here. What if Daddy is nearby and overhears? Don't get me wrong: I want to see Daddy. Eventually. Once I have time to take everything in. But I want to be the one who decides when that moment happens. Not Charles.

"Come here!" he says, motioning me with his hand.

"Okay, okay," I whisper, walking toward him.

He is standing by a pair of double doors that say "Worship Room" on a small sign to their right.

"Behold the chapel," says Charles. "I'm sorry. I mean, the Worship Room."

I push in one of the doors and peek inside.

I can't help but be disappointed by what I see.

Somehow I was thinking the chapel would look like the chapel in Granddaddy's church, which was also Daddy's church before he left. Now, Granddaddy's church wasn't a fancy place; it wasn't like one of those Catholic sanctuaries where they worship statues and graven images and burn incense until no one can breathe. We had a slide show about those churches during Sunday school and our teacher lit some of the incense just so we could smell it and everyone agreed it smelled awful.

No, I wasn't expecting the church to be fancy. Granddaddy's was just the opposite, actually. It was simple, a white wood chapel with six rows of pews running on either side of the aisle, dark wood floors, and a big brass cross erected right behind the pulpit where Granddaddy stood.

Mama once said Granddaddy thought he was the risen Christ standing up there in front of that cross. To be honest, I don't remember all that much about Granddaddy, I was so young when he died. Mama says she can't smell the plain kind of Chap Stick without thinking about him. She says he was always applying it to his lips.

Pastor Finch's church is much bigger than Granddaddy's and it isn't as, well, as pure-looking as Granddaddy's was, but still, it has pews and stained glass windows and a big baptism tub at the front. When you're in there, you know you are in church.

But the inside of Daddy's new church—well, you could be anywhere. In fact, the place it most resembles is the gym from my high school all set up for a pep rally, just a big, windowless room with a couple of mike stands up front and rows and rows of folding chairs where otherwise the basketball court might be.

Hung on the walls are handmade posters, which spell out

"The Way" and "The Truth" and "The Life" and "Believe." I hate to say it, but even the posters remind me of a high school gym. I keep expecting one of them to say "Go, Team, Go!"

"What do you think?" asks Charles.

I shrug, trying not to show him how disappointed I feel.

"It's sure not All Saints Episcopal," he says. "There's not a Tiffany window in sight."

"I bet the acoustics are real good," I say, "when the band plays."

"Yeah," says Charles. "I bet you're right."

He looks at me with such tenderness that I almost think he's going to lean over and kiss my forehead, like a daddy might do.

CHARLES AND I look for the staff offices, where we figure Daddy might be. My heart is beating so fast as we walk through the building it's as if I just ran ten miles. I keep thinking I'm going to turn a corner and bump into Daddy. I hope he thinks I look good. I hope he likes the way I've grown up.

I see Charles open a door labeled "Private" and then he's calling me again, in that loud, aggravating voice he has.

"Here are the stairs," he says.

"Are you sure you want to go down them if they are marked 'Private'?" I ask.

"You're really worried about a little sign after everything you've done to get here?"

"Fine," I say.

Downstairs is a hallway just like the one upstairs, only there are no bulletin boards on the walls. From the end of the hall we hear what sounds like typing.

"Might be Luke working on his sermon," says Charles.

We walk toward the typing noise, passing several closed doors along the way. The door is open to the room where the noise is coming from. Looking in, I see a plump woman with curly red hair pinned and piled on top of her head. And Lord help me, she has a bright green parrot sitting on her left shoulder.

"Hello there," she says, looking up at us from her computer. Her voice is warm and throaty, her accent thick as Meemaw's was. "Buster, say hi."

That bird looks right at us and squawks, "Hello."

"Hey there, Buster," says Charles, and I just know that he is loving every minute of this.

"Buster, we were wondering," says Charles, "is Luke Meadows around today? Pastor Meadows, I mean."

My mouth gets dry. What if the bird woman says, "Why yes he is," and then just pulls Daddy out from some back room?

"Buster says to tell you that Luke is off shooting that program of his today. Do y'all know about it? It's called *Salt of the Earth* and it is as cute as it can be. It's just like a soap opera only it's made for Christians. Pastor Meadows writes, directs, and stars in it."

"Yes ma'am, we've heard of it," says Charles.

First time I've ever heard him say "ma'am."

"Missy and I are just the biggest fans of the show. We even chartered a fan club in Atlanta, where we're from."

"Well dang if Buster and me don't have a cousin down there in Hotlanta! He's in Sewanee to be exact, but we always go to Atlanta when we visit. Buster here just loves the World of Coke."

RD once took Mama and me there. The tour was kind of boring but at the end you go into this big room where they have every flavor of Coke you can imagine, and you can try as many of them as you want. There are also all kinds of weird Fantas, like Fanta Passionfruit and Fanta Melon. And there's this one soda that tastes real bitter. It's from Italy and it is called Beverly. RD said it should be called No Thanks.

What I want to know is, how in the world did she take a big green parrot into the World of Coca-Cola with her?

"Buster was allowed in the World of Coke?" Charles asks, as if he can read my mind.

"Honey, Buster here knows a trick or two about covert operations. For that adventure I just stuffed him into this big ol' purse I have that has polka dots all over it. Nobody notices I've punched out a few of those polka dots to make air holes for Mr. Buster here."

"Wow," says Charles, sounding like he genuinely means it.

"Ma'am," I say, "would you mind telling us where Pastor Meadows films his program?"

I figure if I don't go ahead and ask, Charles is going to forget all about finding Daddy and just want to stay here all day yakking about that bird.

"Sorry, darlin', but that information is top secret. Pastor Meadows will have my hide if I give it out again."

"You have the most amazing hair," says Charles.

Charles, I think to myself, *if you think she is going to fall for such obvious buttering up, then you are a fool.*

Except her face is turning bright as her hair and she's wearing this little smile like Mama used to get when RD was chasing after her.

"Aw, now, don't you go getting too attached to this hair," she says. "It's just a piece I clip on and it's coming out tonight."

Charles claps his hands together and screams with laughter. "You are too fun! You and Buster."

"My name's Carol," she says, running her fingers down the bird's back while he stays perched on her shoulder. "Born on Christmas Day which is why red is my signature color."

"Perfect," murmurs Charles. "Just perfect."

"Where's the bathroom?" I ask, thinking I cannot stand to watch Charles with her for one more minute. He's acting like he really likes her, but the truth is he is just amused by her. Probably he thinks she is "hilarious." She's just one more funny thing to entertain him. Just like Daddy's show. Probably even just like me.

"Take a left out of my office, then it's the third door on your right down the hall," she says.

Reaching into a Wal-Mart bag beside her desk she pulls out an eight-pack of toilet paper. "Would you mind putting this under the sink while you're in there?"

"Sure," I say, but what I'm thinking is, *I lied to Mama and drove all the way to Durham just to be this woman's janitor?*

CHARLES IS WAITING for me outside the bathroom. "Come on," he says. "Let's go to the car."

"I thought you'd still be flirting with Buster and that woman."

"Shh. Come on. I've got some good news, but I need to tell it to you outside."

We make our way back outside and into the car. Charles starts up the engine.

"Guess where we're going?" he asks.

"I don't know, Disney World?" I say, just to be dumb.

"Noo, we are going to visit the set of your favorite Christian soap opera!"

"You found out where Daddy is? Charles, I can't believe she told you!"

He's driving now as if he knows where he's going.

"She said she really shouldn't, but you and I were so sweet and such obvious fans that she would break the rules just this once if I promised not to tell Luke she was the one who told us where the show is filmed."

He turns right.

"How do you know your way around so well?" I ask.

"I've been coming up here since I was little. More to Chapel Hill than Durham, but there's a barbecue place over here my dad always likes to eat at. Plus Carol wrote out the directions. It's just off Five-oh-one."

He picks a piece of paper off his lap and waves it at me. Carol's directions are written in round, curly script; instead of dots she marks her *i*'s with stars.

THE NEIGHBORHOOD CHARLES takes us to is nice enough, nicer than the one Mama and me live in but not by far. It's sure not what you picture when you think of television glamour. Just rows of smallish houses with grassy front lawns and woods in the back. Charles slows down in front of one of them, which has brick on the first floor and vinyl siding on the second. An American flag flies to the side of the red front door.

The numbers on the mailbox say 2620, and that is when I get really excited because I know these numbers, I've seen them on the front of the Praise house when watching the show.

We really are here.

We climb out of the car, Charles shielding the sun from his face with his hand.

I am wearing my white church dress. I made Charles stop at a McDonald's on the way over here so I could change into it. I was going to wait and wear it to services on Sunday, but I decided I wanted it to be the first thing Daddy saw me in. It's a young-looking dress, babyish almost, and maybe I want Daddy to still think of me as a little girl. Maybe it scares me a little for him to see me so grown up, my breasts so big, my legs so long. The problem is that the dress is a little tight in the chest. It's not like I can't breathe or anything. But it's tight enough that Charles raised his eyebrows when I came out of the McDonald's bathroom wearing it.

"Are you sure you want to go for sexy Catholic girl about to take her first communion?" he asked and I had a strong urge both to take off the dress and to punch him in the stomach.

I didn't do either, just pulled down on the skirt a little bit and told him that Jesus loved him but the rest of us found him real hard to take.

Of course now that we are walking up to the house I'm thinking, *Does it look as if I'm trying to be sexy? Is the dress too little for me?* Too late. Charles is already ringing the doorbell, pressing his finger on the buzzer again and again as if our being here constitutes an emergency.

Which it might.

A BLOND MAN wearing a tight T-shirt that shows off his arm muscles opens the door. All I can think is that he looks like a Ken doll. A Christian Ken doll, as he wears a large silver cross on a chain around his neck.

"Aw shoot, I thought y'all was my pizza," he says. "Thought y'all was Domino's."

"Domino's delivers and they want you to, too," says Charles in a singsong voice.

He said the same thing to me once when a Domino's commercial came on while we were watching TV. When I asked him what on earth he was talking about he said that he boycotts Domino's because the founder gives money to pro-life groups. I said, "You just made me a Domino's customer for life."

"Hi," I say, smiling, trying to make up for Charles's rudeness. "We're not the pizza guy, we are just big fans of your TV show."

The man grins. "So Carol told you where to find us?"

"Yeah," says Charles. "She said she hardly ever gives out that information, but Missy here and I are special."

"Lord, that woman is the mouth of the South," says the Christian Ken doll. "Pastor keeps getting on her about her big mouth and she just keeps sending fans over to us."

He's smiling in a way that makes me think he doesn't think it's so bad for Carol to always be spilling the beans.

"Pastor as in Pastor Meadows?" asks Charles, shooting me a look.

"That and Pastor P. It's hard to keep the two straight in my head. I mean, they're both Luke, it's just one is the real live version and the other is the made-for-TV. It's gotten so confusing for all of us, we just call him Pastor and figure that covers both bases."

"Is he here?" I ask, my voice cracking.

"What's that?" asks the man, cupping his ear.

"Missy and I are the biggest *Salt* fans on the planet," says Charles. "So if Pastor is around, maybe we could get his autograph? We drove all the way up from Atlanta just to meet him."

The man starts looking at Charles as if he might be carrying a gun in his pocket.

"You drove all the way from Atlanta just to get Pastor's autograph? Boy, you cain't even get the show in Atlanta. It only plays on a little old cable channel here in Durham."

"Charles has a satellite dish," I say. "To pick up college sports games. One day it picked up *Salt of the Earth*. We think God must have wanted us to see it."

The man is studying me like I'm a math problem he's trying to figure out. He smiles, revealing the whitest teeth I've ever seen.

"You drove all the way up here just to get our John Hancocks? Well, I am flattered."

It feels wrong to be lying to this man. Especially because of that cross he is wearing.

"Look, the truth is—"

Charles cuts me off. "The truth is her daddy lives here in Durham and she comes to visit him on the weekends so we didn't just drive up here to get autographs, but we are very interested in meeting the cast."

"Does your daddy live up here too?" asks the man. Something about his tone makes Charles blush.

"No. But I'm her cousin and I have a car so taking Missy to

see her daddy just seems like the right—the Christian—thing to do."

Why Charles has to go making up all kinds of lies—including saying that he is a Christian—is beyond me.

The man continues to study us, looking back and forth, back and forth, smiling like he knows a little secret.

"Look here," he says. "Luke and just about everyone else are off at Durham General, but why don't y'all come in and I'll get you a Co-Cola and we can get to know each other better while we wait for them to come back."

"Durham General? Is that the hospital? Is Luke—I mean Pastor—is he okay?" I ask.

"They're just shooting a scene. I'd tell you all about it, but it's top secret."

I LIKE THE inside of the *Salt* house. The front door opens right up to the living room, which I recognize immediately from the show. There's the L-shaped sofas and the entertainment center with the big-screen TV. There's the braided rug and the fireplace with the mantel above it lined with photos. I walk over to the mantel and begin looking at the pictures in the frames, hungry to see more of Daddy.

All of the photos are of the *Salt* cast, which disappoints me a little, though I know it shouldn't. (What was I thinking, that Daddy would prop a big old photo of me right on the mantel?) There's the same one of the Praise family that was on the bulletin board at the church, the one where Daddy's arms are slung around Dawn's and Matthew's shoulders. There's something familiar-looking about Matthew and then I realize what it is.

"Oh my Lord!" I say. "You're Matthew. From the show!"

The blond man sits on the sofa looking just as proud and pleased as a cat with a mouse. "Guilty as charged," he says. "I'm surprised you didn't recognize me sooner, seeing as what fans you two are."

"Wowsers," says Charles, who has already made himself comfortable on one of the sofas. "I had no idea we were among celebrity."

"Well you are," says the man who plays Matthew, giving Charles a look that says, *I don't like you.*

"Is Matthew your real name?" I ask.

"My real name's Dwayne. Pastor just thought it was important for me to have a biblical name for the show."

"Like the very biblical moniker Dawn," says Charles.

I don't even know what *moniker* means, but I know Charles is being a real pain in the butt. I shoot him a look like he is my two-year-old and he is one second away from a smack. I swear, it is hard to believe that Charles is Mrs. Parker's son. Even though she sometimes acts like she's better than you just by being so polite all the time, she's a really nice lady while Charles can be such a jerk. Once Mama and me were over at the Parkers' house helping them get ready for their Christmas party, and I overheard Charles's daddy tell him to quit being such a "g.d. smartass." Only he didn't say "g.d." He said the whole word and he sounded like he meant it too.

I remember thinking, *You tell him, Mr. Parker.* But then I also felt kind of sorry for Charles.

"Y'all look like a real family in this photo," I say.

"Thank you, darlin'," says Dwayne. "We've got some extra copies of that picture. I'll sign one for you if you want."

"Ooh, I want one!" cries Charles.

I hope Dwayne doesn't give Charles an autographed photo. If he does, Charles will probably try to sell it on eBay.

The doorbell rings. *Deep breath, take a deep breath.* I start running my fingers through my hair. Then I give the hem of my dress one more tug. I wish it wasn't so short. Dwayne keeps looking at my legs out of the corner of his eyes.

I don't know if I should go sit on the couch or if I should

just stay here by the fireplace or what, but my body decides for me by freezing right up.

Dwayne answers the door. It's the Domino's guy, holding a box of pizza.

"About time, my friend," says Dwayne. "Way over thirty minutes. That means it's free, right?"

"No sir," says the delivery guy, who's sixty if he's a day old. "We changed that policy a long time ago."

"Betcha had to give away too many pizzas, didn't you?"

"That'll be twelve eighty," says the man. I watch as Dwayne takes a ten and two ones out of his wallet and then counts out eighty cents in change.

Charles notices too and shoots me an astonished look. He mouths, "Wouldn't Jesus tip?"

At least I think that's what he's mouthing.

Dwayne shuts the front door and walks toward the kitchen with the Domino's box. "'Scuse me, folks, but I am starving and if Loretta catches me eating this pizza in the living room she will skin me alive."

Charles shoots me another look. This time he mouths, "None for us?" and gives such a sad hound dog look that I have to laugh.

I go over to the sofa and sit by Charles.

"This is weird," I whisper. "I feel like we've tricked our way into here, like we're breaking the law or something."

"If anyone's up shit creek it's your father," whispers Charles.

"That's not what I want!"

He puts his hand on my knee and squeezes. "You're just nervous because it's a big deal to see your dad after so many years. Don't worry. It's going to be okay. Things have gone great so far."

I study his fingers wrapped around my knee. They are long and thin and bony. I like having his hand on me. I wouldn't mind if he just kept it there.

And then I hear a car door slam. And another. And I can hear people talking and laughing in the driveway, saying, "The look that nurse gave us . . ." and "Staci played that scene just right, didn't she?" and "I would have thought she was miscarrying for real," and "Man oh man, I thought that woman was going to call the cops on us." And then the front door opens and a barrel-chested man wearing a T-shirt and baggy shorts comes barging in followed by a tall skinny guy with a ponytail.

"Dwayne, get out here," the barrel-chested guy says, not even noticing us. "Have we got a story for you!"

And right behind him walks Mrs. Praise and the girl who plays Dawn. Dawn is wearing a pair of khaki shorts that look like they have blood all over them and I can't believe that she looks so completely happy and at ease and not at all embarrassed that she obviously is leaking from her period.

Mrs. Praise notices us right away. "Uh, hello," she says. "Who are you?"

Dwayne walks into the living room, a piece of pepperoni pizza hanging from his mouth.

"Want to introduce us to your friends, Dwayne?" asks Mrs. Praise in a voice that makes it clear she's really not interested in meeting us at all.

Dawn is talking to herself, saying she has got to get out of these shorts *right this instant*, now where did her bag with the clean change of clothes go? And Dwayne is saying, "These two are Atlanta's biggest *Salt of the Earth* fans." Two other guys walk in the door, both of them with video cameras slung around their shoulders, and just behind them, in walks Daddy.

Daddy.

Tears press against my eyes. It really is him. Just as handsome as he was in that photo I have of him holding me when I was just a little baby. His curly hair looks too bright in the light of day, on account of its being dyed blond. But oh Lord, those are his eyes. I will never forget those blue eyes framed by those long lashes.

Charles looks at Daddy, looks back at me, and then looks at the guys with the cameras. "I'd start those things going if I were you," he says.

Dwayne is looking strangely at Daddy and then he blurts out, "Pastor, I want you to meet two of your greatest fans; they drove here all the way from Atlanta."

And Daddy. Daddy's been staring at me this whole time like he can't believe it. Like I'm Jesus Christ, come around for the second time to judge the living. Him first.

I stand up and start to walk toward him. I want to put my arms around him. I want to tell him that everything is okay, that I love him. I want to feel that he is real, that his skin is warm, that his heart beats beneath his T-shirt. But he has turned away from me and he is running, running out the door, leaping over the stoop, running down the gravel driveway and into a white pickup truck parked on the street. It starts with a roar. And he must have put the pedal all the way to the metal because the truck jumps and then makes a terrible grinding noise and then it goes. And before I manage to say, "Stop, wait, come back!" the truck is roaring down the street.

I am left just standing in the living room, everyone staring at me. Stunned.

CHAPTER FIFTEEN

Backsliders

(Missy, Fall 2004)

*D*wayne told the rest of the cast and crew that they could go on home, that he would stay with me at the Praise house until Mama came to pick me up. Charles had been gone for a couple of hours by then, headed back to Atlanta, I now know. After everyone else left, Dwayne told me that Durham had some of the best barbecue in the world. He asked did I want to drive out with him to get some. I didn't actually say yes or no, but I followed him to his car. I did not want to be alone at the house.

On the way to get barbecue, Dwayne was playing what used to be one of my favorite songs, "I Bow Down before You" by the Mars Hill Aliens. That night I didn't want to hear it. I did not want to hear about how God has a plan for me, how God knows every thought I've ever had, how God knows my past and my future. *If God knows my future*, I thought, *then why did He let me drive all the way up here with Charles only to have my daddy leave me again?* On that night it seemed to me that God was either a bully or just plain dumb.

At the restaurant Dwayne ordered pulled pork sandwiches

and baked beans and cornbread to go, and then he said that he didn't know if I partook or not, but that there was nothing like a cold beer to accompany smoked meat. I had never tasted beer before in my life, but I told him that I would try one, so we stopped by the Kroger and Dwayne bought a twelve-pack.

We drove back to the house, because that's where we told Mama we would be waiting when she came to pick me up. I asked Dwayne whose house was it exactly and he said the church owned it but Daddy kind of acted like it was his. We went inside to the kitchen and ate our pulled pork sandwiches. I drank one beer and then drank another. At first the beer tasted horrible but then I sort of got used to it. It still didn't taste good, but it got easier to swallow. Dwayne took one of the moistened towelettes that came with our sandwiches and wiped the barbecue stain off his lip and then he said that if this were a real barbecue there would be dancing, and did I want to dance with him?

Now, I'd never been to a barbecue with dancing, so what Dwayne was saying didn't make much sense to me, but I said yeah, I'd dance with him.

He took my hands in his and danced me around the kitchen and I leaned my head against his chest and pretended that everything was okay. I pretended even, for a moment, that Dwayne was my daddy and he and I were dancing together because he was so excited that I found him, he was so excited that I was back in his life.

Dwayne said, "Come on, let's go downstairs and put on some music so we don't look like two fools dancing without a song."

He led me down to the basement, which was wood-paneled and cozy and felt like a living room. In the middle of the room was a brown couch set up in front of an old TV, and in the corner was a desk with a computer on it. Near the desk a guitar leaned against the wall. It was the same one Daddy played in the opening credits of the show.

"That's where Luke writes his scripts," said Dwayne, motioning to the desk. As soon as he said Daddy's name I started to cry. It was just too hard being so near all of his things.

"Hush now, darling," Dwayne said. "I didn't mean to make you upset." He clucked his tongue in his mouth and wiped away my tears with his finger.

"I never knew what a fool your daddy was until today," he said, and then he kissed me on the mouth.

I kissed him back. It was my first kiss, and unlike what I had heard from a girl at school it felt good and not sloppy. It made the hair on my arms pop. It made me want to be kissed more, to be kissed harder, to be swallowed up by Dwayne so that I no longer had to be in my body.

"Oh Missy," he said and we kept kissing and kissing. He led me over to the couch and we sat down on it and he started running his hand on my thigh underneath that stupid dress I wore.

Dwayne kept rubbing and rubbing my thigh with his hand. It felt good. It made my nipples get hard. He pushed up my dress so that it was bunched around my waist and then he sort of pushed me back onto the couch and started unzipping his pants.

Hearing that zip brought me back to earth and I told him that no, I could not do that, I could not have sex with him.

"It's okay, honey," he said, breathing real heavy. "We don't have to do that. We can save that for when we're married. I just want to be near you. That's all. I just want to press up right next to you. Look, I'm keeping on my underwear, you see?"

He took off his khaki shorts but left on his boxers, which were green and printed with the Krispy Kreme logo. I could see the outline of his penis through them and for some reason, at that moment, I thought, *That's why it's called a hard-on. Because it's so hard.*

I lay back and he climbed on top of me. When he pressed his body against mine I could feel his penis pushing into my underwear and I must have looked startled or confused because he said again, "It's okay, honey. This is as far as we are going to go. I just want to feel close to you, okay? We're both going to keep on our underwear."

I admit that at first it felt good to have him rub himself against me. It did. It felt so good that it made me want to kiss him again, and I raised my head so we could do so, but he didn't seem to notice. He was looking past me, his eyes fixed on the wall. He started moving back and forth real fast, bumping against my underwear. And then his face changed so that he looked like he was in pain and he was moving even faster against me and it wasn't that it hurt, it didn't, but it sure didn't feel good and all I could think about was Mrs. Persons's little dog, who always tried to hump my leg whenever I went over there with Mama.

"Dwayne," I said but he said, "Shh, shh, hold on a minute, just a minute," and then he started moving so fast it was like he was shaking, shaking like the washing machine at the end of the spin cycle and he was grunting and chanting to God and I felt a drop of sweat from his face fall on me and then I felt something warm and wet soaking through my underwear and after that Dwayne collapsed on top of me, still.

Chapter Sixteen

Two Letters, One Sent

(Louise, Fall 2004)

November 15, 2004
Dear Caroline,

Now you know that I want to do everything within my power to make your wedding a beautiful and romantic event, and you know that neither your father nor I want you to worry one bit about details like how much the wedding is going to cost. We are going to take care of all that, and we are going to make sure that the champagne and flowers are plentiful and in exquisite taste. With so many guests coming from out of town, you must know that I see it as my duty to show your (soon to be!) California in-laws that Atlanta has all of the sophistication of San Francisco.

But of course, this letter is not about champagne or flowers or any of those things. No, darling, I'm writing in response to the request that you made of Davis's mother and Nanny Rose and me. Since you explicitly asked for our engagement stories *in writing*, I can only assume that you plan to use the written version for some part of your wedding ceremony. Or maybe you will read aloud from them at the bridesmaids' lunch. Perhaps you'll put together a scrapbook for the mothers. I'm sure that whatever you have planned will be just lovely.

Here is the problem. What you want and what I have to offer are two different things. You want the cute stories, the ring in the glass of champagne, the nervous gibberish of a man minutes before he pops the question. You want a story like Tiny has, that she saw Anders for the first time at a Chi O crush party, pointed him out to me, and declared, "I'm going to marry that boy." And of course she did because Tiny was too powerful a force to be denied.

The real story of your father's and my engagement isn't cute. The story that I have always told you about how he proposed— well, it wasn't exactly a lie but I omitted a lot of details. And stole a few from Tiny.

I was not, as I have led you to believe, sassy when your father broke up with me. I did not toss my hair in the wind and say "Sounds like a plan" when he suggested—in the fall of our senior year—that we date other people. That's something Tiny did. I cried and implored John Henry to change his mind. We were sitting on the edge of his bed in the apartment he shared with some of his fraternity brothers. He stood up to usher me out after he delivered his news and I grabbed him around the waist, literally trying to hold on to him. Begging him not to leave me.

I don't much like to think about that afternoon.

It won't come as too much of a surprise that he and I were sleeping together, will it? I wouldn't have done it had I thought he would even consider breaking up with me. I thought, in fact, that our sleeping together guaranteed his intentions. So when he announced that he wanted to be a free man his senior year, well, you can imagine how I felt. Used. Discarded. Utterly bereft.

You have to remember, Caroline, that even though it was

1975 when I was a senior, I was not what was called a "liberated woman." Feminism might have arrived at Chapel Hill, but it sure didn't come to the Chi Omega house. Nor to the apartment I shared with Tiny either. Good Lord, Tiny and I were so innocent that we shared a double bed our senior year of college. You once thought that was hilarious. Way back before you became an engaged woman, during your rebel years, you asked if Tiny and I had ever "hooked up."

I laughed when you asked me that, not because I was making fun of lesbians—as you seemed to think—but because the idea that Tiny and I would have even thought of such a thing was absurd. Tiny? The girl who taught me how to use a tampon, the girl whose underwear I borrowed for four years straight during college? She was like a sister—not a boyfriend—to me.

Anyway. My relationship with Tiny is not why I am writing this letter. You want to hear about your father and me. I don't know why I never told you the real story of the breakup. Maybe I was embarrassed, embarrassed because you, even as a teenager, always had such drive and purpose and I was so woefully unprepared for the world. You were more prepared for the world at sixteen than I was at twenty. You seemed to know it too. As a teenager you seemed to hold a certain contempt for me.

So that was the first thing I lied about, my own feelings about the breakup. I was devastated, in part because I was in love with John Henry (how could I have sex with someone I didn't love?) but also because losing him meant losing my future. We had been dating exclusively since our sophomore year at Chapel Hill. I just assumed we would marry the summer after graduation. I would get a job—tutoring or waiting tables or selling Avon—until he finished law school and his career took off and then we would have a baby and I would become a full-time mother.

I had no idea that there was any other option for me besides marriage and motherhood. The grooves for that track were worn deep. So if I didn't marry John Henry, what would happen to me? I certainly couldn't move back to Atlanta and live with Mother and Daddy. Mother had no feelings for me. It wasn't that she was mean; she was simply neutral. Half of the time she was at "her spa" (as we so graciously put it). Daddy, who adored me as a little girl, became more and more distant as I grew up. It was as if he could no longer love me once I looked like a woman.

I couldn't move back in with them; I would go as crazy as Mother.

And while I had been ready to get a little job during John Henry's time in law school, I had no concept of having a career. What on earth would I have done? Teach school like my old-maid aunt Clare?

What made it even worse was that Tiny and Anders were already engaged, their wedding set for June 10th after graduation, my salmon pink maid of honor dress already picked out. And it wasn't just Tiny who was getting married. Most of the girls from my pledge class were engaged. Night after night I was called to the Chi O house to take part in yet another "candle ceremony" where we stood in a circle and passed around a lighted candle until one of us—the engaged one—blew it out.

I had been looking forward to my candle ceremony. I was well aware that there were only a handful of us left who didn't have engagement rings. Up to that point I had always been one of the insiders. I was popular in high school; I had my pick of sororities at Chapel Hill; I was dating one of the cutest boys on campus, and not only that but a boy from one of the most distinguished families in Atlanta. When John Henry broke up with me, I had my first taste of what it felt like to be an outsider. I thought about my mother's sister, whom Mother always referred to as "poor Clare." Even as a little girl I could sense that Clare laughed too hard when Daddy told a joke, almost as if she wanted Daddy to fall in love with her. Probably she was just flirting by proxy. (And she wasn't a lesbian, Caroline. I know that's usually your first guess about these things but trust me on this one.)

I did not want to become Clare. I did not want to be left behind as Tiny and all of the other girls I knew became women. That was the trick: to be a woman you had to marry a man. Otherwise you were a girl forever.

I cried for days. Not straight through, of course. And not during the few dates that Tiny set me up to go on. But when I was home, at my apartment, I would cry and cry until I was all worn out and then I would be okay for a few hours and then I would start crying again. I cried every time I took a shower, the hot water washing the tears off my face. Tiny would rub my back each night and even though I had usually stopped crying by then I would wake up in the morning with red, puffy eyes.

Caroline, I never told you what a mess I was. Maybe I should have. Maybe I should have told you so that you wouldn't have felt like such a mess yourself during the hard times in your life. Instead I tried to make you so presentable that no one would ever turn you away. I wiped the dirt off your chin, yanked the hair out of your mouth, scolded you for getting a grass stain on your new white dress.

When I told you the story of John Henry's and my temporary breakup, I made it sound as if I was made beautiful by grief. As if my cheeks glowed pink and my lashes grew long and shiny, nourished by all the tears I had cried. The first time I told that story to you was when you were fifteen, a sophomore in high school, devastated because some sorry boy you liked didn't want you as his girlfriend.

Do you remember that afternoon? It was the first hot day of spring and we were in the pool, floating on those clear plastic rafts with the silver base that reflected the sun. You had covered yourself in baby oil and I resisted telling you to put on sunscreen.

We were getting along that afternoon and I did not want to disturb the peace.

And maybe because I didn't, maybe because I just floated along on my raft enjoying the day, you confided in me about Hugh Strokes, who was a senior at Coventry and had asked you on several dates before telling you that he wasn't looking to get involved with anyone because he would be leaving soon for college. He had broken your heart, which struck me as a real waste considering I had known Hugh's daddy, Hugh Senior, for a long time. He was a grossly obese man who owned a chain of carpet stores. I had met him when I was in college, on a trip with John Henry to visit Wallace at UGA. He had been in Wallace's pledge class. He was fat even then, throwing lawn chairs for sport in front of the Chi Psi house.

I knew you could do better, so I told you to brush it off, to be blasé, to date other people. "Your going out with other boys will only make him want you more," I told you. But what I was thinking was that once you dated other boys you would no longer want Hugh Jr.

"Shrug him off," I said. "Like I did with your daddy."

And then I proceeded to tell you Tiny's story as if it were my own.

I'M NOT SURE if I should tell you this next part. It hardly seems relevant anymore, except that it's a piece of my history. In your letter you said that it was your wish to know me as a woman, and not just as your mother.

So here it is, your granted wish: I did not shrug off your father's rejection, but I did stop grieving it. The reason was that I fell in love with another man.

Caroline, please don't share this at the bridesmaids' luncheon. It's a story just for you, a story I should have told you when you were still a girl, so that you would know that a breakup doesn't signify the end of the world. So you would know that our hearts are resilient and capable of change. Of course it used to seem that you knew that without me having to tell you. I saw the way you put your life back together, first after you moved to San Francisco, and then after Frederick moved to New York. I listened to you tell me about all of the boys you dated out there. You never seemed to worry about finding one man to settle down with. You were so filled by your own ambition, your own energy. If I had been asked to make a prediction, I would have guessed that you would have remained wild and free your whole life.

I would have been wrong. And as a bride-to-be you are naturally in a conservative phase of life. I don't mean Republican—I know that you are as upset about this last election as I am—I mean traditional. Weddings bring out nostalgia for all things family-oriented and wholesome. Brides start valuing china and children and engraved invitations. (Knowing this I shouldn't have been surprised when you told me you were going to take Davis's name. I shouldn't have been surprised and yet I was. From your senior year of high school all the way until the summer you introduced us to Davis, how many lectures did you give me about the importance of women's identity, about the importance of not being swallowed up by a man? And now you tell me that Caroline Parker is going to become Mrs. Davis Hamilton? Well—I didn't expect it. That's all.)

IT WAS DURING your father's and my "time off" that I met Ben. Benjamin Ascher. Ben and I were in a music class together, the History of Jazz, otherwise known as "Listening for A's." Ben, however, was a musician and took the class seriously. He took all of his classes seriously; he was attending UNC on a Morehead scholarship, having turned down both Yale and Harvard because he didn't like the cold. Growing up in New Jersey had taught him to hate northeastern winters.

He played piano. He was in two different bands, the UNC jazz quartet and Portnoy, a band he had formed with a group of friends. They were a good enough group that the fraternities used to hire them to play at their parties. I had noticed Ben, way before I ever met him, performing at a Phi Delt mixer. Actually, I might not have noticed him had John Henry not made a joke about Ben's hair, which grew in tight curls into a sort of halo around his head. You can imagine the sort of joke your father made.

Ben was so skinny I could circle his waist with my hands and my fingers would almost touch end-to-end. He was a serious sort of person in a lot of ways, a double major in art history and philosophy, but he had a whimsical, silly side. You would have loved him. His favorite topic was "the real obscenities." It wasn't until years later when I read *Armies of the Night* (at your urging!) that I realized Ben had borrowed a lot from Norman Mailer. But back then, I had never before heard such ideas and thought that all of his were original. To Ben the bombing of villages in Vietnam was a real obscenity while language, no matter how off-color, was not. Whenever he used the f-word, I would suggest to him that it was possible to be obscene in both big and small ways, that the word *fuck* wasn't what ended the war in Vietnam.

"Maybe not," he said. "But it's still fun to rattle people's cages."

Ben, in fact, was the first person I knew who had taken part in protests against the war. I mean you couldn't escape the hippies and the activists strewn about campus, but I didn't know any of them personally. Surely some of the boys in John Henry's fraternity were opposed to the war, but not John Henry's friends. They were all quite militaristic even though none of them went over there to serve. As for Tiny and me, the only way the counterculture really influenced us was we wore bell-bottoms and stopped curling our hair.

Sometimes I wonder how different your childhood would

have been if Ben had been your father. Genetically speaking, of course, you wouldn't have been you—but if he and I had gotten married and had a child, she would have had some of your characteristics. Ben would have been a wonderful father. Attentive and supportive and with you every step of the way, even during the scary teenage years. I'm not saying that John Henry was a bad father—he certainly adored his little girl—but I think it's fair to say that he is a limited man. We both know that. You can't grow up with Nanny Rose for a mother and Wallace for a brother and not be scarred.

I was walking out of our History of Jazz class when Ben called after me. He liked what I had said in class about the similarity between writing formal poetry and playing jazz standards, that the shape for both was in place but the inside needed filling. He asked if I wrote poetry and I told him no, that I had just read a lot of it because I was an English major. He wanted me to teach him different forms of poetry: the sonnet, the villanelle, the sestina. I was pretty sure that he knew the sonnet form—back then most people knew those things—but I was flattered that this boy who was clearly the smartest person in the room had noticed what I'd said. Plus, that afternoon I had been feeling particularly overwhelmed by my single status and had been planning to go home and cry. Going to get a cup of coffee sounded like a better idea.

At the Carolina Coffee Shop we ate pancakes and talked about poetry. It soon became obvious that Ben knew more about it than I did, that he read it for pleasure while I simply read whatever my professors assigned. He suggested I read Gwendolyn Brooks, who at the time I'd never heard of. We got to talking about other books, our favorite books, and I told him that mine was *All the King's Men*. He paused for a moment with a funny look on his face and then said that was his favorite as well, which surprised me because I thought of it as such a southern book. (My father, in fact, always reminded me of Willie Stark, but I didn't get into that with Ben. Not that afternoon.)

He asked if I wanted to go on a walk. Eventually we made our way to the arboretum, where John Henry and I had first kissed three years before, on a spring night when the air was so warm it felt like swimming to walk through it.

Ben and I did not kiss that afternoon. We looked at plants. He noticed things, a beetle crawling on a leaf, a robin high up in a tree, the way a particular shadow hit the ground.

It became our pattern: coffee and then a walk, only after that first walk Ben was always venturing deeper and deeper into unfamiliar neighborhoods, streets with rusted cars parked in the yards and tiny houses, their sinking porches crowded with black people, old and young. Ben would whistle while he walked and wave to people on their porches. Some waved back, some stared at him like they wanted to ask just exactly what did he think he was doing walking over there?

I had always been uncomfortable in black neighborhoods— sorry, darling—but with Ben I wasn't. It wasn't that he was some hulking man or anything; it was that nothing ever quite felt real with him. It just didn't make any sense that I would be spending my time with this Jewish Yankee who wasn't in a fraternity and hadn't been a Boy Scout and in fact seemed to dislike most athletics besides baseball. He was unlike any male I'd ever known, and around him I was a different person than I knew myself to be. Ben was always laughing at things I said, not patronizingly, but laughing in real amusement. You and your father like to tease me for having no wit, but my wit was one of the things Ben liked best about me.

But there was another reason why things never felt quite real with Ben and that was because I knew, from the very beginning, that he and I could never get married. There just wasn't much mixing and matching between Jews and Protestants back then, at least not in North Carolina, not for a girl in Chi O. We were just so ignorant. There was this girl, Margaret Bath, who was also from Atlanta. She had gone to Lovett. She was Protestant, Episcopalian I think, or maybe Presbyterian. One or the other. Sophomore year her daddy put her on a strict allowance after she spent $500 at Saks during a trip to New York, and because of her new budget and consequent stinginess, we all started calling her Margaret Bathberg. As if that was funny.

It cut both ways too. Ben told me that when he left for Chapel Hill his mother made him promise her two things: that he would go to Hillel, and that he would not bring home a *shiksa* for her to meet. (Of course Ben had to explain to me what a *shiksa* was. "A Jewish mother's worst nightmare," he said.)

Maybe he would have defied her. He certainly had the gumption to do so, but I didn't want to have a mother-in-law who didn't want me. It would have all been so complicated. Daddy would have refused—refused—to pay for the wedding. He wouldn't have even attended it. Daddy was a segregationist through and through, and that didn't just apply to whites and blacks.

DURING THE TIME that Ben and I dated, I felt as if I were split into two selves. When I was with him—even though I knew there was no future between us—I was buoyant and hopeful, but as soon as he dropped me off and I was alone, away from him, I lost all my energy and I would mope around the apartment and sometimes cry. What a pitiful girl I was. Tiny tried to remind me that I had only dated Ben to make John Henry jealous in the first place. And there was some truth in that. After your father and I broke up but before I met Ben, I took any date Tiny could find for me, hoping to run into John Henry while I was in the middle of a good laugh with one of his fraternity brothers. Hoping to make him jealous enough to want me.

I never slept with Ben. I knew that if I did I wouldn't be able to say good-bye to him. But we would kiss for hours and hours on the front porch of the house he rented with his bandmates on McCauley Street. I still remember that. But even more so, I remember our talks. I remember how, talking to him, I felt such a sense of connection that for the first time in years, since I was a girl, I wondered if there might really be a God. Ben and Tiny were the only two people who I ever felt actually listened to me. If I ever tried to have an opinion around Daddy he dismissed it as naïve, and John Henry just seemed distracted when I talked.

Ben saw the world as wide open and was shocked to learn that I had no plans for after graduation. "But you're so smart," he would say. We made a list of things I might do: get a PhD in English, join the Peace Corps (his idea), move to New York City (mine). Because he was a Morehead scholar he had all sorts of connections. And even though I wasn't sure I wanted to do any of the things he suggested, the fact that there were options made me start thinking, for the first time, about what I might like to do besides care for a husband and children.

(Don't get me wrong, Caroline. I don't mean to imply that nurturing a family is in any way a secondary or inferior thing to do, but perhaps doing so should have felt more like a choice and less like a mandate for me. I mean, my God. I was twenty-one years old and ready to pledge allegiance to one man for the rest of my life. And what did I know about commitment and compromise? All I knew of married life was a cliché from television: my husband would return home at the end of the day and I would be waiting at the front door, eager to kiss him on the lips. And why I thought that, given the state of my parents' own marriage, I will never know.)

IT TOOK ME by surprise when John Henry finally called. I always said it was shortly after we broke up, but really, it had been months. He called right before Chapel Hill let out for Christmas break. It was two in the morning. I assumed he was drunk. He had been every time I'd run into him at a party after we broke up. Drunk and with his arm wrapped around a different girl each night. I started to tell him to call me back once he sobered up, but he cried out, "Wait. Just wait. I'm stone-cold sober. I just . . ."

In that moment while he choked back a sob, I felt my skin prickle and I knew that my life was about to change.

And then your father told me that Wallace, his twin, had shot himself in the head.

I won't go into the details. You know them already.

JOHN HENRY WANTED to drive home to Atlanta that night (morning, really) but I convinced him to come to our apartment instead. He was a mess at my front door, broken, hunching his shoulders like a boy in trouble. Tiny was out, sleeping at Anders's. I was wearing a white cotton nightgown and when he stepped inside the apartment he backed me against the wall and wrapped his arms around my middle, got down on his knees, and wept until my nightgown stuck to my skin.

Later, in bed, it was as if our months apart were a fantasy, some other life that I had accidentally stepped into, before finding my way back into the real. He smelled the same, like Ivory soap and bourbon.

WE TRIED TO sleep in anticipation of the long drive to Atlanta the next day, but neither of us did. We didn't talk either, just held each other and cried. It was impossible that Wallace was dead. Impossible that John Henry's twin would put a bullet in his brain. Impossible, except for all the signs. Wallace's expulsion from two boarding schools, the coma he went into his freshman year at Georgia after downing two bottles of bourbon, the money he would borrow from John Henry, with no explanation as to what it was for. I wondered who would clean up his apartment. I wondered if we would need to go to Athens and do it ourselves. We left the next morning at 6 a.m., exhausted and unwashed. There was no discussion of whether or not I would go with him. Of course I would.

BEN AND I had plans to go to a movie the night after John Henry and I left for Atlanta. He showed up at my apartment and Tiny told him what had happened. He sent flowers, roses, but they had turned brown and limp by the time I returned to Chapel Hill a week later to take my final exams. He came by our apartment the first night I got back. He was always so happy to see me; he would run up the porch stairs to get to the front door. I always made him ring the bell. I liked the excitement of opening the door and seeing him, allowing him inside.

That night I waited for him on the front porch after he called to say he was coming by. He walked up the steps and when he saw me, on the swing, he smiled. I couldn't talk. I started to cry. He thought I was crying out of grief, grief for Wallace. He tried to comfort me, but I could not be comforted. Not by him. Your father and I were already engaged. That was why I was crying. Your father proposed to me the night of Wallace's funeral. He needed me to stand beside him, to hold his hand, to hold it together for him, to make things nice. He was the last Parker, now that Wallace was gone. He needed me fiercely, and I loved feeling needed, feeling as if he couldn't get through the months after Wallace's death without me. Also I worried that maybe he had inherited some of Wallace's bad genes. They were, after all, identical twins, the same egg split in half. If I refused to marry him, might he put a bullet through his own brain? It didn't seem possible, not John Henry, who was nothing if not rational and calm. But in the days following Wallace's funeral, I saw your father break.

The next year, on the day of our wedding, I cried down the aisle, thinking of Ben. And the minister, the man who married John Henry and me, looked at me, and said, "It's wonderful these days to see a young person taking her wedding vows seriously. . . ."

November 16, 2004
Dear Caroline,

I am so sorry it has taken me so long to respond to your sweet letter. Ever since I received it I have been meaning to sit down and write out the story you asked for, but there has just been so much going on around here I have not had a spare minute! Most distracting has been the home improvement project that we are in the middle of—replacing *all* of the toilets. We should have done it years ago, but we knew how expensive it would be and how much of a mess it would cause. Last week we reached our tipping point when the toilet in Charles's bathroom overflowed *five* times in one day! I felt as if the plagues were upon us.

It will be a relief to have the new plumbing, but as for now, there is a team of workmen at the house from morning until night. I don't mind their company of course but the crew manager, Rodriguez, *loves* to talk. Not that I'm complaining—he's as sweet as he can be and has such fascinating stories about growing up in Guatemala—but it has gotten so that I spend so much time talking with him that the day goes by without me getting around to any of my work.

Not that writing to you feels like work! I'm thrilled to have the chance to record your daddy's and my engagement story. It's something I should have done a long time ago so that when I'm an old senile woman I'll be able to look up my memories. Your daddy and I are also just *thrilled* that you and Davis have definitely decided to have the wedding in Atlanta. And I think it is going to be just perfect to have the ceremony at our house and then have everyone walk over to the Driving Club for the reception. Of course we might want to hire a shuttle or two just to transport any old or feeble guests.

Did you ever meet Tiny's darling little gardener, Nancy? Well, I managed to book her after Tiny moved to Sea Island, which is no small feat. Nancy has a waitlist a mile long, and there I was, jumping to the top of it. But you know how Tiny is. When she puts her mind to something, it gets done, and Tiny wanted me to have Nancy for your wedding.

Nancy and I have been thick as thieves plotting the design of the back garden for the wedding. She is going to dig up all the bulbs from last fall and plant a new collection of only white flowers, all timed to bloom for the big event! Can you imagine how stunning it will look? And we are going to start a vine of jasmine over the stone archway that leads into the garden. It will work perfectly for the wedding party to make its entrance under-neath the arch. Gives me goose bumps just thinking about it!

I could go on and on about how lovely your ceremony is going to be. But I guess I should get down to business and give you that story you've been asking for! Of course, by now you've probably heard it so many times you could write it yourself, but here goes: It was the fall of my senior year at Chapel Hill. Your daddy was also a senior and was in the middle of filling out his law school applications. Tiny, whom I was sharing an apartment with (our first apartment ever, we had lived before in the dorms and then in the Chi O house), had gotten engaged to Anders just a few weeks back. He had given her a beautiful ring that had belonged to his grandmother. Though it was as simple as could be and only had a teeny little stone (he later upgraded the diamond), it looked so beautiful on Tiny's hand that I noticed it always.

I thought that your daddy and I were headed in the same

direction as Tiny and Anders. We had been dating for over two years, we were in love, and we were about to graduate. Back then, those things spelled e-n-g-a-g-e-m-e-n-t, so much so that anytime John Henry took me to a halfway decent restaurant I became convinced that he was going to pull a ring box out of his pocket. I mean, over half the girls from my pledge class were already engaged! Honey, I was behind.

Unfortunately, your daddy had other plans. Plans of independence.

One night your daddy and I were listening to records at his fraternity house when he said that he had something serious to discuss with me. My heart started beating faster and my hands started to sweat. *This is it,* I told myself. But instead of asking me if I would be his wife, your daddy asked me—or rather, informed me—that he thought we might ought to date other people, seeing as how it was our senior year and the last time we would be able "to play the field."

I wanted to die. I was so embarrassed that I thought he was going to propose and instead he was breaking up with me! But instead of crying or getting all upset about it, I channeled Tiny. I squared my shoulders, tossed back my hair, and said, "Sounds like a plan." I knew that was just what she would do.

Your daddy looked a little stunned, but then he coughed and said, "Okay then." I went home and told Tiny all about it. She reminded me of how Anders had put her through the exact same thing.

"You," she said, brushing my hair out of my eyes with her hand, "are going to do exactly what I did and go on a date every night until John Henry becomes so jealous he comes to his senses and proposes."

IN THE BEGINNING Tiny and my sorority sisters had to set me up with dates. But once the word got out that I was free and available, well, boys just kept calling me up on their own! I went on so many dates that my sorority sisters nicknamed me "date girl." Your poor daddy. I don't know how many times he ran into me out with another fellow. Once I was even out with one of his fraternity brothers! Well, this went on for a little while, up until the time I ran into your daddy at an afternoon football game. I was on a date (of course!) and he was there with his roommates. As luck would have it, our seats were right next to his. Oh Caroline, you should have seen his face when I made my way down the aisle he was sitting in with my Saturday date.

Poor John Henry. He had brought a little flask of bourbon with him to the game and he kept mixing himself bourbon and ginger ales. That was his all-time favorite drink back then. Honey, by the time halftime rolled around, your daddy was drunker than I had ever seen him. He was three sheets to the wind, totally and absolutely schnookered.

And it was during halftime that he came stumbling up to where I was sitting with date #551 and plopped right down next to me. When he put his head on my shoulder I had to use every ounce of strength I had not to put my arm around him. But I resisted. I had decided that I was not going to go back to him until he could offer me a firm commitment.

Finally he turned his head so that he was looking at me, his breath soaked with alcohol.

"Louise," he said, "I don't think this dating other people thing is such a good idea."

Oh how I wanted to jump up and do a victory dance, to run in circles and holler like a madwoman! Instead, I kept my cool. I even found it within me to flick back my hair before answering, "Fine by me. Sounds like a plan."

A week later he officially proposed. Which really was good timing considering what would soon happen to Wallace. He needed me to help him get through all that.

• • •

I HOPE THAT if they hear this story Davis's parents won't be too shocked by what a trickster I was! But maybe they should be warned early of the ways of southern women—after all, they're going to have one for a daughter-in-law!

Just teasing. Don't read that last part aloud if you are planning to read this at the bridesmaids' luncheon or the rehearsal dinner. And do call me when you get this. I want to talk to you about menus for the reception. You would not believe how sophisticated the food has become at the Driving Club. I'm afraid Nanny Rose might not recognize half of what she's served!

Love you,
Mom

CHAPTER SEVENTEEN

The Inevitable Occurs

(Louise, Winter 2005)

*G*ood Lord. What that poor child is going to do with a baby, I don't know. If she hadn't been raised in such a narrow, narrow church the fact that she is pregnant would not necessarily mean that her life is ruined. And even her mother, a member of that church, agrees that abortion is the best solution. When I called Faye to see if Missy had accepted my offer to pay for one, Faye said that when she suggested terminating the pregnancy Missy looked at her like she had suggested she abort Christ Jesus himself.

It seems that the man who got Missy pregnant did not ejaculate inside her, and so Missy has convinced herself that because they did not technically have sex, but instead his semen seeped through her underwear and up into her while they were, well, humping without penetration, that God has destined this child to be born. Faye said she wanted to slap her child's face when Missy told her that this was God's baby.

"You think God's going to pay for its diapers?" she asked me (as if I needed convincing). "You think God's going to be the one who has to drop out of school and take care of it?"

John Henry and I will help out, of course, though frankly, Missy's pregnancy is coming at a bad time for us financially. We've got Caroline's wedding this spring *and* we'll have Charles's college tuition next fall, which depending on where he is accepted might be even more expensive than tuition at Coventry, if you can believe it. Not to mention the fact that we had to redo *all* of the ancient plumbing in our house, which cost a fortune.

But obviously I feel somewhat responsible for Missy having gotten herself involved with that horrible man considering it was Charles, my son, who literally drove Missy to him. What was he thinking taking her to North Carolina like he did, not stopping for one minute to consider how Faye would feel when she discovered Missy was gone, let alone how Missy would feel upon encountering her father after so many years of absence? And how about how John Henry and I would feel—did feel!—when we were told, by our housekeeper, months after the fact, that all this had happened while we were away on vacation?

Charles wasn't thinking, that's the answer, and really, how can I blame him? We all make foolish choices. It was a foolish choice on my part to hire Faye in the first place. I should never have let Mother talk me into it. I knew it was a messy situation, I knew I should have stayed out of it, but Mother was so adamant and I was so busy with Charles and Caroline, who were then five and ten, that I acquiesced as I always seemed to do with my parents and said sure, I could use the extra help.

Talk about foolish. Who hires the daughter-in-law of a woman who years ago had an affair with your father?

Of course everything is more complicated than it first appears. Thinking back on my decision to hire Faye all those years ago, it seems to me that I must have been unduly influenced by the fact that Mother was so much better. It must have somehow affected my sense of possibility. Just imagine: after a lifetime of crippling mental illness, one of Mother's doctors said that he had a new drug that might help alleviate her depression. The drug was Prozac, and after she was on it two months Mother's moods stabilized and she became, for the most part, a normal, functioning adult. Mother's change must have turned me into an optimist. I thought that if Mother could be fixed, any situation could be.

The call from Mother about Faye came on an unusually peaceful summer afternoon. Charles was taking his nap while Caroline watched TV downstairs in the sunporch. I was in John Henry's and my room, folding clothes. (That is one of the main memories I have of Caroline and Charles's childhood: me folding laundry. That and having to drive them places constantly.)

The phone rang, and when I picked it up, it was Mother, sounding so excited, so hyper, that for a moment, I worried that she might have skipped a dose of her medication or perhaps taken too much of it.

"You will not believe who I bumped into at Sam's Club," she said.

"Sam Walt—"

She interrupted my joke. "Winnie Meadows. Can you believe that? Winnie Meadows."

"Who?" I asked.

"Winnie Meadows. You remember her. The lady who came over to our house once when you were a little girl. She gave me a necklace. How could you forget?"

Of course, of course, I remembered, it just had been so long since I heard her name that it took me a moment to place it. Winnie Meadows. Miss Winnie, the pretty woman who visited our house *twice* when I was little, once to see Daddy and once to see Mother. I remembered too the necklace she brought

Mother, though I hadn't seen Mother wear it since Daddy's death. She wore it every day until then, despite the fact that Daddy despised it.

"I didn't realize you two were still in touch."

"Winnie and I haven't been in touch, not at all. I haven't seen her since that day at our house, thirty-some-odd years ago. Our meeting today was entirely providential. There I was at Sam's Club, making my way down the aisle, when I practically collided into her, her shopping cart loaded with cleaning supplies and her cute-as-a-button granddaughter riding up top. I was only picking up a few things, some Co-Cola and toothpaste and toilet paper, and I had just started down the detergent aisle to get my Cascade, and there she was."

Mother could have survived a nuclear attack with all the bulk goods she kept in her condo. Besides the closets and pantry packed tight with nonperishables, I once discovered eight cases of canned peaches under her bed, at which point I wondered if Prozac had really cured her of her craziness at all.

"Are you sure it was her? I mean, it's been a long time."

"You think I wouldn't recognize her? Her face certainly looks a little run over, but it was Winnie all right. Same dark eyes, same cheekbones. Even thinner than she was thirty years ago, if you can believe that."

"Did you talk? Did she know that Daddy died?"

It was only after Daddy made a pass at one of my sorority sisters, Melissa Reynolds, during parents' weekend sophomore year at Chapel Hill, that I put two and two together about Miss Winnie. *Of course,* I thought, sipping my third Bloody Mary at the Phi Delt pregame party while trying to avoid both Daddy and Melissa, *that woman and Daddy slept together. That was why she kept showing up at the house. They had been having an affair.*

"Why would she know anything about your father? She had no contact with him."

"She could have read his obituary in the newspaper. They ran a big enough one."

"Louise, forget about her connection with Ernie. What happened between the two of them—that's ancient history. It doesn't even matter. What's important is, I saw her again. And listen, Louise, I think I willed our meeting into being. That or it was, I don't know, divine intervention. I mean, ever since I've been better, I haven't been able to stop thinking about her, wondering how she's doing, wishing I could tell her thank you for the kindness she showed me. And there she was! Just as real as day, looking over the boxes of dishwashing detergent."

"Mother, she had an affair with your husband. That's not kind."

That was the first time I had ever spoken directly with Mother about one of Daddy's affairs and it made my heart beat faster just to acknowledge that yes, it had happened. They had happened.

"Louise, you know I forgave her for that. The day she came to me, I forgave her. And I'll tell you why: during all that time when I was not myself, when I was suffering so terribly, she was the only person who treated me with compassion, who treated me like a human being."

I tried not to let it hurt my feelings that Mother didn't include me as someone who treated her like a human being during those years. But then again, how could I have? I was a child. To me, Mother was beyond human, she was a discontented god whom I was forever trying to please. Besides which, Mother was being dramatic, a trait she was known for (and a trait which my daughter surely inherited). Miss Winnie could not have been the only person who showed her kindness; there must have been a nurse at one of Mother's hospitals who treated her well.

"Anyway, I called to tell you about the difficulties Winnie and her family are facing. Winnie's husband, the preacher—he died last year. They'd been married for over thirty years and now he's gone. Then just last month, her only son, who was living at her house along with the rest of his family, he just up and left, abandoning his wife and child, *and* mother, leaving nothing but a note saying they were better off without him. But of course his leaving means they no longer have his paycheck, small as it probably was, so obviously they're *not* better off without him."

"Mother, how much money did you give her?" I asked. Mother was always giving away her money. Thank God Daddy established a trust fund for me or she would have given away all my money too.

"I didn't give her money, I gave her a job. I told her that you would hire her daughter-in-law, Faye, as your housekeeper."

"Are you crazy?" I asked, stepping into my own joke. Yes, she was crazy. Certified by a multitude of doctors.

"I am compassionate," she said, her voice icy. "I am showing compassion for a twenty-one-year-old woman with a four-year-old to support and no husband to help with the bills."

"Hire her yourself, then," I said. "Surely your condo needs a maid as much as my house does."

Right after Daddy died, Mother sold the house I grew up in, declaring that owning a grand old home had always been Daddy's vision and not hers and that, frankly, she was tired of all the maintenance the house on the Prado required.

"Sofie already comes twice a week," she said. "I can't have somebody in my home more often than that."

"Then have Sofie come once a week and have Winnie's daughter-in-law come the other day."

"Poor Sofie already lives paycheck to paycheck! I can't cut back on her hours."

"Mother, I already have a housekeeper too, remember? Remember Sandy?"

"Yes, but Rose Parker pays for her so it's not as if you've exhausted your household budget. Please, darling, just hire Faye once a week, and if she's good at what she does, give her number to Tiny and the other girls you're friends with and in no time at all she will have a full schedule."

"What if she's no good?" I asked.

There was a pause.

"She'll be good, Louise, believe me."

"Oh, Mother."

She began to tell me again about all the misfortune Winnie and her daughter-in-law were facing, misfortune that she somehow believed I could take away if only I allowed Faye to clean for me.

That was the thing about Mother. Despite a life that usually pointed to the contrary, she had faith that there was hope in every human interaction. It was the dormant Catholic in her, though she became an Episcopalian when she married Daddy. Still, she retained her Catholic worldview, to the point of reminding me of that woman in *Grey Gardens*, the crazy one—well, they were both crazy—who left Wonder bread in her attic so that the raccoons who lived up there wouldn't starve.

When I was growing up, Mother was similarly tenderhearted toward animals. She never killed the spiders that built webs on our front porch (she would stand for what seemed like hours marveling at a single web), and consequently our house was infested every spring. She fed stray cats, who would then leave presents of dead mice and voles for us on the front steps. That would drive Daddy absolutely crazy; after all, he was the one who had to dispose of their carcasses, too upsetting were they for Mother to handle. What most infuriated Daddy was when she would reach her hand through our neighbor's fence to pet their German shepherd, who was often left outside alone on a chain. Even after she was bit, she continued to do it.

("He must have thought I was an intruder," she said, while Daddy bandaged her mauled hand. "Poor thing.")

Again and again Mother defended her actions by claiming it was the Catholic in her that made her do it. Daddy said that she acted the way she did not out of any Catholic reverence for life but out of a childish foolishness. Of course, my father thought that religion, for the most part, *was* childish foolishness, so I'm not sure why he needed to make the distinction between the two. Though he attended church, he was skeptical of all faiths that involved more commitment than a monthly check and the recitation of the Apostles' Creed. He used to joke that if the meek inherited the earth it would only take ten minutes for the strong to get it back.

Mother talked on and on about Winnie and her daughter-in-law's troubles while I folded the last few pieces of clothing left in the basket.

"It's not as if this girl has had every advantage in the world like you. She's only twenty-one, poor as a church mouse, and hardworking. I just don't see what harm it's going to do you to hire her."

"It's odd, that's all," I said, wishing my voice didn't sound so prim. "Admit that it's a little odd."

"I don't see why. Winnie will stay at home and look after her granddaughter, so you won't have to worry about Faye canceling on you because of childcare problems."

"That's not what I'm worried about," I said.

"Louise, I will pay for this woman to come clean your house. What more can I offer?"

There it was, dangling in front of me, mine for the taking, a service that would help me out tremendously—I had two children to care for, after all, and Sandy did only come once a week—despite the inherent strangeness of the situation.

Quickly, I rationalized: This was a young woman, who had absolutely nothing to do with Daddy, who needed work. Her mother-in-law, who just happened to have crossed my family's path many years before, happened to have crossed our path once again. And it was fortunate she did: the girl needed help and I needed help. (I had so much laundry to fold!)

In retrospect, I should have waited a day or two to make my decision. I should have hung up the phone and thought it over. But despite the fact that Mother often drove me up the wall, there was a part of me that was as desperate to please her as I had been when I was a little girl. There was a part of me that worried that if I refused her generosity, she might never be generous with me again. She might once again recede into herself.

"Okay," I said. "I'll hire her. I mean, I'll let you hire her for me. Okay?"

"Oh I am so glad, Louise! This is going to mean so much to Winnie's family, it really is. And it will help you out too. I know it will!"

Faye never was that good a housecleaner. Certainly not compared to Sandy. And her daughter, much as I adored her, was trouble from the beginning. But I tried with Missy, I really did. I tried to reach out to her, to show her that it was possible to have a worldview uncorrupted by fundamentalism. During that talk I had with her after she stole my bird, I told her that I would give her five thousand dollars if she graduated from high school. You see, it seemed to me that she took the bird because she was attracted to nice things, and I decided to use that attraction to try and encourage her to work for a better life for herself.

But let's face it. The formula is pretty much already set: if your mother had you when she was very young, you'll get pregnant when you are young too. Add those inane virginity pledges into the mix and you're pretty much guaranteed a spate of teen moms. That's the horrible irony about those pledges, isn't it? The kids feel so bad about breaking their promises when they are about to have sex that they don't use any protection, because at least then they didn't *plan* to sin. Lord help us all.

I spoke with Caroline about the situation this morning. Not about our family's distant connection to Winnie—I've never gone into that with her—but about Missy's pregnancy.

"I offered to pay for an abortion," I said.

"She's going to have one?" asked Caroline, sounding surprised.

"She's not. It's a shame, but she's not."

Caroline was silent.

"Don't tell me, you think she should have the baby?" I asked.

"She should if that's what she thinks is right. It's her body, her choice."

"It won't be her body for long," I said. "When you have a child, your body is no longer your own."

"I know, Mom," she said. "Believe me, you've made the difficulty of child rearing abundantly clear."

Well. That stung a little. I've just always tried to be honest with Caroline. I haven't wanted to set her up with false expectations like I had. It never occurred to me that she might be offended to know that child rearing was not a walk in the park.

She'll understand once she has one of her own.

CHAPTER EIGHTEEN

Body and Soul

(Caroline, Spring 2006)

I feel such affection now, thinking back on Frederick. Which is a minor miracle given what a mess we were, from the drama of our exile to the drama of our life in San Francisco.

I'm proud of him now. So much prouder from a distance than I would have been had he succeeded near me. Ultimately, that was what blew us up. His relative success compared to mine. He had a BA in theater from Yale and consequently arrived out here with tons of connections to the San Francisco (and Berkeley) theater scene. Of *course* he was the one people recognized as the actor. Of course he was the one getting parts (albeit parts that paid little or no money). He would come home late from rehearsal, smelling of cigarettes and alcohol, and I would promise myself that I would throw my arms around him the minute he walked through the door, that I would make his homecoming a good thing. But after a lonely night brooding and drinking, more often than not when he walked through the door I picked, picked, picked until we fought, fought, fought. Once I saw that I had thoroughly exhausted him, had thoroughly beaten him down, I was ready to make up.

We had a few very bad months but then he got smart and applied for acting programs on the East Coast. He got into the best one, the MFA program at Tisch, and soon after he heard the congratulatory message left on our answering machine by the head of the program, he moved to New York.

(I was the first to hear the message and considered—briefly—erasing it before he came home.)

The day he sent in his deposit to Tisch, I smashed every wine glass on the floor—except for the two expensive ones Mom had given me. But things got so much better for me after Frederick moved away. I felt less embarrassed about the little productions I auditioned for, and because of my newfound confidence, I started getting callbacks and then parts. I enrolled at SF State and asked two friends of mine from my class to move into my apartment and take over Frederick's half of the lease. A year later I got a place of my own in the Mission. (When I called my father to ask if he could help me a little with the rent, he agreed so readily that I understood, maybe for the first time, unconditional love.) I started dating, realized I *could* have orgasms, that there had been something not quite clicking when Frederick and I had sex, that the buildup had always been more exciting than the actual event.

My first few years in San Francisco were all about discarding the things about me that bespoke my rich-girl background. It was a thrilling time because I thought I was becoming my true self. I thought that people in San Francisco had found their Eden, had discovered the key to authenticity. (Eat organic and boycott the Gap!)

I sold most of my cashmere sweaters (Mom's favorite gift to give) to Crossroads Trading Company, cut off all my hair (I did it myself one night after listening to too much Ani DiFranco and drinking too much beer). I discovered secondhand stores for work pants and T-shirts. I ate vegetarian (though I loved cheese too much to go vegan); I rode my bike all through the city, slapping my hand aggressively on the hoods of cars that blocked the crossing lane when they stopped for traffic lights.

"Asshole!" I would yell.

I felt, during that time, so buoyed by how far I had moved from my parents' world. I believed myself to be safe—saved—from the traps I saw adults, especially southern women, get stuck in. One night I went to a dyke bar with a friend and ended up meeting a woman there, Miriam, whom I dated briefly. On our first date, after dinner at Greens (her treat, at the time I had no money), we made out in the parking lot and then went back to her place in Oakland. She lived in the rear apartment on the third story of a converted Victorian and we had to walk up the rickety fire escape—all three flights—to get inside. It was thrilling making my way up those unfamiliar steps. At the top we could see the San Francisco skyline twinkling on the other side of the bay and there I was, in this place I'd never been before, not sure where to hold on, not sure where I was, and yet pulsing with the excitement of uncharted territory.

How liberating to have another woman's mouth against my vagina! Surely it meant that I would never have monogrammed towels or a subscription to *Southern Living*, let alone move back to Atlanta and join the Driving Club. And yet Miriam and I broke up after I had a series of dreams about living in a yellow house with a man and a baby. I didn't know—still don't know—if the dreams meant that deep down I was straight or deep down I was too scared of marginalization to let myself really enter a sexual relationship with a woman.

Soon after I broke up with Miriam, Davis came into the restaurant where I was waiting tables, asked me out, and precipitated my exile from the land of San Francisco cool kids. None of my friends liked Davis. Wait. That's not quite true. They liked that he would often treat at dinner; they liked that he would offer to drive people home after a play or a show; they liked that he always volunteered his apartment for cast parties. But they made fun of him behind his back, called him Pac-man (for Pacific Heights). Which he was. But also he was sexy and competent and had enough money to take me to Zuni every night of the week if I wanted to go. And after two years of eating vegetarian burritos and cheap Indian (and a few good meals with Miriam), it was wonderful to be so well treated.

I never intended to stop acting when I got married. I was only twenty-two, certainly not the age to retire. From the very beginning I told Davis that acting was my passion, my calling, that I would still do experimental theater, that I still would do nudity if the piece called for it.

"And I'm not going to stop watching football," he said. So we shook on it and I went on an audition the day we returned to San Francisco from our honeymoon in Fiji. But with each audition I went to, I found myself becoming more and more critical of the scripts, of the "siege the palace" tone of them. Is it simply that money corrupts? I had access to so much more of it now that I was with Davis. I had an ATM card to our joint checking account, restocked twice a month with deposits from his hefty salary.

Also, I had been unexpectedly affected by my father. When I described the plot of a play Davis and I had seen at the ACT as "just another piece about rich white people," he said, "Caroline, do the rich not bleed?"

It affected me, yes—His eye is on the sparrow, both fat and lean—but still I tried to defend my position.

"Sure they bleed. And when they do they act like they are the only ones who have ever hurt."

"My little Bolshevik," he said. "You are so much like your mother."

I was nothing like my mother.

I was so far away.

268 · Susan Rebecca White

I was getting fat. My mother would never have allowed herself to get fat. When I was in high school she once warned me about the few pounds I had put on my senior year. I told her that my body was my own, to keep her opinions about it to herself. She snapped that aesthetics were important to her, that it was important for her to be surrounded by pretty things. Including her daughter.

God.

It happened quickly, the weight. It was as if my body—which, since that talk with Mom, I had underfed—suddenly resisted and pushed itself out, claiming space it always wanted. My hips grew and soon none of my jeans or pants fit. Men would stare at my (newly rounded) ass while I waited for the N train. Davis teased, "Baby got back." (That was before he started eyeing me critically when I ordered dessert at a restaurant or put out cheese after dinner.) I thought what the hell, I'd go with it; it was sexy to be a little hippy. I started using butter when I cooked. I bought *The Gift of Southern Cooking* and learned to fry chicken after brining it for two days, first in salt water then in buttermilk. No butcher in San Francisco sold lard, so I fried the chicken in peanut oil instead. I made cheese straws with double the cheese and twice the cayenne pepper. I made Mom's brownies with the three kinds of chocolate. One rainy night I taught myself how to make the baked buttered saltines they serve at the Driving Club.

The fat piled on. Directors started asking me to audition for different sorts of parts, for the mother or the friend or (when I auditioned for Shakespeare at Stinson) the nurse. I was no longer ingenue material.

There was a group of women, all overweight, who called themselves Fat Positive Actresses and performed pieces that included only big women. I did not want to join their troupe. Not that I didn't think what they were doing was interesting, but God, I didn't see being fat as my mission in life. I did not feel a need to proselytize pounds. (And would I even qualify? I was padded and curvy but I did have a waist.) What I *was* interested in was learning how to cook a goose so I could render its fat to fry potatoes.

I read cookbooks at night the way I used to read novels. I dreamed of food. I figured that at some point I would join the gym and hire a personal trainer. Being fat would just be one of my many experiences, much as lesbianism had been.

What I didn't realize was, it was all leading up to something.

You see, it was necessary for me to lose my girl self, my lithe body, my ability to get parts that kept the audience's eyes riveted on me, all of their easy, superficial love anesthetizing my yearnings for something more.

He had been chasing me for years but my girl self could not be caught.

I had to be fattened before I was ready.

IN THE DREAM that changed everything I visited a church, dark and hidden within a foreign city. The pews were filled with young people, most of whom looked like girls I went to school with at Coventry. White, well dressed, pretty in an understated sort of way. There were a few gay boys in the corner pews and one radiant black girl in the center aisle.

The church was on its feet singing and the black girl's voice dominated. She was large and her voice seemed to swell in her body before she let it out of her mouth. We sang softer so we could hear her. Everyone pressed up against each other to get a little nearer her spirit.

And then it was later, another service, and I was at the church early. The pews were worn and scratched. One of the gay boys was at the church, his hair spiked the way Charles wore his the last time I saw him. He was thin, this boy. He seemed shy.

"Do you like it here?" I asked. "Do they accept you?"

"I like a challenge," he said.

I sat in the middle of the pews, hoping to be near the black girl. She came and sat in the pew in front of me. I could smell the oil in her braids. A group of girls wearing houndstooth coats came to the pew and glared at me. I was in one of their seats. I did not move, instead staring at the neck of the beautiful singer. And then people pushed in around me and suddenly we were up on our feet, singing. The minister came out, an Indian man with dark hair, and held above his head a garishly madeup baby doll with bright red cheeks and long gold earrings. And then we were moving, moving in a line up and down the aisles, worshipping and extolling the baby doll. I reached my hand out to touch the side of the pew and found it covered in something sticky. I looked down and saw that the pocket built into the back of the pews where the hymnals are kept was filled with dates and nuts and honey. I reached in and pulled out a handful. Everyone in the church was still moving and singing.

I knew, holding the honey, that I was not supposed to eat it. That the pastor was supposed to tell us how and when to do so. But I knew also that the honey and dates were gifts from God, that they were abundant, that they were here for the taking.

I lifted my hand to my mouth but woke up before tasting anything.

And so I hunger for Him still.

CHAPTER NINETEEN

You Can't Be a Fag and a Parker

(Louise, Spring 2006)

*J*ohn Henry and I are sitting in the library after supper when we hear the doorbell ring. We're not expecting anybody. We've settled in for the night, he in front of the TV and me with a lap full of catalogs to flip through. I consider not answering the bell. I don't know a soul who would drop by unannounced after dark; in fact, now that Tiny is gone, I don't know anyone who would drop by at all.

The doorbell rings again. John Henry shows no intention of moving from the sofa where he is stretched out, the newspaper crumpled on his lap, his hand holding the remote.

"I'd get it," I say, "but I'm worried it might be a burglar."

Without taking his eyes off the baseball game on TV he says, "I'll come rescue you if it's someone menacing."

Hmm. I'm willing to bet that if the Braves were about to hit a home run, John Henry would have a hard time pulling himself away from the game. Regardless of what was going on with me.

Finally I stand up and walk to the front door. Before opening it I ask, "Who is it?"

"It's me."

It sounds like Charles, but that's impossible because Charles is five hundred miles away in Chapel Hill, at college. Admittedly, his getting in there surprised us. His grades at Coventry, after all, were far from admirable. But his SAT scores were fabulous (he got a perfect score on verbal!), and he was a legacy going back to John Henry's granddaddy. And so, as with Caroline, I had to take back everything I had said about him not living up to potential, setting himself up for great disappointment in life, letting down his father and myself, etc., etc.

Probably my children should just ignore every word I say.

I open the door and lo and behold, there is Charles, a duffel bag slung over his shoulder as if he were on leave from the army.

"My God. Sweetheart, what are you doing here? Did something happen? Are you okay?"

"Surprise," he says.

John Henry comes up from behind me. "Who is it, Louise?" he asks, but he reaches the door before I have a chance to answer.

"Charles," he says.

"Hi, Dad."

"Gracious," I say. It still doesn't seem real that he is here, that I can reach out my hand and touch him. "When did you get here? How did you get here?"

"I drove."

Neither John Henry nor I move from the door frame.

I am thinking that something terrible must have happened. He must have flunked out of school or gotten a girl pregnant or—God help him—walked into his dorm room and found his roommate with his head shot off.

(It was Wallace's roommate, after all, who discovered him.)

"Um, folks, can I come in?" asks Charles. "This bag weighs, like, two hundred pounds."

"Oh honey, I'm sorry. We're just so surprised to see you. Come in! Come in!"

I step aside to make room for him to walk through the front hall. He drops his bag on the floor.

"God, I'm starving," he says. "I drove this whole way without stopping."

"You drove your car?" asks John Henry. "The Accord?"

"That's the only car I've got," says Charles.

"From Chapel Hill to here is a pretty far drive. Your lease only allows ten thousand miles a year, you know."

Oh good God.

"Come on, sweetheart," I say, trying to put my arm around Charles's shoulder but only reaching his upper arm. (Could he have grown even taller since the last time I saw him?) "Let's get you something to eat."

I reheat the leftover butternut squash soup from dinner and make Charles a piece of cheese toast, his favorite food from since he was a little boy. I sit at the table with him while he eats. I let him have a glass of wine from the open bottle of pinot gris. I know that something must be wrong for him to have come home so unexpectedly, but I am so enjoying the experience of sitting with my boy, watching him eat food that I prepared, that I just push all concern and worry right out of my mind.

"Darling, it's time."

John Henry clicks off the TV with a sigh and follows me into the living room with the slumped shoulders of a man being dragged somewhere he doesn't want to go.

"I don't understand this meeting," he says.

"Shush," I say. I don't know where Charles is and I don't want him to overhear his father's negativity. The living room doors—original pocket doors that slide to open—are perennially shut to guard against animal damage, even though our cat, who would have torn up the good furniture, died years ago.

John Henry and I sit on one of the living room sofas, directly across from the Earl LeTrouve portrait of the Drag Jesus. John Henry is jiggling his leg like crazy, which is what he always does when he is agitated. It probably doesn't help to have him facing the LeTrouve.

Charles walks into the living room just as the grandfather clock strikes seven. He is freshly showered, his hair still damp. There's no denying it. He has grown even taller this semester. He's taller now than his father. I look at my husband, and I look at my son, and I feel astonished to realize that they are *both* men.

Charles sits in the upholstered chair opposite our sofa. The expression on his face is as grim as his father's. The two of them look as if they are about to be shipped off to war.

John Henry, who brought the newspaper into the living room with him, continues reading it, even though we all are here for the meeting. I'm not entirely sure why he is being so hostile toward his son. Could he *still* be annoyed with Charles for refusing not only to pledge John Henry's fraternity but to join one at all?

"I just hate to think of all the networking he'll miss out on," John Henry had said.

"Um, Dad?" asks Charles. "Are you ready?"

John Henry holds up one finger, signifying, I suppose, that he needs a minute to finish reading his article.

"Put down the paper, dear," I say.

"Just let me finish this last line," says John Henry, stretching out the word *last* so he can sneak in more reading while he says it.

"Okay," he says. He puts the paper in his lap, close enough to him so that he can still read it if he looks down.

"Well?" says John Henry. "What's so important that you put five hundred superfluous miles on your Honda?"

Why my husband can't treat his own son with a little kindness, I will never know. John Henry's own father, Judge Parker, was always jovial. (Although to be fair, he was usually drunk.)

"Okay," says Charles, rubbing the palms of his hands on the thigh of his jeans. "There's something about me that I think you both should know. I just, I'm trying to be honest and I just, I just want to have an open relationship with you and so I thought you should know . . ."

A bead of sweat runs from his hairline down the side of his face.

And just like that, I do know.

Oh my Lord. I know what he is going to say.

What I can't figure out is why on earth I didn't guess it before.

I remember him as a little boy, how sweet and open he was, how he looked at me with such unbridled adoration. And then I remember him in middle school, too skinny, with dark circles under his eyes and no plans for the weekend. He was even more miserable in high school, his dark hair dyed platinum, his smirks and sarcasm, the tight T-shirts he wore with ironic captions, the way he would jerk away anytime I tried to lay a hand on his shoulder, as if he couldn't stand to be near me because he couldn't stand himself.

I squeeze his knee. "Honey, I think I know what you are going to say and I want you to know that your father and I always have and always will love you."

The tears in my eyes are about to spill over and run down my cheeks. I don't blink, trying to keep them in. I don't want Charles to think that I'm upset by his news.

Charles turns toward me with a look of such gratitude that I allow myself the pleasure of knowing that yes, at this crucial time, I have done right by my child.

Charles turns to his father and says, "I'm gay."

And then Charles starts crying, his shoulders shaking, wails coming from some choked place inside him that doesn't want to let the pain out.

He cried like this when he was a child, forgetting to breathe between sobs until he finally has to gasp for air, his mouth gaping like that of some wounded animal.

John Henry looks at the newspaper on his lap, his expression flat.

"Baby," I say, "we love you. And we are so glad you trusted us with this."

I look to my husband to confirm my statement. He is silent.

"Aren't we glad he trusted us with this?" I ask him.

John Henry stands, the newspaper falling from his lap onto the floor. "Is that all of your news?" he asks.

Charles and I just stare at him.

"Because if it is, I say we adjourn this meeting."

"What are you doing?" I ask.

Charles has not taken a breath since his father stood up.

"I'm going to watch the rest of the game," he says.

And then he walks out of the room.

SOMETHING ABOUT JOHN Henry's callousness seems to calm Charles. Perhaps the familiarity of it reminds him how to cope. He wipes his eyes and straightens his spine and says, "That could have been worse."

"I'm sorry," I say. "He'll come around."

Charles shrugs. "Maybe."

Suddenly I feel very awkward. I'm not sure what I'm supposed to do or say.

"Do you want something to drink?" I ask. "Some iced tea or a Coke or something? Or if you want a beer I'll get you a beer."

Does my son even drink beer? Fraternity boys drink beer. Gay men do what? Sip martinis?

"I could make us gimlets," he says. "They're fun."

My God. A gimlet?

"I don't even know what alcohol is in that."

"Gin," he says. "They're fabulous."

My son says "fabulous." My gay son says "fabulous." I have a gay son. I have a gay son who makes himself mixed drinks. Oh Lord. Am I one day going to be one of those blue-haired old ladies wearing ancient Armani who gets taken out to lunch at the Colonnade by her son and his partner?

I wonder if I should try and fix Charles up with Chevre.

CHARLES BRINGS ME a gimlet—in a chilled glass—and we sit in the living room together sipping our drinks. I have a hundred questions I want to ask, but I'm not sure which ones are appropriate and which are not.

"Maybe," I say, "your father and I can go to a PFLAG meeting."

Charles barks out a laugh. "Puh-flag," he says. "I'm *beginning* to like the sound of that."

As usual, I am on the outside of one of Charle's inside jokes, an inside joke he has with himself.

"You can go if you want," says Charles. "It will probably just be a bunch of mothers crying because their butch daughters refuse to be debutantes."

He's probably right. Bootsey Brook's daughter, Sally, shaved off all her hair after her first year at Hollins and brought some girl who looks just like a twelve-year-old boy home for Christmas break. Not that Bootsey went running off to a PFLAG meeting. She just insisted—even though Bootsey's house has countless bedrooms in it—that Sally and her "friend" stay at a hotel.

I take another sip of my gimlet. Charles must have stuck the martini glasses he's using into the freezer. It is frosty. The gimlet tastes more of gin than anything, but it's nice and cold and with every sip I feel more comfortable sitting here with him.

"I just have one question, sweetheart." (A lie. I have a thousand questions.) "Why did you decide you had to tell us this weekend? Why drive home so suddenly?"

Charles presses his lips together. "Do you want the truth or something more palatable?" he asks.

Oh Lord.

"I want the truth, of course," I say, not sure if I really do.

"I dropped out of school. I'm not going back to Chapel Hill."

I have no idea what to say to that. I am shocked, obviously. He can't drop out of school. I mean, is he even allowed to do that without our permission? I take a good long sip of my drink.

"Look," says Charles, talking fast. "It wasn't working for me, it really wasn't. Chapel Hill is cute but face it, it's a backwater. The big thing to do on the weekends is to go to frat parties and watch white kids dry hump to hip-hop."

It's funny to hear him say that: "dry hump." We used that term when we were in college, although it's certainly not something I would have said in front of my parents.

"Charles, you were only there for a semester and a half. I'm sure there are other groups besides the fraternities."

"Okay, let's see. There are the environmentalists who seem to think that having body odor equals a political movement, there are the freaks from Campus Crusade for Christ, and of course there are oodles of good moderate North Carolinians who bore me to tears anytime they open their mouths," he says.

"Darling, you sound very judgmental."

"Well there's a lot of judgment out there against gay men. Especially in the South."

"But you're not a man!" I say.

Charles puts a finger to his cheek. "And I wonder why he went queer," he says, as if he is at a cocktail party talking about himself.

"Your father is going to kill you," I say.

"No, he'll just ignore and belittle me."

Well, that was correct. At least his brain is still functioning in some sort of realistic manner.

"He's not going to give you any money."

"I haven't asked for any," says Charles.

I keep my mouth shut, but I'm thinking, *You will.*

"Look," he says. "I've talked to Caroline. She told me that I could sleep on their couch for as long as I want. So all I'm going to need is a plane ticket to San Francisco."

"Caroline knows about this?"

Charles nods.

"And her newfound religious leanings don't—you know—conflict with your . . . with who you are?"

"I don't see how they could considering she lives in a city chock full of fags."

"I wish you wouldn't say that word," I say.

"Oh Louise," says Charles. He drains the rest of his gimlet. "You're priceless."

Who would have thought that I would raise a born-again daughter (although I'm assuming this phase of Caroline's will soon pass; she's certainly gone through stages before) and a gay son? To be perfectly honest, I prefer the gay son. Or rather, I think I'll be more comfortable with a gay son. I just don't know what to say to Caroline when she starts talking about God. When she confesses as she did one time on the phone—I think she might have had too much to drink—that Christ is with her, always guiding her choices if she takes the time to "discern his presence." I suppose I should try and take joy in her joy. (Although she doesn't *seem* joyful. She seems burdened.) I just find her religious language a little, well, embarrassing.

"Oh dear," I say, looking in my martini glass. "I guess all my children are leaving me."

"It's not you I'm leaving," says Charles. "It's the Confederacy."

How he can say that when we are sitting in the middle of Ansley Park, the border of Midtown, the gayest place in the South, I will never know.

I suppose he has a natural tendency toward the dramatic.

AND WHAT ABOUT my husband? What of him? Does he even want to know of Charles's big plans to be a college dropout sleeping on his God-obsessed sister's sofa in San Francisco? Should I even bother to pass on that information? I suppose at some point he'll notice that he's stopped receiving tuition bills from Chapel Hill. I suppose then he might make an inquiry or two as to the whereabouts of his son.

Oh Lord. It's just going to be John Henry and me and Nanny Rose around Atlanta. Now that Tiny's divorce is finalized she has moved to Sea Island for good. Not that it really even matters. All she wants to talk about anymore is the huge settlement her lawyer got for her. (She threatened to reveal all of Anders's misallocation of firm funds—including the personal use of Jose—if Anders didn't give her half of his future earnings. Anders, knowing he was beat, acquiesced.) That or Ray, her forty-two-year-old boyfriend, who I swear uses self-tanner (or else why would his skin be so orange?).

I am going to wind up old and alone, my only accomplishment that I drove my children as far from Atlanta as possible and stayed married to a man who is incapable of feeling one iota of sympathy for his own flesh and blood. Why have I not made more of my life? If I had married Ben Ascher instead of John Henry, maybe things would be different. Maybe I would have had a thriving and stimulating marriage instead of this thing—this stale compromise—that John Henry and I have come up with (except for sex, we've always been good in that department); maybe my children wouldn't have felt the need to adopt such extreme personalities, to move such extreme distances away from me.

After Charles finishes his drink and leaves the house for God knows where, I walk around looking at all my pretty things. The carved wooden bowls by Philip Moulthrop, the piece of Tiffany stained glass above the round window in the hallway, the George the Second mahogany dining room chairs, and all our gorgeous hand-knotted rugs. These things bring me comfort, I swear to God they do.

JOHN HENRY IS already in our bed, under the covers. The lamp on my bedside table has been turned on, a thoughtful gesture on his part, not that I really want to feel appreciative toward him at this particular moment. I lie down on top of the covers, near him but not touching. We have not talked since he left the living room after Charles's revelation, hours ago.

"I wish you could have given him more," I say, knowing he is still awake.

I hear John Henry sigh beside me. Everything seems softer in bed, quieter.

"I did the best I could," he says, opening his eyes. "Believe me, if I had told my father what Charles told me, he wouldn't have reacted as calmly as I did."

"Did Wallace ever tell your father?" I ask.

I can *feel* John Henry's muscles tighten, the way they always do when I bring up Wallace.

"We don't know for sure about him," he says.

"We know what was in his apartment in Athens," I say. "When we went down there to pack up his stuff."

"I've got to get some sleep," says John Henry. "I've got a big day tomorrow."

My heart is pushing against my chest. I want to talk about this. I want to talk about Wallace. I want to talk about the thing we never talk about on the rare occasions when we do actually talk about him.

"He was such a sweet man," I say. "Do you remember how he always brought me flowers for my hair? Every single time we went out with him? Do you remember how he used to throw his head back and laugh when someone told a joke, how he just gave over to it completely?"

"He was always more outgoing than I was," says John Henry.

"You were outgoing. After a few drinks."

"Thanks."

I turn on my side and smile at him, just to let him know I was teasing. He smiles back.

"Do you think Wallace would have shot himself if he could have lived an openly gay life like he could now?"

My husband is no longer smiling. He sits up, looming over me, his eyes cold.

"Louise, I don't know why you're insisting on that interpretation of him. It's like you are obsessed."

This is as far as we ever get. This is where John Henry raises his voice and I back off because God knows I don't want to cause

John Henry further grief. Wallace, after all, was his brother, his identical twin.

"Darling," I say, sitting up so I can be at eye level with him again. "Those magazines in his room, his diary for God's sake. He couldn't have been more explicit if he had spelled it out in a suicide note."

John Henry is silent and then I hear a gasp and he is crying hard just for a moment before he stops, the expression on his face returning to impassivity.

I surprise myself by feeling sorry for him. It is as if I feel my heart plumping after scrunching itself so tight against him. I place my hand on his chest, over his heart.

"His suicide was not our fault," I say. "We gave Wallace a lot of love. But we can do better by our son."

"You don't know that," he says.

"We *can* do better by our son."

"You don't know it wasn't our fault. My fault. Wallace's suicide."

"Oh darling," I say. I rub his forearm. "You know, even if he was gay, most likely that wasn't what made him kill himself. Most likely he had some sort of chemical imbalance. I mean, think about my mother. Think about how much better she was once the doctors finally discovered Prozac."

It breaks my heart, still. To think that my mother had a treatable form of mental illness, to think that she didn't have to spend all that time at those hospitals, having electric shock treatments and sitting around in a housecoat playing bingo with other crazy rich ladies.

John Henry whispers something.

"What?"

"I said it was my fault about Wallace."

"Of course it wasn't your fault," I say.

"The week before he killed himself Wallace visited me at Chapel Hill and told me he might be a homosexual."

Not once have I ever heard John Henry even mention the idea that his brother might be gay. Not once in our thirty years of marriage. I don't know what to say. I didn't even know that Wallace visited our senior year. I don't remember him ever having done so.

As if he can read my mind, John Henry says, "It was during that break we took, when we dated other people. Before I came to my senses."

It's funny. I've told that story so many times the way I *wished* it had happened that even John Henry believes it. He's probably forgotten the real details. He's probably forgotten that we got back together the night of Wallace's death. He probably thinks it happened just like I told Caroline, at a football game one afternoon when he was drunk as a skunk. Lord knows he doesn't dwell on the time around Wallace's suicide.

How strange to think of Wallace, with whom I was always so close, running around Chapel Hill without making plans to see me. It is ridiculous I know, but I feel hurt all these years later. I wonder if Wallace didn't want to see me or if John Henry instructed him not to.

"I can't believe he admitted that to you."

"He was depressed. He talked about breaking up with Heather."

"My God, I'd forgotten about her. Do you remember how irritating she was with her baby talk?"

John Henry continues talking, as if I hadn't said anything. It's not that he's being rude exactly, more like he's on a mission, a soldier carrying out an order.

"We'd been at Phi Delt for most of the night, just playing cards and drinking. Around two a.m. we headed back to our apartment, cutting through campus to get to Franklin Street. There was hardly anyone on the main quad, just an occasional couple that would pass by. That was when he told me that he was thinking about breaking up with Heather. He wasn't attracted to her. They had tried to have sex—several times—and it hadn't ever worked."

"He told you that?"

"He told me he didn't think he was attracted to girls."

God, I can see them. Wallace and John Henry walking across campus together, Wallace's shoulders hunched the way they always were when he was upset. John Henry wearing a T-shirt, maybe even wearing it inside out the way he would when he'd forgotten to do laundry. The tall trees of the campus making a canopy above them, not that either of them would have looked up, not during such a confession.

"What did you say?" I asked. "What did you say when he told you he wasn't attracted to girls?"

John Henry is silent for so long I begin to think he did not hear me. Just as I am about to ask again, he says, "I tried to make a joke. I told him that there were no fags allowed on campus after sunset."

Apparently there used to be signs that said that, outside small southern towns. Except it wasn't fags they were warning, but black people. "Niggers" the signs would say.

"What happened?" I asked. "After you said that, what did he say?"

John Henry covers his face with his hands. I stare at his wedding ring, thinking of how startling it was to see it on his finger those first few months of our marriage. How shiny it was back then.

"What did he say?"

"I don't want to talk about it."

"For God's sake, John Henry, just go ahead and tell me. What did he say when you told him that fags weren't allowed on campus after sunset?"

John Henry lowers his hands from his face. He sighs, defeated.

"He didn't say anything so I kept talking. I told him that there were a million girls he could date, that he just must not have been dating his type. I told him that I could set him up with any girl on campus, that he could come up any weekend and I'd have a sure thing for him, and he interrupted me and said that he was a homosexual."

Oh my God. Poor Wallace.

"So I told him that he needed to do whatever he had to do to get over it because you couldn't be a Parker and a fag. And then he started shouting at me that he *was* a Parker and he *was* a faggot. I told him to shut the hell up but he kept yelling it, kept yelling, 'I'm a goddamn Parker and I'm a goddamn faggot.' He wouldn't stop yelling, Louise. He wouldn't shut up. And then I saw two guys from Phi Delt stumbling across campus toward us and I sort of lunged at Wallace just to shut him up. I knocked him to the ground and I put my knee on his chest and I looked down at him below me, half expecting him to be crying, half wanting him to be crying so I could knock the shit out of him for it, but he wasn't. He was just staring up at me with this strange look on his face, like I wasn't even there. Like I didn't even exist."

I wonder where Wallace was at that moment.

"Did you knock the shit out of him?"

"No. I didn't. I stood, gave him a hand to help him up, though he didn't take it. I said something about us being drunk and it being late and why don't we go home and sleep it off. And he sort of waved me away, said he'd meet up with me later, back at the apartment. But he must have had his car keys on him because he didn't come back to my place that night or the next day. I didn't talk to him that week but I knew he was back in Athens because he had called Mother from there to tell her he loved her. She called to tell me that, like it was the most wonderful thing in the world that Wallace had done so. She thought it meant he forgave her for having sent him to military school after he got kicked out of Fox Hill."

His face crumples and he is crying hard again. This time I think he will keep crying. This time I think he might not ever stop.

Perhaps I should hate my husband for the story he has told me, but I don't. I feel—I feel sad for him and sad for Wallace. Sorry for them both. What has holding this in done to his spirit all these years? I wrap my arms around him and he grabs onto me, crying into my neck, his tears wetting my skin and my hair. It is like the night he came to tell me of Wallace's death.

And as I hold my husband I am floating back in time, back before Wallace shot himself, back before I met Ben Ascher, back before John Henry tried to end things between us our senior year. Back to that first sweet summer after we started dating, when John Henry looked at me like a man in love and Wallace brought flowers for my hair. We were all in Atlanta. We would spend most days at the Driving Club, swimming. My body was sleek and taut, John Henry's nearly hairless and tan. He would sit in a lounge chair and watch me dive from the high board, his eyes trained on me even as I pulled myself out of the pool.

Afterwards we would play tennis, or rather, John Henry and Wallace would play. Occasionally we would find a partner for me and play doubles, but mostly, I watched. I didn't mind.

They were perfectly matched, those two, in their tennis whites. Wallace had such a powerful serve, his body a straight line just before he drove the ball over the net. And there was John Henry, eyes focused, feet nimble, whacking it back to his brother.

It seemed sometimes that they would go for hours before either of them lost the point.

Imagine their young bodies, lithe and sure, nailing the ball, stroke after stroke. The sun that shone upon them made the white of their shirts almost blinding.

CHAPTER TWENTY

Coming-Out Party

(Louise, Spring 2006)

$\mathcal{C}$harles and I sit at the kitchen table eating a late breakfast of croissants and coffee. (The croissants I order from Williams-Sonoma. They arrive frozen and uncooked and you set them out the night before to let the dough rise. Hot out of the oven they are buttery and flaky—absolutely to die for—and worth every penny of their admittedly exorbitant price.)

"Charles," I say. "I have been thinking long and hard about this and I have decided that you absolutely may not drop out of college."

"Is that a Freudian slip?" he asks. "Long and hard?"

"Oh good Lord, be serious," I say, dabbing a tiny bit of jam on the end of my croissant. "You know that I don't care one bit that you are gay. I love you and I'm happy that you trusted me enough to be honest about your life. But I have already had one child drop out of school and move across the country. I am not going to have my other child do the exact same thing."

Charles crunches into his croissant. He seems to be considering my words while he chews.

He swallows.

"Would you like more coffee?" he asks.

I look down at my cup. It's already empty. Even though I only drink decaf, I'm a coffee addict.

"Yes, please," I say. He stands to fetch the coffeepot, my sweet, evasive boy. He is still in his pajamas, even though it is eleven in the morning. Of course I can't judge; I'm still in my silk robe. (I wonder if Charles has had as much trouble sleeping as John Henry and I have. For the fifth night in a row we have stayed up past 2 a.m. talking about things, talking about Wallace mainly.)

Charles pours hot coffee into my mug.

"Is that decaf?" I ask, looking up at him. I made two pots, decaf for me and caffeinated for him.

"Of course it is," he says, sitting back down at the table. "Look, my situation is entirely different from Caroline's. She dropped out of high school—not college—and in case you don't remember, she was embroiled in *le grand scandal de Coventry*."

"Oh I remember," I say. "Believe me, I remember. Listen. Consider this. Just go back for the rest of the year and then you can transfer anywhere you want. NYU or Oberlin or Berkeley or wherever. Your father and I will pay the tuition wherever you get in."

"I don't *want* to go back to Chapel Hill!" says Charles, sounding for all the world like a three-year-old on the brink of a tantrum.

"Well stay here then," I say, although this is not something that John Henry and I discussed. "Stay here and apply to transfer to a college that's better suited to you. Or transfer to Emory."

"Emory!" says Charles, disdain in his voice.

CHARLES MAY OBJECT to Emory—Lord knows why—but bringing up Emory gets me thinking about Stephen Pollard, Tiny's framer. Ever since he framed my first two Earl LeTrouve paintings I've been on Stephen's mailing list for gallery shows and art lectures and such. And I've bumped into him at Whole Foods on Ponce so many times it seems as if we are destined to be friends.

Stephen went to Emory. In fact, he has a group of male friends from Emory who get together in the Hamptons every few months. The last time I bumped into Stephen he was picking up chocolate truffles to take for that weekend's trip.

What I should do is have Charles meet Stephen so that Stephen can sort of show him the gay scene around town. Charles should be able to find it on his own considering that we live within a stone's throw of Midtown, but maybe he needs someone who is actually "out" to introduce him to the action. I don't mean the sex action; I mean, well, I mean whatever it is gay men do in Atlanta besides go to Outwrite Books.

What I'm thinking is that maybe I could have Stephen and his partner over for drinks or dinner, and then maybe see if Chevre could come, and then I could ask that nice couple—Ricky and Jim, I think their names are—who live just down the street and whose gorgeous house was on the Tour of Homes last year.

Drinks might work best, something very casual, just to let Charles meet everybody and see that his father and I really are okay with his lifestyle (at least John Henry is pretending to be) and that there are gay people in Atlanta living full and rich lives.

The big question is, Should we have champagne or cocktails?

And what in the world will I serve for nibbles?

And then it hits me: gay men love retro. I'll make old-fashioned country club goodies, the kind of stuff served for appetizers at a southern wedding. And I'll let Charles be in charge of the drinks—gimlets!—so that he can interact with everyone.

I AM AS NERVOUS as a girl before her first date. It's silly, really, we're only having three people over (Ricky and Jim had tickets to the symphony and couldn't make it), but still, I've never hosted a party for gay men before. I have to hold myself back from running to the hall mirror to check my hair one more time before my guests arrive. In honor of my retro-sixties appetizers and drinks, I bought myself a wig that gives me a perfect teased flip. I hope I'm not overdoing it. Charles will probably think I am, if he ever gets home. (I am going to kill him if he doesn't show up soon. He's been gone all afternoon. I don't even know if he's showered.)

Chevre is going to scream when he sees me, he is so used to my short hair. (I decided to cut it all off when I turned fifty. And you know what? The new cut took ten years off me.) Keeping with my retro theme, I'm wearing a simple blue A-line shift that looks like something my mother might have worn to a cocktail party when I was a little girl. Except my dress is new.

John Henry is in the library watching the Braves on TV. I told him he has to turn the game off when the guests get here but that he can do whatever he wants in the meantime. Really, he is being a good sport about all this. He even went out and bought us a new bottle of premium gin for the gimlets. And he didn't make fun of my wig.

The doorbell rings.

My first guests!

And no Charles.

I quickly scan the living room to make sure everything is in place. I decided to make things simple and just to put the hors d'oeuvres directly on the coffee table so that people can serve themselves: baked and buttered saltines, spicy cheese straws from a recipe Caroline gave me, sticky stacks of caramelized bacon, shrimp with cocktail sauce, and for the nonretro folks, a big tray of cheeses (Epoisses, aged Gouda, Brillat-Savarin, and Saint Agur) from Alon's with crackers, walnut bread, and apples. And of course I put out a platter of my famous brownies.

John Henry is at the front door before I get there. He looks

nice in his brown corduroy sports coat and chinos. Ever since he
turned fifty the man has let me pick out most of his clothes and I
have to say, I do a good job. And—hallelujah!—he finally got rid
of his comb-over.

"Ready?"

"Of course," I say. "Open the door!"

It's Stephen and Bob.

"Welcome!" I say.

"Thank you so much for having us," says Stephen. "We're
thrilled to get the chance to peek at your gorgeous house!"

"And to enjoy the evening with you," says Bob, nudging
Stephen.

Stephen laughs. "That goes without saying. Louise, this is for
you."

He hands me a bottle of Perrier-Jouët champagne. I am delighted to feel that it has been chilled. In fact, I think I'll open it
up right now.

Stephen is short, about my height, his gray hair trimmed close
to his head. He has perennially ruddy cheeks, which make him
look as if he's always just coming in out of the cold. Bob is the
beauty of the two. His eyelashes are so long, Nanny Rose would
say, "they are wasted on a man." He is about six inches taller than
Stephen. He wears his hair long enough so that you can see the
wave in it. His blue eyes are piercing.

(It occurs to me that if Bob were just a little younger, Charles
might try to steal him away.)

"I absolutely adore champagne," I say, leading them into the
hallway. "Do y'all mind if we go ahead and open this?"

"Please do!" says Bob.

John Henry asks if he can take coats from anyone, but the
men are only wearing their suit jackets.

"What a gorgeous grandfather clock!" says Stephen. "Is it an
antique?"

"Why yes," I say. "It's a church clock, from the George the Second era, I believe."

I hand the bottle of champagne to John Henry. "Darling, why don't you go open this and bring us each a glass. And I'll just give Stephen and Bob a little tour."

John Henry goes off dutifully to the kitchen. I show Stephen the tiny renditions of Matthew, Mark, Luke, and John, one painted on each corner of the clock face.

"It's so rare to have an old English clock that actually runs," says Stephen.

I hope my father—wherever his spirit is—hears that. I inherited the grandfather clock from him. He was so protective of it that he left instructions in his will detailing how and when to wind it.

The bell rings again. "Excuse me," I say.

I answer the door and there is Chevre, the top of his Afro nearly brushing the archway above the door.

"Oh my God!" he screams. "Look at you!"

He reaches out to touch my hair while I smile and blush. "This is perfect, Louise," he says. "I really think we need to grow your hair out again so it can do this on its own."

"Come on, come in," I say. "I can't grow my hair out, Chevre. Long hair on an older woman looks like mutton dressed like lamb."

"Please," he says. "You can't be a day older than thirty-five."

"You are a liar and I adore you for it," I say.

Stephen and Bob, who have turned away from the clock to face Chevre, stand waiting for an introduction. Chevre is a good foot taller than Stephen and he is probably twenty-five years younger. Perhaps this wasn't the best pairing of guests. Oh well. Maybe Chevre and Charles will entertain each other while the rest of us go off and be old together. If Charles ever arrives.

I introduce Chevre to the couple just as John Henry walks in with three glasses of champagne.

"And one more, sweetheart," I say, taking a glass from him. "Thank you."

"Oh, none for me, thanks," says Chevre.

"Would you like something else?" I ask. "We've got wine and bourbon and my son should be home soon to fix anyone who wants one a gimlet."

"Gimlets!" says Bob, obviously pleased.

"Just some sparkling water for me," says Chevre.

Aha. He doesn't drink. Maybe that is how he stays so skinny. John Henry heads back to the kitchen to get Chevre's water.

"I'm sorry to say that the guest of honor isn't here yet," I say. "But please, let's go into the living room, somebody make a toast, and we can all have a bite to eat."

"What are we toasting?" asks Chevre.

"We're toasting champagne," says Stephen.

"Yes!" I say. "Champagne every day!"

I am, I realize, a bit keyed up.

NEVER IN MY life have I felt so appreciated for my culinary prowess. Stephen says my brownies are the best he has ever, ever tasted and Chevre keeps slapping his own hand away from the cheese straws but then taking one anyway. John Henry, not surprisingly, hasn't said a word this whole evening, besides asking our guests if anyone needs another drink. From what I can tell, anytime he goes to the kitchen to fetch another bottle of champagne (we decided to stick to what we started with and so we dug around in the wine rack and found a couple of bottles of Nicolas Feuillatte to serve) he refills his own glass first. I hope he doesn't get drunk and fall asleep in his chair. Then again, I'm not sure if Chevre, Bob, and Stephen would notice, they are paying so much attention to me.

"Louise, this is such a beautiful room," says Stephen. "You have a gift for decorating."

"John Henry nearly filed for divorce when I hung that," I say, nodding toward my Jesus.

"Oh John Henry! It's wonderful!" says Stephen. "My only suggestion would be to install a light above it so that people can really take in the gorgeous hues of the piece."

"You want to draw *more* attention to it?" says John Henry, looking incredulous.

Chevre throws back his head and laughs. "Uh oh," he says. "You're pushing it, Stephen."

"I'm so sorry that Charles is missing all this," I say. "I hope nothing wrong has happened."

"Does he have a cell phone?" asks Bob.

I mock slap my forehead. "Of course!" I say. "Excuse me, gentlemen, I am just going to run and give him a call."

Both Bob and Stephen stand when I get up. I haven't seen a man do that since my father used to stand for my mother during nice dinners out, when she would excuse herself to go to the ladies' room.

In the kitchen I dial Charles's number. His voicemail picks up after the first ring, and I don't leave a message. I'm too annoyed with him to do so and if—God forbid—he has been in an accident I don't want him to listen to a recording of me yelling at him after it's all over.

I walk to the back door and press my forehead against the glass. I am a little woozy from all of the champagne. I look outside toward the garage, at first only seeing darkness until my eyes adjust. There is Charles's Honda Accord, parked in the driveway since our garage only fits two cars.

I have a momentary flash of panic, thinking that Charles might be in his car killing himself with carbon monoxide. But I shake it off. Charles is not Wallace.

I open the back door and walk outside, enjoying the feel of the night air against my skin.

"Charles?" I call. "Charles?"

No one answers. I walk to the gate that leads to the pool. Peering through it I spy the red glow of a cigarette being smoked in the distance.

"Charles?"

I open the gate and walk toward the pool. The light is gone, but I know he is down there. I can smell the cigarette smoke.

"I know you're down there," I say. I am reminded of his childhood, how he used to hide from me anytime he did something bad. Which was funny, sort of, that he felt the need to hide, because I never remember punishing him the way I did Caroline. I can't remember ever having spanked him.

I take my time walking to him. My eyesight is not at its best in the dark, and I don't want to trip over anything and land on the concrete. Finally I make my way to the edge of the pool, where he sits, his pants rolled up, his legs in the water.

"I didn't know you smoke," I say.

"I try not to," he says.

"Well that's good."

He looks up at me. "Are you wearing a wig?"

"Yes," I say, adding impulsively, "I have cancer."

He looks up quickly, his face stricken.

"I'm sorry," I say. "That was a joke. Not a funny one."

"Stranger and stranger," he says.

"Look, Charles, you and I need to talk and I can't sit down on this concrete because it will tear the fabric of my dress."

"I don't want to go inside to your party," he says.

"Well obviously," I say. "Why else would you be hiding out here? Just come into the kitchen with me. No one is in there."

He stands, drops his cigarette on the ground, and uses his foot to unroll the bottom of his pants.

"Are you sure your cigarette is out?" I ask.

He steps on the butt. "Now it is."

We walk to the kitchen. Stephen is at the counter, pouring himself another glass of champagne. John Henry must have passed out.

I feel Charles tense up behind me.

"Stephen, this is my son, Charles Parker."

Stephen lifts his glass of champagne. "Delighted to meet you, Charles," he says. And then he walks out of the kitchen as if he knows that Charles doesn't want to meet him.

Charles sits at the kitchen table, his shoulders slumped.

"I went to a lot of trouble to put this party together," I say. "And you don't even have the courtesy to tell me that you don't want to come."

I feel myself choking up. I hate yelling at my son.

He rolls his eyes. "I'm *sorry*," he says, "but I didn't ask you to do this. I didn't want you to do this. I mean, God, Mom, I'm not going to become best friends with a bunch of fifty-year-old gay guys."

"Bob and Stephen are not some 'bunch of guys.' And Chevre is no older than twenty-five, I'm sure of it."

"Yeah, and he's also, like, a queeny colorist from your salon. Jesus. Talk about central casting. What made you assume we'd have anything to talk about? I mean, what if I assumed that you wanted to be friends with every woman out there who also happens to like fucking men?"

I stand from the table, blinking back tears.

"You are being snotty and rude, and I have a party to host," I say.

"That's right," he says. "*You* have a party. Just admit that it's *your* party."

• • •

I AM WALKING back to the living room when I feel someone grab my arm. I jump.

"Louise."

It's Stephen.

"I'm sorry, I didn't mean to scare you, I just wanted to get to you before you had to go back in front of everybody."

"Oh Stephen," I say, and to my terrible embarrassment, I start to cry.

Stephen clucks his tongue and pulls me in for a hug. He rubs my back, murmuring words of comfort.

"Oh hon," he says. "You tried so hard."

I pull myself away from his embrace. "Was I wrong to have all of you over? Am I just a fool?"

Stephen reaches into his pants pocket and pulls out a travel-size pack of Kleenex. He hands it to me. I take one and dab my eyes.

"I for one am very glad you invited us over," he says. "I had a hunch about you but now that I have seen your house I know for sure."

"What do you mean?" I ask.

"Well, first of all, I hope that you and I are going to be friends. Real friends, not just bump-into-each-other-in-the-chocolate-aisle-at-Whole-Foods friends. And second of all, I hope I can convince you to go in on a little project with me."

I can't help but feel suspicious, as if he is about to ask me to loan him money.

"Louise, you have a gift for collecting and cultivating beauty. Every single room I've seen tonight is put together better than a team of decorators could have done."

A look of worry crosses his face. "You didn't hire decorators, did you?"

I shake my head. No.

"I adore the LeTrouve pieces that you picked out, the party

Christ *and* those delicate egg temperas you have displayed in the entrance hall. And I was stunned by the two original portraits by Hank Huffington, and those blue marble Buddhas you have in the living room, and the kilim and Tabriz rugs and the Moulthrop bowls, and I adore how everything is arranged just so—the gorgeous flowers included—and well, I just think you have a real vision."

I smile despite my frustration with Charles.

"Now this might sound a little cuckoo, but have you ever thought about turning your house into an intimate little gallery? You could host shows the same way you would host a party. My God, if you had the time you could cater your own affairs: I've never tasted anything like your brownies, and believe me, I'm a chocolate connoisseur."

"You think I should be a caterer?"

"No, no, you would hire caterers. I'm just saying that you *could* do it, if you needed to. No. Your job would be to curate the shows. It would be like throwing parties for a living but people would come and buy the art you had displayed."

"Stephen, I'm flattered. But I love my art. I don't want to sell it."

Stephen flaps his hands back and forth as if waving away a bad smell. "God no, darling. You wouldn't sell *your* art. That would be part of the permanent collection—no price tags affixed. What you would do is have shows and borrow—display—art directly from the artists themselves. Granted, you might have to rearrange some of your own pieces during the shows, but I'd help you. And I'd help you connect with artists too."

"I'm not sure that John Henry would be willing to have his home turned into a stage, but . . ."

"But isn't it your home too?" asks Stephen.

Yes. Yes it is.

And haven't I thrown a zillion firm parties for John Henry

where after getting the house in tip-top shape, after getting myself plucked and preened and jeweled, all I ended up doing was talking to the other partners' wives? And not the interesting ones, oh no. No, as host I would inevitably get stuck (for hours, it seemed!) in conversation with Rosalie Henderson, whose favorite topic seems to be "how affirmative action *nearly* kept my son out of Dartmouth."

Lord.

I imagine the guests at Stephen's and my parties will be a much more interesting bunch, and there will be so much to look at and admire, no one will grow bored. Plus, we can hire musicians, a jazz trio, or maybe even a DJ to set the mood so that every show feels like a party, so that people will be encouraged to let down their hair, to drink too much, to dance even, all before buying up every piece of art that Stephen and I have for sale.

And suddenly I am saying, "Yes, yes, let's do it, yes," as if this wonderful possibility before me is elusive, as if it might evaporate as suddenly as smoke.

CHAPTER TWENTY-ONE

The Exile

(Caroline, Summer 2006)

*O*f all the things hindering my spiritual growth, my addiction to ZipRealty.com is the most arresting. I cannot stop looking at homes in Atlanta. I will type in different zip codes around the city (30306, 30307, 30312) and up pops photo after photo of homes Davis and I could easily afford to buy.

In San Francisco we rent. We could purchase an apartment, but Davis refuses to "blow" our house money (his house money, really, considering I don't have a job and therefore contribute nothing) on only one thousand square feet of space, which is about what we'd get if we bought in any of the areas of the city where Davis feels comfortable. Davis's comfort zone is small. Bernal is out. The Mission is out. Potrero Hill is out. Hayes Valley is out. The Outer Sunset is fine, but Davis says if we moved out there we might as well move to the suburbs. He makes it sound as if moving to the suburbs is a sad inevitability, when in fact it is his greatest fantasy.

Lately he's been taking me to this neighborhood in Lafayette called Happy Valley, which is in the East Bay, where his parents live. Real estate in Happy Valley is insanely expensive, but Davis says his parents would be willing to help out significantly if we bought a house near them. (But not if we bought a house in the city.) Honestly, I wouldn't mind living in the East Bay. I'd be fine with Berkeley or Oakland. But Happy Valley? It sounds like a joke. To get there you have to drive through a tunnel. This is after you've already crossed the Bay Bridge. You drive past all the places where the weird people live—Berkeley and its outposts—and then you drive through a tunnel and when you come out you are in the land of the clean, the straight, the safe, the new. What you leave behind is soul—at least my kind of soul—though I will probably find myself in Happy Valley before too long, as Davis has quite a strong will and quite an incentive from his folks.

I never imagined that I—just like my mother—would be in this position. Dependent upon my husband to make our money. It's just that it seems to come so easily to him, the corporate world and its financial payoff. And giving it away seems to come so easily to me! I tried, in fact, to get Davis to pledge to tithing, but he threw a fit. He hasn't yet seemed to notice that about one percent of our income is sucked out of our banking account each month by automatic withdrawal. Sucked out and deposited into the accounts of Doctors Without Borders, the Heifer Foundation, AHOPE Ethiopia, and my favorite, Saint Anthony's.

Saint Anthony's is where I volunteer once a week, me and the Catholic retirees, most of whom detest Bush's policies more strongly than any hipster from the Mission. One fiery redhead clenched her fists while talking about domestic spying. "The nerve!" she said. "The nerve of them spying on the Quakers!"

Besides politics, the ladies at Saint Anthony's talk of their grandchildren, their knee aches, and how expensive housing now is in the city. The Tenderloin, where the majority of San Francisco's homeless live, is now growing in its elderly population. Old people living on fixed incomes have had to move into SROs (single room occupancies) in order not to be on the street. One of the men who volunteers in the dining room three days a week lives in an SRO on Tenth Street.

Saint Anthony's is where I most clearly feel Jesus. Some of the time. In flashes. Even though each Friday, as I take the N train down to the Civic Center exit, I dread what I am about to do, even though many of the people whom we serve smell deeply of dirt and urine, even though occasionally I've been yelled at or flicked off, there is almost always a breakthrough. Some moment when you realize your contentedness. If Jesus was right, then the Kingdom of God resembles the dining room at Saint Anthony's. The last shall be first; a privileged daughter of the South shall serve the ignored man from the street.

I don't mean to sound pious. The truth is, I do it for me. For my own sanity. One man asked why I was volunteering. I said it was to be a part of something. How lonely I often feel in this city, in my apartment, within the confines of my marriage. Davis and I—we don't fight, we don't talk. We lead separate lives in the same few rooms. Every night after dinner he watches TV by himself and I catalog houses we will never, ever buy on Zip.

I have a feeling that Davis and I are not unlike most married couples. I have a feeling that very few people feel genuinely connected. And if he were to reach out—how can he go where I am headed? I don't mean heaven—I'm not a literalist—I mean centering my life on the Gospel. Davis finds the idea of Christianity abhorrent (he ought to get together with my mother). I find myself longing to pray with him, to start the day with a prayer, or an intention at least. To end it with attention paid to each other. Some kind of ritual to keep us tuned in. A ritual better than Letterman after the news.

We hardly ever have sex.

• • •

I WANT TO go home to Atlanta. A place I haven't lived in for over five years. A place I've returned to fewer than ten times since I first left: every other Christmas, the occasional Thanksgiving, my mother's fiftieth birthday party, Charles's high school graduation. Louise tells me everything in Atlanta has changed. To note, she and my father went out to dinner in Cabbagetown the other night. Cabbagetown! The neighborhood surrounding the old cotton mill where all the folks brought down from Appalachia to work in the factory stayed on even after the mill closed. They were a mile from downtown but hardly ever seemed to leave their front porches. They were my first glimpse of poor whites (usually, in Atlanta, when you drive through a poor neighborhood, black people live in it). Years ago I went to Cabbagetown with my youth group from church. We took turkeys to the families for Thanksgiving. Now artists live in the houses and the mill has been turned into upscale lofts. And John Henry and Louise go there to dine.

Davis would never move with me to Atlanta. I know. His job, his family, his center of gravity—they're all here. I wonder how he would cope without me if I were to divorce him and move home. I wonder how long it would take him to start dating again. Probably not long at all. He's thirty-three and attractive. He makes money. He wants a child. In fact, if our marriage is to work, I imagine I'll need to provide him with one soon, but I have no desire—no yearning at all—to care for an infant. And I have to keep reminding him, *Honey, you've got nine years on me. Your biological clock is ticking faster than mine.*

It would never work for me to go home. Not without Davis. First of all, I have no money. Second, I'm too fat. My mother would hate how I look; she *does* hate how I look. And who would I be friends with? Amanda from Coventry? Jim? (Ha.)

But what if Davis agreed to go? What if I could talk him into it from a financial standpoint? My God, we could buy a perfectly fixed-up bungalow in Candler Park for a fraction of what we'd pay in Happy Valley. He could work for SunTrust or Wachovia or some other southern bank and I could—oh you might as well go there as long as you're fantasizing—I could go to seminary. Like Davis would ever agree to be a minister's husband. He is not at all spiritual. He thinks that the fact that religion is contradictory, confusing, and illogical is reason to eschew it. Whereas I say, "Yeah, and so? How would you describe the human heart?"

Seminary. I floated the idea with my mother and she suggested I be a psychologist instead. "Isn't that the same thing?" she asked. "Just with better pay?"

Well, maybe. Maybe so. It's a half-baked thought, anyway. I'm still not even entirely comfortable admitting that I'm a Christian. There are just so many disclaimers you have to add, as in, "But I like gay people, and I don't think you are going to hell."

NOT LONG AGO I confessed to a friend that I was reconciled to always being in a state of exile. I can't go home—what home do I have in Atlanta besides my mother's house, which is hers, not mine?—and yet I long for it. And I've yet to find a church community that feels right, that feels as searing and raw as the dream that sent me on this search in the first place. (I'm expecting too much, I know. I've always wanted more than anything or anyone could ever give me.) The only thing the mainline churches in San Francisco seem passionate about is gay marriage. Which is fine, admirable even; I just wish they expressed an equal passion for transcendence. And the more hard-core evangelical church that I went to, well, it weirded me out. It started out promisingly enough; the minister was Indian like the one in my dream, but the whole sermon focused on the literality of the Resurrection. "Without the real, physical resurrection of His once-dead body, Christianity doesn't have a leg to stand on," said the minister. (His joke, I think, was intentional.)

It seems to me that it's unnecessarily exclusive to say that in order to be a Christian you *must* believe certain doctrine. Especially if that doctrine comes from taking the Gospel at its literal word. The smartest thing I ever heard about the Bible is that if you want to take it seriously, you can't take it literally. And I want to take it seriously. I *do* take it seriously.

And so, I pick and I choose and I find outlets for my longing—candlelit Taizé services on Wednesday nights, Saint Anthony's every Friday, ZipRealty.com for God knows how many hours during the day. I fantasize about Davis and me in a bungalow, members of a leftist Christian community in Atlanta, and yet I know I am envisioning myself with someone other than my husband. My husband does not like change. He does not want to be moved. Well, maybe to Marin. Or Walnut Creek. Or God forbid, Happy Valley.

(I do not mean to make an easy target of suburbia. I know the hearts that beat inside those homes are just as red and real. It's my own heart I worry about. What will happen to it on the other side of that tunnel?)

LAST NIGHT STARTED with one of those meals that makes me want to throw things just to add energy to the event. Davis cooked—spinach salad with poached chicken and dried cranberries, low calorie for my benefit I am sure. At dinner we went over the day's business (yes, I had called the landlord about the leak in the showerhead; yes, he had made dinner reservations for that Saturday at Delfina).

And then we sat and chewed in silence. He poured himself more wine without offering me any (did he think it was too caloric?) and proceeded to study the bottle. I sneezed and he didn't say "Bless you." After eating we stared at each other for a moment or two before he began clearing the table.

"I'll do the dishes," I said. "You cooked."

He went to the living room to watch TV; I looked out the

kitchen window while I rinsed off the plates. The hills behind our apartment building had turned yellow and dry from the arid summer.

The yellow hills make Davis nostalgic. They speak to him of summertime and youth: baseball games played until nine at night, cookouts by his parents' pool, hikes up Mount Diablo. To me, they will always be foreign.

I started to cry. I was thinking about Frederick, how much we shared, how he and I had the same reference points, the same inside jokes about Atlanta. I remembered with clarity the pain of his leaving, how some days it literally was hard to breathe I was so shocked by his absence. How cold he had been leading up to his departure. How he informed me one night in bed, just as I was going to sleep, that he had accepted Tisch's offer of admission. There was no affect in his voice. There was no longer any love.

I started crying for the eventual heartache that I would feel over Davis; whether we parted through divorce or death, we would part. And then I felt so lonely I started thinking about the loneliest people, and my mind went to the prisoners, as it often does when I'm overwhelmed, to the prisoners in the worst conditions. I read an article once about Sing Sing, an article that haunted me. A former guard wrote it and he talked about the men kept for months (months!) in solitary confinement, in a box deep below the earth, in the bowels of the prison, cut off from everything and everyone. My chest contracted thinking of them there, now, breathing. How do they breathe in such conditions? Right now, in this moment while I wash dishes, they are kept there, buried alive.

I don't think I believe in hell after death but I know it exists on this earth. Christians with more faith than I believe that Jesus manages to squeeze Himself into those tight spaces where our earthly damned are kept. God, I hope so. I prayed that it was so, even though my chest was tight and constricted just from thinking about the possibility of my own confinement. (What if some secret agent from the Bush administration whisked me away to some undisclosed place for signing too many MoveOn petitions?)

I breathed in and breathed out until I was no longer overtaken.

I was still crying, but softly now.

I finished the dishes and headed toward the office, where our computer is, where I spend hours looking up houses on Zip. I wanted to be absorbed in the search for a house I would never live in. I wanted to lose myself in the distraction of virtual tours and bathroom counts. But as I entered the office I heard a voice tell me not to. To turn around and talk to my husband. I sound like a loon, I know, but the voice was firm. I was not to check out in front of the computer that night. I was to tell my husband of my loneliness.

I walked into the living room and stood in front of the TV.

"I don't like this," I said.

Davis looked at me. "This show?"

"I don't like that every night after dinner you come in here and watch TV and I go in the other room to use the computer. It's like we're roommates, sharing the same space."

He looked tired. (I wear him out; I know.) He reached for the remote and muted the sound of the TV. He sighed. "Do you want to talk?"

I nodded and sat down at the end of the sofa. He was stretched out over most of it. At an earlier stage in our relationship, back when I was skinny, I could have stretched out beside him.

"I'd like to turn the TV all the way off."

He clicked it off with the remote.

"I feel so far away from you."

"I'm right here," he said.

"I mean spiritually. I feel disconnected."

"Caroline, you and I spend a lot of time together. Breakfast every morning, dinner most evenings, a date on Saturday night."

"I know, I know . . ."

"Look around at other couples," he said. "We're doing really well compared to most people. Think about how well we get along compared to—well—compared to them."

He looked toward the ceiling, indicating our upstairs neighbors, whose screaming fights sometimes keep us awake at night.

"If we could just incorporate a ritual," I said. "Something we do every day to keep us tuned in and focused on each other."

I wasn't saying what it was I really wanted. I wanted him to listen to me with more rapt attention. To look at me the way he did when we first started dating.

"Honey," said Davis, "this is marriage. The quotidian details are what it's about. I'm sorry if I was out of it during dinner. I had a tough day. I'm tired. On Saturday I'll be sparklier, okay? We can dress up for dinner. We can really enjoy our night out on the town. But tonight, I'm not very good entertainment."

I felt like I was drowning. I felt that we would never understand each other. How well *can* any two people understand each other? We're so trapped in these bodies, these egos. As if my loneliness stemmed from his not cracking more jokes! From his not dancing the soft-shoe to entertain me!

I used to complain of the same thing to Frederick. I wanted more of his attention. I wanted his eyes fixed on me. I wanted him to be enraptured. He said I couldn't always have the spotlight. He said I was too used to the concentrated attention of the audience.

I started to cry, again, and Davis, who once upon a time would have jumped to comfort me, stayed put.

I knew that no human could ever love me the way I wanted to be loved.

"I wish we could pray together," I said.

"You can say a prayer if you want," said Davis. "I'll bow my head."

I smiled. I felt so pathetic. "What if we're praying to different gods?" I asked. "The god of the atheists and the god of the believers."

"You want me to believe not just in God but in multiple gods?"

I smiled. And then I made the leap. You cannot imagine how self-conscious I felt. "Will you say a prayer for me and I'll say a prayer for you?" I asked. I sounded like a goddamn Michael W. Smith song. I sounded like one of the Crispy Christians from Coventry.

"Can we do it in bed?" he asked. "I'm so tired."

A part of me wanted to lash out at that, at what I so easily could have read as rejection. But I took two deep breaths and was able to say, "Okay."

Yoga breathing. A trick of my mother's.

I MET HIM in bed after brushing and flossing. I figured I might as well get ready to go to sleep if I was going to lie down. I lay beside him, on my side. I held both his hands with mine.

"Hello," I said.

"Hello."

"I'm probably going to sound really disingenuous and cheesy," I said. "I've never prayed out loud before."

"You don't have to do it," he said, "if it makes you feel self-conscious."

Again I felt a flash of irritation. I wasn't saying I didn't want to do it, simply that I was aware I might sound sanctimonious or silly.

"I'm doing it," I said. "Okay. Here we go. Dear God, thank you for giving Davis life. Please bless him and keep him safe. Please let him feel loved and cared for, both by me and by others . . ."

I kept going. The words came easily. How different it is to pray aloud for a person rather than to simmer in silence, angry that he won't change to suit your needs. When I got to "amen" my feelings were softer and kinder toward Davis than they had been when I started the prayer. Softer and kinder and perhaps even a little more distant. A little more distanced from my own pit of need. I was aware, for a moment, of his needs and desires. I was aware, for a moment, that his life mattered independently of mine.

CHAPTER TWENTY-TWO

The Accidental Catholic

(Missy, Summer 2006)

During a time in my pregnancy when it seemed my belly grew bigger by the minute, a girl in my English class, Fatima Ramos, gave me a card with the Virgin Mary's picture on it. The card was blue and Mary, who wore a gold crown and cradled the infant Jesus in her arms, looked Hispanic like Fati. Fatima said that her sister carried a card just like mine every day during her pregnancy. I asked Fati if her sister had a girl or a boy and she said a boy. I asked how old her sister was and she said fourteen.

I kept that card with me during the nine months I carried Grace, wearing out its edges by constantly rubbing it with my fingers. I even took it to the hospital with me when it was time to deliver.

Before I got pregnant, I'd never considered how young Mary was when she had Jesus. She was even younger than me, and she wasn't married either, at least not when she first got pregnant. I wouldn't dare tell anyone that I sometimes compare myself to her, that it comforts me to do so, because they'd shoot back that she was a virgin (me too, sort of) and she was chosen by God to bear His only Son while all I am is a damn fool who let herself get knocked up by a stranger whose phone was disconnected by the time I called to tell him the news.

I COULD SPEND all day pressing my nose against Grace's belly, just taking in that smell of baby powder and new life. Of course I don't have all day to spend; I'm lucky if I get a few hours with her when she's not sleeping. RD is still mad at me for quitting school, but after a month of trying to go to class, do my assignments, take care of Grace, *and* earn enough money to keep her in diapers, I realized I was failing half my subjects, and what was the point in going if I wasn't going to pass? It was hard enough going through eleventh grade pregnant: once I had Grace, school became impossible. I'll never forget that first day back in class when I thought about Gracie and my breasts started leaking. I didn't have a clean shirt to change into either.

Truth be told, I'm learning more from being a mama than I ever learned in the classroom. Not that that's going to help me when an employer wants to see my diploma, which is why RD says I have to get my GED.

THE NIGHT THE e.p.t made a plus sign, Mama started yelling that she was going to kill that Charles Parker for knocking me up.

"This explains it all," she said. "That's why he ran off before RD and I even arrived in town. He was too ashamed to look us in the face after what he did to you."

"Mama," I said, "Charles Parker may be a lot of things, but he ain't the daddy of this baby."

"That's why he drove you all the way to North Carolina. He knew you'd give him a return on the favor, didn't he?"

"He took me because he wanted to be on *Salt*, least that's what he said."

Mama humphed. "You're sure you two never got together?

Not once? The Parkers have a lot of money, you know, and if you're carrying their grandchild they're bound to help you out."

"Mama, Charles was about as interested in having sex with me as a cat is in taking a bath. He doesn't like girls. He's not interested in them."

"I never heard of a seventeen-year-old boy who wasn't interested in girls, unless he's queer. Is he queer?"

I nodded.

"Oh good Lord. I should have figured. Well, whose is it, then? You better go ahead and tell me because there ain't no use hiding it now."

I tried to explain to Mama exactly what happened between Dwayne and me, that we didn't have sex but that he did spill himself all over my underwear. I told her that I thought of the baby as God's, since Dwayne and I didn't have sex but I still got pregnant. Angry as I've been with Him, I figured He meant for Gracie to be born. Mama just looked at me like I'd sprouted a second head.

"It don't matter *how* Dwayne's junk got in you, it did, and that means he's the father of the child. Not God. Girl, you have got to get a little realistic about life. You have got to learn how to be a Christian and still know what's what. You have got to learn to apply the rules of church to church and the rules of the world to life. Every Christian does it. Think about it, if we didn't, all we'd do is give away our money and get slapped on both sides of the face.

"You ain't the Virgin Mary, girl. You just got humped by a man with fast sperm."

After that Mama started making all kinds of commotion about suing my Daddy or suing Dwayne or suing the church that financed *Salt*. But then RD, who'd been listening quietly from his seat in the La-Z-Boy, told her to calm down, saying that the last thing we needed to do was to chase two deadbeats into a courthouse, that regardless of who was to blame for this, when you got right down to it there was nothing a judge or lawyer could do about the fact that I was the one who was pregnant and I was the one who was going to have to bear and raise this baby.

I WONDER IF after that angel told Mary she was pregnant, Mary lied and told people the baby was Joseph's. It might have been easier that way, easier to have people think she was a slut rather than crazy. Don't get me wrong, I know that there's a big difference between Mary and me. She was pure and I am not. Still, I bet a lot of people thought she just got knocked up like any other girl.

WHEN WE FIRST got back from North Carolina, before we realized I was pregnant, Mama didn't tell Mrs. Parker about anything that had happened while she and Mr. Parker were off in San Francisco. Telling Mrs. Parker about Charles and me would only complicate things, Mama said, and it might even put her job in jeopardy because Mrs. Parker might think I was bad news.

"After all," said Mama, "I'm sure she hasn't forgotten about the time you stole from her."

I didn't argue with Mama, but in my heart I really didn't think there was much I could do that Mrs. Parker wouldn't forgive me for. Sure, when she first realized I took her bird she said she didn't want me coming to her house anymore, but a couple of days later she called back and said she hoped Mama hadn't been too hard on me about it (I didn't tell her that I got a whipping). Mrs. Parker said that she had probably made too big a deal about it, and that while it was important that I respect other people's property, she understood "how awful it is to be surrounded by things you can't have." To tell the truth, her saying that hurt me worse than Mama's strap.

Anyhow, Mama figured that since I made it home from Durham safe and with Daddy "out of my system for good," everything was okay and it wasn't necessary to spill the beans. Then I missed two periods and started to get fat, and we realized everything wasn't.

When Mama finally did tell Mrs. Parker about all that had happened between Charles and me and Dwayne and me, Mrs. Parker was understanding and kind, the way she always is. She apologized again and again for her son having taken me to North Carolina without telling anyone where we were going. She even said that she and her husband were considering sending Charles to a military academy for his final semester of high school.

Guess what? They didn't.

Then she told Mama that she would pay for me to have an abortion since I never would have gotten pregnant had Charles not delivered me to Dwayne's door.

"Let me help fix the damage my son caused," she said.

Mrs. Parker even told Mama that we could hire a private doctor to perform the operation so I wouldn't have to have it done at a clinic where there might be protesters.

Mama came home from Mrs. Parker's house that night and told me what had been offered. She said she thought I should do it. "It might be a sin," Mama said. "Probably is. But so is having a baby you can't take care of."

But Mama took care of me, and she was only seventeen when I was born, the same age I was when I had Grace.

Besides which, I knew I couldn't kill a life that was already growing inside of me, the life that was making me crave mustard and that kind of lunch meat with the olives stuck in it. I had never liked either of those foods before. Matter of fact, I used to tease RD about the fact that he ate monkey meat.

My cravings proved that there was someone else, someone

living inside of me, who was running the show. How could I kill that other being?

Think about what would have happened to the world if Mary had slipped off somewhere and aborted baby Jesus just to make things easier for herself. What then? I was angry with God— I still am—but that doesn't mean I can turn away from His plan altogether.

Mrs. Parker was upset when she learned that I was going to keep Grace, but after a couple of weeks of looking at Mama with sad eyes, Mama said, Mrs. Parker went back to her normal, cheerful self. And that was what finally soured Mama on her, that Mrs. Parker was able to recover so quickly from the disappointment she felt over my life.

"You getting knocked up gave that woman maybe ten minutes of worry," said Mama. "And then she was back to her old ways, all cooing and crooning over every little thing."

In fact, Mrs. Parker's good fortune seemed to grow with my belly. Charles was accepted at the college where she and Mr. Parker went: "Oh Faye, isn't it thrilling?" she asked while Mama loaded the dishwasher. Her daughter was having her wedding in Atlanta, which meant Mrs. Parker got to plan it: "Faye, what do you think about passing around martini glasses filled with grits casserole? Is that fun or unappetizing?"

After I recovered from Gracie's birth, RD got me a job working at Chick-fil-A twenty hours a week, the same one where he's assistant manager. That was when Mama told Mrs. Parker that she was quitting her so that she could be at home, to take care of Grace while I was at work. Mama lied. She does help care for Gracie when she can, but she also lined up a cleaning job on Mondays and Thursdays. Her new client lives in Lawrenceville, which isn't that far away from Loganville and is a lot closer to us than Mrs. Parker's neighborhood. We try to schedule ourselves so someone is always home for Gracie, but when days get crazy there's a lady down the street who keeps kids. She only charges three dollars an hour, which is about all she's worth. If she does more than plop Grace in the playpen and turn on the TV, I'd be surprised.

Mrs. Parker gave Mama a check for one thousand dollars on her last day of work. She told Mama to put it in a savings account for Grace, but that money is long gone by now. The bills ate it right up.

WHEN I GO to her crib each morning, she smiles and gurgles and reaches out her arms, thrilled to see me. I worry sometimes that she must think I've deserted her when I leave her room at night after singing lullabies. Mama says you have to let a baby cry herself to sleep or else she'll never learn how to get to sleep on her own. Some nights it seems Gracie never stops crying, even after I sneak back in her room and pick her up again. One time when she wouldn't stop crying I started up alongside her, the two of us wailing away with no end in sight.

If Mama would allow it, I'd let Gracie sleep in my bed with me. That way she'd know I'm never going to leave her. That way she might not start crying in the first place.

In the mornings when I scoop her up into my arms, her warm little body molds itself against mine.

RD LOVES GRACIE. She is the first person he goes to when he comes home from work, asking, "How's our baby doing?"

Sometimes I get the feeling that he forgets that she's Dwayne's, that he thinks of Grace as his. To tell the truth, it doesn't much bother me that he does.

To tell the truth, he'd have made a good daddy.

He don't even mind changing her diapers, which Mama says is unusual for a man.

"I can count on one hand the number of times your daddy

changed yours," she said. "And your granddaddy, ha. He never once changed a diaper, even though by the time you were born he'd retired from preaching. All he did was sit around in that old ratty robe of his watching *The 700 Club* on TV. Never even occurred to him that he could have helped Meemaw out with you."

Before I ran off looking for Daddy, Mama never spoke much about him or Granddaddy. But once I came back from Durham, she talked about them more and more, Granddaddy especially. I never knew how much she hated him. He could be real inspiring behind the pulpit, Mama said, but at home he was a bully.

"Granddaddy Meadows—though I called him Pastor Meadows back then—he literally had a shotgun by his side when he called Luke and me into his office to 'discuss' my pregnancy. He said Luke had two options: a wedding or a funeral, and he didn't seem to care much which option Luke took. In fact, he looked a little disappointed when Luke said, 'Guess we're having a wedding.'"

Mama said that Granddaddy Meadows was forever disappointed in Daddy, that he shook his head every time he talked about him. Granddaddy used to say that his son had a decadent streak that, regardless of countless attempts, no belt could beat out, that it resided in him the way the Holy Ghost resides in others, that it was what allowed him to impregnate a seventeen-year-old girl, and that it was what would ultimately cause his ruination.

MY FAVORITE THING to do is to watch Gracie while she sleeps, her belly rising up and down with her breaths. Standing over her crib, I cannot for the life of me imagine talking about her the way Granddaddy used to talk about my father. Maybe as babies grow up you start to feel less attached to them, but I don't see how. I don't hardly feel whole anymore unless I've got Gracie nuzzled up next to me. I put my hand on her belly and let it ride up and down with her inhale and exhale, wishing that I could breathe like she does, slow and assured, as if I knew for certain that someone was watching out for me.

I'M NOT READY to talk to God yet, but sometimes I talk to Mary. It's funny. We learned once in Sunday school that Catholics aren't real Christians because they worship the mother more than the Son. I believed that then, but now I don't really know.

Sometimes I imagine that Mary watches over me the way I watch over Gracie in her crib after everyone has gone to sleep and I sneak back in her room just to look at her.

Maybe it's wrong, but standing over Gracie's crib, I pray to Mary. I ask for the bitterness I feel toward Daddy and Dwayne and yes, even God, to dissolve. I ask that we don't have any un-expected bills this month, though more often than not, we do. I give thanks for the blessing of RD, thanks also that I can finally see that he is a blessing, to Mama and to me.

And finally, I pray that Gracie don't fall in love with her miss-ing Daddy like I once did with mine. I pray that Mama, RD, and me, tired and broke as we are, might somehow offer her enough.

CHAPTER TWENTY-THREE

Swallowing the Raspberry

(Louise, Spring 2008)

*A*fter we learned of Nanny Rose's death and began making plans for her funeral, I called Caroline in Oakland to make sure that she could come home for it. Caroline said that it is actually great timing, that the public school where she is student teaching is going to be on spring break and that it won't be a huge deal for her to miss a couple of her classes at Mills, where she is earning her credential. She said that maybe she will ask Sam, her boyfriend of six months, if he would like to come too, as the school where he teaches is also on break.

The only problem with Sam coming is that I was planning to fix a big sausage, egg, and cheese casserole to serve at breakfast the morning of the funeral. And Sam is Jewish. Though I assume he can't be too, too religious considering he is dating a woman who wears a cross around her neck—or at least, Caroline was wearing one the last time I saw her.

So I went ahead and asked Caroline, "Does the boy eat pork?"

"The boy?" she said. "He's three years older than I was when I got married."

"Yes, and you were a baby. Much too young. It's okay if he doesn't, I just need to know so I can plan meals."

"The boy eats pork," she said. "The boy loves pork. The boy thinks there is nothing on God's green earth that can't be improved with a slice of bacon."

"Really?" I replied, thinking that if they are still dating by next Christmas I might enroll him in the Bacon of the Month club, just for fun.

"His logic goes: he's a bad Jew for eating it, but he feels guilty about it, so that makes him a good Jew."

I smiled. Sounds like something Ben Ascher would have said.

When I called Charles in New York to tell him about Nanny Rose, he groaned. "Well, shit. She just had to go and die on the weekend of the prom, didn't she?"

"I'm surprised NYU has one," I said, ignoring his lack of sentiment toward his grandmother. "I thought prom was for high school."

"It's called the Prom You Never Had. It's an LGBT thing."

Oh. LGBT stands for Lesbian, Gay, Bisexual, something. I can never remember the last part. Transsexual. Or maybe transgender. Whatever Sandy was—I think—though don't quote me on that. Charles gets so irritated when I get my gay terms wrong.

I told Charles I was sorry that the funeral conflicts with his party and he sighed and said it's no big deal, that this way he'll get to see the dogwoods in bloom, which is one of the few things he misses about Atlanta.

Nanny Rose left instructions in her will stating her desire to be cremated, which shocks me. How could she not want to be buried next to her husband and her son? One hint might be that in her will she specifies that her ashes be mixed with the ashes of Gunther, who was cremated last fall after a long decline and an assisted death. I am convinced that that dog's death brought about Nanny Rose's. After all, he was her constant companion in that big old house of hers on Peachtree Battle Avenue. Not that she was completely isolated there. I visited once a week and she had a housekeeper come almost every day—it was her house-keeper who found her slumped over on her kitchen table, her cup of coffee still hot beside her—but come evening Nanny Rose was always alone.

For years John Henry and I tried to get her to move into a home for active seniors, but Nanny Rose refused, and there was really no medical reason that would mandate her doing so. In fact, whenever I accompanied her to her annual physical, the doc-tor always gushed over what good shape she was in.

"She's healthier than most fifty-year-olds!" he would exclaim, and I would think to myself, *Good Lord, she's going to outlive us all.*

THE FUNERAL IS held at Trinity Presbyterian, Nanny Rose's church. Trinity is a very solid place, made of red brick and situ-ated on a big, grassy hill. You can be sure that no matter how hard a wolf might huff and puff, he would not blow Trinity Presbyterian down. Nanny Rose was so upset when I did not join Trinity after John Henry and I got married. I made John Henry join All Saints instead. To me the decision was perfectly reasonable. All Saints was the church where I was baptized, it was near Ansley Park—where I knew we would end up living once we moved out of our starter house—it was where we were married, and its chapel, which includes seven stained glass win-dows designed by Tiffany Studios, is stunning.

Don't get me wrong. Trinity is a fine church and I'm sure we would have been happy there, especially considering how seldom we attend services. But not becoming a Presbyterian was one of my few open rebellions against Nanny Rose, one of the few barriers I managed to erect that she didn't bulldoze right through.

In retrospect, I imagine she admired my firm resolve.

AT THE MEMORIAL service the minister says that Nanny Rose was "both gracious *and* a force to be reckoned with," which is pretty much true, though occasionally she dropped her gracious side. Still, I am relieved that he seems to have actually known her. Too often you go to funerals and it is just so obvious that the minister has no understanding of the person behind his or her eulogy. (I wonder how much Sandy's minister knew about him/her?)

Because Nanny Rose is to be cremated, there is no body—or even coffin—to view, but dozens of people come to the service to show their respect, including the well-powdered ladies from her circle and the remaining members of her bridge game. Also attending are several members of John Henry's firm, other business associates of his, tons of our old friends, and most of my new ones. Stephen and Chevre attend, of course. Bob, Stephen's partner, would be here but he's taking care of his own sick mother, who lives in Highlands, North Carolina.

Tiny is here. She drove up from Sea Island last night. She's still single. A few months after she and Ray started dating, she found out that Ray and his friends were part of a pool, placing bets on how many "beach widows" they could sleep with. When Tiny called to tell me this revelation, I jokingly told her that she should never, ever have trusted a man who uses self-tanner.

"Easy for you to say," she said, and I could hear the bitterness in her voice.

My comment about self-tanner had only been an attempt at levity. But then I realized something: Tiny is jealous of my lasting relationship with John Henry. Which is so strange considering that before they got divorced I always viewed her relationship with Anders as ideal, while my relationship with my husband was so tenuous. Or rather, my feelings toward him were tenuous. There was sexual passion, yes, but otherwise I felt such anger toward him so much of the time.

I'm not as angry anymore.

AFTER THE MEMORIAL we go to the Houston's on Peachtree, just south of Peachtree Battle shopping center, where Nanny Rose used to run all her errands. Our group at Houston's—John Henry and his high school friend Jack, Caroline and Sam, Charles, Stephen, Tiny, and me—is certainly an eclectic bunch.

We arrive at the restaurant at 6:00 p.m., expecting to be early enough to avoid the crowds. The very elegant hostess, a black woman with her hair pulled back into a chignon, tells us that we will have to wait until two tables open up.

"May we please have one big table?" I ask.

"I'm sorry, ma'am," she says. "Our tables can only accommodate up to six guests."

"Honey, two of our guests are so skinny they only count as one, and if you'll just pull up an itty, bitty chair for me at the end of the table I'm sure we will all be able to squeeze in," says Tiny.

I swear you would think she was flirting with a man.

"I really am sorry to inconvenience you," says the woman, "but we can't pull chairs up to the booths. It creates a hazard for the servers."

I consider slipping her a twenty but decide to use sympathy instead. "Listen, if you could possibly find a way to seat us all at one table—and we really don't mind squeezing—we would so appreciate it. You see, we just came from the funeral of my husband's mother, and he really needs all of his family gathered around him at this time."

"I'm so sorry for your loss," says the hostess. She pauses and looks around the restaurant, which is built to resemble a hip fifties ranch with low wood-beamed ceilings and big plate-glass windows looking out onto Peachtree. "Let me see what I can do."

She hands me a beeper, informing me that it will vibrate when the table is ready.

Tiny grabs the beeper from me and slips it into my front pocket. "No sense not taking full advantage of the buzz," she whispers.

I try not to laugh, but I can't help myself, and then Tiny starts laughing too. I turn away from the hostess, whom I just told I was in mourning. My shoulders are shaking. Hopefully she will think I am overcome with grief.

"Let's wait outside," says Tiny, once she collects herself. "I need a cigarette."

"When did you start smoking again?" I ask, surprised. Tiny smoked in high school and college, but she quit right before Helen was born.

She sighs. "Oh, I don't know, Louise. I guess I picked it back up in Sea Island. I'm not a chain-smoker or anything; it's just an occasional pleasure."

I look around to make sure everyone else is doing okay before I disappear outside. Charles, Caroline, and Sam sit on one of the benches in the inside waiting area, talking. John Henry, Jack, and Stephen make their way to the bar. Good. Let them all drink and have a good time. John Henry especially, as he is the one who has lost his mother. Though considering the fact that we all must die someday, Nanny Rose certainly made a splendid exit.

After a lifetime of health, she died of a massive (and most likely instantaneous, according to the doctor at Piedmont) heart attack. She couldn't have had a better ending if she had planned it herself, and knowing Nanny Rose, she probably did. She probably left instructions to God in writing.

• • •

Tiny and I stand outside, leaning against the stacked stone exterior of the restaurant, watching the other groups of people who are waiting for tables. Many of the patrons are African American, and many of them are dressed better, and far more expensively, than either Tiny or I. One woman in particular stands out. Over knee-high black leather boots she wears a short-sleeved, scoop-neck, cream-colored sweater dress that is made entirely of cashmere. (I know because I saw it at Neiman's. I thought about getting it for Caroline, for her to teach in, but it cost $695.) Around this woman's neck hangs a long gold necklace, a diamond-encrusted circle dangling from its end. Usually I don't care for logo bags, but her Louis Vuitton works. Her hair falls just to her shoulders. Her diamond studs are simple but *big*. Her posture is impeccable, her body slim and fit, though not at all bony. She is with a group of all black women, and they are all dressed to the nines, from their salon-styled hair to their expensive boots and heels. And surely every toenail in that group has been recently clipped, filed, and painted.

"I had no idea this Houston's was so diverse," whispers Tiny.

"Stephen says that this Houston's and Justin's—the restaurant P. Diddy owns, which is just across the street—tie for being the epicenter of black power in Atlanta," I whisper, pleased to have such knowledge.

"Well aren't you a fount of information," says Tiny, blowing out smoke rings like she used to do in high school.

When the vibrator buzzes I jump it startles me so.

"Not used to that?" asks Tiny, leering.

We walk into the restaurant and gather up our crew, motioning to everyone to come on. Charles has joined the other men at the bar. He, John Henry, and Jack all drink beers out of the bottle, while Stephen holds a martini glass. I bet John Henry ordered Charles's drink for him, without even asking what he wanted, because even if Charles did want a beer, I doubt he would have ordered a Budweiser. Caroline and Sam are still sitting on their bench, squeezed as close as can be. Ever since they've arrived home I've been noticing the private looks they give each other, while pretending to listen to others talk. Their glances are so sweet, so intimate, that I almost want to say, "Hey, let me in on your secrets!"

THE HOSTESS HONORS my request and seats us at one booth instead of two, which means we are all squeezed rather tightly against each other. Immediately we order more drinks—another round of beer for John Henry and Jack, martinis for Charles and Stephen, a margarita on the rocks for Tiny, and wine for Sam, Caroline, and me. Then Caroline suggests we tell stories about Nanny Rose.

"I'm sure everyone has a good one," she says.

Everyone says yes, yes, though in truth neither Sam nor Stephen knew Nanny Rose at all, and probably the last time Jack saw her was at John Henry's and my wedding. They are just here for support.

"Darling, you start," I say to John Henry, but then the waitress returns because she can't remember whether we ordered two or three spinach and artichoke dips for appetizers.

Once that is settled I prompt John Henry again, and all eyes turn to him, except Jack's; he is looking around with a quizzical expression on his face, probably wondering how he wound up packed so tightly into a booth with two gay men.

"Mother was a real firecracker," says John Henry.

"That's for sure," says Jack. "She was one tough lady."

"Here's to firecrackers!" says Stephen.

We raise our glasses and clink them against each other.

"She was always on time," I say.

"Pathologically so," mumbles Charles.

"When I was a kid she believed there was nothing that couldn't be cured by an enema," says John Henry.

"Christ," says Jack, shaking his head.

"You poor thing," says Stephen.

"If I had a cold, she gave me an enema. If I had a stomach-ache, she gave me an enema. If I had a sprained wrist . . ."

"She gave you an enema!" say Stephen, Tiny, and I.

"Nice timing," says Sam.

OUR WAITRESS RETURNS with the drinks and the dip, and then it is time for everyone to give their dinner orders, which always takes a long time because no one ever remembers what kind of salad dressings and soups are offered, so the poor waitress has to keep repeating the options again and again.

She starts with me—I have the dubious honor of being the oldest woman at the table—and I order the hickory burger with fries. Thank God I managed to go to Bodypump this morning.

While people are busy studying the menu and ordering, I study Sam. Compared to Davis, he seems very, very young. Which he *is*, though he's not a boy. He's youthful but not im-mature. Caroline says he graduated from Berkeley when he was twenty-one, spent two years in the Peace Corps in Peru, and is now in his second year at the teaching program at Mills College, working on his masters at night while teaching math to middle school kids during the day. Caroline is in her first year at Mills, becoming credentialed to teach elementary students.

I would never say this to Caroline's face, but it saddens me that she gave up acting or at least pursuing some kind of art. And I regret that at each critical stage in her life it was a man who got in her way: Frederick by diverting her from Juilliard, Davis by making her so damn comfortable she forgot how hungry she was to be on the stage. Don't get me wrong, I'm not blaming either Frederick or Davis, I just think she's had—well—shitty timing with men.

And I know that teaching is a noble career, but I also know how passionate she was about theater, and sometimes I wish that she would just get her old selfish gene back, that she would say "to hell with duty!" and try to find her way to the spotlight again.

But maybe I'm just nostalgic for my thin, young daughter who seemed to have the world before her, who seemed ready to fight any person or thing that got in her way. She's become so calm, so assured, so settled in her own (substantial) body. Which is a good thing, I suppose. It just makes me feel old.

John Henry and I are footing the bill for her Mills tuition, same as we did for her divorce lawyer. It was a noncontested divorce—very clean as far as those things go. She did get a little money out of it, which she offered to use to help pay her tuition, but John Henry told her to either invest it in mutual funds or put it into a high-interest savings account, ING or Emigrant Direct.

"A woman needs money of her own," he said, which promptly caused me to open my own checking account, where I keep all the money I make on art sales. (I had been keeping it in our joint account, but doing so made me feel as if I had to ask for John Henry's permission every time I wanted to spend it.)

Caroline and Sam both say that they are dedicated to working in the Oakland public schools, despite all the known difficulties of overcrowding and underfunding. I say good luck and keep me posted. What I don't say is that I have my doubts as to the sustainability of their career plans—not to mention the sustainability of Caroline's dedication. Still, I wish them well.

BEFORE SAM AND Caroline arrived home I asked John Henry how he felt about Sam being Jewish. We were sitting on our front porch swing, enjoying the warm spring evening while eating strawberries I bought at the Morningside market.

John Henry finished chewing his berry, swallowed, and said, "It's probably not a bad idea to mix up the gene pool."

Funny he should say that. Funny because it epitomizes what I have come to think of as the "kinder, gentler John Henry," and funny because it brought up, indirectly, something I have been worrying about for over a year now, whether or not our gene pool has already—if not mixed—at least taken a detour.

I made the discovery last fall, after Charles left for NYU. I had decided to turn his bedroom into a den so that I could use the entire downstairs for my shows. While I was boxing up all Charles's remaining things, I came across a photo slipped into the pages of his senior yearbook from Coventry. It was a photo of the cast of *Salt of the Earth*, the show that starred Missy's father. And there, in the center of the picture, was a man who looked startlingly like a young version of my father. A curly-haired man just like Daddy, he had the same intense eyes framed by the same long lashes, the same elegant nose, a broader smile but the same large teeth behind it.

There was no doubt the man who looked so much like Daddy was Luke Meadows, the star of *Salt of the Earth*. And just from looking at his photo, I could understand why Missy wanted him back so desperately, even after he'd been gone for so many years. It was obvious the man had real charisma.

I had to sit down on Charles's bed I was breathing so hard. And my mind was spinning with questions: could Daddy have gotten Miss Winnie pregnant all those years ago?

I thought to myself, *Holy Christ*. If Luke Meadows was actually Daddy's son, and not the son of the man Miss Winnie married, the preacher, then that would make Luke Meadows my half-brother, and that would make Missy a cousin of Caroline and Charles.

But no. It didn't make sense. Because if Luke had been Daddy's son, wouldn't we have found out about it? Wouldn't Miss Winnie have made sure Mother knew? Instead of giving Mother a gold necklace, wouldn't she have taken the money Mother offered? And even if she refused the money out of pride, wouldn't she at least have told Mother about Luke all those years later, when Mother ran into her at Sam's Club?

And isn't it possible for two men—two white, Protestant men—to look similar to each other without being related?

I put the photo back in the yearbook, put the yearbook in one of the brown cardboard boxes already filled with books, taped it shut, and stuck it in the attic with the mice. At dinner when John Henry asked me about my day, I mentioned nothing.

But I had insomnia that night, my mind continuing to spin out questions: What if Luke is Daddy's son? What does that mean? How should it affect our lives? *Should* it affect our lives? Is there not a statute of limitation on Daddy's transgressions, on the ever-generating consequences of his having taken Miss Winnie for a convertible ride, so many years ago, on that gorgeous spring day? Considering that Luke was in no way raised as a part of our family, that no one even knows where he currently is, that Missy's mother voluntarily cut off her connection with our family before Missy's baby was born, and that before she did, my family's involvement with theirs only caused them greater problems—a child born to a child!—does it matter that we might be related?

During that sleepless night, for the thousandth time, I asked myself, *Was there anything I could have done to change the trajectory of Missy's life?* I offered encouragement to her as a child. I loaned her mother money whenever she needed it. And after she went to Durham, I offered money for an abortion. I gave her mother a thousand dollars—a thousand dollars!—when she quit.

But do I owe them more?

Caroline would say that yes, I should offer all I have to give, regardless of DNA. I should treat Missy and her mother and her mother's husband as family, simply because they were a part of our lives, and because Charles's actions irrevocably altered theirs. Nanny Rose would have voiced an unequivocal no, damn the blood if it's not legitimate. In Nanny Rose's world, the only children that matter in one's genealogy are those born safely within the confines of marriage, and preferably a marriage for which the reception was held at the Driving Club.

And where does that leave me? Philosophically, somewhere in between Nanny Rose and Caroline. Also suspicious of interference. Afraid it will do more harm than good. Afraid of the old adage: "No good deed goes unpunished." Wondering if maybe it's time my family leaves the Meadows family in peace. A continued withdrawal, regardless of the damage previously wrought.

(Though maybe some sort of trust fund for the child, for Grace? Arranged, perhaps, without the knowledge of my husband?)

"Louise?" asks John Henry.

"Yes," I say, smiling, aware that I have been caught spacing out.

"Would you like another glass of wine with your meal?" he asks.

I look down and see that my hamburger has been set before me. I look up and realize that our waitress is standing by my chair, obviously having asked me about wine multiple times.

"Sure," I say. "I'm having the pinot. And may I also have a glass of iced tea? Unsweet with lemon?"

"I didn't realize people in the South drank anything but sweet tea," says Sam as the waitress puts his bacon cheeseburger before him.

"Well I must not be a real southerner," I say, "because I can't stand it sweet."

"Believe me, Mom, if anyone is a real southerner, you are," says Caroline.

"Mother was a sweet-tea drinker," says John Henry.

"She would put *four* cups of sugar in every pitcher. It was *so* good," says Charles.

"Was your mother a big sweet-tea drinker?" I ask Jack, who has been mostly silent.

"My mother liked sweet tea but her staple was Coca-Cola, in the eight-ounce glass bottle."

"Not Co-Cola?" asks Stephen, with a smile. He shifts in his chair so the waitress can place a plate of prime rib with french fries in front of him.

"Oh, you know that's affectation," I say, shaking salt on my own fries. "No one really says it that way anymore unless they're *trying* to be southern."

"My mother mixed her Co-Cola with rum and drank her Coca-Cola straight," says Tiny.

Sam laughs and Tiny flashes me a look, which I interpret to mean, *Encourage Caroline to keep this one around.* Tiny adores anyone who will laugh at her jokes.

"I love Coke in the eight-ounce glass bottles," says Caroline. "I can sometimes find them at Safeway, but a six-pack costs about five bucks."

"I remember when you could get one for five cents," says Stephen. He holds his martini glass up, signaling to the waiter that he wants another.

"Five cents a six-pack?" asks Caroline.

"Five cents a bottle."

I wait until I have swallowed my fry before saying, "*I* remember when people actually responded to RSVPs, wrote thank-you notes after parties, and didn't have private phone conversations in public."

Clearly I have decided to cast my lot with the grumpy old ladies.

"I smell imperialist nostalgia," says Charles, in a singsong voice.

I take a sip from my new glass of wine. "Sweetheart, how can I be an imperialist when I've never lived anywhere but in the United States?"

"Ha!" Charles barks. "You think that it's possible to be a wealthy citizen of the United States and *not* be considered an imperialist?"

"Why don't we hit the brakes on this train before it wrecks, and get back to our dinner?" suggests John Henry. The plate of food before him certainly looks worth getting back to, pieces of seasoned chicken stacked on top of one another, with a side of dirty rice.

"Why don't we get back to stories about Nanny Rose?" says Caroline. She is having the grilled chicken salad with peanut sauce. When she first ordered it I was tempted to tell her that even though it's a salad, it's not low-cal.

I held my tongue.

"I want to hear more about her," says Sam. "She sounds like a real character."

I glance at John Henry, wondering if it irritates him to hear his deceased mother described as a character. He puts a big bite of chicken in his mouth. He doesn't look too concerned.

"*You* think the United States is an imperialist nation, don't you?" Charles asks Sam.

I cannot wait for my son to outgrow this confrontational phase.

"I think it's a complicated nation," says Sam.

"Like the South!" I say, trying once again to get Charles off subject. "Like Atlanta."

"Louise, honey, Atlanta isn't the South anymore," says

Tiny, eating her ribs with a knife and fork. "It's L.A. with no beach."

"You just read that somewhere," I say. "Atlanta is the South. I'm drinking iced tea, right?"

"Unsweet," Sam and Caroline say at the same time.

There goes one of their looks again.

"I think the South might have died with Mother," says John Henry.

"Look away, look away . . . ," sings Charles.

"Well I'm southern," says Stephen, "and you haven't buried me yet. I still write thank-you notes and let people know whether or not I'm coming to their parties, and I don't answer my cell phone in public unless it's an emergency."

"That's why we love you, darling," says Tiny.

"I just realized something," I say. "I don't think the South is dead at all. I think gay men have simply replaced the old southern matrons."

"I love it," says Tiny.

"Here, here," says Stephen, lifting his martini glass.

Charles is wearing his most scornful face. "Hello, Mom? I don't really aspire to be an old southern matron."

"Attaboy," says Jack, raising his beer bottle to Charles.

Sam laughs again. "Y'all are such fun," he says.

I'm glad he perceives this conversation as fun, though Charles is actually making me a little tense.

"People from California say *y'all*?" asks Tiny.

"No, it's just that Sam has an obsession with all things southern. He's already made me take him to Krispy Kreme twice since we've been in Atlanta, even though there's one near the San Francisco airport," says Caroline.

I wonder: if Sam is obsessed with all things southern, does that mean Sam might want to live in the South one day?

"Okay, I have the true test of whether or not one is really southern," says Caroline.

"Is it whether or not you're a racist?" asks Charles, sitting up straight and blinking his eyes like an earnest student.

"For goodness' sake, Charles!" I scold. "What a terrible thing to say."

I want to remind him that there are black people sitting at tables all around us and maybe he should be a little more sensitive. But Charles will jump all over me if I say that; he'll say something about how my being uncomfortable talking about race in front of black people proves that I am a racist.

I look to John Henry, but he is busy taking a swig of beer, probably to help alleviate his irritation with his son. I follow his lead and drain my glass of wine in one long sip.

"I don't mean to make a speech . . . ," says Sam.

"But you're going to anyway," says Caroline, smiling.

"From my experience working in a predominantly black public school in Oakland, I'm willing to say that it's much, much tougher to be black in America than it is to be white. There are exceptions to every rule of course, but the bottom line is even if people don't mean to be racist, our system privileges white people—at least, white people who aren't really poor—and a lot of white people refuse to acknowledge that.

"That said, I think some white southerners, because they are so aware of the South's history, *do* acknowledge that. More so than, say, white people from New Hampshire, where I'm originally from. So, Charles, man, I hate to say it, but I don't think whether or not one is a racist is a litmus test for southern citizenship. Now, whether or not it's a litmus test for American citizenship might be a discussion worth having."

"'Might be,'" says Caroline, laughing. "As if you don't initiate that discussion every other day or so!"

"I think Sam's point is well made," John Henry says, which is surprising, given that John Henry is usually more interested in discussing his own hard work than in acknowledging the privileges he has been granted. My guess is he's just happy to have someone at the table who can win an argument with Charles.

I'm tempted to ask Sam about the exquisitely dressed black people eating all around us, to see where they fit into his theory on race. What if you're wealthy and black? Or what if you're poor and white, like Missy? I'm not trying to be contentious. It's a question I think about a lot, knowing that Atlanta is considered a mecca of opportunity for middle- and upper-class African Americans, but also knowing that many of those working menial jobs around the city, and the majority of homeless people I pass on the street, are black.

Is the bottom line always money? Does wealth trump everything? I know that I certainly feel more powerful now that I'm earning money of my own.

"There are plenty of white southerners who don't acknowledge their privilege," says Charles. "Or who do, but who only discuss race with white people."

He arches an eyebrow and looks at us all.

"I've got to tell you, son," says Jack, "I'm not big on discussing race with anyone."

"Is that right?" asks Charles, his voice oozing derision.

"Can I *please* give my test that will reveal who at this table is a real southern dame?" asks Caroline.

"I don't think I'll qualify, sweetheart," says John Henry.

Caroline smiles. "You're absolutely right, Dad. You will not qualify. But for the rest of you, here goes. Pretend it is Thanksgiving and you have just enjoyed a multiple-course turkey dinner including two servings of cornbread stuffing, sweet potatoes with marshmallows, green beans almandine, and a big old piece of pecan pie with real whipped cream."

Good Lord, if that's the way Caroline eats no wonder she has gained so much weight.

Stop it, Louise, I tell myself.

"After dinner you retire to your daughter-in-law's living room, where your son and she and their two gorgeous, darling children all sprawl about, letting their food digest. You notice that sitting on the coffee table is a pretty wooden bowl with twelve perfectly ripe raspberries in it. You think to yourself, *A nice juicy raspberry is just what I need to cap off my wonderful Thanksgiving feast.* So you reach over and pop the raspberry into your mouth."

Oh! Suddenly I recognize the story she is telling, and I get a little jolt of excitement. It's a good one.

"But suddenly you are quite aware that the raspberry in your mouth did not grow on any bush. And there is nothing juicy or succulent about it. Indeed, it is hard and cold on your tongue, for it is made of painted porcelain."

"Twenty dollars a raspberry," I add, interrupting Caroline. "Hand-painted."

"Oh no," says Stephen.

Caroline continues, "Once you realize that the raspberry you have placed in your mouth is porcelain, you look around the room and notice that your eleven-year-old granddaughter is staring right at you, and you are pretty sure she witnessed you eating the porcelain berry. So the question is, What do you do if you are a true southern dame?"

I look around the table. John Henry looks confused. Jack is yawning. Charles is still glaring at Jack. Stephen and Tiny are on the edge of their seats.

"Honey, you swallow that berry," says Stephen. "Because if there's no evidence that it ever went in your mouth, then your nosy little granddaughter can't tell on you. And if she *does,* you just deny the charges. You claim that the one *you* ate was real."

"Yes!" cries Caroline. "Exactly! Nanny Rose looked right at

me and then she swallowed the raspberry. I saw it go down her throat."

"Mother did that?" asks John Henry.

"She did," I say. "Caroline told me about it afterwards and when I counted the berries, there were only eleven in the bowl instead of the twelve I had originally purchased."

"She didn't!" cries Tiny, clapping her hands and laughing.

"Isn't that perfect?" says Caroline.

"You never told me that story," says Sam.

"I haven't thought about it in years."

"I guess I'm not a real southern lady," says Tiny. "I would not swallow glass just to get out of looking like a fool."

"Don't look at me," I say. "I would never have swallowed something that expensive unless it was caviar."

"I think it's fair to say that none of us are dedicated to putting on as dignified a front as Nanny Rose was," says Stephen.

"To Mother," says John Henry. "The last of her kind."

"Here, here!" I say.

We raise our glasses and clink them against each other.

Our separate yearnings lift and collide.

Acknowledgments

Thank you to Suzanne Gluck at William Morris for introducing me to the lovely and intrepid Shana Kelly, who read nascent drafts of *Bound South* and encouraged me to keep going. Shana, your enduring faith in me, and your willingness to read my work at all stages, contributed enormously to my ability to bring this book to fruition. You are a treasure, and Miss Ella is one lucky lady.

Endless thanks to the amazing Trish Grader, whose highly developed sense of story and impeccable editing helped make *Bound South* the book it was meant to be. Trish, you were a pleasure to work with and I look forward to our next collaboration!

A special thanks to the editors of the magazines and journals that previously published portions of this book: Youmna Chlala and Brent Foster Jones at *Eleven Eleven;* Agnes Scott College's Lisa Alembik, who edited *Blackbird on your shoulder: stories and other truths from the South;* and Rebecca Burns and Paige Williams at *Atlanta* magazine.

Had I not attended the graduate program in creative writing at Hollins University, I would probably still be dreaming of being a writer, instead of actually being one. Thanks especially to Wayne Johnston, for insisting that I allow the novel to find its own shape.

The Hambidge Center provided a gorgeous refuge while I made the final edits on this book. Thanks especially to Bob, Debbie, and Ray, who are fast becoming my mountain family away from home.

I am grateful for my wonderful group of friends, both near and far. Special thanks to the continual spiritual, psychological, and creative support offered by Kasey Foster, Laura Reynolds, and Katharine Powell. Thank you also to the members of my fabulous writing group, Sheri Joseph, Beth Gylys, Megan Sexton, and Peter McDade, who have inspired me with their talent and generosity, and who have helped me transfer my creative life—almost seamlessly—from San Francisco to Atlanta. And thank you so much to Susan Bridges, southern dame extraordinaire, who represents everything I love about Atlanta, and who has helped my creative journey in endless ways.

I am blessed with wonderful in-laws, Hal and Elaine Deutschman, who by their overflowing love and support have truly taught me the meaning of the word *kvell*.

Thanks to my large and loving family. Special thanks to the friendship and guidance provided by my brilliant sister, Lauren Myracle.

Thanks to my parents, Ruth and Tim White. Dad, thank you for your off-center humor and your generous heart. And thank you, Mom, for letting me know you not just as a mother but also as a woman, and for passing your "artist gene" on to me. We both know that you are not Louise Parker, but you sure provided me with some of Louise's best lines.

And finally, I am endlessly astonished at my luck in getting to share my life with my wonderful, darling husband, Alan Deutschman. Alan, you have nurtured both this book and me since the very beginning of our relationship. Life with you is a journey and an adventure.

Bound South

For Discussion

1. *Bound South* is told from the first-person perspective of three different characters: Louise, Caroline, and Missy. Why do you think the author chose to give voice to multiple characters? How did hearing from each woman shape your understanding of the novel? Did you believe all three women to be reliable narrators? Why or why not? Of the twenty-two chapters in the novel, Louise narrates thirteen. Ultimately, is this her story? Discuss why or why not.

2. In chapter one, Louise tells us that her Sunday school class once discussed "how it is internalized racism that makes us scared of those who are—in fact—quite often the most vulnerable and disadvantaged" (page 14). What is internalized racism? In what ways has Louise Parker internalized racist thinking? In what ways has she resisted racist thinking? Do you think that Louise's attitudes about race and class are particular to the South? What are Caroline's attitudes about race and class? What are Missy's?

3. Describe the relationship between Louise and Caroline. How does their dynamic change as Caroline grows older? Do you know of mother-daughter relationships like the one between Caroline and Louise? Do you think this type of relationship

is specific to mothers and their daughters? If so, why? What was Louise's relationship like with her own mother? What is Missy's relationship like with hers?

4. After meeting Louise, Deidre (Caroline's friend) declares that Caroline and Louise are "two of a kind" (page 200). And later (on page 267), John Henry says to his daughter, "You are so much like your mother." Do you agree with Deidre's and John Henry's assessments? Why or why not? In what ways does Caroline become more like her mother as she grows up? In what ways does she become less like her mother?

5. In the book's beginning, Caroline is a sexy, caustic teenager who runs away to San Francisco with her high school theater teacher. By the book's end, she is a more subdued, divorced Christian woman planning to teach in urban public schools. In what ways does the trajectory of Caroline's life surprise you? Why do you think Louise, who battled wills with Caroline throughout her childhood, wishes that as an adult Caroline "would say 'to Hell with duty!' and try to find her way to the spotlight again" (page 331)? Do you share Louise's wish that Caroline return to a more "selfish" self?

6. In the final chapter of the novel, Louise tells us "it saddens me that [Caroline] gave up acting, or at least pursuing some kind of art. And I regret that at each critical stage in her life it was a man who got in her way" (page 330). Do you agree with Louise that Caroline's pursuit of art has been crippled by her various romances? In what ways did Caroline's romances change her for the better, and in what ways did they hurt her? How did her romantic relationships seem to alter her personality? What character traits did she maintain throughout her varied relationships?

7. Why do you think Missy stole the clay bird from Louise's collection (page 54)? Did it surprise you that Missy stole the bird, considering her strong religious convictions?

8. After Missy's mother, Faye, discovers that Missy has stolen the bird, she tells Louise Parker, "That girl is going to get the belt" (page 66). Louise tells us that she "wanted to suggest some other form of punishment but I had to remind myself that that was not my place, that people from other cultures and classes handle things differently" (page 66). What do you think about Louise's reticence on this matter? When is it acceptable to interfere with the way someone raises his or her child? When is it not acceptable? Do you believe that there are certain child-rearing practices that are indisputably better than others? In what ways does socioeconomic class affect child-rearing practices?

9. What was your reaction to *Every Woman Has Some Jesus in Her*, the Earl LeTrouve painting of Jesus in a ball gown that hangs in Louise and John Henry's home? How do your own feelings about religion factor into your reaction to this piece of folk art?

10. Tiny, Louise's best friend, is an avowed Christian, a staunch Republican, and in possession of a dominant personality; Louise is openly agnostic, a yellow-dog Democrat, and accepting of the fact that "Tiny's will has always been stronger than mine" (page 69). Yet Louise and Tiny are lifelong friends. Why do you think their relationship has remained so strong despite their significant differences in personality and worldview? What are some of the factors that allow them to remain so close? How do you think their friendship will be altered by Tiny's divorce and move to Sea Island?

11. Louise still thinks wistfully about her brief college romance with Ben Ascher. What do you think Louise's adult life would have been like had she married him? Do you think a marriage between Ben Ascher and Louise would have worked out?

12. While talking with Tiny (page 156), Louise says, "Sometimes I wish John Henry would cheat on me and then we could just get a divorce." Why do you think Louise felt such dissatisfaction in her marriage? Were you surprised that she and John Henry were still married by the novel's end? In what ways did their relationship change over the course of the novel?

13. Discuss the role of religion in the novel. Which character's religious beliefs—or lack thereof—resonate most strongly with your own? In what ways does religion unite the different characters? In what ways does religion divide them? By the novel's end, both Missy and Caroline identify themselves as Christians. Do you believe that Missy would recognize Caroline as a Christian? Would Caroline recognize Missy as one? What do you think of the way the novel treats the subject of Christianity? What do you think of the way the novel treats Judaism?

14. Were you surprised by John Henry's reaction to Charles after Charles told him that he was gay? Why or why not? Were you surprised by Louise's reaction to Charles's news? Why or why not? If you had a son who came out to you, how do you think you might respond? Would it make a difference whether it was your son or your daughter who was gay?

15. After John Henry tells the story of the intense fight he had with his brother the last time he saw him alive, Louise says, "Perhaps I should hate my husband for the story he has told me, but I don't. I feel—I feel sad for him and sad for Wallace... What has holding this in done to [John Henry's] spirit all of these years?" (page 289). In what ways did Louise's response to John Henry's story surprise you? Do you think that Louise and John Henry might have had a happier earlier marriage had Wallace not killed himself? In what ways did Charles's coming out ultimately improve John Henry and Louise's relationship?

16. When Missy and Charles first watched *Salt of the Earth*, did you believe that Pastor Praise was really Missy's dad? Why or why not? Why do you think Missy is so focused on finding her father, even though he has been gone for so many years? In what way is Missy's relationship to Jesus connected to her relationship with her missing father?

17. Why do you think Charles was so interested in the Christian soap opera, *Salt of the Earth*?

18. While watching him chat with Carol, the receptionist at Luke Meadow's church, Missy feels frustrated with Charles. "He's acting like he really likes [Carol], but the truth is he is just amused by her. Probably, he thinks she is 'hilarious.' She's just one more funny thing to entertain him. Just like Daddy's show. Probably even just like me" (page 221). Do you agree with Missy's evaluation of Charles? Do you believe that Charles legitimately liked Missy? Why do you think he agreed to drive her to North Carolina? Why do you think he returned to Atlanta without her once their plans didn't go as expected? By the novel's end, what are your feelings toward Charles?

19. In chapter sixteen, Louise writes two letters responding to Caroline's request to hear about her engagement story. Why do you think that Louise decides to send the abridged, sugared letter, instead of the more honest and difficult one? How might it have affected Caroline to be told the truth about her parents' courtship and engagement? Which letter would you have sent were you in Louise's place? Do you believe that parents have an obligation to be completely honest about their lives with their children after the children reach a certain age? Why or why not?

20. After Nanny Rose's funeral, Caroline tells the story of Nanny Rose swallowing a porcelain raspberry rather than admitting that she had mistaken it for a real one. And Louise's mother, Amelia, also of Nanny Rose's generation, advised Louise "to keep up with the little things, to say your *ma'ams* and *sirs*, to write your thank-you cards on time, so that people would feel generous toward you when the big things happen that you can't control" (page 124). In what ways do you agree with Nanny Rose and Amelia that appearances really do matter? In what ways has "keeping up appearances" limited the life choices of the characters in *Bound South*?

21. Do you think that *Bound South* has a happy ending? Why or why not?

A Conversation with Susan Rebecca White

When you sat down to write *Bound South*, did you know that you were going to have three different women narrating it, each from the first-person point of view? Do you think of one particular woman as the protagonist, or do the three women share this role? You obviously care about all of your characters, but are you especially attached to a particular one?

I did not initially plan on having all three women narrate *Bound South* from the first-person point of view. In fact, initially I opened each section of the book with a story told from third-person point of view. But my editor convinced me, rightly, that the occasional switch to the third person was jarring, and that it was important to let the women of the book narrate their stories completely.

It's interesting to think back on my process of writing this novel. The first piece I wrote was about Missy stealing Louise Parker's clay bird. I wrote that in graduate school as a stand-alone short story, but when I was finished with it I still had Missy's voice in my head, and I wanted to write more about her and find out what happened to her dad. (I tend to find out what happens to my characters through the process of writing their stories, letting my subconscious mind do all of the work.) And then one day I wrote a piece called "Louise Parker Speaks," and there was Louise, just as alive as could be, springing up from the page. And of course writing about Louise led me to writing about Caroline, because Caroline needed to have her say. And so, piece by piece, the book came together.

In my mind Louise is the major protagonist, as she is the one who is directly connected to almost all of the characters in the story. And while I love Caroline, I have to say that both Missy and Louise hold a special place in my heart. They are both just so vulnerable and yet resilient.

You were born and raised in Atlanta, where *Bound South* takes place. How did your personal relationship with Atlanta find its way into the novel? Do you consider yourself a Southern author?

I'll start with the second question: I didn't really think of myself as a Southern author until after I wrote *Bound South*, and then I realized that yes, indeed, the South has shaped me, and my understanding of the South helps my writing. Here's what I mean: When I was in college in the Northeast, and then later when I was living in San Francisco, I wrote a lot of stories, but they weren't really place-specific, unless you consider a bar in either New York or San Francisco a specific place. And then I got to graduate school and I realized that a lot of writers set their stories in urban bars. I remember thinking: *I am not going to write another story that takes place in a bar or on a date.* Not because such stories are inherently bad, but because I realized I didn't really have anything new or interesting to say on the subject, whereas other writers do. And I guess it was around that time that I also realized that while plenty of other authors could write about New York or California better than I could, I really, really knew Atlanta, or at least one slice of it, and I should try writing about it. And that led me to Missy and Louise, who I think are both products of their environment—Caroline, a little less so, perhaps, though in the end she finds she can't escape feeling real nostalgia for the South.

I wrote much of *Bound South* while living away from Atlanta, and my yearnings for home made their way into the book. For example, Caroline is always trying out recipes from *The Gift of Southern Cooking,* and of course that was the cookbook I turned to every time I felt homesick. Even Missy and RD's love affair with Chick-fil-A sandwiches was a reflection of my own cravings.

Writing about Atlanta also allowed me to explore different parts of the city whenever I returned home to visit my parents. It's quite feasible that a woman like Louise Parker would live in

Ansley Park, but I also situated her there because I really like that neighborhood, and I thought it was fun to research its architecture and history, and to walk its streets whenever I was in town.

After living away from Atlanta for more than a decade, you are now living there once again. What is it like to have returned to your hometown as an adult? Do you believe the saying "You can never go home again" to be true?

It's complicated being back, and I have to admit there are times when I think longingly of San Francisco. Part of that is because by the time I returned to Atlanta I was fully an adult, so living in Atlanta came with all of these adult responsibilities, like owning an old house that seems to be in constant need of repair—not that to be an adult one has to own an old house, but I certainly took that route.

In this city, I feel very known, which is a mixed blessing. I can't tell you how often I run into people who knew me when I was a little girl. It's lovely, to an extent, but I do think nostalgically of the blank slate I had in San Francisco—how I could create whatever identity I wanted for myself because no one there knew me as a kid.

That said, I do live in a different—and decidedly more progressive—neighborhood than the one I grew up in. I'm married and involved in my community, both in girly ways (I'm in a gourmet group and a book club) and in more overtly political ways. For the most part, my adult life in Atlanta does not mirror the world that I grew up in—although I definitely spend more time here at furniture stores than I ever did in San Francisco! But in an effort to recruit more ex-pats to return home, I am always telling friends who have moved away that there are "lots of Atlantas," and that almost everyone can find some sort of a niche here.

During your twenties you lived in San Francisco, where part of the novel takes place. How was living in San Francisco different from living in Atlanta? Had you been born and raised in San Francisco, do you think you would have written a novel like *Bound South*?

Hmm, I probably would not have written a novel like *Bound South* had I grown up in San Francisco. Hopefully I would still be a writer, but my leading lady would most likely have been cut from a different cloth than Louise. In fact, I am currently working on a novel where one of the characters is born in Atlanta but moves to San Francisco at a young age. The move changes her entirely. That said, San Francisco and Atlanta share some qualities: neither city has terrible winters, people in both places tend to be fairly friendly, and each town has amazing restaurants. And neighborhood really matters in both places—where you live says a lot about who you are, or at least people will make a lot of assumptions about you based on the neighborhood you live in.

The city of San Francisco does seem to dedicate more energy toward preserving and beautifying public spaces, whereas in Atlanta the focus is definitely on private space (read: one's home and garden).

Besides being a writer, what other jobs have you held?

I'll start with the most ridiculous. For two days I was an associate at a high-tech PR firm in Silicon Valley. I guess you have to know me to grasp the absurdity. I am about the least high-tech person on the planet: I don't get cable, I don't text, I have no idea what a BlackBerry even does. After the PR firm, I started cleaning houses. My job as a housekeeper was equally absurd, mainly because I'm allergic to dust and just about as allergic to doing housework. But my friend and I came up with a cute name, "The Mop Squad" (which I'm sure has been used by cleaning services before). We made funny posters featuring photos of us holding feather dusters like weapons, à la Charlie's Angels, and we posted an ad on craigslist and we got quite a few gigs. But the thing is—we were rarely asked back twice! Instead people would hire us and then would never call us back.

For two years I waited tables at a Middle Eastern restaurant in San Francisco. I loved that job, mostly because the staff was so nice, and the woman who ran the place, Ellen Sinaiko, is smart and funny and, in general, just a joy to be around. Also, I've taught junior high and high school English. I really love teaching.

Is there a character from *Bound South* to whom you most relate? Is *Bound South* in any way autobiographical?

Bound South is not autobiographical, but it is based on my understanding of the people of Atlanta. It's funny—I tried to write an autobiographical story and found that I wasn't very good at it. I took myself—or perhaps I should say my viewpoint—too seriously. So I started writing about people different from me, first Missy and then Louise. Which isn't to say that I don't take either of them seriously, just that I'm able to see their foibles, and I'm able to see how their specific backgrounds influence who they are and what choices they make, and how each character knows truths about life that come into direct conflict with the other's truth. (For example, Missy knows that she *cannot* have an abortion, while Louise knows that Missy's life will be infinitely more difficult because she doesn't have an abortion. Both women are correct but neither was really able to see the other's point of view.)

In terms of relating to any specific character, to be honest, I relate to them all. While we have somewhat different worldviews, like Louise I try to be honest about acknowledging uncomfortable and painful truths about myself. And I really like living in a pretty environment, as does Louise. I'm a big cook, like Caroline, and I've always been drawn to religion, though I've never bought a cross to wear around my neck. And like Missy, I've had my heart broken (although not by my father), and I understand how we can create gods and ghosts out of those people who break our hearts, the way that Missy did with her daddy, Luke Meadows.

Art plays such a pivotal role in *Bound South.* **What role does art play in your own life? Do you personally know, or collect the art of, anyone like Mr. Earl Le Trouve?**

I have a distinct aesthetic sensibility—can't say if it's good or not—and I usually have an immediate response when I see a piece of art for the first time. Either I am instantly drawn in—as Louise was drawn to Earl's egg tempera pieces—or I am left cold.

I have a very odd photo that I just adore. I bought it for my husband's birthday, and he was nice enough to let me pretend that it was a gift for him and not really for me. The photo is huge—at least three feet long—and in it an old beat-up sofa is on fire. The fire is just raging. And in front of this burning sofa is a stuffed (but very real-looking) fox, whose hair is being blown by the gusts from the fire. When I first saw the fox I thought it was alive, but then I realized that all of the animals in this artist's work are taxidermied. (The artist's name is Jody Fausett.) Anyway, I looked at that photo and I just loved the statement of the fire, the intensity of it, the lack of ambiguity, the clearing away. And so I bought it and hung it in my dining room, justifying the central placement by saying that it's a conversation piece.

My friend Susan Bridges runs an art gallery (named whitespace) out of the carriage house behind her home. Through her I have met some eccentric Southern artists, though none quite like Mr. LeTrouve.

Bound South does not shy away from either serious or controversial topics, including transgenderism, teen pregnancy, suicide, the treatment of prisoners at Abu Ghraib, sexual harassment, and even a mother's own violent thoughts toward her daughter. Yet the book is laced with humor. How did you manage to write about such weighty topics and still write a funny book?

When I was growing up my father often said something to the effect "very few things in life constitute an emergency," and I suppose that attitude got somewhat ingrained in me. (Although if you ever sit next to me on a plane you will experience a not-so-Zen girl. I am a panicky freak on planes.) Also, I'm not writing about war or genocide or imprisonment (though there have been funny books written about war). Anyway, while some experiences are inextricably difficult and sad, how we deal with them is often laced with humor. I am reminded of the time that my grandmother, who had been diagnosed with Alzheimer's, started to sit and then froze halfway down because she couldn't remember whether or not she was in the middle of standing up or sitting down. It was a horribly sad moment, and a harbinger of many more terrible moments to come, yet she and my mother started laughing hysterically because it was all so ridiculous and darkly comic. And it seems to me that that is how life is. There are ridiculous moments even in the middle of big and serious events.

Caroline, Missy, and—to a lesser extent—Louise all struggle with their religious beliefs. Does this reflect a struggle in

your life with religion? Do you consider yourself a religious person?

I have a genuine desire for religious experience in my life, and I am quite envious of those who have it. And though I'm not always comfortable calling myself a Christian, I do—most of the time—believe in God and I do practice elements of the faith. And yet, I am fundamentally put off by any religion that claims its followers have backstage passes to the God show, as it seems most major religions do.

The times I feel most spiritually connected are during times of service (volunteering at the homeless shelter), times of meditation, and times spent in nature. I wish I had a more solid religious core, and yet I often feel that people who are very religious erect a certain boundary around themselves that no one can enter except those of their own faith. And that seems a shame.

Will you share with us the titles of some of your all-time favorite books and explain why you love those particular ones? Are there any books you've read lately that you are itching to recommend?

Oh yes! I just read *The World to Come* by Dara Horn and I absolutely loved it. The prose is gorgeous and smart, and the book is such a page-turner! I have also just recently discovered the novels of Gail Godwin, who started writing books around the time I was born and is still going at it. I admire her so much. To me she is an artist who has fully embraced her craft, someone who has stretched herself to her potential. I will forever love *A Confederacy of Dunces* by John Kennedy Toole, as it makes me laugh out loud every time I read it. And I love *The Assistant* by Bernard Malamud, in part because my husband bought it for me when we were first falling in love, but also because there is nothing clever or cynical about it, it's just about human love and human failings. And, man, do I love Flannery O'Connor's short stories, though I think you really do need to understand her views on faith in order to understand them. *Ellen Foster* by Kaye Gibbons is important to me because Ellen's moment of becoming fully human, when she realizes Starletta is as intrinsically valuable as she, made me stop reading, put the book down, and just let her epiphany wash over me like a baptism. And speaking of baptisms, there is a strange sort of cookbook, *The Supper of the Lamb*, by Episcopal priest Robert Farrar Capon that is truly odd and truly life-affirming.

You earned your MFA in creative writing from Hollins University. There is a lot of discussion among writers about the value and merit of these programs. Are you glad that you attended one? Do you think your time at Hollins helped you to become a better writer?

Absolutely. There is nothing like having two years during which your only real responsibility is to write. The danger with MFA programs, I think, is that you can start writing for your little bitty circle of readers and forget that there is a larger audience out there who might not have the same preferences as the small sample of people in your writing workshop. But all that means is that you learn to take criticism with a grain of salt, which isn't a bad skill to develop if you want to be a professional writer.

Will you tell us anything about what you are working on now?

I am writing a story about a modern-day patched-together family who, through tragic circumstances, gets ripped apart. It is a comedy. (Just kidding! But it does have its funny moments.)

Enhance Your Book Club

1. *Bound South* highlights the friendship between Tiny and Louise, which has been in place since childhood. Bring in a picture of a childhood friend, or even have that friend join your book club and share memories of growing up.

2. Louise has a deep appreciation for art, especially art created by Southern eccentrics. Do a Google image search for art created by Southerners, particularly those who are untrained. You might want to start by looking at images of art created by Howard Finster, Thornton Dial, and Nellie Mae Rowe. Print out images of some of this art and bring it with you to your book club.

3. If you are hosting the club, consider serving (or asking others to bring) traditional Southern foods to your meeting. Some ideas for foods to serve are: cheese straws, ham biscuits, spiced pecans, celery sticks stuffed with pimiento cheese, and preacher cookies. Check out Scott Peacock's *The Gift of Southern Cooking* for recipes. Or you can just order a case of MoonPies off the Internet and serve those! (You can order them from Southernconnoisseur.com.)